Not Dead Enough

Books by Warren C Easley

The Cal Claxton Oregon Mysteries
Matters of Doubt
Dead Float
Never Look Down
Not Dead Enough

Not Dead Enough

A Cal Claxton Oregon Mystery

Warren C. Easley

Poisoned Pen Press

Poisoned Pen Press
6962 E. First Ave., Ste. 103
Scottsdale, AZ 85251
www.poisonedpenpress.com
info@poisonedpenpress.com

Printed in the United States of America

For Dick and Bettie

Acknowledgments

Marge Easley and Kate Easley, my first line of defense, kept me on track during this project in more ways than I can count. My editor, Barbara Peters, worked her usual magic, which resulted in a stronger, better focused manuscript, and the crew at Poisoned Pen Press followed through with their usual cheerful competence. I'm lucky to be part of a highly talented and perceptive critique group. Thanks once again to Lisa Alber, Kate Scott, LeeAnn McLennan, Janice Maxson, Debby Dodds, and Alison Jaekel. You guys rock!

Finally, to people everywhere who are fighting for clean water, free-flowing rivers, and fish-friendly habitat, I say, keep up the good fight!

Prologue

Celilo Falls
Columbia River Gorge
March 10, 1957

Nelson Queah told himself he would not watch, but there he stood, his eyes drawn to the rising river like some fool gawking at a car wreck. He watched, transfixed, as the water rose, taking the small, rocky islands first, then the south bank of the river where his village had stood, and finally the falls. He would never again stand in the spray and deafening roar of the falls, waiting to take the next salmon like his father and his grandfather and his people stretching back to the beginning of their collective memory.

He glanced at his watch when it was over. Four hours had elapsed. Less than the blink of an eye for a river that had flowed unfettered since the Ice Age torrents, yet gradual—like watching a loved one die a slow death. But it was more than that. Snuffed like a candle in the east winds of the Gorge, the light burning in Nelson Queah's heart went out that day, and he could feel his soul begin to wither around the edges.

The silence. The awful silence.

Had Nelson been in the bowels of The Dalles Dam that morning, he would have heard the "gates down" command. He would have seen twenty-two white men—each selected for the honor by the Army Corps of Engineers—press the buttons that simultaneously closed twenty-two massive steel and concrete floodgates. He would have experienced the exact moment when millions of gallons of water roiled in mad confusion before reversing course and surging upriver through the Long Narrows to the mighty falls at Celilo, sacred fishing grounds of his people for ten thousand years.

Nearly all the villagers, some thirty families, along with members of other tribes who had fishing rights at the site, stood on the river bank with Nelson. Some wept openly and others sang funeral dirges in the Sahaptin and Kiksht languages to the rhythmic thrum of rawhide drums. Behind them and across the Columbia River on the Washington side, thousands of curious onlookers lined the highways. A new lake—named Celilo for the falls it buried—had formed behind the dam. The name is another insult, Nelson told himself. It would be a constant reminder of what his people, the Wasco, and all the tribes who fished the falls, had lost.

When the river was nothing but a flat expanse of slack, rain-pocked water, Nelson turned to leave. He vowed that he would never allow himself to look at a photograph of what had been. Instead, he willed an image of the place into his mind— weathered basalt cliffs on the horizon, the placid sweep of water before the violent funneling down, which sent the entire volume of the river hurtling over a narrow lip of jagged rocks. Below the falls, wooden scaffolds jutted precariously above the rapids amidst a web of cables that carried fishermen across in hand-pulled chairs. He pictured his family's scaffold. There was his father, straining at the long-handled net dipped deep in the boil. At his feet, Nelson saw himself as a young boy, spreading sand to reduce the slickness under his father's feet.

This is what he would remember.

Nelson made his way slowly toward the village, which had been unceremoniously relocated by the Corps of Engineers across the railroad tracks and the highway to a piece of rocky, uneven ground with no power, water, or sewage services. Only a handful of families had chosen to remain there. The rest were scattered around the area, most going eighty miles south to the Warm Springs Reservation.

When he reached the highway, a voice called to him, "Hey, Queah, what happened to your waterfall? I don't see it."

Nelson spun around to face two men leaning on the side of a black Cadillac gaudy with chrome. The speaker was Cecil Ferguson. He stood on the left, a large, well-muscled man with a scarred and pitted face, flaming red hair and light blue, almost colorless eyes. The other man was a big Yakama Indian named Sherman Watlamet. He laughed like the gutless ass-kisser Nelson knew he was.

"Go to hell, Ferguson," he spat back at them, not bothering to even acknowledge Watlamet's presence.

The two men pushed themselves away from the Cadillac in unison. Ferguson said, "Well, maybe now their women won't smell of fish all the time." Ferguson erupted in laughter at his comment. Watlamet smiled uncertainly, and then when Ferguson poked him in the ribs with his elbow, joined in.

The sight of Sherman Watlamet laughing with the white man sickened Nelson, and blood rose in his neck. He closed half the ground between them and stopped, expecting them to do the same. But to his surprise, Ferguson nodded in the direction of the Cadillac, and they both turned on their heels. Apparently this would be settled another day.

But Nelson couldn't resist a parting shot. "You shame your own people, Sherman. You're lower than a goat's tit." Then he turned and crossed the highway without looking back.

He entered the Army surplus house he'd been given. It reminded him of the barracks at Quantico, where he had done his basic training during the war. He let the dog out, took a can of beer from the icebox and sat down. He was still seething with anger. Deep down he was disappointed Ferguson hadn't followed him across the highway, although he knew that if that had happened, one of them would probably be dead now.

Nelson dropped in a chair, held the cold beer can against his cheek and let out a long breath. Thoughts of war came to him. Despite the trail of broken treaties, the racial slights, the failed BIA policies, he joined up and hit the beaches of Sicily with the 5th Marine Division. But Sicily was a walk in the park compared to Anzio. He could still feel the grenade fragment in his leg when the weather turned, and flashbacks of the slaughter of his reconnaissance troop were never far behind. He had taken out a machine gun nest single-handedly that day, and for that his commanders gave him a Silver Star.

But fighting to stop the dam was not like fighting the Germans. It was no fight for a warrior. Nothing but endless hearings and testimony, lies and deceit. Treaty talk. All of it. His people knew about treaty talk. He had stood shoulder to shoulder with his brothers and even some white fishermen who understood what the dam would do to the migrating salmon populations. But the Corps of Engineers and the white politicians were clever. They fought with numbers and words and promises. The dam would bring cheap power and prosperity to the cities along the Columbia, the salmon would be protected, and the tribes would be fairly compensated. How could he make his people understand what was being taken? No. This had been no fight for a warrior.

He sipped at his beer but didn't begin to relax until he thought of his girls. His ten-year-old daughter, Rebecca, was visiting her cousins at Warm Springs, where his beloved wife, Tilda, was recuperating in the TB ward of the hospital. He missed them both, especially at this moment, although he was thankful they had missed the flooding of the falls and the ugliness afterward.

Because of Tilda's quarantine, he'd resolved to write her at least once a week, and it was Sunday, the day he had set aside for the task. What would he say to her, today of all days? How could he hide the deadness he felt in his heart, the humiliation?

Nelson drained his beer, sighed deeply, and got up to fetch pen and paper. *Tilda must not hear your sorrow. Lie if you have to*, he told himself.

March 10, 1957

Dearest Tilda,

I hope you are feeling much better, my dear. You have been in my thoughts constantly. I am driving down to Warm Springs tomorrow to pick up Rebecca. I am sure she is having fun with her cousins. She will probably not want to come home with me. I will drop this note at the hospital. Perhaps they'll allow a brief visit tomorrow. I long to see your face!

We had a feast in the longhouse last night in honor of the falls. Everyone was there except Chief Thompson, who is still ill. Many people asked about you. Oliver Tam told us all the story of how the salmon were first released in the river to be shared by all people. Do you remember the story? Two old women were hoarding them behind an earthen dam. Coyote disguised himself as an infant and tricked them into going to pick huckleberries for him. While they were busy, Coyote destroyed the dam and released the salmon. We all howled and screamed at this!

There is a silence in the village now, Tilda, but there is no cause for despair. The salmon will find new ways to their spawning grounds. Our people will still fish, and perhaps Coyote still has a few tricks up his sleeve.

Your loving husband,
Nelson.

Nelson started to set the letter aside then below his signature he added—

P.S. I am waiting for the young man I told you about last week, Timothy Wiiks. He has promised to bring the evidence he found about money being stolen at the dam. I saw the man he is accusing today on the river, but there was no trouble. I told the newspaperman about the stealing. He is anxious to meet with Timothy and me tomorrow. I think this is the right thing to do.

Nelson awoke in the chair later that night, the finished letter resting in his lap. He tore it from the pad and laid it on the kitchen table. He had let the dog back in, and it was now standing at the door growling. He looked at his watch. It was nine-twenty. Hoping it was the young man, Timothy, he went to the door and nudged the dog away with his knee. If it was a deer instead, he didn't want the dog off chasing it at this hour.

He opened the door and stepped outside. It had stopped raining, there was no moon, and it was deathly quiet. He had only gotten a few steps down the path when he heard a boot scuff behind him. The blow that followed was decisive, buckling his knees and driving a shard of bone deep into his brain.

Chapter One

Fifty Years Later

"Come on, give the steelheads a break. I've got hot coffee."

It was my friend, Philip Lone Deer. He'd come up behind me on the riverbank. We were on the Deschutes River, just south of the Warm Springs Reservation boundary, on the Indian side. It was mid-morning and brutally cold, but the sun sparkled and danced off the river. I was standing hip-deep in fast-moving water. "Wait a sec. I'm feeling it here."

I was a novice fly-fisherman, so my comment made him laugh. Fly fishing for steelhead is the big leagues. "In your dreams, Claxton." Then with sudden urgency, he added, "*Whoa,* you're right. There's a fish out there. I can see him from up here. Cast out about forty feet and swing your fly to the bank. He's at three o'clock. A big one."

I flicked the lure—a big fly called a fire butt skunk—off the surface and back behind me and then cranked it forward, hoping for a decent cast. The fly hit downriver at about the right distance. I lowered the rod tip and began working the lure toward the bank. Sure enough, at three o'clock a big steelhead crunched the lure on a violent upward pass. The surface erupted, and the fish came out of the water like a chrome-plated missile.

"All right!" Philip cried. A Paiute who lives off reservation, Philip was a professional fishing guide, one of the best in the

Northwest. I'd hired him to teach me to fly-fish after I arrived in Oregon, making good on a promise to my daughter that I would find a hobby. Our friendship had grown from there, and now we fished together as friends when our schedules permitted it.

With my heart rapping against my ribs, I set the hook at the top of the leap. The fish re-entered the water and wrenched the tip of my rod downward as it ran for the center of the river. It took me a good five minutes to bring it alongside. I slipped out the barbless hook and gently supported the fish from underneath with my hand until its crimson gills pumped hard. It rolled on its side, and its iridescent scales flashed in the sunlight. My heart swelled at the sight of such a beautiful creature, my first steelhead. I said, "Thanks, big boy," then watched it vanish with a flick of its powerful tail.

Afterwards, up on the bank as we huddled in the sun sipping coffee, Philip said, "Next Saturday there's going to be a commemoration of the fiftieth anniversary of the flooding of Celilo Falls. If you're free, why don't you come over to the Gorge and join me."

"Won't it be more of a wake than a commemoration?" I knew the story of how the construction of The Dalles Dam on the Columbia River had led to the flooding of the great Native American fishing grounds and village, and what that had meant to the tribes in the region.

"Nah, not really. We Indians know how to put things behind us. A matter of necessity. It'll be some speeches, some dances, a lot of good food. But don't come for all that. I want you to come and feel lots of guilt for what the white man did to us, man."

"But what about all those casinos we've given you?"

"Seriously, I want you to come, Cal. You can check out the work on the new village and the longhouse. The Corps finally admitted they'd screwed up the original relocation and coughed up millions of bucks to rebuild everything."

I whistled. "I don't feel so guilty anymore."

"Besides, you've got to see my father. He's going to wear his full headdress."

I told my friend I would go but intended to avoid the speeches if I could. I didn't see how anything good could be made out of what had happened and didn't want to hear any of the great white fathers from Oregon and Washington, D.C., try to spin it that way. To me, the flooding of the falls was just another gut shot to the Indians, and it was the dams that spelled the slow but steady decline of the migrating salmon populations, the lifeblood of the Columbia River tribes for millennia.

I headed out for the commemoration that following Saturday from my place in the hills above Dundee, a small town perched some twenty-five miles south of Portland at the epicenter of Oregon's wine country. I'd moved to an old farmhouse there six months earlier after taking an early retirement from the city of Los Angeles. Celilo Village was better than a hundred miles to the northeast, but it was a good day for a drive. The air had been scrubbed to a sparkle by a hard shower the night before, and the sky had that color, that achingly pure blue that seemed peculiar to the Northwest and always lifted my spirits. Of course, there's more rain than sun up here in Oregon, but I was beginning to realize that one day like this one was worth at least thirty days of rain.

Traffic was light when I reached Portland. Its handsome, compact center was cleaved east from west by the Willamette River and stitched back together by a series of eight bridges, earning it the nickname Bridgetown. As I cleared the river high atop the I-5 Bridge, I found myself wondering what an earthquake would do to the aging structure and quickly suppressed the thought. A reflex from my L.A. days, I suppose.

I took the I-84 turnoff and headed east toward the Columbia River Gorge, a passage carved through sheer basalt cliffs that funneled the mighty river for over eighty miles. A low cloud cover had formed, but when I entered the Gorge the sun broke through and began playing off the whitecaps flecking the gray-verging-into-blue water. I played tag with heavily laden eighteen-wheelers for ninety minutes before The Dalles Dam came into view—its low profile set against the humped, treeless hills on the Washington side of the river. White water from half a dozen open floodgates cascaded down the center of the dam and stretched downriver like a huge, white tongue.

I arrived at Celilo Village at quarter past one. It must've been a sellout crowd, because I had to park out near the highway and walk in on the frontage road. I knew lunch was scheduled for two, and the aroma of meat and fish being cooked over open fires greeted me at the edge of the village. Calling the place a "village" was a stretch, since what I saw was maybe a dozen manufactured houses jammed in on either side of a short dirt road off to my left. A single basketball hoop and a couple of dirt bikes leaning against the supporting pole were the only suggestions that kids lived there. On either side of the broad road, stakes and plywood forms gave me a sense of the shape of the village to come. It promised to be a real upgrade, but then again almost anything would be.

I followed the rich aromas to the large wooden building that I took to be the longhouse. An elongated A-frame structure, it sported a set of huge, old-growth timbers that crossed at the roofline, tepee style. A small army of cooks was busy preparing lunch along one side of the building. I slipped into the front entryway, stood at the back, and scanned the standing-room-only crowd for Philip.

I didn't spot Philip but saw his father immediately. He was the one on stage wearing all the eagle feathers. He sat with the other tribal leaders next to an American flag and the four flags of the sovereign nations affected by the loss of the falls—Umatilla, Yakama, Nez Perce, and Warm Springs. Several white dignitaries sat with them, including a gray-haired man in military dress with lots of ribbons and medals. The brass from the Corps, no doubt. A man in a blue suit and red power tie stood at the podium, reading what I quickly realized was a proclamation from the Governor of Oregon. To my surprise, the words were refreshingly honest and forthright, and I found myself wanting to believe the promise that government had learned a lesson, that something like this could never happen today. I wondered.

After a brief closing ceremony, the crowd emptied out and began queuing up for lunch.

"Cal. Good to see you, buddy," Philip said as he emerged from the throng and met me with a fist bump. "How long you been here?"

"Oh, quite a while. Nice ceremony. Your dad was looking good up there."

Philip flashed a brilliant smile. He had turn-your-head looks but none of the vanity that could have generated. Black hair pulled back in a ponytail, a chin like a block of granite, and obligatory high cheekbones were all Paiute warrior. But his green eyes and narrow, almost delicate, nose came from his white mother. "Bullshit," he said. "I saw you sneak in a few minutes ago." He was still smiling. "Let me guess—car trouble?"

I shrugged. "Give me a break. I did catch some of the Gov's proclamation."

"Impressive speech, huh? Makes me confident that if you ever take our land again, you'll do it with much more sensitivity."

"Well, don't take our word for it. Make sure you get a signed treaty."

Philip threw his head back and laughed. "Come on, let's get something to eat."

We piled our plates high with salmon, venison, corn on the cob, and salad and sat down at a table, joining another party of three. The man I sat down next to extended his hand and said, "Hello, I'm Jason Townsend," and then introduced us to the other two. Townsend was tall and blond and strikingly handsome. His yellow V-neck sweater with a button-down underneath, chinos, and spotless jogging shoes signaled a failed attempt at dressing down, Oregon style. He looked vaguely familiar to me. I scanned my memory banks but came up empty. "So, what brings you two to the commemoration?" he asked as we tucked into our food.

Philip looked at me to answer Townsend's question. "Well, Philip's a member of the Confederated Tribes at Warm Springs. I'm just here to pay my respects for the loss of the falls."

Townsend looked directly at Philip. "I'm truly sorry for your loss. Based on what we know today, we probably wouldn't have built The Dalles Dam."

Philip lowered his fork and looked back, not quite knowing what to make of the man. "Yeah, well, it screwed up the best fishing hole in North America." Townsend laughed at this, albeit a bit cautiously, and waited for Philip to continue.

After a pause, I filled the vacuum. I was used to doing this for my laconic friend. "I wish I could have seen Celilo Falls with my own eyes. Imagine all the migrating salmon in the Columbia squeezed into one spot."

Townsend leaned in. "I wish I could have seen it, too. The pictures don't do it justice. They say the roar of the falls shook the earth." He looked at Philip again, but he didn't respond. He'd spoken his piece. "Now we know the dams are killing off the salmon," Townsend went on. "I think they need to go."

That rang a bell with me. Is this the guy who's thinking about a run for the U.S. Senate, the guy who's advocating dam removal? Wasn't his name Townsend? I took another look at him. Could be. The other two are probably aides, I decided. The thin, well-dressed man across from Townsend, introduced earlier as David Hanson, said, "People in the Northwest don't want to give up their cheap power, and they shouldn't have to. We have so many new options now—solar, wind power, geothermal, wave. The dams can be phased out over time."

"That's right, David," Townsend added, coming in as if on cue. "I think we can find less ecologically damaging sources of power in the Northwest. But it's going to take new leadership."

I glanced at the other aide, Sam DeSilva, and caught him rolling his eyes at the comment. Sam was short and stoutly built with a closely shaved head that glistened in the sunlight. He obviously wasn't a true believer.

I looked back at Townsend. "Philip and I are fly-fishermen. We daydream about free-flowing rivers. Does this dam-removal idea stand a chance?"

Townsend squared his shoulders and looked me in the eye. "I think it does. It won't happen overnight, and we can't remove all the dams, but big changes always start with a dream."

We continued the conversation in this quixotic vein while we ate our lunches. I had to admit it felt good to think about the possibility of the Columbia River flowing freely again, but I still didn't give the idea a snowball's chance in hell. By this time, I was sure who Townsend was. I said, "You're thinking about a run for the Senate, aren't you? I read about you a while back." Philip shot me a surprised look that turned pained. He put white politicians right up there with people who fish with dynamite.

Before Townsend could answer, a reporter butted in and asked him for an interview. Philip took the opportunity to jump up and grab me by the arm. As we turned to go, Townsend slipped me a business card and said hastily, "Sorry for this, Cal. Great meeting you. I *am* running for the Senate. And I'm serious about the dams. Call me if you want to help."

Chapter Two

As I caught up with Philip, he said, "Come on. I want you to meet my cousin." He guided me through a crowd that had formed around a drumming circle to a booth fronted by a banner that read "Learn about Pacific Salmon." There, a group of Native American kids listened to a woman wearing a fringed buckskin dress trimmed in turquoise and white beads. She was tall and willowy with her hair in traditional braids that hung past her shoulders. The kids seemed to hang on her every word, even the older boys standing at the back, although their interest probably had more to do with her figure than the subject matter.

"Okay," the woman said, "I've been doing all the talking. Now it's your turn."

The kids clapped and chattered excitedly.

She looked at the younger kids sitting up close. "Who can tell me why the salmon is such a special fish?"

A thin little girl wearing heavy glasses shot her hand up. "Um, they go back to have their babies in the same place they were born. Sometimes it's a really long swim back to that place, but they never forget where it is."

"*Very good.* What are fish called that do this?"

A boy in the second row called out, "Ana...uh, anadromous."

The woman smiled brightly. "*That's right.* She looked at the boys in the back. "What do you guys think about a fish that swims a thousand miles up a river just to spawn?"

A tall boy in gangbanger pants and a black tee-shirt said, "They're damn tough."

The woman's face lit up. "Wonderful point. Tell me more. Why are they so tough?"

"Well, look at all the stuff they have to fight against—fishermen, dams, sea lions, pollution, people messing up their spawning grounds, stuff like that. But they keep coming back every year. My dad says there's no quit in them."

I looked at those kids huddled around the woman, tough survivors, too. No wonder they have such a strong bond with the fish they hold sacred. After all, they've lived together along this river for thousands of years. And then I had another, less comforting thought. What if our stupidity wins out and we allow Columbia River salmon to become extinct? Could these people cope? Shit. Could I?

The woman ended the discussion with an old Wasco story of how Coyote freed the salmon for the benefit of all the river peoples by fooling two old women who were hoarding the fish. The kids laughed and clapped when she told them Coyote did this by destroying a dam that was holding the fish captive. The irony of the story wasn't lost on them. Not one bit.

Philip and I waited in the back until she finished her talk, and the kids began to drift away. Philip waved and she came over to us.

"Hi, Winona," Philip said as he hugged her. "Meet Cal Claxton. Cal, this is my cousin, Winona Cloud."

Her face was unadorned with makeup, and her smile was as modest as it was brief, showing the hint of two honest-to-goodness dimples. Her eyes were almond-shaped and hazel-going-to-green. They regarded me with intelligence and obvious curiosity as she offered her hand.

"I enjoyed your talk, Winona. You had those kids eating out of your hand."

"She knows her stuff," Philip interjected, gazing at her proudly. "She has a PhD in biology from Stanford."

Winona showed another hint of a smile, and I thought she might actually be blushing.

"What are you doing with your degree?" I asked.

"I work for a nonprofit, Pacific Salmon Watch."

I nodded to let her know I'd heard of the organization.

"I'm heading up a project on river habitat restoration. We're working with the Columbia tribes on this. She glanced back at the booth, stacked with literature and decorated with photos and illustrations of salmon. Part of my job's education."

"I liked the way you mixed the science with the Indian lore," I told her.

She smiled more fully, deepening the dimples. I thought of the sun breaking through somewhere in rainy Oregon. She said, "I grew up with that particular story of Coyote. It was my grandmother's favorite."

"I've told Winona a little bit about what you do, Cal. I think there's something she wants to discuss with you. I need to find my father, so I'll look you two up later, okay?" Philip turned to leave but not before he gave me that look he has when he thinks he's done something clever. God, I hate that look.

We lingered in an awkward pause after Philip walked away. Finally, I said, "So, Winona, what did you want to talk to me about?"

She glanced at her watch. "Would you mind if we took a walk? It will take a while to explain, and I'm not comfortable talking around all these people."

"Fine. I'm no lover of crowds. Can we walk to the river from here?"

"Sure. The park's not far."

We took the frontage road under I-84 and five minutes later were strolling through Celilo Park, a rocky spit squeezed between the railroad tracks and the river. The wind had picked up and cloud shadows darted across the water like schools of dark fish. Winona caught her skirt in a gust, laughed, and said, "One thing that hasn't changed in the Gorge is the wind." We found a picnic table partially sheltered behind a stand of gnarled cedars and sat down.

"Where exactly were the falls?" I asked.

"Out there," she said, pointing west and downriver. Then she swung her arm southward. "The original village was over there. My grandfather, Nelson Queah, had a fishing platform right below the falls."

"Does he live in the village now?" I asked eagerly. I was dying to talk to one of the Celilo old-timers to hear firsthand what the fishing was really like.

Winona drew her mouth into a straight line and looked out across the water. "No. He's gone."

"Oh. I'm sorry."

"Thank you. He disappeared fifty years ago today."

"The day they flooded the falls?"

"That night."

"What happened?"

"Well, that's what I wanted to talk to you about."

Chapter Three

Winona looked out at the water as she began to speak. White-caps blanketed Celilo Lake now, glittering in the afternoon light like silver coins. Downriver, a low-riding barge slogged silently toward us. "I never knew my grandfather. He disappeared nine years before I was born. But I grew up on stories about him, told mostly by my grandmother. He was a man of principle and a political activist." She smiled with a tinge of bitterness and waved a hand toward the water. "He fought hard to prevent this back in the fifties. He was a warrior, too, a Marine during World War II. He earned a Silver Star and a Purple Heart overseas. Italy, I think. When he came back he had no tolerance for the racism that was prevalent around The Dalles at the time."

I frowned and waited for her to continue.

"My grandmother loved to tell about the time he went into The Dalles for a haircut shortly after being discharged. He waited patiently for his turn and was denied service. He refused to leave the shop, and when three men tried to throw him out, he beat the hell out of them, all three."

I laughed out loud, the scene playing in my head like a movie clip.

Winona smiled, shook her head, and looked back out on the river. "He spent ninety days in jail for that. He was well respected in the village and became a member of the Celilo Fish Committee. The committee managed the fishing at the falls. You know—who could fish, where they could fish, that sort of thing. He also worked with the fishermen and the cannery to settle disputes. There was a lot of cheating going on at both ends. When the dam became an issue, he threw himself into opposing it. He wrote letters, gave talks locally, traveled all the way to Washington to testify at congressional hearings. He was uncompromising. He urged the tribes to refuse a buy-off from Washington. 'Don't trade the falls for money,' he used to say. 'You can't put a price on the falls.'"

"I think he was right about that. You must be very proud of him."

"I am. That's why I wanted to talk to you."

I raised my eyebrows and waited again, wondering where she was going with this.

"That night, after the flooding of the falls, my grandfather disappeared. Without a trace."

"Oh." I nodded and waited for her to continue.

"One man claims he saw him that night out by the river, stumbling around like a drunk. So the police assumed he got drunk, fell in what had become a lake, and drowned in typical Indian fashion. Case closed."

"They didn't find his body?"

She looked out at the lake. "No. The lake isn't particularly deep, but the Narrows, where the river used to run, is a deep trench. And the turbines at the dam, of course…"

"You don't believe it was an accident?"

"No. And neither did my grandmother. She had to live with the shame of the accusation—you know, just another drunk Indian—but she never believed it. Not for a minute." Winona looked at the barge out on the lake and hesitated for a moment, as if weighing what to say next. "I…I didn't know my grandfather, but I feel like his spirit lives within me. I *know* he didn't die like they said." She clinched a fist and put it to her chest. "And the anger I feel at him being remembered like that sits in my heart like a heavy stone." Her eyes narrowed and the muscles along the line of her jaw rippled. She was right. I could sense the warrior in her.

My prosecutor instincts kicked in. "Who was this witness?"

"His name's Sherman Watlamet, a Yakama."

"Still living?"

"I think so."

I waited, and when she didn't continue, said, "So, Winona, how can I help you?"

"I want you to try to find out what *really* happened to my grandfather. I want to know the truth."

I started to laugh but caught myself. "Uh, that would be next to impossible, I'm afraid. Except for one possible witness, any physical evidence is probably long gone after fifty years. Besides, I'm just a small-town lawyer. What you need is a private investigator."

"Philip told me that you went to law school at Berkeley and that you were a prosecutor for the city of Los Angeles."

"That was a while ago, Winona, another world." What I didn't tell her was that it was a world I'd left and didn't care to revisit.

"Well, Philip said that if anyone could help, it would be you. He said you're brilliant."

I laughed. "He must have been talking about my fly fishing."

She didn't smile. "I'll pay you, of course." Then she lifted a hand, palm out. "Before you make up your mind, let me tell you the rest."

"Okay, I'm listening."

"I found something the other day I think might be important." She raised her eyes to meet mine. Hers were filled with an eagerness that made me uncomfortable. "I was going through some of my grandmother's papers. She, uh, died two weeks ago."

"I'm sorry to hear that."

Winona nodded, a weak smile creasing her lips, and surveyed the lake again. "She raised me. My father was killed in a logging accident when I was two. My mother has never been in the picture much. Alcohol and drugs. I think she's somewhere in Eastern Oregon now. She didn't make it to the funeral. Anyway, last Wednesday I came across a trunk in Grandmother's bedroom closet. This dress was in it," she said, looking into her lap as she swept her hands downward in a gesture of display.

"It's beautiful."

"Thank you. She was married in it. I also found a packet of letters my grandfather wrote to my grandmother. She had TB during the time the falls were flooded and was in a sanatorium in Warm Springs. Grandfather was a faithful letter writer, and he told her what was going on in Celilo Village in great detail."

I leaned in a little.

"I mentioned the letters to Philip, and that's when your name came up. Cal, I think there's new information in the letters. My grandfather had enemies, and the so-called witness, Sherman Watlamet, was one of them. I don't think it was an accident. I think someone murdered him."

"Why did your grandmother keep the letters to herself if they shed light on what happened to him?"

She smiled wistfully. "Grandma Tilda was a very private person. I don't think she could bring herself to let anyone else read the letters. But I'll never know for sure."

I looked out at the lake this time. A ragged row of gulls followed above the wake of the barge, which had moved well to the west. Trying to solve a fifty-year-old cold case—even with a handful of chatty love letters—is undoubtedly a fool's errand, I told myself. But what could I say? Even if she wasn't the cousin of the first good friend I'd made in Oregon, the earnestness of her request made it hard to say no.

I exhaled a long breath. "Tell you what, I'll take a look at the letters and make a few inquiries, and then we'll decide if there's anything we can do here. How does that sound?"

She gave me the full radiance of her smile. "Thank you, Cal. I...uh...have read the letters a couple of times and put some notes together. Do you want to see those, too?

I paused to consider her question. "No. Hang on to those for now. I want to read the letters with fresh eyes. We'll compare notes afterwards."

A quick read. A few phone calls. That would be the extent of it. Or so I thought.

Chapter Four

I was hunched over a pile of papers at my law office in the middle of the following week when my phone rang. "I didn't catch you working, did I?" It was Philip Lone Deer. My friend had this deeply ingrained notion that unless you're out rowing drift boats through white water or felling trees, you're not *really* working.

"Actually, I was just finishing my manicure."

Laughter. After some additional banter, he said, "Thanks for talking to Winona, Cal. You think you can help her? Nelson Queah's disappearance has been eating at her for years."

"Too early to tell. Fifty years is a helluva long time, Philip. A lot of the people who might've known something are dead and gone by now."

"Yeah. I guess you're right." He paused. "You think there's anything in those letters she found that might help?"

"I've been jammed up and haven't gotten around to them yet." I felt a stab of guilt. "I was planning to take a look tonight." In truth, I was having a hard time getting started, despite my promise to Winona Cloud. The accordion folder she gave me still sat on my desk at home, untouched.

"You don't really want to help her, do you."

It wasn't a question. I tried to come up with the right response but couldn't seem to find it. "Uh, not really."

"Goddamnit, Cal, I—"

"*Okay*, I'm on it tonight. It's just that you both need to understand that the chances of this going anywhere are slim to none. Fifty years is an eternity in a case like this."

"I get that, and I'm sure Winona does, too. Just give it a shot. And look, if you need any help, anything at all, just let me know."

I thought for a moment. "As a matter of fact, there is one thing. Winona mentioned a witness, allegedly the last person to see Nelson Queah alive. Name's, uh, Sherman Wat-something."

"Watlamet. Sherman Watlamet. I remember her telling me."

"Yeah. That's the guy. She said he was a Yakama. Could you try to get a line on him? I'd like to talk to him if he's still breathing."

"Consider it done."

I locked up my law office around five and headed for home with my pup, Archie, in the backseat. Dundee and its three thousand inhabitants sat wedged between the Willamette River and the Dundee Hills, thirty-five miles southwest of Portland on the Pacific Highway. A blue-collar farm town careening down the path of gentrification, it was becoming known as the center of the Oregon wine country, at least by those owning vineyards there. I urged my old BMW out of town and up into the hills, which rose sharply on the west side of the highway, the road winding through orderly rows of pinot noir grapevines whose buds were swollen but had not yet unfurled into leaves.

Archie, a six-month-old Australian shepherd, began to whimper as we turned off and made the final climb up Eagle Nest, the graveled lane that serves my house and that of my only neighbor. When I let him out to open the gate, he jumped from the backseat without hesitation and landed chin-first. Undeterred, he picked himself up and, ignoring my laughter, shot past me to scatter a covey of quail grazing up by the weeds that marked the vegetable garden of the previous owner.

I'm perched on five acres that slant down to a ridgeline overlooking an abandoned gravel quarry. My old farmhouse, a four-square with a wraparound porch and the original shiplap siding, sits with its back to the ridge. The view out the back is straight south and carries the eye down through the vineyards and out to the Willamette Valley, a hundred-and-fifty-mile-long agricultural cornucopia that's squeezed between the Cascade Mountains and the Coastal Range.

The old farmhouse is no treasure, but the view's worth a million bucks, as far as I'm concerned.

Archie followed me through the front door, and we both headed for the kitchen. I fed him, let him out, and then opened a bottle of pinot noir. I was still acquainting myself with the local wines. This particular bottle was made from grapes grown in a vineyard I could see from my kitchen window. I poured some, swirled it, and held it up. Not inky like a typical cabernet sauvignon, it scattered the light like a jewel. I sipped it, enjoying the complex flavor that belied its lighter color. "This will do nicely."

My stomach grumbled, which started me thinking of dinner. My cooking skills were severely limited. Not because I was indifferent to good food. Just the opposite. My wife had been an exceptional cook, but I'm ashamed to say I took her skills for granted. Now I found myself trying to recreate some of the magic she worked in the kitchen, but with decidedly mixed results. My daughter, Claire, had insisted I bring Nancy's cookbooks in the move from L.A., but they remained packed in a box up in the attic. I thought about bringing them down every now and then but hadn't gotten around to it. Too many ghosts up there.

I hated to shop more than anything, so it was no surprise that the fridge was nearly bare that particular night. I settled for two grilled cheese sandwiches made with the last slices from a block of Gruyere I'd picked up at a shop in McMinnville. A couple of sliced tomatoes, cucumbers, and Kalamata olives dressed with olive oil and balsamic vinegar completed the meal. At least I had a good wine to go with it.

After dinner, I carried a second glass of wine down the hall to my study and slid the contents of Winona Cloud's file onto my desk. Three curled and yellowed newspaper articles from *The Dalles Chronicle* were on top. The first was dated March 13, 1957—a small item noting that Nelson Queah, resident of Celilo Village, was missing. He'd failed to pick up his daughter,

Rebecca, at the Warm Springs Reservation on March 11 and had not been seen in Celilo Village since the falls were inundated on the 10th.

A follow-up piece two days later quoted Sherman Watlamet, a fellow falls fisherman: "I saw Nelson Queah cross the highway and head toward the river at about 9:10 p.m. on the night of March 10th. He was weaving and staggering, and I figured he was very drunk." The article also said that Queah's house in the village had been broken into and apparently burglarized, although his daughter, Rebecca, stated that nothing seemed to be missing.

The article went on to describe dragging operations performed by the police in newly formed Lake Celilo and the fact that no body was recovered. The final piece described a memorial ceremony held in Queah's honor at the village a month later. His war record was highlighted, and a huge turnout of Native Americans from around the region was noted.

I attacked her grandfather's letters next. The envelopes had been opened carefully with a letter opener, and I could read most of the postmarks. The letters themselves had been written on cheap paper that had turned the color of dead leaves and was nearly as brittle. The ink was faded sepia, but Nelson's handwriting was precise and legible. There were forty-six letters in the stack, and they were arranged in chronological order. The first was dated April 9, 1956, and the last, March 3, 1957, a week before the falls were flooded.

I went over to the sound system looking for something mellow to work by. I put on Coltrane's *Blue Train* and added one of Monk's solo CDs behind it. By the time Monk came in on "Ruby, My Dear," I'd finished reading the letters. My first reaction was full-on admiration for Nelson Queah. The Dalles Dam was nearing completion as he wrote the letters, and the social order at the falls and in the village was disintegrating as longtime residents drifted away, and the tribes began jockeying for compensation from the Corps of Engineers for the loss of their fishing grounds. But as Winona had told me, Queah was unwavering.

In May of 1956 he wrote,

> *"…Some of the tribes can't wait to get their hands on the white man's money. I told them today at the meeting I would take no money. It would be like putting a price on the moon and the stars. I cannot do that, Tilda…"*

There was precious little to go on. I had tossed the pages that might contain leads in a separate pile. When I finished reading I had only a half dozen pages.

In August of 1956 Queah wrote,

> *"…Chief Thompson has been sick this week. I am in charge of the fish committee, but some do not care to listen anymore. Sherman Watlamet told me I was a fool and that he would fish wherever he wanted. I told him as long as the falls are there, we would fish as it has always been done. I went to the river and put a lock on his cable chair. This made him furious, and I thought we were going to fight right there…"*

I imagined the scene unfolding. I knew the cable chairs were rickety affairs used by the fishermen to pull themselves by hand across the rapids to their fishing platforms. By locking the chair, Queah had denied Watlamet access to the other bank, where his fishing platform apparently was located. I set the item aside.

The next page I set aside was from a letter sent in October of 1956,

> *"…I ran into Cecil Ferguson and two other white men today. Ferguson is the man who offered me a job before construction of the dam started if I would stop speaking out against the project. He was angry when I turned him down. Do you remember this, Tilda? They were drunk and if Sam Katchia and Sonny Jim had not been with me, I think there would have been bad trouble. Dearest, I am trying hard to keep my promise to you not to fight, but I will not let this man Ferguson bully me…"*

Another item of interest was from a letter in late February of 1957,

"...I met with the newspaperman I told you about, Tilda. His name is Fletcher Dunn. He works for the big Portland newspaper, The Journal, I believe it is called. He is writing a story about the falls and the dam, and he interviewed me for a long time today. I like this young man. He seems to be sympathetic to our side. It is too late to save the falls, but perhaps he will tell the truth about what is happening to us.

I culled two entries from the last letter of the series, dated March 3, 1957. On the first page he wrote,

"...The newspaperman came by this morning. He brought me a copy of his first article on the dam and the falls. I think it tells our story well, although I don't think many white people can truly understand what losing the falls means to us. He also writes about what the whites are saying, that we need the dam to keep the country strong. I think he had to write this because mostly whites read the paper. I am enclosing the article for you to read. I hope you are proud of the words I spoke for our people, Tilda..."

On the back of the second page he wrote,

"...Something surprising happened tonight, Tilda. A young man named Timothy Wiiks came to see me here at the house. He is the nephew of a man I served in the war with, Jacob Morning Owl of the Umatilla Tribe. Jacob was killed in Sicily. Timothy works at the dam and has discovered that a contractor there has been cheating the Corps out of a great deal of money. He is afraid to go to the police and asked for my help. I told him I would talk to the newspaper reporter who interviewed me. I trust the reporter and I think he might know what to do about this..."

I scanned back through the key pages and jotted down some actions on a single sheet of paper. It was a short list.

1. Can Philip locate the witness Watlamet? This is key!

2. Who is Cecil Ferguson? Who did he work for? Try to locate and interview him. Ditto for Timothy Wiiks.

3. Find Fletcher Dunn and the articles he wrote about the dam and the falls.

4. Assess possibility of an accident or suicide. Queah's mental history? Drinking? Tribal attitudes toward suicide? Talk to Winona.

I stepped out on the side porch to watch the sunset through a stand of Douglas firs on the west edge of my property. A Rufus hummingbird buzzed my ear on a last trip to the feeder. I watched through the trees as the sun sank in a pool of orange and red fire, the firs stark silhouettes against a violet glow.

I still wasn't optimistic. But after reading the letters, I was no longer indifferent. Winona was right—Nelson Queah deserved to have the truth told about him.

Chapter Five

Jake

Later that same week, a man sat dozing in a camp chair with his cowboy hat shading his face when a text pinged him awake. Jake didn't recognize the incoming number, and the message wasn't signed, but he knew who the sender was. It read:

> We have a problem. The Old Man needs a favor and he needs it right away.

Jake texted back: What kind of favor?

> You'll be briefed at the guest house tonight.

What the fuck? Jake said, "Tonight?" and texted back: I'd have to leave right away.

This response came back: The Old Man's counting on you and there's good money in it.

Jake sat up a little straighter. How much good money?

> Enough to make your trip very worthwhile. Trust me.

Things were slack at the moment, and money, or the lack of it, hung like a damn noose around his neck. He exhaled a sigh and replied: Okay. What do I need to bring?

> A change of clothes or two. Motels are out so bring your camping gear. You'll have to do some fieldwork, so pack

your binoculars and your Remington, the one with the scope.

Why the artillery?

Just bring it. Not a word about this to anyone. Do not call me, do not call the Old Man. All communications thru this number, text only. Am I clear?

Text only? What's that all about? Jake wondered. Some kind of security thing? He texted back:

No problem. See you tonight. I'll be in late, between 9 and 10.

As Jake packed up his truck, he played the exchange back, coming around to the term "good money" several times. He was hanging on by a couple of fingernails right now. A good payday for a short job was just what the doctor ordered. Shit, who knows? He asked himself. Maybe it'll be enough to get things turned around. God knows he could use some good luck.

But something gnawed at him, deep down in his gut. He knew "good money" came with a price, a stiff price of its own. He'd done some bad shit in his life for money, but never, ever had he been asked to bring a gun to the party. *What the hell am I getting myself into?*

Chapter Six

"I found Watlamet."

The voice cut through the fog of deep, pre-dawn sleep. Had the phone rung? I wasn't sure, but I had it pressed to my ear... My head cleared enough for me to know who it was. "Damn it, Lone Deer. Is that you? What the hell time is it?" I struggled to sit up and looked at the clock.

"It's five. I waited 'til five to call you, man. I found him. I found your boy, Sherman Watlamet."

A long pause ensued while I cleared my head and tried to figure out who he was talking about. Five a.m. was late for my friend, the quintessential morning person. "Oh, yeah," I finally stammered, "the guy who claimed he saw Queah down by the river the night he disappeared."

"Right. He lives on a ranch out near a little town called Clarno on the John Day River. Been there for years. I popped over there yesterday and had a talk with him."

That cleared the cobwebs. "You did *what?* What the hell did you say to him?" I knew from experience that it was damn easy to scare off a witness or cause him to clam up.

"Hey, no worries. I didn't spook him. All I told him was that you wanted to talk to him about the disappearance of Nelson Queah. I didn't get into any of it with him."

"That's a lot, Philip."

"Jesus, Cal. I had to tell him *something.*"

"Okay. So what did he say?"

"Well, it took him a while to make up his mind, but he's willing to see you. I got the impression this is a touchy subject for him."

I breathed a sigh of relief. "Touchy?"

"I don't know. When I mentioned Queah's name, it was like I hit a nerve. But he came around okay."

"Was he hard to find?"

"Did Custer get his ass kicked? I had to cast a broad net. Apparently, he left the Yakama Rez when he got his payoff from the feds after the falls were flooded. Lives alone out on the John Day River. A real recluse."

"When can I see him?"

"He said he'll be around Friday. It's a long drive out there for you, so I'd plan to get there early. That way you might catch him before he decides to go into town or something."

"Did you get a phone number?"

"Didn't see a phone in his place. Didn't think to ask him."

"Okay. I'll have to take my chances. I'll try to get out there Friday. How far is it?"

"From Dundee, oh, a hundred and seventy, eighty miles."

"Listen, Philip, I need another favor."

"Shoot."

"I need you to try to find another person. His name's Timothy Wiiks." I spelled it for him. "He's probably in his early seventies by now. His uncle was a Umatilla named Jacob Morning Owl. The uncle was killed in World War II."

"Wiiks isn't exactly a Umatilla name."

"I know that. His mother was probably Morning Owl's sister. His father was Scandinavian, by the sound of it."

"Hmm. Okay. I'll see what I can do."

Giving up on any more sleep, I stumbled out of bed and took the back stairs down to the kitchen. Archie was right behind me, having just learned to navigate the steep stairs with big puppy paws he'd yet to grow into.

I fed Arch, ground some coffee beans, and made my usual double cappuccino using the one appliance I brought with me in the move. I had left most of the furniture, too. A clean getaway. The night's rain had let up, and the cloud-churned sky looked congealed, almost solid, the only evidence of the sun a yellow stain bleeding through in the east. A few birds fluttered at the feeder, the stout ones willing to brave the sodden air. I made a second cappuccino—my antidote for the rains—and padded down the hall to the study to check my e-mail.

A message from Winona Cloud sat right on top. I'd left her a voicemail the day before suggesting we meet to discuss the letters. The note said she had a two-thirty meeting in McMinnville, and since she'd be driving right through Dundee to get there, she wondered if we could meet for lunch somewhere. I tapped back a quick reply suggesting the Brasserie Dundee, a little eatery north of town with great food.

My fledgling, one-man law practice was struggling to take root. After all, I was an outsider in a small, agricultural community, and being from Los Angeles didn't help my cause, either. That morning I did get a walk-in—an Hispanic man who wanted me to defend his son in juvenile court for shoplifting a pair of expensive cross-trainers at a shoe warehouse in Newberg. The only hitch was the dad was strapped for cash. He said he'd heard I had some acreage up in the hills and offered his son to work off the bill. I told him we could probably work something out.

Taking barter was no way to get solidly into the black, but what was I going to do?

At a little before twelve-thirty I parked behind the Brasserie and went in the back door of the place, a beautiful old Craftsman-style home converted to a restaurant and bar. The owner—a black woman named Bettie James—was the first friend I'd made in Dundee. Like me, she'd fled the stress of a big city—Seattle in her case—where she'd owned a successful, upscale restaurant. A handsome, big-boned woman, Bettie had a ready laugh, a keen intellect, and an ocean of compassion concealed behind a street-smart demeanor.

I found her behind the bar. "How you been keepin', Calvin?"

"Good, Bettie. Yourself?"

"Oh, can't complain. Wouldn't do me any good if I did." A deep laugh and flash of white teeth. "How's Claire doin' down there in Beserk-ley?"

I laughed. Bettie loved to tease me about Claire's school and my alma mater. "She's fine. Swamped with midterms at the moment." We were still talking about Claire when Winona walked in. I introduced them and after some small talk, Bettie excused herself.

Winona wore jeans, a turquoise silk blouse with a plain silver necklace, and a blue blazer. Her raven hair was pulled back, the long ponytail held with a silver clasp, and she carried a soft-sided leather briefcase.

A striking woman, by any measure. I tried not to notice.

First off, she asked about my fee, and I told her she owed me nothing at this point, and that I'd bill her at my attorney rate less twenty percent plus any expenses incurred going forward.

Her eyes narrowed a bit. "Why the discount?"

I shrugged. "This really isn't legal work, more like investigation. If we get into some legal issues, I'll adjust my fee. Sound fair?" She agreed and I told her I'd e-mail her a contract, which I'd forgotten to bring along. A paying customer!

She placed a sheaf of notes from her briefcase on the table and took a pen from her coat pocket. "So, what do you think of the letters, Cal?" She was all business, and her expectant look worried me a bit, like I was supposed to pull a rabbit out of a hat or something.

"Your grandfather was a good man. I can understand why you want to know what happened to him."

She smiled, but only briefly, and waited for me to continue.

The waitress arrived. "The salade niçoise is great here," I said. "That's what I'm having."

"Fine. A salad's good," she answered with a curt nod to the waitress.

I opened my folder and glanced down at the single page to-do list on top of the stack of letters. The list now seemed woefully inadequate given the apparent level of her interest. I decided to lead with the good news. "Philip located Sherman Watlamet already. He's still alive. I can talk to him Friday if you give me the go-ahead."

Her face brightened, threatening to expose the dimples. "That's good news, Cal. Yes, by all means, talk to him. Where is he?"

"Out in the high desert on the John Day River. Lives alone on a ranch."

"You saw the references to him in the letters. He and Grandfather were not on good terms. Do you think he'll talk to you?"

"Good question. Maybe time has erased the hard feelings. People tend to open up as they get older, you know, to put things right. But I can't promise anything."

"He *must* know more, Cal. He wouldn't have lied like that about Grandfather unless he knew what really happened."

I nodded, although I still had my doubts. I cleared my throat. "Look, Winona, bear with me for a moment. I need to go back over some stuff."

She eyed me cautiously. "Okay."

"Did your grandfather have any history of drinking? Did you ever hear anything about that from your grandmother or anyone else?"

Her eyes narrowed, and she slowed the cadence of her speech. "I already told you. Sherman Watlamet was *lying* when he said he saw my grandfather drunk that night."

I smiled to ease the tension. "I know what you told me. I just want to be sure."

Our lunch arrived at this point. After squeezing some lemon juice on her salad and forking a chunk of rare ahi tuna and a slice of egg, she answered. "Grandmother Tilda was very religious. She didn't drink. Grandfather drank some, after all, he was an ex-Marine. But I *never* saw or heard of a problem. He was always a good provider."

"Good." I paused for a moment and decided to risk the next question. "How likely would it have been for a Wasco man to take his life back in the fifties?"

She laughed derisively, looked down at the green beans impaled on her fork, then back up at me. "Maybe some, but not Grandfather. That would have been a cowardly act, and he was no coward. He was raising my mother while Grandmother Tilda was in the hospital, for God's sake. He never would have taken his own life. That would have left my mother with no one to care for her." She paused, her eyes burning with something just short of anger.

I held her gaze for a beat. "Sorry about the tough questions, but I don't think you hired me to tell you what you want to hear. We're after the truth, right?"

"Right," she answered, but her look told me she hadn't ceded an inch of ground.

I glanced down at my notes. "Uh, this white guy who tried to buy off your grandfather—Cecil Ferguson. Any thoughts on how to locate him?"

She scrunched up her brow. "I know who you're referring to, but no, Grandmother Tilda never spoke of anyone by that name. I wouldn't know how to find him."

"What about Timothy Wiiks, the kid who discovered the theft at the dam? Any thoughts on him?"

She frowned and shook her head.

"I asked Philip to see if he could find him," I said. "Wiiks' mother's a Umatilla. We'll see what he comes up with."

"Great idea. Philip has such good contacts in the tribes." Her look turned wistful. "I'm afraid I've been out of touch too long."

"Well, maybe this exercise we're about to undertake will help bring you back."

She nodded, managing a smile. "Maybe so."

I went on to tell her I would also try to locate the newspaper man, Fletcher Dunn, and as we continued to compare notes in detail, I was disappointed to find that she hadn't noticed anything or anyone that I hadn't. That left me feeling even less optimistic about our chances.

Winona had a different take. As we finished up she said, "I can't help feeling encouraged by this, Cal. I just know that one of these people must have the key. Like you said, people want to make things right as they get older."

"Yeah, well, it's early days."

After Winona left, I sat at the table sipping my coffee. I had to laugh when I thought about how she'd left—all cheery and optimistic, like I was going to clear this thing up tomorrow. I thought about my upcoming meeting with Sherman Watlamet. *Did you really agree to drive a hundred and eighty miles to talk to this guy?* I asked myself. *I'm afraid it's going to be a long drive for a short meeting.*

Chapter Seven

In my book, the only decent reason for getting up before dawn is to fly-fish. But there I was, fumbling around with the coffee machine at four-thirty on Friday morning. Philip was right about an early start. I sure as hell didn't want to miss Sherman Watlamet after driving all the way out there. But I had to admit I was looking forward to the drive to a part of Oregon I'd only read about. I would go through the Gorge again, this time well past Celilo Village, and then climb out into the high desert. Out there, the landscape was formed, not by the ice age torrents that carved the Gorge, but by millennia of erupting volcanoes that sculpted a sprawling, starkly beautiful landscape.

Archie was in the backseat, a happy puppy. He loved to ride in the car, so I'd decided to take him with me, his first serious road trip. He was large for his breed, with a black coat trimmed in copper and white and big, expressive eyes that matched the coppery color of his trim. Not high strung like most Aussies, he was calm, inquisitive, and utterly undeterred by any obstacles he encountered. He had a way of winning people over, too—even folks who thought they didn't like dogs.

We were twenty miles into the Gorge when the sun ignited the horizon in gold and orange light filtered through a low bank of thin clouds. A profusion of sharply etched silhouettes emerged upriver—knife-edged cliffs, blunt headlands serrated with firs, and smooth, humpbacked peaks. In first light, the scene was a study in purple, with the distance of the shapes marked by the depth of their hues. The river materialized almost simultaneously as a smooth, rose colored band that ran through the center of it all.

We exited the Gorge at Biggs and made a pit stop before heading south on Route 97. The sky had turned vivid blue and was featureless except for the blurred arcs of two crossing contrails. I smelled sagebrush and juniper as we sped through the high desert, slowing only for a couple of one-stop towns and one big coyote on the side of the road that set Archie off in a fit of barking.

Just before Clarno I turned off the highway onto a dirt road that ran more or less parallel to the John Day River. A mile in I slowed down as I approached a thick line of junipers on my left, which, according to Philip's directions, marked an intersecting road without a street sign. I was to turn there, toward the river. A pickup suddenly emerged from the shielded road, swung into the intersection, and blew by me in the direction I'd come from. Fearing it was Watlamet on his way out, I craned my neck to get a look at the driver, a man in a cowboy hat. As we passed each other, our eyes met for a moment before he turned away. "Too young," I said, feeling relieved. I was sure he wasn't the man I'd driven all this way to see.

I took the left at the trees and a quarter mile further in saw a rusty mailbox marking a deeply rutted driveway, just as Philip had described it. The driveway led up a low knoll. I stopped at the top and took in the view of Watlamet's place—a weathered, ranch-style house, a barn behind the house with an old tractor parked alongside, and pasture land behind the barn, where at least a dozen head of cattle were grazing. Two horses were corralled next to the barn, and a cherry red Toyota pickup sat in front of the house.

I eased down the drive and parked well back from the truck so that I could be seen from the house. Philip had reminded me that it was bad manners to barge in on an Indian household unannounced. The proper etiquette was to wait outside several minutes, which I did before leaving Arch in the car with the windows partway down. The house was quiet, and no one answered the door, so I started around the house toward the barn.

That's when I saw him.

He was slumped in an old rocker on the side porch, his chin resting on his chest, arms dangling at his sides. The back of his head was a dark red mass. I moved in for a better look. The wall directly behind his head was sprayed with bloody pulp, gray hair, and bits of bone. I said something out loud—I think it was, "*My God!*" My knees quaked, and my mouth filled with saliva as the coffee and cereal in my stomach threatened to come up.

I took a deep breath, exhaled, and looked again at his head and at the deposit on the wall. Definitely not blunt trauma. I moved around him carefully, looking for a gun but saw none. Not a suicide, but a bullet for sure. High caliber, from the damage done. The round had entered about mid-forehead and judging from the blood still oozing from the cavity, I guessed the shooting happened no more than ten minutes earlier.

I stepped back. This was a crime scene, and I didn't want to disturb anything.

I followed the probable trajectory of the bullet with my eyes to a stand of cottonwoods maybe seventy yards off toward the river. The shot probably came in from those trees. A moment later Archie began to whine and bark, the way he does when he's heard something outside and wants to be let out. A spike of adrenaline shot through my body. I thought of the pickup that had passed me and the fact that I'd heard a car approaching out on the road just as I got out of the car to knock on Watlamet's door.

Had the shooter circled back?

Archie whined again, and every hair on my neck stood in unison. *The house. Take cover in the house.* I reached the side door just as two shots rang out. The door frame next to my head exploded. I fumbled with the doorknob, flung the door open, and dove into Watlamet's dining room. Two more bullets hissed over my head, ripping into an interior wall. I hadn't served in the military, but those shots taught me all I needed to know about combat. It was personal. Those rounds were meant for *me.*

I rolled behind a wall below a window, aware now that Archie was still barking. "*Archie, lay down, boy! Lay down now!*" I yelled out, keeping my head down and hoping my dog would obey me. Another shot rang out, and I heard the distinctive crunch of auto glass, which shatters without disintegrating. The barking stopped.

I couldn't let myself think about what Archie's silence meant and fought back the urge to go to him, which would have been suicide. *Focus,* I told myself. Watlamet's a rancher. There must be a gun in this house. *Find his goddamn gun!* I glanced around. Nothing in the dining room. I started down a narrow hall to what I figured was a bedroom and nearly ran into it— a gun rack on the wall bearing several rifles and a shotgun. The rifles looked intimidating, because I didn't know much about guns. The shotgun, an old double barrel breach loader, looked like one my grandfather had.

I took the shotgun out, and after fumbling around with shaking fingers for what seemed an eternity, pushed a lever mounted between the stock and the barrels to snap open the breach. The shiny brass heads of two shotgun shells stared back at me—a welcome sight. I closed the breach and moved quickly to a side window in the living room just in time to see a figure dash from one stand of trees to another, closer in. My attacker was coming in for the kill. I punched the barrel through the glass and pointed it in his general direction.

Kaboom. Kaboom. The buckshot sprayed out, kicking up dust well short of the trees, and the recoil knocked the gun out of my loose grip. I didn't care. I just wanted the son of a bitch to know I was armed. As soon as I fired I rolled out of the way and two more rounds punched through the window where I'd just been. I dashed back to the gun rack, found a box of shotgun shells, and dropped in two more shells.

The scene fell silent and nothing moved. I kept watching, my ears ringing from the shotgun blasts and my nostrils stinging from the stench of exploded gun powder. Then I heard the whine of a transmission out on the road, the sound of a car driving away at a high rate of speed.

I was pretty sure my attacker had fled, but I watched anxiously for several more minutes before checking the house for a landline. I didn't find one. My cell phone was in the car. I opened the front door a crack and peered out. Nothing stirred except the birds, which began singing again. I wanted to call out to Archie but stopped myself. If he was okay, I didn't want him sticking his head up.

I pocketed a half dozen shotgun shells and dashed first to the Toyota and then to my car, keeping both between me and the cottonwoods. I snapped the rear door open, my mouth so full of my heart I couldn't speak. Archie was on the back seat. Light winked off bits of glass in his dark coat. His ears were back and his eyes met mine with a look of relief. He was unharmed.

He whimpered and wagged his stub of a tail. I held my hand out, palm down. "Stay down, big guy. Stay down." He obeyed and kept whining softly. I retrieved my cell phone from the front seat, but there was no signal. "*Shit.*"

I got in the car and, keeping as low as possible, turned it around and gunned it to the top of the knoll. There was no sign of the shooter, but I felt terribly exposed up there.

A single bar showed on my phone. I dialed 911. "There's been a homicide out on Clarno Road." I looked at the directions Philip had given me, read off the address, and told them that I'd exchanged gunfire with the shooter. At this point I noticed a stinging on my neck below my right ear and the fact that my collar was sticking to my skin. I reached up and touched the still wet blood and realized I had a nest of splinters embedded deeply in my neck. Not a nest, actually—more like a lumberyard. The wound began to burn, but the good news was I was still breathing.

I drove back down the knoll and parked between the house and the Toyota. I scooped up the shotgun and Archie, who was still trembling, and hustled back into the relative safety of Watlamet's house to wait for the officers to arrive.

Damn, I thought, *what in hell have I gotten myself into?*

Chapter Eight

Jake

Jake started sprinting toward his truck after firing two final rounds at the man in Watlamet's house, the man with the double barrel shotgun. *I hope to hell I hit the bastard but no way I'm waiting around to find out. Time to get out of Dodge.* He reached the truck, stuffed his rifle behind the seat, and took off in the direction of his campsite.

He pounded the steering wheel as he sped away. "Goddammit. Goddamnit. That dude saw me. This was supposed to be *easy.*"

It wasn't until he pulled off the highway and began the climb into the narrow canyon that he stopped talking to himself. And only after he pulled off the road below the mouth of the abandoned mine and tucked his truck in behind a pile of tailings did his pulse come back to normal.

He double-timed up a steep ridge to where he knew there was a cell phone signal and tapped out a text to the number he'd been given: Target is down. One problem. Someone saw me as I was leaving. Not sure if I took care of him. I'm back at campsite. Need guidance.

Seventeen agonizing minutes later he received a reply: Stay where you are. Check back tomorrow, mid-morning.

After hiking back down, he slipped under the shade of the low tarp he'd rigged earlier, took a long pull on a bottle of water, and lit up a Camel. But the cigarette did nothing to calm him. He laid back using his backpack for a pillow and let out a deep sigh that turned into a moan. *You fool. You never should have agreed to this.*

His thoughts flashed back to the night he'd arrived at the guest house...

He'd let himself in, like the text said. But no one was there. Instead, he found two envelopes with his name on them, and he almost giggled. "Damn, this is like some kind of spy shit." He opened the thick envelope first, whistled softly, and sat down on shaky legs. It was stuffed with money—a wad of crisp, new one-hundred dollar bills a couple of inches thick. One hundred and fifty of the little beauties. He counted them twice and did the math. A cool fifteen thousand.

A note tucked into the bills read: *"Down payment. Another $15,000 paid upon completion of task."* When he tore open the second envelope his hand shook slightly, and he felt a sinking feeling in his gut. The details of his job—what he was to do, who he was to do it to, and how—were precisely laid out on two pieces of typed paper. There was an explanation, too. It made him feel a little better. Some crazy old Indian hermit was going to dredge up the past and hurt a lot of innocent people. This was unacceptable to the Old Man, and he needed Jake to put a stop to it. The Old Man would consider it a great personal favor.

But Jake still felt shitty after it all sank in. Kill a man? Sure, he'd killed his share of big game—long horns, elk, deer, even a couple of bears. But a man? That was different. Then he glanced over at that stack of bills. Thirty thousand bucks would change his life, big time. He could pay off some debts, get caught up on his alimony. A sliver of hope slipped into his thoughts. *Maybe Amy would change her mind after this. Maybe we could start over...*

But then the thought of the awful task in front of him came back in full force. He sat there in the guesthouse for a long time, going back and forth. What finally swung it for him was the Old Man, what was said in the note about doing him a personal favor. *Maybe this would really count for something. God knows, nothing I ever do is good enough.* Sure, the money was great, but he knew deep down he would have done the job for nothing, just to please the old bastard.

And besides, the job's a no-brainer, and no one will miss the old Indian, anyway.

Jake's thoughts were brought back to the here and now by a gust of wind that slammed into the weathered tarp above him. He sat up. "No-brainer, my ass. Now there may be a witness out there. I hope to hell I killed that son of a bitch, too."

When the sun finally sank behind the rim of the canyon, he fired up the propane stove inside the protective ring of rocks he'd built and waited for a pot of water to boil. Freeze-dried beef stroganoff with noodles was his favorite camp food, but this particular night it didn't taste that good. As a matter of fact, the food caught in his throat and the only thing that went down easy was a fifth of I. W. Harper.

But the whiskey didn't keep him from seeing the old Indian's face in the scope of his rifle. Over and over again.

He woke the next morning with a splitting headache, but as he hiked back up the ridge he felt more hopeful. *I pumped two rounds in right where I saw the muzzle flash of that shotgun. I must have hit him. Hell, they can just pay me the rest and I'll go home, lay low and let this thing blow over.*

But the text that came in read: There's a loose end. Sit tight for 24 hrs.

Jake's throat constricted as he read the text, and he had difficulty swallowing. *Shit. Missed the bastard. This ain't over. Not by a long shot.*

Chapter Nine

Once inside Watlamet's house, I put Arch and the shotgun down, pressed a handkerchief to the wound on my neck, and rummaged through his kitchen for a clean towel. Still trembling, Archie shook himself and came over to me. I dropped to one knee and brushed the remaining bits of glass from his coat using the towel. When I finished he scrubbed my face with puppy kisses while I hugged his neck with one arm. "Thanks, big boy," I said in a husky voice. "You saved my life."

I flopped down on a threadbare couch and leaned back for a moment. The shock of what had just happened sunk in. It was my turn to tremble, the shakes starting in my gut and rippling down my legs. I felt like an idiot and was glad no one was around to see me like this.

After I calmed down I started poking around the house. I glanced at my watch and figured I had, at the outside, a couple of minutes. In any case, I'd hear their sirens coming in. I felt a twinge of guilt at the prospect of mucking around in a crime scene. After all, I'd spent a career in law enforcement. On the other hand, I wasn't going to disturb anything. And I felt like I'd earned the right to know if there were any clues in Watlamet's house that might tell me who had killed him and nearly blown my head off.

I saw nothing of interest in the living and dining rooms. A desk containing a pile of papers—mostly bills, credit card receipts, and copies of a church newsletter—stood in a corner of the kitchen. I glanced through them without spotting anything.

In the bedroom I found a cell phone that I'd missed in my earlier search. It lay on a nightstand, partially obscured by a lamp and a large, leather-bound Bible. Using a pencil, I flipped it open and scrolled down to *Recent Calls*. Under *Calls Made*, there were two numbers, under *Calls Received*, three. I jotted the numbers down on a business card from my wallet. As I closed the phone, I heard a siren in the distance.

I waved with both hands to the Wasco County Sheriff's cruiser that came down Sherman Watlamet's dirt drive. I knew they'd be on high alert and wanted to make damn sure they saw I was unarmed and had no reason to confuse me for the gunman who'd shot the Indian rancher through the head.

I gave a deputy—C. Grooms by her name tag—a quick run-down on what had just happened. She seemed satisfied that I was the innocent bystander I claimed to be, and when I told her I didn't want an ambulance, offered to give me first aid. Her partner was, by this time, over in the cottonwoods looking for shell casings. The medical examiner and forensic team hadn't arrived yet.

A big woman with blond hair combed up in front, Grooms had biceps that filled her short-sleeved shirt and small gray eyes that were hard, like ball bearings. She retrieved a first aid kit from her patrol car, took a closer look at my neck, and made a face. "I'll bandage this up for you, but you're gonna need to get those splinters removed." I nodded and she set about the task as she began questioning me. "So, Mr. Claxton, you said you got a look at the man in the truck who passed you comin' in here?"

Thinking of all the witnesses I'd questioned in my career, all the expectations I'd had about their ability to remember important details, I had to laugh inwardly. Now the tables were turned, and I wasn't so sure how much I'd picked up in my quick encounter with the man I assumed was the shooter. "Yeah, I did get a look, and then he turned away. He looked surprised as hell to see me. Not a lot of traffic out here."

"Seein' the way he circled back on you, he must consider you a witness, for sure."

I nodded. "I'm afraid you're right about that."

She smiled and snipped off a piece of tape. When the tip of the scissors touched my neck, I flinched. "Hold still," she said sternly. "Tell me what you saw, Mr. Claxton."

"He was Caucasian, mid to late forties, give or take. Big eyes in a long, narrow face. Prominent nose. Dark, heavy sideburns, long hair, maybe. Couldn't tell for sure because of the cowboy hat." I closed my eyes to picture the fleeting moment better. "Uh, medium build, maybe, fairly broad shoulders. That's about it."

"Good. What was he wearing?"

"The cowboy hat was gray, and he wore a dark shirt, blue maybe."

"I see," Grooms said, not looking up from a pad she was jotting notes on. "Could you identify this man if you saw him again?"

"Yeah, I'm pretty sure I could."

"Do you think you could help our artist come up with a sketch of this man?"

"I suppose I could do that. It'll be pretty rough."

"But better than nothin'. How about the truck?"

I puffed a breath through my lips and shook my head. "Late model, dark blue pickup. Nondescript...Ford or Chevy, maybe."

Deputy Grooms rolled her eyes at my inability to differentiate between a Ford and a Chevy but didn't comment. "Did you see the plates?"

"Nope. I was worried about him being the man I'd come to see— the victim, Mr. Watlamet—so I really didn't focus on the truck."

She snapped her notebook shut and said, "Excuse me," and then walked briskly over to the squad car. I knew she was going to call in a BOLO for the truck and the man I described. There was a good chance he was still on the road.

When she came back she asked me more questions about why I happened to be visiting Sherman Watlamet. I laid out the entire story and told her that Philip Lone Deer had helped me find Watlamet. I gave her Philip's phone number and address. She asked me who my client was. I told her that was privileged, but if she felt she needed it, I would seek my client's permission to give it to her. She told me to go ahead and do that.

"Do you think this killin' here's connected to the disappearance of Mr. Queah in any way?" she asked when I'd finished.

"I don't see how it could be, but you know what they say about coincidences."

She allowed a faint smile. "Right. You gonna keep workin' on the disappearance?"

I shrugged. "It'll depend on what my client wants to do now."

Grooms locked onto me with those hard, gray eyes. "You might want to consider quittin' while you're ahead, Mr. Claxton. But if you learn anything new, you be sure to call me."

Later that afternoon I was sitting on a park bench in The Dalles watching Archie sniff around. I had just finished up with the sheriff department's artist, a young woman who quickly and deftly captured the essence of the face of the man I saw. To be honest, I was more than a little skittish about this. The sketch was bound to get into the papers and reinforce the shooter's notion that I was a star witness. Of course, I didn't know whether he knew who I was, and that was something I needed to talk to Philip about. Just what had he told people in his search for Watlamet? Had he used my name? I wondered. As if on cue, my phone chirped. It was Philip returning my call.

"How'd it go with Watlamet?"

"Uh, not too well."

"Why? What happened?"

"He's dead. Someone shot him with a rifle at long range just before I got there."

"*What?* You're kidding."

I went on to tell him what I'd found and how Archie had saved me from getting my brains blown out, too. After I finished he said, "Where are you now?"

"I'm sitting in a park in The Dalles watching Archie take a leak."

"Don't go home. Bring the hero dog and come to my place. We can talk about this. You can go home in the morning. I'm glad you're okay, man."

"Me, too."

Chapter Ten

"Hold still, damn it!" Philip was bent down next to me with a large magnifying glass in one hand and a pair of tweezers in the other. The tools came from his fly tying workshop. "I don't know whether I can do this, Cal. Maybe you should go to the hospital."

"Come on. Tying a number sixteen fly's a lot harder than extracting a few splinters from my neck. You can do this."

"You got something against hospitals?"

"Just not a big fan. Carry me in to one, okay. Otherwise I'm looking for a work-around."

Philip shook his head. "Okay, but this work-around's going to hurt. The next little bastard's straight in like an arrow. I'm going to have to dig it out."

I gritted my teeth at the stab of pain as he began probing around in the wound.

"Got it. Now, hold on. This next one's the size of small log."

When the last splinter was out and I was rebandaged, we went into the kitchen and popped two beers. Philip said, "My wife's visiting her sister, and I only cook camp food. We can go out if you want."

"Tell you what, if we can find something in the fridge, I'll cook. I owe you for medical services."

Philip opened the refrigerator and pulled out a package of ground beef. "Uh, how about hamburgers?" Archie eyed the meat, sat down at Philip's feet, looked up at him and whimpered.

I smiled. "Looks like Arch has first dibs on that."

Philip laughed. "Good point. The hero dog deserves a special treat tonight."

"You got any pasta?"

"Yeah. Should be some in the pantry."

"Smoked salmon?"

He looked insulted. "Of course. In the fridge."

I found a nice chunk wrapped in foil along with some green onions and white wine, and after rummaging through his wife's spices I picked out some dried dill.

I started heating a pot of water for the pasta. "So, tell me how you found Watlamet." I handed him the onions and nodded toward the chopping block between us. "Chop these while you're talking, and if you've got a couple of cloves of garlic, chop those, too."

"I tried every contact I had over at Yakama Rez," Philip began. "They asked around to their friends. You know how it goes. All dead ends. They knew of him, but nobody had a clue where he was living."

"Did you tell them what it was about or mention my name?"

"I didn't use your name at all with those guys, just said someone wanted to talk to Watlamet about the disappearance of a Wasco Indian, Nelson Queah, to get their attention. Of course, I used your name with Watlamet, so he'd know who to expect."

"So how did you find him?"

"My father remembered Watlamet used to be a hunting guide. He suggested I call Henry Johnson. Henry's a Yakama who used to hunt elk with Dad in the Wallowas. He got back to me a day later. Said he had to make about a dozen calls to track Watlamet down. He'd pretty much dropped out." Philip handed me the chopping block.

I scraped the now-chopped garlic and onions into a skillet of hot olive oil that spattered and sizzled. "What was your take on Watlamet when you met him?"

Philip stroked his chin and thought for a moment. "Like I said, the guy's a loner, or *was* a loner. Some of the people I talked to used the term 'apple.' You know, red on the outside, white on the inside. I was a little surprised by his spread. He was living above the poverty line, for sure."

I nodded as I added some wine and dill to the skillet. I was pretty sure that's what my wife put in the sauté. Then I added the pasta to the big pot of water, which was now at a roiling boil. "You said he seemed a little reluctant at first—"

"Yeah. When I mentioned Nelson Queah he seemed to react, you know, his eyes kind of flared. But then he nodded and said something like, "Yes, I will talk to this friend of yours.""

I crumbled the smoked salmon into the sauté, and then I remembered the secret ingredient—lemon zest. Luckily, there was a lonely lemon in the fridge, so after adding some chopped lemon peel, lemon juice, salt, and pepper, I let the whole thing simmer while the pasta cooked.

We went back over everyone Philip had talked to about Sherman Watlamet one more time, but nothing else of interest surfaced. By this time, the pasta was ready. I drained it, put it back in the pot, and dumped in the sauce. "Got any parmesan cheese?" Philip found a small hunk, which I grated and added to the pot. All that remained was tasting my masterpiece and announcing that dinner was ready.

Philip opened a cheap cab and poured two glasses. We both ate hungrily and silently for several minutes. He said, "This is great, man. I didn't know you could cook like this."

"I didn't either. I got tired of eating crap food, so I've been dabbling in the kitchen. Sometimes a recipe just comes back to me. I guess I'd paid more attention to my wife's cooking than I realized. I exhaled a breath. "She was a great cook. To her, food was the glue that held our family together. Of course, it really wasn't. *She* was the glue." I felt a surge of emotion and caught myself. "Anyway, I'm getting better at cooking, I think."

"For sure," Philip said as he piled on a second helping.

Perhaps sensing my discomfort, Philip changed the subject. "What's the deal with this sketch you helped make? Will it be in the papers?"

"Uh, it'll circulate through the law enforcement systems for sure. I don't know about the papers."

"Hmm. So, what're you going do to protect yourself from this guy?"

I shrugged. "Any suggestions?"

"I think you have to assume the shooter knows who you are. So, don't make yourself a target. Stay away from the windows at your place, keep the blinds drawn, that sort of thing."

I nodded and frowned. The thought of having to skulk around at my own place was disquieting.

"You have a weapon at home?"

"Nope."

My friend shot me an incredulous look. "Why not?"

I shrugged. "Never felt compelled to own one. In my last job I became familiar with what a bullet can do to a human body. Too familiar."

He cranked his brows down and shook his head. "That's the whole idea, Cal. I've got a .357 Magnum I can loan you."

"Thanks, but I'll pass." I knew I probably should take the gun, but at the time the threat to me personally still seemed pretty abstract.

After we finished eating, I asked to use Philip's computer to see what I could learn from the numbers I'd taken off Watlamet's phone. I reminded Philip that Grooms was probably going to contact him, and when she did, he wasn't to mention I had the numbers. Cops get pissy about people messing around in their crime scenes, I told him.

I pulled up the reverse phone number directory and punched in the first of the three outgoing numbers I'd jotted down. It corresponded to a Methodist Church in Shaniko, the nearest meaningful town from Watlamet's ranch. The second number was the residence of a minister named Aldus Hinkley in Shaniko, and the third was the Rose City Senior Living Center in Portland.

Looking on over my shoulder, Philip said, "What do you make of that?"

"Not much." I checked the dates of the calls again. "But it's interesting that Watlamet seemed anxious to talk to the reverend at a church in Shaniko after you talked to him about me. Maybe I'll drop by there tomorrow on my way home and see what I can find out."

"Wouldn't hurt. It's not too far out of your way."

I tried the numbers of the two incoming calls next. The first belonged to a doctor's office in Shaniko and the second to a veterinarian in Fossil, a larger town north of Clarno.

We went back in the kitchen and poured some more wine. Philip said, "What about Winona. Have you talked to her since the shooting?"

I scratched my head and frowned. "Nah. Not yet. I guess I'm just putting it off. It's bad news for her. The last person to see her grandfather alive is dead now." I retrieved her card from my wallet and called her. When she didn't answer, I left a message to call me but gave no details.

Philip eyed me appraisingly. "I know you've had a couple of meetings with her, but you haven't told me much about them. She's quite a woman, huh?"

I kept a poker face. I didn't want to encourage Philip to do me favors when it came to women. I wasn't looking for that kind of help. "She's been all business when I've talked to her. Are you two really related?"

"Well, we didn't hang out together as kids. I think she's a second cousin, once removed."

"She seems pretty private. What's she really like?"

Philip shrugged. "From what I hear she's, uh, complicated. Married some Klickitat from over in Washington, a political activist. That didn't work. Lives alone in Portland now."

"What's complicated about that?"

Philip smiled and shook his head. You know, the same old story—she's conflicted, caught between two cultures, all that bullshit. And she probably feels a ton of pressure because of the expectations, Stanford PhD and all."

I thought of Philip. Half white, half Indian. He was caught in the middle, too. "Sounds familiar."

Philip looked at me and laughed. "She's got it worse than me, man, a lot worse. Nobody expects me to change the world. For me, it's simple. Live in the moment. Screw the rest. That's how to survive."

"Words to live by," I said and instantly regretted it.

My friend looked at me again and held my eyes with an impatient, almost scolding look. "You're like her, Cal. Complicated. I know that what happened down in L.A. was bad. I'm not saying it wasn't. But at some point, you need to shrug it off and get on with your life."

I nodded. "Yeah, you're right," but inside I was screaming, *shrug it off? How could I possibly shrug it off?*

I was utterly exhausted and turned in early that night, but sleep didn't come quickly. I lay there in the dark listening to Archie breathe and thinking about what had happened— Watlamet's rag-doll body, his shattered skull, those incoming rounds with my name on them, and the question of whether I was now the target of some maniac sniper.

Fragments of that scene spiraled in my head like debris in a tornado. It was a feeling I'd experienced once before, and I manned the firewall separating me from those old memories with all my strength.

I finally fell into a fitful sleep, which was, thank God, dreamless.

Chapter Eleven

The next morning Archie and I sat in the car across the street from the Shaniko Methodist Church waiting for someone to show up. A modest, single-story structure sided with board and batten hewn from old growth firs, it looked at least a hundred years old. The sign out on the highway told me the population of Shaniko was four hundred sixty-nine, but right now, at eight-forty, it looked more like five or six, max. I sipped a cup of black coffee I'd bought at a little diner just outside town. The coffee was better than I expected, which boded well for the rest of the day. I'm off my game without a decent cup or two in the morning.

At eight-fifty a dusty green pickup pulled into the church parking lot. A big man with a mashed potatoes and gravy waistline got out. He wore dark slacks, a faded cowboy shirt and freshly polished boots. I told Arch to stay put and intercepted him as he was unlocking the back door.

"Excuse me. Are you Reverend Hinkley, by any chance?"

He looked around at me and smiled without any effort. "In the flesh. What can I do for you?" He had combed-over, black, thinning hair and a lopsided nose that made me wonder if he'd ever boxed. His eyes were a soft brown, his gaze disarmingly friendly.

I offered my hand. "My name's Cal Claxton. I was wondering if I could talk to you about Sherman Watlamet."

His face clouded over. "Is Sherman a friend of yours?"

"No, Reverend. I take it you heard what happened yesterday."

"Yes. I'm afraid I have. It's all over town."

"I was the one who found him. I'd driven out to his ranch to talk to him."

He shook his head and looked at me in bewilderment. "My Lord, what a terrible thing. Who would shoot a kind man like that? Our whole congregation's in shock." He paused for a moment and appraised me. "Are you with the Sheriff's Department, Mr. Claxton?"

"No, I'm not. I'm an attorney." I handed him a card. "Could we talk for a few minutes?"

Reverend Hinkley's office was a small cubicle cluttered with books and papers. There was a single picture on the wall of Jesus praying in the Garden, light streaming down from the heavens onto his upturned face. One of the books on his credenza was Richard Dawkins' *The God Delusion*, and I wondered whether the Reverend had an open mind or was preparing to tell the local library to remove the book from its shelves.

He offered me a seat. I said, "I have a client who has asked me to look into the disappearance of her grandfather, a Wasco Indian named Nelson Queah. Mr. Watlamet and Mr. Queah were seen together the day of the disappearance. I'd gone out to Watlamet's ranch to talk to him about this. That's when I discovered his body."

He leaned forward in his chair. "That must have been horrible for you. I understand he was shot from long range with a rifle."

"It was a high caliber weapon, for sure."

He nodded in my direction. "I see you're injured." He wasn't probing like a gossip or voyeur. There was genuine concern in his eyes.

I shifted in my seat. "Yeah, the killer shot at me but missed. I took some splinters when the bullets hit the house. I'm fine."

His eyes got larger. "Dear God. Something happens like that must make you wonder about mankind."

There was an invitation in the statement. I almost dumped the feelings that the shooting had stirred up in me but caught myself. I was here to get information from the Reverend, not the other way around. "Well, I was a district attorney for the city of Los Angeles for many years, so I've seen a lot, Reverend. But, in all honesty, you never get used to something like this."

"I'm sure you don't, Mr. Claxton. I'm sure you don't."

I cleared my throat. "I'm wondering if Mr. Watlamet happened to say anything about the disappearance of Nelson Queah to you or anyone else in the church?"

The wariness returned to his eyes. "Are the shooting and this disappearance related?"

"I have no reason to believe that's the case. The disappearance happened quite a while ago." I hoped he wouldn't ask how long. The answer might cause him to doubt my sanity.

He leaned back in his chair, laced his fingers together on his belly, and looked straight into my eyes. "Mr. Claxton, words are often spoken to me in confidence."

"I know, Reverend. And I respect that. It's just that Mr. Queah's granddaughter cares deeply about him, and she's been suffering in his absence. Mr. Watlamet was one of the last persons to see him alive."

He kept his eyes on me. They had softened again. "I see. Are you a religious man, Mr. Claxton?"

As a lapsed agnostic, I was afraid the conversation might veer in this direction. I stroked my mustache with my thumb and forefinger to buy a little time. "Uh, not in the conventional sense, Reverend. I sometimes feel spiritual when I'm out in nature. When I'm fly fishing, mostly."

Smile lines sprang from the corners of his eyes. "Christ is in all things, especially nature, don't you think?"

I wasn't sure I could put a name on it, but I nodded in agreement.

"Where do you fish?"

"Oh, I'm just a beginner, but I like the Deschutes. That's my favorite river."

"It's a great river. The salmon fly hatch's superb, and the winter steelhead, oh my. I love the John Day, too. Can't beat the smallmouth bass there."

I smiled and nodded in agreement. "Haven't had the pleasure, but I've heard that."

Reverend Hinkley's smile was now a broad grin. "You know, last July we had a trip on the Day you wouldn't believe. A big mayfly hatch brought every smallie in the river to the surface. Lordy. You should have seen it, Mr. Claxton. The river was *boiling*." He leaned back in his chair, and a laugh roared from his chest like a thunderclap.

He went on to tell me about the trip, which led into a lengthy exchange of fly fishing stories, mainly from his end. It was a relief to think about something other than bloody murder, and to tell the truth I almost forgot why I'd come to see the Reverend, whom I learned was an uncommonly good fly fisherman. No user of foam poppers and treble-hook spinners, the good reverend fished the right way—using dry flies that float on the surface.

The fact that I was a fly fisherman must have compensated for my shaky religious underpinnings, because when I finally steered the conversation back to the subject of Sherman Watlamet, Reverend Hinkley leaned forward and said, "You know, Mr. Claxton, what Sherman told me the other night *is* confidential. But since he's now in the Lord's hands and since you're an honorable man, I'm going to share some of what he said to me."

"Thank you, Reverend. I'll treat the information with great discretion."

"Sherman joined our church a couple of years ago. He's been a blessing. Our only Native American." He gazed down at the blotter on his desk for a few moments and then chuckled. "You know, there's nothing like the passion of the newly converted, Mr. Claxton. Sherman was no exception. He loved Jesus with all his heart."

I smiled. "I'm sure he did."

"A couple of nights ago he called me and said he wanted to come by to talk about something important. About setting something right, I think is the way he said it."

A small current of excitement went down my spine. I nodded but kept quiet, fearing if I said anything I might break the spell.

"His soul was in great torment. Said he'd done things that were wrong, that he was ashamed of. Said he wanted to get it off his chest." The Reverend closed his eyes and shook his head at the memory of it. "He wanted to know if it was right to tell the truth, even if it hurt someone, a friend."

"Couldn't the truth hurt him as well?"

Reverend Hinkley smiled. "He didn't care about himself, Mr. Claxton. When you have the fire of the Lord in your heart, you're fearless. I told him the Lord spoke only the truth, and if he wanted to be like Jesus, he would have to do the same thing, no matter what the consequences." Reverend Hinkley's eyes brightened with a film of moisture. "He cried when I said this. I told him to talk to his friend. To ask his forgiveness."

"Did he mention any names, Reverend?" I asked as gently as I could.

"He didn't mention anyone named Queah. He was worried the truth might hurt a man named Cecil. Cecil was an old friend of his."

"Cecil?" I recognized that name. "Did he mention a last name?"

The Reverend paused for a moment and wrinkled his forehead. "No. I don't believe he did, Mr. Claxton. All I remember is the name Cecil."

"Did he tell you what it was he wanted to set right?"

"No. I'm afraid he didn't. All he said was the passing of a man's wife got him thinking, a man he had wronged in the past. I didn't probe." Then he paused again and met my eyes. "This could have something to do with Sherman's death, couldn't it, Mr. Claxton?"

"I honestly don't know, Reverend. But I think you should consider passing this information along to the Sheriff's Department. They may contact you, but if they don't, I'd call Deputy Grooms, and tell her what you just told me." I wrote the name down for him.

◇◇◇

Frampton? Farmer? What the hell was Cecil's last name? Archie and I were back on the highway, heading north toward I-84. Out on the horizon, white clouds scudded east to west like a thawing ice floe. I figured the wind was up in the Gorge, and hoped it wouldn't rain now that I was missing a back window. I couldn't for the life of me remember the last name of the Cecil mentioned in Nelson Queah's letters—the guy who had offered him a job if he would stop protesting against construction of the dam. I thought about calling Winona when it came to me—*Ferguson.* That was it—Cecil *Ferguson.*

I pulled off the road and let Archie out to stretch his legs. An eighteen wheeler whooshed by, and my dog instinctively moved away from the highway. We walked a few yards into the sage brush, and I dialed one of the numbers I retrieved off Watlamet's phone. A female receptionist answered at the Rose City Senior Living Center. "Uh, this is Jim Smith from Fed Ex," I said. "I've got a package here for a Cecil Ferguson. Just checking to make sure I've got the right address."

"Yes," she answered brightly, "he's one of our residents."

Bingo. "Thank you. Uh, do you have a room number?"

"He's on the fourth floor, four-oh-two, but you can leave the package at the desk."

Well, well, every now and then I get lucky.

We got back in the car, and I Googled the address of the Rose City. I looked back at Archie. "You up for one more stop, big boy?"

Chapter Twelve

The Rose City Senior Living Center was on Eighty-second Avenue in Southeast Portland, an area known not so affectionately as Felony Flats. Across from a used car lot and wedged between a beer joint and a mini-mart, the building had a weather-stained façade, squinty little windows, and a low, covered portico propped up with faux Greek columns needing paint. A large, free-form sculpture made from bent tubes of stainless steel welded together stood on one side of the entrance—the builder's contribution to the arts, no doubt. It looked like a train wreck to me.

As I approached the entrance, I fell in with a middle-aged couple. When they were buzzed in, I smiled, held the door, and then followed them into the elevator and got off on the fourth floor.

Cecil Ferguson had been a big man once, but age and some wasting disease had stooped him at the shoulders and taken most of his body mass except for what held him together, skin stretched over bone, mostly. He had thinning, red-gone-to-gray hair, and his wavy nose and hollow cheeks swarmed with tiny blood vessels, most of them broken. His pale blue eyes blazed at me, as if all the life left in him had retreated there to make a final stand.

"Who the hell are you?" He stood in the doorway, his bony fingers gripping the edge of the door, his hoarse words stalling between us from lack of breath.

"My name's Cal Claxton, Mr. Ferguson. I was wondering if I might speak to you for a few minutes."

"How'd you get in here?" The eyes got hotter. The anger that burned there seemed endemic, like something he'd carried around most of his life.

"I came in with some folks who're visiting one of your neighbors."

He considered that for a moment. "What do you want to talk about?"

I hesitated for a couple of beats and decided to go straight at him. "Your old friend, Sherman Watlamet." A momentary image of Watlamet's shattered skull and wall-spattered brains flashed through my head.

He laughed. "The chief? You know the chief?"

"Uh, I met him the other day, yes."

He didn't move. "You a cop?"

"No. I'm a lawyer." I handed him my card. "I just want to ask you a few questions, Mr. Ferguson. It won't take long."

He stepped aside. "What the fuck. I'm not going anywhere."

Light filtered into the sparsely furnished room through soiled, gauzy curtains. The image of a female judge in a courtroom was frozen on a TV screen in the corner, and the warm air reeked of cigarettes and urine. Ferguson flicked off the TV and sat down in a recliner that had an oxygen cylinder propped against it. I sat across from him in a hard-backed chair. He fished a pack of cigarettes from his shirt pocket and lit up with the casual grace of a longtime smoker.

With the smoldering cigarette dangling from his lips he said, "Doc says I gotta quit these coffin nails, but I figure what's the point?"

I smiled and nodded. "Tough habit to quit."

He inhaled deeply and blew a cloud of blue smoke out of the corner of his mouth. His eyes burned like tiny gas flames. "The chief called me a couple of nights ago all hopped up on Jesus. Said he was gonna unburden himself or some shit like that. Is that what you want to talk about, Mr. Lawyer?"

"Yeah, I think it is. I represent the granddaughter of Nelson Queah. I believe you knew Mr. Queah back when the Columbia dams were being built." I paused and waited for a reaction.

The line that was Ferguson's mouth turned up at the ends like a smiling serpent, and he remained silent.

"Queah disappeared the day they flooded the falls at Celilo. His granddaughter wants to know what really happened to him, you know, to put the matter to rest for the family and the tribe."

Ferguson leaned back in the recliner, took a drag on his cigarette, and appraised me. Then he smiled again, showing yellowed teeth and stretching the skin on his chin to translucence. "You can't prove a damn thing, you know."

I struggled to hide my surprise. "I know that, Mr. Ferguson. This isn't a criminal investigation. All I'm after here is the truth about the disappearance of Nelson Queah. We don't think he killed himself or fell in the river. We think it was foul play."

"Why should I give a rat's ass about some Indian or his granddaughter?" He laughed, a single "hah." "Talk to the chief, Mr. Lawyer. He's the one who wants to *unburden* himself."

"I can't do that, Mr. Ferguson. Sherman Watlamet was murdered yesterday. Someone shot him with a high-powered rifle. I found the body."

"*What?*"

"He's dead."

Ferguson looked at me in disbelief for a long time, as if the words circled in his head with no place to land. "*No*, they wouldn't do something like that." He shook his head adamantly. "*No*. You're wrong. It was some sort of accident."

"I can assure you it was no accident. The shooter took a couple of shots at me as well. Do you know something about this, Mr. Ferguson? Who's *they*?"

Ignoring the question, he wrapped his chest with his arms, closed his eyes, and began rocking back and forth. In a low, barely audible voice, he said, "Should've kept my fucking mouth shut." He shook his head. "Ah, Sherman, you dumb son of a bitch." Then he stopped rocking and covered his face with his hands.

I leaned forward in my chair and spoke softly. "Who killed your friend, Mr. Ferguson?"

After a long pause, he looked up slowly and gave me the serpentine smile again. Then he started to laugh, and the laugh turned to a deep, hacking cough. When he removed his hand from his mouth, a thin rope of spittle trailed down his chin. He drew himself up and looked at me, his eyes burning. "I'm no rat, Mr. Lawyer. And you can't trace nothin'. I called 'em from a payphone."

"You're not a rat if you tell me about it. These people killed your friend."

"Not gonna happen." He paused again, and I waited, sensing he had something more he wanted to say. "But I'll tell you this. The Chief did some pretty bad stuff in his day, but he never killed nobody, not directly, anyway."

"What did he want to confess?"

Ferguson puffed a breath through his lips and smiled. "I don't know. Probably that he took money to lie about what happened to Queah, maybe some other stuff he did to his Indian brothers he wasn't too proud of. I suppose for an Indian that's a big deal. Nobody else gives a shit."

"What happened to Queah?"

He looked at me again with those blazing eyes and struggled to get up. "You need to get outa here now." I got up and he followed me. When I turned at the door he smiled a knowing smile. "Tell his granddaughter he's resting at his favorite spot—the bottom of the falls. I cracked his skull and put him there. Now get the hell out of here." He shut the door with more strength than I thought he had.

Chapter Thirteen

I walked out of Ferguson's apartment, not believing what I'd just heard. At my car, I leashed up Archie. We both needed a walk. We stopped at a little coffee shop three blocks down, where I bought a double cappuccino and took a seat at an outside table. I called Deputy Sheriff Grooms first and told her about my talk with Reverend Hinkley, careful to give the white lie that I'd noticed his name on a church bulletin in Watlamet's house, not his number in the dead man's cell phone. Then I filled her in on my visit with Cecil Ferguson, his reaction to Watlamet's death, and the apparent confession he'd made.

When I finished, Grooms paused a couple of beats before responding. "Well, looks like we got our answer on whether the murder's related to that missing fella you're investigating."

"Queah. His name's Nelson Queah."

"Right. You're right smack in the middle of this, aren't you, Mr. Claxton?"

"Not intentionally. I was just following up for my client. I didn't expect Ferguson to know anything about the Watlamet homicide, and I sure as hell didn't expect him to confess to killing Queah."

"Let me get this straight now. You're saying that Ferguson told someone that Watlamet was gonna make some sort of confession about the missing man Queah?"

"That's right. He was going to admit that he lied about what happened all those years ago."

"And Ferguson told someone about this, then someone killed Watlamet to keep him quiet?"

"Yeah, that's what it sounded like to me."

"And this fella Ferguson knows who did it?"

"I think so, yes."

After I gave her the address of the senior center, she said, "I'm gonna need another formal statement from you covering this new development, okay?"

"I need to go home first so I can feed my dog and change my underwear."

She chuckled. "You make sure you do that now. You owe that pup of yours, you know. By the way, did you see The Dalles newspaper today? Our boy's sketch's on the front page, thanks to you. Who knows? Maybe we'll get lucky and wrap this thing up quick."

My chest tightened a little. I didn't feel quite as enthusiastic about the sketch going public as Grooms did. "I sure hope so," was all I managed to say.

Afterwards, I wondered if Watlamet's murder had been picked up by *The Oregonian*. If it had, there was a good chance Winona had seen it, which wouldn't be cool since I should've been the one to break the news. I went back into the coffee shop and found a paper, just to make sure. To my relief there wasn't anything on the killing, which tended to bear out the complaint by the eastern part of the state that its news went essentially unreported by the Portland paper.

I called Winona and got her this time. She said she'd been swamped all day and apologized for not getting back to me. I told her I had some news but didn't want to discuss it on the phone. She said she was still working, suggested we meet at her office, and gave me directions.

Pacific Salmon Watch was located in a tastefully renovated building in the Pearl, a warehouse district in Northwest Portland that was undergoing full-blown gentrification. When I cut the ignition Archie whined softly a couple of times. I turned around and took his head in my hands. "I promise, big boy, no matter what happens next, we're going home tonight. You sit tight. I'll be back with something to eat."

The receptionist told me "Dr. Cloud" was in a meeting and showed me to a small waiting area down the hall from her office. I thumbed through a spiffy four-color brochure describing the place and was comforted that an organization with such seeming clout was on the side of the fish. On the other hand, I wondered why the furniture was so damn nice.

Her office door opened, and a familiar-looking man stepped out with Winona behind him. I watched unobserved as he turned to face her. He said, "Thanks so much, Win. Your help really means a lot to me."

She looked up at him and smiled, and I looked back down at the brochure.

"Will I see you this weekend?" The man asked.

"We'll see." Then she glanced over at me, smiled, and said, "Oh, Jason, I want you to meet someone."

I stood up. With the exception of a worn knit shirt I'd borrowed from Philip, I had on the same clothes I'd worn the day before, and I sported a large, blood-soaked bandage on my neck. To top it off, my Merrells were spattered with the dark stains of my own blood.

"Jason, this is Cal Claxton. Cal, Jason Townsend. Cal's the lawyer I told you about. The one helping me look into what happened to Grandfather."

He smiled broadly and shook my hand with the same firm grip of a week earlier. "Of course. You're the lawyer from Dundee. Good to see you again, Cal." He wore sharply pressed gray slacks and an expensive looking leather jacket, and his tan suggested he hadn't spent the entire winter in Portland.

"How's the Senate race shaping up?"

The smile became an ah-shucks grin. "We're making progress, but it's going to be an uphill fight." Then he looked at Winona, who had let go of his hand. "Dr. Cloud, here, has been helping us define some of the environmental issues Oregon faces. I'm thankful to have her in my camp."

"I can understand why."

Townsend glanced at his watch. "Well, gotta run. Nice to see you again, Cal. I could sure use your help. Call me." Then to Winona with an endearing look, "I'll be in touch."

I followed her into her office and closed the door behind me. Her hair was pulled up and piled in a loose bun that accentuated her oval face and big, luminous eyes. We sat down and she smiled, although her eyes held concern. "What in the world happened to your neck, Cal?"

"Uh, it's quite a story." I took her briefly through the events surrounding my discovery of Watlamet's body and the aftermath.

She sat rigidly in her chair, the color draining from her face. "My God, Watlamet's dead, and you were nearly killed. Oh, Cal I'm so sorry. And this all started because he heard about my grandmother's death and it triggered his conscience?"

"Reverend Hinkley didn't hear the name Queah, but I assume that's what happened. Watlament wanted to get right with the Lord."

"This person, this killer, he's still out there?"

I nodded. "There's more." I described my meeting with Cecil Ferguson. When I finished, Winona lowered her head and clasped it in her hands. When she raised her head, her eyes were damp, her expression dazed. "So quickly? I can't believe you unraveled this so quickly." She took a tissue from a box on her desk and dabbed her eyes. "Thank you, Cal. I wish Grandmother could be here now. We knew all along Sherman Watlamet lied, and now we know he was paid to do it. What shame he brings to his family and his people. And this man, this Cecil Ferguson." Her face grew rigid as she spoke the name. "He admitted killing Grandfather?"

I nodded and repeated what he said, leaving out the part about where he put the body. "But apparently he doesn't think anyone can prove it."

"Will the police arrest him?"

"I've already talked to them. They're going to pick him up for questioning. But I'm afraid they'll be more interested in finding out who shot Watlamet than what happened to your grandfather, at least initially."

She nodded. "Do you think Ferguson will tell them what he told you?"

I stroked my mustache and gathered my thoughts for a moment. "Hard to say. He was stunned by the news of Watlamet's death. Maybe he'll decide to tell all after he thinks about it. I think the man's dying—emphysema or something—so maybe he'll figure he has nothing to lose. Then, again, he might deny saying anything to me."

The muscles in her jaw flexed. "I want proof, Cal. I want something to take to the tribe."

"I know. We'll just have to wait and see."

"*Wait and see?* Why do we have to just wait and see?" Her eyes grew huge, her lower lip trembled.

I blanched and fought back an irrational feeling that Watlamet's death was somehow my fault, that I should've prevented it. "Look, Winona, the deputy investigating the killing knows about your grandfather. I think she'll work with us on getting some kind of statement from Ferguson. Trust me on this."

"Okay."

"Uh, there's one more thing, Winona. Ferguson also told me where he put your grandfather's body. He said he put him in his favorite place, at the bottom of Celilo Falls."

She looked down, seeming to study a ballpoint pen on her desk. Her eyes filled again, and a single tear fell to the desk like a raindrop. "Well, he's in good company. A lot of good men died in those rapids fishing for salmon. And when the flood waters rose, the bones of our ancestors on the burial islands upriver were swept into the channel as well." She nodded and showed a wisp of a smile. "Grandfather's not alone down there."

Then she looked up. The smile was gone, and her eyes shone flat and hard. "Cecil Ferguson will pay for this."

The woman meant it. No doubt about it.

Chapter Fourteen

After leaving Winona's office in the Pearl, I stopped at a Plaid Pantry and bought a bag of dog kibbles, two prepackaged turkey sandwiches, and a twelve ounce cup of black coffee. There was some light left, so Arch and I ate dinner in Tom McCall Park, a green belt that ran along the west side of the Willamette River in the center of Portland. The air was crisp with a hint of plum blossoms mingled with the smell of freshly cut grass. The low light had a soft reddish cast, and when the lights of the Morrison Bridge winked on they were reflected in the mirror that was the quiescent river.

An hour and a half later, as we turned onto the gravel road leading up to my place, Archie was sitting up straight in the back seat and softly whimpering. The moon was full, but low and to the east, so the house was shrouded in deep shadow. I let Arch out when I opened the gate, and he ran next to the car as I taxied in. As soon as my headlights illuminated the front of the house I stopped the car, hit the brights, and took stock. Nothing caught my eye, and Archie gave no indication anything was amiss. Still, after I'd put the car in the garage I made a quick circuit of the house, carrying a flashlight and crowbar, rethinking all the while my decision to turn down Philip's offer of a gun.

I took a long, hot shower, being careful to keep the water off the bandage on my neck. Afterwards, I scrubbed off the condensation on the mirror with a fist, lifted one side of the bandage, and with a handheld mirror took a look. The wound was red and angry and possibly on its way to becoming infected. I might need to have it looked at after all, I conceded. I towel-dried my hair, suddenly flecked with more gray it seemed, and made a mental note to trim my mustache in the morning. I couldn't help noticing a thickening in my waist and vowed to add a couple more miles to my jogging route.

At eight the next morning I stood at my north fence line, a cup of coffee in hand. My house stood below me near the edge of the ridge. We'd had a pretty good blow in February, and I could see that some of the shingles on the roof had lifted. I wondered how much longer the old cedar roof would last and how much it would cost to replace. Behind me, my neighbor's south pasture stretched up to her house, which was partially screened by a stand of Douglas firs. I saw Gertrude Johnson out by her barn and waved. To the east and west were large tracks of undeveloped land, thick with fir and cedar that ran up to my fences and were rendered nearly impenetrable by dense thickets of blackberry, silal, and poison oak.

My phone chirped, and I dug it out of my jeans. "What's up, Philip?"

"He's pigeon-toed."

"*What?*"

"The sniper. I'm over at Watlamet's ranch right now. I got to wondering about the scene out here, so I came over to have a look around. I figured the sheriffs might have missed something."

"Yeah. Go on." He had my attention. Philip had mentioned in passing once that he was an expert tracker, a skill learned from his father and grandfather and one that was probably embedded in his DNA. The Paiutes, after all, were legendary Plains hunters. But it hadn't occurred to me to ask him to examine the crime scene.

"Anyway, I found the spot where I think he nailed Watlamet. A stand of cottonwoods. Some idiot had tromped all over the ground there, so I couldn't tell much."

"Right. Grooms' partner was looking for shell casings." I waited for my friend to continue, knowing it was not wise to rush him.

"There's another stand closer in toward the house. Something happened there, too, but I couldn't make sense of it. Same idiot."

"Yeah, that's where he was when I shot back with the shotgun. I think he fired two more rounds at me from there."

"Okay, could've been. But here's the deal—there was *another* spot further up the knoll. I figured he might have stopped at that spot, you know, to take cover on his way in."

There was a long pause. Finally I said, "And?"

"There they were. A couple of nice boot prints right behind one of the trees where the ground was firm. Our boy's as pigeon-toed as they come."

"How do you know the prints belong to the shooter?"

Philip laughed. "Once I knew what to look for, it was easy to track him back to the road, where he parked his car. It was in some trees, maybe a half mile away. Then I doubled back and found his tracks between the two stands of trees. They were faint as hell but unmistakable. It's gotta be him, Cal. Who else would have parked out there, walked into Watlamet's property, and just happened to wind up where the shots were fired? By the way, I found some nice tire tracks, too."

"Nice work, Philip."

"Yeah, well, this guy needs to go down. What should I do now?"

"Call Grooms and tell her what you've got. She talked to you, right?"

"Yeah. She drove over yesterday. How much do you think that woman can bench press?"

I had to chuckle. "More than you, for sure. This could be huge. They may be able to make molds from the boot and tire prints."

"Okay, I'll call her right now. Is she going to be pissed I was nosing around in her sandbox?"

"You didn't cross any crime scene tape, did you?"

"Nope. Didn't see any."

"Then you're good."

And that was a fact. My friend was good.

Chapter Fifteen

It wasn't fear, but Philip's call dredged up an acute feeling of vulnerability in me. He was right when he said I needed to assume the shooter knew who I was, and now the solitude of my sanctuary and the long, unobstructed views of the valley seemed more of a threat than a comfort.

I walked through the vegetable garden, thick with winter weeds, down to the house and around to the side porch. The valley floor was suffused with early spring colors—soft greens, yellows, and ochres—but my eyes fixed on the bare, rocky cliff edge of the abandoned quarry in the foreground, directly below the ridgeline. Most of the quarry was beneath my line of sight, but I could see the top of the cliff, where decades ago miners had chased a sinking vein of blue basalt into the ground, forming a deep trough that ran along my property line. A lake choked with pea-green algae lay at the bottom of the trough. Left of center on the cliff edge was a single copse of scraggly cedars whose growth had been stunted by the rocky soil.

No question, I decided. That's the spot a sniper would pick, aided no doubt by a satellite image pulled off the Internet.

I heard a beep inside the house, causing Archie to yelp and telling me someone had triggered the motion sensor at the front gate. This was the first day the young man accused of stealing the shoes was supposed to work for me. Archie led me around to the front of the house, just as the boy and his dad were getting out of their truck, a beat-up Chevy with a rough-running V-8 engine. I shuddered at the thought of gassing up that guzzler.

The boy's name was Santos Araya. His dad and I had agreed he would work five Saturdays, and that, combined with a hundred bucks, would cover my retainer fee. Archie gave Santos the once-over, and by the time his dad was pulling away, my dog was standing next to him, tail wagging in a gesture of acceptance. Santos was taken by Archie as well but struggled not to show it as he appraised me warily with dark, expressive eyes set in a face that was just beginning to know the scrape of a razor.

He wore baggy jeans, battered sneakers, and a large black and red jersey with *Blazers* written across the front and the number 7 below the letters.

I looked him over and said, "You a Brandon Roy fan?"

He nodded.

I smiled. "Me, too. You play?"

He nodded again.

We were standing in front of the garage, which had a backboard and hoop mounted above the door by the previous owner. I went into the garage, rummaged around, and finally came out with a basketball that belonged to Claire. It had made the move up from L.A., because my daughter and I had spent hours playing one on one, and I couldn't bear to throw it out. It was dusty and low on air but still bounced reasonably well. I snapped Santos a crisp chest pass. "Let's see what you got."

He stood holding the ball for a moment, trying to figure out if I was serious or not. Wasn't he here to work? Finally he shrugged, dribbled tentatively a couple of times, and put up a soft shot that caromed out of the basket.

I think he missed one other shot that day. When I backed away from him, he put the ball in the bottom of the net with the prettiest jump shot you've ever seen. If I came out to block it, he slipped around and laid it in like I was planted in the ground.

Gasping for breath after an hour, I said, "Okay, Santos, I've taken enough punishment for one day. We've got to get some work done around here." Then I pointed at him and said, "But next week I'm going to kick your butt." He suppressed a smile and remained silent. I thought of my laconic friend, Philip.

I helped him load the wheelbarrow with tools, took him out to the garden, and introduced him to the weeds. I was walking back down to the house to make another cup of coffee when the idea hit me. I veered off into the garage, grabbed a screwdriver, and headed up my long driveway toward the front gate. I unscrewed the bracket holding the cheap motion sensor I'd mounted on a fence post. It was concealed in a big rhododendron next to the gate, placed high to avoid being triggered by coyotes and skunks. Deer hadn't been a problem, since they avoided my property because of Archie, who liked nothing better than to try herding them.

I unscrewed the cap and checked the batteries. They were operable but badly corroded, so I went back to the house and replaced them. I called Santos down from the garden, poured him a glass of orange juice, and showed him the motion sensor. I then walked him down the hall and pointed out the wireless receiver in the laundry room, explaining in simple terms how the whole thing worked. "I'm going to mount this motion sensor in those trees over there," I said, pointing out at the quarry. I put my hand in front of the aperture and wagged it back and forth. "When something blocks the beam out there like this, it'll cause the receiver to buzz."

He nodded, but his face registered confusion.

"It'll tell me when animals are over there, you know, like a deer or a fox. I like to watch them," I said, answering the question I figured he wanted to ask. I saw a flicker of interest in his eyes, but he remained silent.

"When I get over there, I'll call the house phone on my cell. I want to know if the signal carries far enough to trigger the alarm. Okay?"

"Okay."

I left Archie with Santos, loaded a backpack with some tools, and walked out to a trail that ran along the quarry property, parallel to the main road. A quarter of a mile down I turned into a narrow, rutted access road that was fenced on either side and led into the quarry. I scaled a locked gate blocking the entrance and picked my way through a field littered with rotting timbers and parts of an old rock-crusher to the edge of the pit and the twisted stand of trees I was interested in.

I worked my way through the tangle of tree trunks, rocks, and dead branches. When I reached the edge of the cliff, my house burst into view, standing maybe a hundred unobstructed yards away. I looked down and instinctively stepped back. Fifty feet below me lay the putrid lake. Its bottom wasn't visible and its steep, rocky sides had probably trapped its share of unwary animals.

Crouching at the edge, I dialed my land line. "I'm going to test it now," I told Santos. "Let me know if you hear the alarm." I waited, then put my hand in front of the beam. I didn't need him to tell me. I heard the high-pitched buzz over my phone.

"Great," I told him. "I'll call you back as soon as I figure out where to put this thing." The white plastic casing would be too visible attached to a tree. I opted, instead, to wedge it securely between two large rocks at the cliff edge, positioning it so that the beam would aim up and cut across the only clear access through the trees to a spot affording a clear view of my place. Then I arranged some smaller rocks and a dead branch to hide it. I stood back and appraised my work. "Not bad at all."

I backed out of the trees, called Santos back, and then followed the path a shooter would most likely take. The sensor was off to my right, essentially invisible. I heard another satisfying buzz when I crossed the path of the beam.

"Damn," I muttered, "this just might work."

I had just scrambled back over the locked gate when my cell chirped. "Mr. Claxton? This is Deputy Sheriff Grooms."

"Yes, Deputy Grooms. How are you?"

"Well, I've been better. I'm down here at the Portland Police Bureau in Southeast. We were wonderin' if you could come in for another interview."

"Why? What's the problem?"

"Cecil Ferguson's dead. He was murdered in that retirement home last night. You were apparently the last one to see him alive."

I told Grooms I'd leave for Portland right away and punched off. I stood there for a while, rocked by the news. It felt like something was gathering momentum. Trouble is, I had no idea what it was.

Chapter Sixteen

I explained the afternoon chores to Santos and left him out in the garden, hoe in hand, and when Archie started to follow me to the car, told him to stay, a command he was starting to understand. After hearing the news about Cecil Ferguson, I didn't feel so foolish about rigging the alarm system over in the quarry. Somebody was taking witnesses off the board and like it or not, I was a witness.

I decided not to call Winona until I knew more about what had happened to Ferguson. I was beginning to wonder just how far this thing would spread. Is it conceivable, I asked myself, that *she's* in danger, too? I knew she didn't know much about what the hell was going on, but was it safe to assume the murderer knew that as well?

There was little traffic, and forty-five minutes later the Portland skyline loomed in front of me as I came out of the Terwilliger curves on I-5. A gondola from the city's brand new aerial tram dangled over the freeway in front of me like a piece of silver fruit. I wondered what the tram cost and thought of kids in the city schools who were going without computers.

I was learning the traffic patterns in Portland and took the Hawthorne Bridge to the east side instead of chancing I-84, which was frequently jammed like an L.A. freeway. I worked my way up to Burnside and found a parking space on SE Forty-sixth, pleasantly surprised by the lack of parking meters on the east side of the river. I spotted Grooms slumped in a chair halfway down a dimly light corridor. She smiled wearily and stood up as I cleared the metal detector.

"Thanks for comin' in, Mr. Claxton. You made good time."

"No problem, Deputy Grooms. Shame about Ferguson. He knew a lot more than he told me."

She looked at me with steel gray eyes. "Who's next on your visit list?"

I shook my head. "Yeah, I'm feeling like the angel of death here. Find anything that points to our boy with the cowboy hat?"

Her smile let me know she wasn't going to tell me anything I didn't need to know. "Portland wants to talk to you first. This is their murder. When they finish, I want to tie up some loose ends with you. Come on, I'll take you up there."

The two detectives who interviewed me were cranky and generally pissed off. A murder on a pleasant Sunday will do that to you. I went through the whole story with them in great detail. At one point Detective Adams, an old warhorse with thick, stubbly jowls and a florid complexion, said, "How did you get into the building to see Ferguson?

"I waited 'til a couple was buzzed in and went in with them. There's not much security there."

"You in the habit of sneaking into private buildings, Mr. Claxton?"

I smiled. "No, of course not. It was just that Ferguson didn't know me, and I figured it was my only shot at talking to him. You know, just show up at his door."

Adams glanced at his partner and back at me. "No. I *don't* know. You were trespassing, Mr. Claxton." His partner, a younger black man named Hamilton, shifted in his seat and nodded in agreement.

"Mr. Ferguson invited me into his apartment."

"I was talking about the building, not his apartment," Adams snapped back.

I kept my mouth shut. Technically, he was right.

"So, Ferguson proceeds to suggest he knows who killed the guy out in eastern Oregon—"

"Who you also just happened to pop in on," his partner, Hamilton, interjected, leaning forward in his chair.

Adams warned him off with a look and continued, "Did Ferguson say *how* he talked to this party? In person? E-mail? By phone?"

"Yes, like I said, he mentioned a pay phone." Out of frustration I added, "Look, gentlemen, we've been over this already in great detail. I've told you everything I know."

Adams nodded grudgingly. "And you've done all this investigative work on behalf of a client you're going to make available to us to question."

"Right. No problem. I'll pursue that as soon as we finish up here."

"Fine," Adams replied.

The two detectives left, and I stayed in the interview room waiting for Deputy Grooms. I didn't enjoy it, but I wasn't surprised at the hard grilling they'd given me. At this point I remembered the look in Winona's eyes and her comment after I told her what Ferguson had said about her grandfather's resting place. How much of a warrior was she? I didn't know the answer, and I brushed away the thoughts the question conjured up.

I spent another forty minutes giving a statement on tape to Grooms about my meeting with Ferguson. I tried to get her to reciprocate with some information on the murder, but all she told me was that he was beaten to death that night after I left. I gathered that no one had heard or seen anything suspicious, and there were no surveillance cameras at the retirement home. At least I hadn't seen any. When we finished, Grooms said, "Where does your client live?"

"Here in Portland."

"Any chance you can get that person over here? It would save us all a lot of trouble."

"Right. I already told the Portland detectives I'd try to do that. Hang on." I took out my cell phone and speed-dialed Winona. She didn't pick up, so I left a message for her to call me.

We decided to wait for a while. Grooms went out and brought back two cups of coffee. I blew on mine, took a sip, and looked at her over the cup. She had sturdy legs and surprisingly narrow hips that fanned into a thick upper body with well-muscled arms and broad, beefy shoulders. She moved with the kind of physical assurance top athletes have. I guessed softball. I could picture her hitting the cover off the ball or windmilling a fastball that rose a half foot before it got to the plate. Her face was round and fleshy with a small nose and large, full lips, but it was her steel-hard eyes that you remembered.

"So, teaming up with Portland's finest to solve interconnected cases, huh?"

"Right."

"I couldn't help notice you didn't sit in on my interview."

"Wasn't invited. Adams and what's his face won't give me the time of day. I might as well be from Afghanistan."

I wasn't surprised. I knew from experience that expecting different law enforcement groups to cooperate was a stretch in the best of circumstances. And combining a couple of Portland male detectives with a deputy sheriff from Wasco County—and a female to boot—was hardly the best of circumstances. "Hmm. This can't be good. I'm probably next in line to get hit. I'm hoping you folks will find this guy first."

She forced a smile. "Well, I intend to hold up my end of the log." Then she took a sip of her coffee and stared into the space between us. "Might take those two awhile to come around, though."

I smiled and shook my head. "It could be worse. You could be dealing with L.A. cops."

She looked at me and cocked her head slightly. "You've had the pleasure?"

"I used to be a prosecutor down there. Retired early. The city cops treated the county sheriffs like crap. A favorite pastime."

She chuckled and sipped some more coffee. "Seems to be the way of the world."

"What's the C stand for?"

She looked at me for a couple of beats with those eyes. "Cleta. But my friends call me Big C."

"My friends call me Cal."

We were on our second cup of coffee when Winona called back. I took the call out in the hall, telling her only that the police wanted to talk to her about Ferguson, without giving any details. She said she was free, so I gave her directions and told her to meet me in front of the building.

Winona arrived wearing jeans, cowboy boots, and an oversized cotton sweater. Her hair was down, and she wore no makeup. She extended her hand, and I held on to it after we finished shaking. "Thanks for coming, Winona. Uh, I'm afraid the news isn't good. Cecil Ferguson was murdered last night. Somebody beat him to death."

She withdrew her hand and stepped back like I'd slapped her. "No! Not again!" "What happened?" When I finished telling her, she said, "Why do they want to talk to me?" She had lost most of the color in her face.

"Like I said on the phone, they know I was working on your behalf. So they want to see what you know and to cross-check my story, too." I paused for a moment, searching for the right words. "When they realize you're Nelson Queah's granddaughter, they might consider you a suspect, as well."

"*Me?*"

I laughed. "Right. You do have a motive, you know."

"Oh."

"They're going to ask you where you were last night."

He eyes widened ever so slightly, which gave me a pang of discomfort. She smiled weakly and brushed a strand of hair from her face. "I was home. Alone."

"Fine. Anyone see you?"

She shot me an annoyed look. "Not that I know of. What, I need to prove I was home?"

I smiled. "They're cops investigating a murder, Winona. They suspect everyone. I'd sit in with you, but I'm a witness in this thing, too."

"You mean as my attorney? Wouldn't that look a little weird?"

"It would raise some eyebrows, but you don't need an attorney, anyway."

She paused for a couple of beats. "Uh, there is one thing…"

"What's that?"

"I, uh, after you phoned me yesterday, I went over to the senior center to see Ferguson."

"You did? *Why?*"

She scrunched up her brow and opened her hands. "I don't know. I guess I thought maybe he'd talk to me if I came in person. I wanted to hear the truth, you know, from his mouth. Anyway, you mentioned he was on the fourth floor, so I figured I'd just take the stairs and pop in like you did. But no one was coming in or out, and I couldn't figure out how to get in."

"What did you do then?"

"I left. But, uh, when I was standing there out front one of the staff members happened to come out. She asked if she could help me."

"Where did you go after that?"

"Home."

"Okay. Just tell them the truth and you'll be fine." I took her inside and introduced her to Grooms, who escorted her up to the interview room. As she stepped into the elevator, she turned and said, "Cal, will you wait for me?"

"You read my mind."

Chapter Seventeen

Winona Cloud came out of the interview with Adams and Hamilton with a forced smile that didn't begin to hide the stress around her eyes. She told me it went fine, but I took one look at her and said, "Come on. I'll buy you a cup of coffee and we can talk." I wondered what could have happened in the interview to make her so uptight.

"I think I'd rather have a drink."

"Sure. We can do that. You know of a place around here?"

"I don't know this neighborhood." She paused for a moment. "Why don't you just come over to my place? I'm just across the river."

On the way to Winona's apartment, I called my neighbor, Gertrude Johnson, and she agreed to feed Archie for me. Winona lived in a loft on NW Flanders in the Pearl District. I parked next to her car in front of what was once a long loading dock and climbed steep stairs to the second floor of the converted warehouse. Drenched in late afternoon light, her apartment had work-scarred oak floors, exposed laminated beams, ducts and conduits fourteen feet up, vibrantly green plants in big pots and a profusion of art hung on a perimeter of gouged and chipped brick walls. The only separate room was the bathroom, and her bed was three steps up on a landing on the west wall. The place was as neat as a military barracks, and I found myself hoping she never dropped in on me unexpectedly.

"Nice place."

"Thanks. This was one of the first warehouses to get converted in the Pearl. They stored whiskey here. If you breathe deeply enough you can still smell the bourbon."

I inhaled heartily through my nose. "Jim Beam, I think."

She smiled and her dimples appeared and then disappeared like tentative little whirlpools. "I don't have any hard stuff, but I have a good Oregon pinot. You want some? That's what I'm having."

I told her yes, and while she fetched our wines I walked the perimeter looking at the art—mainly originals with Native American themes. I liked her taste, an interesting mix of traditional and abstract works. I stopped to admire a watercolor of a woman in buckskins sitting on a tree stump. A pale moon hung over her right shoulder, and over her left an owl in flight was silhouetted against a lavender sky.

"Some people save their money. I buy art."

I turned around and Winona handed me a glass of wine.

"That's a Dana Tiger. She paints Indian women, strong ones. That one's a medicine woman. Don't mess with her."

The woman in the painting gazed at me with fierce eyes, her left hand extended as if summoning the owl. "I wouldn't dream of it."

We stopped at a cluster of photographs next. In the center was a large picture of Celilo Falls—the iconic image of two men dip-netting from opposing platforms over the narrows with the falls thundering behind them. On either side were hung a series of what I took to be family photographs. Winona pointed at a shot of an imposing woman with a serious, almost defiant look and a smiling child holding a small doll. "That's Grandmother Tilda and me."

I leaned into the photo. "Where're the dimples?"

She smiled again, broader this time. "They're there. You just can't see them." She pointed to another photograph. "That's Grandfather Nelson in his Marine uniform with all his medals."

Nelson Queah had wavy, black hair, a strong jaw and cheek bones that ramped steeply to his eyes, which blazed against his coppery skin with the intensity of a man who believed in himself and the future. Something stirred in me, a kind of reinforcement of the admiration I felt after reading his letters. "He looks like a very proud man."

Winona sighed and smiled wistfully. "The picture was taken after the war. He'd just finished a purification ceremony."

"What's that?"

"In our culture we believe war poisons the spirit, and warriors return tainted. So it's necessary to cleanse their souls before they re-enter their families and communities."

"How's it done?"

"Oh, our family had a shaman do it. You know, lots of sweat lodge time, fasting, praying, that sort of thing."

"Huh. We should do something like that for our vets coming back from Iraq. Might cut down on post-traumatic stress."

"There are many things white culture could learn from us. It's a shame most of the teaching has been in one direction."

I thought of our battered environment and beleaguered wildlife. "Amen to that." Then I looked at the picture of Nelson Queah again. "You favor him."

She nodded and smiled demurely. "I know. Everyone says that."

"It's the eyes. You have his eyes."

She dropped hers for a moment, deflecting the comment. Then she showed me the rest of her family, including a shot of her father taken a few months before he was killed in a logging accident up near Mount Hood. She skipped over a couple of pictures of a young woman bearing a striking resemblance to her. I didn't press it, knowing she had her reasons for ignoring her mother.

At one point she put a hand on my arm, leaned into me slightly and pointed to a thin, young girl standing in front of an old shed. "That's my favorite cousin, Mirrie."

"Philip told me *he* was your favorite cousin."

She squeezed my arm and laughed. "He did *not*. I hardly knew him growing up."

She let go of my arm, but the sensation of her touch lingered on my skin. I was anxious to hear about the interview, but I hadn't eaten since breakfast and the wine had stimulated my appetite. "Are you hungry?" I asked.

"Yes, but there isn't a thing to eat here. I'm not domestic at all."

"We can go out," I offered.

"How about takeout? Do you like Thai?"

"Can't beat the Thai food in Portland."

After we called our order in and were sitting on the couch, I said, "You seemed a little tense after the interview, Winona. Are you sure it went okay with Adams and Hamilton?"

She took a sip of her wine and held my eyes for a moment. I sensed she was running some kind of calculus in her head. "They took my fingerprints and a couple of mug shots—"

"Not mug shots. They didn't arrest you."

"Whatever. The white detective asked me if I was upset that Ferguson killed my grandfather."

"What did you tell him?"

"I said I was upset about what he said, but I didn't know for certain whether he killed Grandfather. I mean, he could have just been bragging or something. And then the black one says something like, 'Well, I wouldn't blame you a bit if you were upset, I'd be upset, too.' I thought it was kind of sneaky."

I nodded. "They were trying to provoke a reaction."

"And they kept asking me if anyone saw me at home last night. Like I needed this airtight alibi to satisfy them." She gestured toward the windows. "Is anyone going to see me in here? I don't think so."

She looked a little flustered, and I got a sense of how she probably came across during the questioning. I was beginning to wonder how Adams and Hamilton had read her. "Did you order in last night? Make or receive any calls?"

"No and no."

"Anyone see you park your car when you came back from the retirement home?"

"Not that I know of." She turned her palms up in a gesture of frustration. They don't actually think I killed Ferguson, do they?"

"Like I said, they're trained to be suspicious of everyone. That's what makes them so likeable."

She puffed a breath out. "The Gestapo's more likeable than those two."

When the food arrived, we spread the cartons out on a round oak table in her kitchen alcove and helped ourselves to spring rolls with plum sauce, tom yum soup, fried noodles, and a curry and mango dish we spread over white rice. Winona picked at her food, and I ate for both of us.

After dinner we talked for a while longer, and I decided to head for home. She walked me to the door, and when I turned to face her, a big tear hesitated halfway down her cheek. It glistened in the overhead track light.

"You okay?"

She dropped her head. "I'm just upset about everything, I guess." She raised her head back up, and tears welled up in both eyes.

Without thinking I hugged her. She sighed, and we stood there for a few moments in soft, tentative contact. I felt her quiver ever so slightly and stepped back. "No wonder you feel like this. You've been on an emotional roller coaster. Things will look better in the morning."

She sniffed. "I know." Then she looked up at me, her eyes moist and shiny. "Do you charge extra for hugging your clients?"

I chuckled. "I believe I put you on the free hug plan." As I said that, footsteps sounded in the hall outside her apartment followed by a sharp rapping on the door.

Winona looked puzzled and said in a hushed voice, "Who in the world could that be?"

I shrugged, but I had a pretty good idea who it was.

Chapter Eighteen

It must have been a slow crime night in Portland for Adams and Hamilton to be able to generate a search warrant and find a judge to sign it so fast. I figured that if they came at all it would be some time the next day. After all, probable cause based on revenge for something that might have gone down fifty years ago would be a stretch for just about any judge. The fact that Winona had gone to see Ferguson probably tipped it. It looked like she was casing the place, after all. In any case, there they were, documents in hand when Winona opened the door. When he saw me standing behind Winona, Adams smirked. "Working late, counselor?"

I shrugged. "Looks like you're the ones working late."

It took the two detectives and three uniforms a little more than one hour to complete the search of Winona's loft. She held up pretty well as they bagged the clothes in her dirty laundry hamper and most of her shoes, and she managed to shrug when they announced they were impounding her car. After all, she could walk to work. But when they went for her laptop, she exploded. "You can't take my computer, damn it. It has all my work on it, my e-mail, my documents, *everything.*"

"That's the idea," Hamilton said as he slipped it into a large evidence bag and labeled it.

"When can she expect it back?" I interjected.

"Our forensics guy should clear it in a couple of days. She can probably pick it up on Wednesday."

"Wednesday! I have work to do tomorrow," Winona shot back. "What am I supposed to do? I've got a presentation to give, and it's on that machine."

Hamilton shrugged. "Sorry for the inconvenience, ma'am, but that's the best we can do."

When the cops finally left, we wandered into the kitchen area. Winona poured us each another glass of wine. She ran a finger along the edge of the table and looked at me over her glass. "What happens now?"

"They'll be looking for any forensic evidence that can connect you to the crime scene. You didn't make it to his apartment, so no worries. The good news is they didn't have enough to arrest you, and once they complete the lab work, you'll be eliminated as a suspect."

"That's a relief," she said, but with a decided lack of conviction.

"Uh, is there anything else you need to tell me about this?"

She held my gaze, and her eyes flared for just an instant before she looked away. "No. There's nothing else I can think of."

We chatted a while longer, finished our wines, and as I was leaving, said, "There's one other thing, Winona." She looked at me and arched her eyebrows. "I don't want to frighten you, but you need to be careful. I don't know what the hell's going on, but two murders in a row is not a good trend. Keep your doors locked and don't let any strangers in, okay?"

She gave me an amused look. "Why would they want to hurt *me*?"

I shrugged. "I don't know. And that's what worries me. None of this makes any sense." I searched her face to see if what I'd said frightened her.

I needn't have worried. Winona Cloud was clearly not one to frighten easily.

You'd have thought I'd been gone for a month by the way Archie carried on when I got home that night. He spun around me barking wildly and yelping at a pitch so high it made me wince. I was reassured by his behavior that no one was lurking in the shadows, but I gave the perimeter of the house a quick check just to be sure nothing had been tampered with. I took him inside and gave him his weekly bone a few days early as a special treat.

I went into my study, read my e-mail, and then scanned the online *New York Times*. I was wide awake, so I got out my notes on the Queah case and looked them over again. There were only two more names on my list that warranted checking into. The first was Timothy Wiiks, the young man who approached Queah about the corruption at the dam. I'd asked Philip to find him but hadn't heard anything. I Googled his name and came up empty, except for the fact that Wiiks was a Norwegian name. Then I searched the online white pages and found nothing there either.

Fletcher Dunn, the journalist who'd interviewed Queah just before he disappeared, was a different story. I learned he'd stayed on with *The Portland Journal*, which later became *The Oregonian*, and retired five years earlier. He spent the last fifteen years of his career writing a column called *Dunn's Doings*, which judging from a few samples I skimmed, was a broad-ranging commentary on things going on in Portland and the state. I also found an address for him in Lake Oswego, a suburb south of Portland. None of the early *Journal* articles were archived online, so I was unable to locate the articles Dunn had written about Celilo Falls that were mentioned by Queah in the letter to his wife. I wondered if Fletcher Dunn would remember anything about the man he interviewed so long ago, the man who saw something in him to trust.

The buzz of the day's events finally began to wear off, so I took the back staircase up to my bedroom with Archie leading the way. I rummaged through my CDs for something mellow and slipped in an early Bonnie Raitt, recorded before she won a Grammy. I fell asleep somewhere in the middle of "Everybody's Cryin' Mercy." But it was a shallow, restless kind of sleep, and sometime before dawn I did something I hardly ever do—I woke up and couldn't get back to sleep.

This case was different than anything I'd handled as a prosecutor down in L.A. Sure, back then I was driven, immersing myself in every detail, following every lead, grilling every witness. But there was always a boundary between me and the case I was working. I didn't do it nearly enough, but I could always go home and leave the crime and all its sordid details at the Parker Center. Not now, not with this case. I was living this one, and the stakes went way beyond nailing some bad guy and advancing my so-called career. It was an unsettling feeling, but at the same time I don't think I ever felt quite as alive as I did at that moment.

Chapter Nineteen

I saw a bald eagle kill an osprey once. I was wading the Deschutes River on my first fishing trip with Philip. The eagle swooped down out of nowhere and hit the smaller bird in mid-flight with a single, vicious blow to the head. The osprey fell into the river like a puppet with its strings cut. That's one way to deal with the competition.

It was the next morning. I sat on the side porch musing over that memory while sipping a cup of coffee and watching finches, chickadees, and nuthatches take turns at the feeders. Each tiny bird snacked on niger seeds for a while, then gave way to another waiting patiently for its turn in a nearby maple tree. It seemed an avian version of musical chairs, an orderly plan of sharing agreed to by the birds.

Birds that committed homicide, birds that willingly shared their food—all part of a natural system that was at once beautiful and violent just like the world I inhabited.

My reverie was broken by the high-pitched whine of the alarm I'd jury-rigged out in the quarry. I jerked to attention, spilling hot coffee down the front of my sweatshirt. I ducked down, hustled back into the house, and took the backstairs two at a time, all the while feeling stupid for presenting such an easy target in the first place and wondering if the coffee was going to raise blisters on my chest.

My bedroom window offered the best view of the quarry, and I'd stashed an old pair of binoculars next to it for just such an occasion, although in truth I never thought the day would come. I edged up to the window, slowly raised the blinds a couple of inches and focused in on the thicket of cedars where I'd stashed the motion sensor.

Something moved just out of my field of vision. I tensed up, refocused, and then…laughed out loud. A big red-tailed hawk sat on a bare cedar branch, staring back at me. It fluttered its wings, and the alarm in the kitchen sounded on cue. Then the raptor launched and dove out of my vision, into the deep cut that housed the narrow, putrid lake. A few moments later it re-emerged carrying a squirming field mouse.

I held a cold, wet washcloth against my reddened chest for a few minutes and then changed into a dry shirt. The thought of having to sneak around in my own house for any length of time was unthinkable, and I began to wonder if I was overreacting. After all, I didn't have any evidence the shooter knew who I was, and if he did, would he *really* come after me? The alarm system I'd jury-rigged seemed to work for hawks all right, but it was still a flimsy line of defense. And there was another more critical question I hadn't had a chance to address yet—what the hell do I do if there's a human over there instead of a bird?

I mulled this over as I munched a bowl of cereal and then reluctantly made a phone call to the Yamhill County Sheriff's office and asked for Sheriff Don Talbot. I say reluctantly, because Don Talbot and I had some history, and it wasn't good history. The first case I'd landed in Dundee was representing a migrant worker in a police brutality case against a couple of his deputies. The preliminary hearing and the accompanying publicity had resulted in one of his deputies, a ten-year veteran, being placed on unpaid leave.

"Sheriff Talbot." He answered curtly, as if he knew in advance this was going to be an annoying call.

"Hello, Sheriff. It's Cal Claxton."

Long pause. "What can I do for you, Claxton?"

"Uh, I got a situation I might need some help with." There was another pause, and I finally spoke into the silence, apprising him of the threat I thought I might be facing and the steps I'd taken to protect myself.

"So, let me see if I'm understanding this," Talbot responded with an edge to his voice. "If you call after some half-assed driveway alarm goes off, you want me to drop everything and send a team of officers in to seal off the McCallister Quarry and apprehend a sniper who'll be hiding in there somewhere, waiting to take a shot at you. Is that right?"

"Uh, more or less." My story sounded a little sketchy when he played it back to me.

Another long pause. "Claxton, you've got more nerve than a bad tooth, asking me something like this. Get back to me when you've got something concrete I can deal with. Thanks to you, I'm short a good deputy, anyway." He hung up before I could get another word in. Just as well, because what I'd planned to say next wouldn't have fallen into the realm of civil discourse.

I sat there looking at the phone in my hand as a mix of anger and embarrassment washed over me. Okay, my request was a little unorthodox, but he can't just blow me off like that, I told myself. And there shouldn't be anything embarrassing about asking for help, for Christ's sake.

But of course, the good sheriff can blow me off, and that's exactly what he did. If the alarm sounds, I'd definitely be on my own.

Chapter Twenty

To my delight, two new clients walked into my office that morning in Dundee and actually wrote retainer checks to secure my services. But business slowed to a halt that afternoon, so I locked up, packed Arch in the car, and drove to the address I had for Fletcher Dunn in Lake Oswego. L.O.'s a tony suburb concentrated around a narrow finger of a lake that lies between the Willamette and Tualatin Rivers eight miles south of Portland. I'd called ahead and caught him at home in the midst of what appeared to be an early happy hour. But he said he remembered Nelson Queah and agreed to talk to me.

His house had been nice once, but now it was an ugly duckling in a row of swans. Paint sloughed from the wood trim, and splotches of moss dotted the roof like green islands in a black sea. The lawn was shin-deep in weeds. The front steps were wobbly, and a crude ramp provided access to the side of the porch from the driveway, where a van with handicap plates was parked. After I rang the bell, I heard what I thought was the whir of a motorized wheelchair.

The front door swung inward accompanied by more whirring. I couldn't see who was behind the screen due to the glare of the afternoon sun. "Calvin Claxton, attorney at law, I presume." The voice was deep and resonant, the words slightly slurred and mildly mocking.

I squinted into the glare. "Yes. I'm Cal Claxton. Are you Fletcher Dunn?"

"What's left of me," he answered. "Come in. The screen's unlocked."

I stepped into the hallway, my pupils dilating in the dim light. Dunn sat in front of me in a wheelchair, sporting a quizzical expression. He was small of stature with a face dominated by a set of inquisitive eyes magnified by John Lennon wire rims. He had a neatly trimmed goatee and wore a black turtleneck, chinos and a pair of thoroughly worn jogging shoes. His legs barely filled his trousers and hung limply in the chair.

Before I could speak, he said, "Let's deal with the elephant in the room first. Four years ago my wife and I were driving up to ski at Mount Hood. Some idiot in an SUV without chains came across both lanes and nailed us head on. He walked away, but my wife died at the scene and I lost the use of my legs. Any questions?"

"I'm sorry to hear about that, Mr. Dunn. I, uh—"

"Cut the mister shit. It's Fletch. So you're interested in what happened to Nelson Queah, huh? Let's go to my study where we can talk." He deftly spun his chair around and led me down the hall. Over his shoulder he said, "Want a drink? With the sun out today, I decided to have a gin and tonic, or a couple, I should say." He chuckled again. "You know, to celebrate the coming solstice."

"Uh, no thanks. I'm good."

What I could see of the rest of the house looked sadly neglected, but his study was neat and orderly. One wall was covered with photographs of Dunn rubbing elbows with an array of important looking people, a testament to his journalistic prowess, no doubt. I was new to who's who in Oregon, but I did glimpse the sitting Governor as well as Clyde Drexler and Bill Walton, two former Blazer stars who stood on either side of a smiling Dorn, making him look comically small. The opposite wall held a large bookcase crammed with books. I glimpsed a couple of titles—Bob Dylan's *Chronicles*, Fischer's *The Life of Mahatma Gandhi*, plus *The Road* by Cormac McCarthy.

He motored over to his desk, which sat in front of a window looking out on a backyard choked with weeds and blackberry vines. A large photograph of a younger Fletcher Dunn with an attractive, dark haired woman looked back at us from the desk. Fletch picked up a half-filled glass with a lime wedge floating in it and took a long pull.

I sat down in a leather chair facing him and watched as he lowered the glass and dabbed a drop on the corner of his mouth with his thumb. I said, "I appreciate your taking the time to talk with me. As I mentioned on the phone, I'm working for Nelson Queah's granddaughter. We know from Queah's letters that you interviewed him before the falls were flooded. We're trying to find out what happened to him."

"You don't believe he got drunk and fell in the river?"

The comment caught me by surprise. I hadn't expected Dunn to remember that kind of detail about Queah's disappearance. "No," I answered.

Dunn shook his head and smiled wistfully. "I never bought it either. Nelson Queah was a classy guy. That explanation the cops gave was total bullshit. They didn't give a damn if an Indian went missing and everybody knew it." Then he met my eyes. "Do you have any theories on what happened to him?"

"We think he was murdered by a man named Cecil Ferguson, with the possible assistance of an Indian named Sherman Watlamet."

Dunn's magnified eyes got even bigger. "Well, I'll be damned. I *knew* it was foul play. You have evidence to support that?"

Sensing I could trust this man, I went on to lay out what I'd uncovered and to describe the murders of both Ferguson and Watlamet. When I finished, I said, "Do you remember Nelson Queah telling you about some kind of theft going on at the dam?"

Dunn nodded. "I certainly do." He picked up a thick file lying on his desk. "This is the file with all my notes on The Dalles Dam and Celilo Falls. First thing they teach you in journalism school, take detailed notes and keep them. I have all my files stored under the staircase. I dug this out after you called." He opened the file up and thumbed through it. "Here's the entry right here." He glanced down at the file. "He called me on

March 4th. Said he wanted to talk to me about money being stolen from the government out at the dam. I agreed to meet with him and another gentleman on March 11th, the day after they closed the flood gates. I drove out to talk to them that day, but they weren't there and neither was anyone else."

"The other person was named Wiiks, Timothy Wiiks." I spelled the name for him. "He was working at the dam when he discovered the theft ring. He went to Queah for advice. Do you have any information on him?"

Dunn scanned through his notes. "No. I don't see any other names in connection with this. Apparently Queah didn't share the name with me."

"What about Cecil Ferguson? I think he worked at the dam or somewhere in the area around The Dalles. I'd like to know who he worked for."

"If he had a management job at the dam I should be able to find him. I collected all the organization charts for the contractors so I'd know who the players were." He pulled a sheaf of papers from the back of the file and began thumbing through it.

I held my breath.

"Here he is." He pointed to the center of the fourth page in. "C. Ferguson, project manager for Gage Cement. Gage was a major contractor. Rock and cement. Ferguson worked for Braxton Gage."

I jotted the name down. "Good. Uh, what about Wiiks? Can you find him in there?"

Dunn went back through the charts but came up empty. "If he was down in one of the organizations somewhere, this wouldn't show him. I just have the major players here."

"So what can you tell me about this Braxton Gage?"

Dunn drained his gin and tonic, set the glass down, and smiled. "Braxton Gage is a legend in the Gorge. If I'm not mistaken, he still lives in The Dalles. Hell, he owns half the town. I heard he's retired but still goes to the office every day. You know the type."

I nodded. I did know the type.

"His daddy had a bunch of saw mills, but they went into rock and cement at just the right time to cash in on the dams being built in the Gorge. Braxton parlayed that into shipping on the Columbia, and now he's the biggest carrier on the river. Has been for a long time."

"So he made a killing by supplying cement for the dams. Maybe more than he should have?"

Dunn laughed. "Wouldn't surprise me. You know, I told my boss I wanted to look into that after Queah disappeared. Fat chance. I remember exactly what he told me. 'Listen, Fletcher,' he says, 'you're a new broom. Stay in the corner until I tell you where to sweep.'" He smiled, stared at the space between us and shook his head slowly. "That was the drill at the *Journal* back then—don't rake any muck up unless it's politically safe. And going after a project like The Dalles Dam didn't fall in the safe category by a long shot. It was the darling of Portland and Washington, one of tricky Dick Nixon's favorites."

"So, nobody ever tried to contact you about the alleged scam after that?"

"No. I didn't hear another thing after Queah vanished. I would've remembered that for sure."

"What else can you tell me about Braxton Gage?"

Dunn picked up the now empty glass and drank some melted ice with a noisy slurp. "Well, they used to call him the young Turk. I mean he was in his late twenties, probably, and calling all the shots in his dad's company. Actually, there were two young Turks that made fortunes in the Gorge back then. The other was a guy named Royce Townsend. His brother ran the construction company and put Royce in charge of the dam construction."

A slight tremor went down my back. Townsend? I recognized that name. "Does he have a relative named Jason Townsend?"

"Yep, his son. Jason's contemplating a run for the U.S. Senate. Nothing would make the father happier than to have a son who's a U.S. senator."

I nodded. "So, Gage was a subcontractor for Townsend during the construction phase?"

"Right. They were both young, brash, and smart as whips, so naturally they became rivals. Still are, I suppose, but mainly in the political arena now." He chuckled for a moment before continuing. "Townsend became a leftie with a fat checkbook.

"What about Gage?"

"He's a cantankerous old fart. Way to the right of Attila the Hun."

"Any other players at that time that come to mind?"

Dunn drained his glass, paused, and then smiled almost lasciviously. "I do remember one thing about Townsend. He was quite the lady's man. Had an affair with a singer who worked at one of the hotels in Portland. Kind of an open secret at the paper, but in those days we protected people's secrets. All the guys in the newsroom were green with envy. She was one sexy broad."

"You remember her name?"

"Nah, not off hand." He looked down at his glass. "I'm empty. Sure you don't want to join me?"

"Okay, talked me into it. Can I—?"

"Stay there," Dunn interrupted, making it clear he didn't want any help. "I can handle the drinks."

Grateful for a few moments alone to think, I sifted hurriedly through what I'd just learned. Cecil Ferguson worked for Braxton Gage at the dam. Was Gage in on the swindle? And who the hell did Wiiks work for? Royce Townsend managed the whole construction project, so Gage, in effect, worked for him. Then there was the link between Winona and Townsend through his son, Jason, and the exquisite irony that the son now wants to tear down what the father built.

Like that girl in Wonderland once said, curiouser and curiouser.

When Dunn returned with the drinks, I said, "Do you have any other sources or records you could check or direct me to that might help me get a line on Timothy Wiiks?"

Dunn pulled down a third of his fresh drink, lowered it and looked at me with wet, magnified eyes. "Yeah, I have some other places I can look. Hell, I can access all the archives at *The*

Oregonian on my computer. Give me some time and I'll see what I can come up with."

Our talk drifted away from the Queah disappearance. Toward the end of my drink—it was at least a double—I nodded at the photograph of him and his wife and said, "You must miss her greatly."

He took a drink. "Every day."

"I can tell she was a good woman." I meant it. It was the way she looked directly into the camera, a level, no-nonsense look, but softened by a smile that conveyed both warmth and confidence.

Dunn flinched slightly, then appraised me for sincerity. It was like being painted with radar before a missile's launched. Apparently satisfied, he said, "She *was* a good woman. The best. And I sure as hell didn't deserve her."

I nodded. "Survivor's guilt's a bitch." The comment just sort of slipped out of me.

"Survivor's guilt? What the hell do you know about survivor's guilt?"

"I've been there." It was more of an admission than I intended to make. Not really one to share, I was habitually tight-lipped about the situation surrounding my wife's death.

But I needn't have worried that I opened the door to questions from Dunn. He said, "Well, somehow, I don't think that qualifies you to judge me. Spare me the pop psychology, okay?" With that, he spun his chair around and began furiously tapping on his keyboard.

Talking to his back, I apologized for my remarks, thanked him for the information, and slunk out of there like a kid who'd been expelled from school.

Nice work, Claxton, I told myself as I pulled away. Fletcher Dunn's a walking history book, and you manage to insult him. You can kiss off getting any more help from this guy.

But Dunn was wrong to think I didn't know anything about survivor's guilt. I was drowning in it.

Chapter Twenty-one

Getting chewed out by a drunk shouldn't be grounds for introspection, but when I left Fletcher Dunn's place, that's exactly what I found myself doing. I couldn't figure out why I was so stung by his tongue lashing. Could it be that his reaction reminded me of my behavior? How many times had I cut off Philip and Claire when their advice hit too close to home? Too many to count. Was I protecting my guilt and shame just like he seemed to be doing? Perhaps. How else could one assure the punishment continues unabated?

These insights demanded more thought, but I found it easy to push them back. Flush with new information and not that far from where Winona worked, I called to see if I could catch her. She told me to stop by, and she would squeeze me in.

The waiting room at Pacific Salmon Watch was empty, and the receptionist said Dr. Cloud was expecting me. Winona's hair was pulled back, and a piece of uncut turquoise hung on a slender silver chain against a black cotton blouse. The color of the stone brought out the hint of green in her hazel eyes. But she looked distracted and had a half moon below each eye a shade darker than her mahogany-tinted skin.

"Are you okay?" I asked.

She managed a weak smile. "Trying to cope without a computer's no fun. I told everyone here my computer crashed. I'm kind of embarrassed about last night."

"You shouldn't be, and don't worry. I doubt anything will get out before this is all resolved," I said, trying to convey more conviction than I felt.

Another weak smile. "I hope so. What's up?"

"I just finished talking to the reporter, Fletcher Dunn. It was pretty interesting."

I began sketching in the key points of my conversation, and when I told her about Ferguson working for Braxton Gage, her eyes flashed. "Could Gage be trying to cover something up?"

I shrugged. "I don't know. But it's certainly a possibility. Your grandfather definitely called Fletcher Dunn and set up a meeting to talk about the theft that was going on at the dam. Dunn confirmed that. And he drove out to the village from Portland the day after the flood, but your grandfather wasn't home. He'd already disappeared." The muscles in Winona's face tensed noticeably. I said, "Do you know anything about this guy, Gage?"

"He's the darling of the extreme right in this state. You know, the folks who swear global warming's a hoax, old growth forests need to be clear cut, and salmon are a nuisance." She made a face. "You get the picture. He bankrolled a string of right wing candidates over the years, but hardly any of them got elected, so he started playing with ballot initiatives, capping tax rates, mandating prison sentences, that sort of thing. He's made himself felt."

I nodded. "Do you know Royce Townsend?"

"Yes." She laughed. "He's at the other end of the spectrum, on the good side of environmental and global warming issues. He's got money, too, and donates to a lot of nonprofits, including my employer, Pacific Salmon Watch. That's how I met Jason, through his father, at a fundraiser."

"Did you know Royce managed The Dalles Dam project back in the fifties?"

Her eyebrows lifted in surprise. "You're kidding."

"Nope." I took her through what Dunn had told me about the elder Townsend and then said, "How does Royce feel about dam removal?"

She shrugged. "I assume he's supportive." Then the irony hit her, and she raised a hand to her mouth. "Oh, my. The son wants to tear down what the father built."

I nodded. "It was a long time ago. Attitudes change."

"I hope you're right." She glanced at her watch. "Uh, I'm getting a little tight on time, Cal. What's the next step?"

I stood up to leave. "I'm going to let Grooms and the Portland cops know what Fletcher Dunn told me. Let them work it from their angle. Meanwhile, Philip's still looking for Timothy Wiiks, the only other witness we have. I'll keep you in the loop."

When I got in my car, I sat there thinking for a while. Sure, Ferguson worked for Gage, but then again, as a contractor at the dam Gage worked for Townsend. That fact got glossed over in our conversation. If somebody put Ferguson up to killing Nelson Queah, then Townsend was as good a suspect as Gage. I fished the card Jason Townsend had given me from my wallet and called him. I caught him on the road—I could hear traffic noises—and told him I'd be delighted to join his volunteer staff, an offer he enthusiastically accepted. As I pulled away in my dusty Beemer, a shiny new Prius cruised in to take my slot. I glanced in the rear view mirror and saw a familiar profile. It was Jason Townsend. He hadn't recognized me, intent as he was on not being late to pick up Winona Cloud.

That night I read until well past midnight, then slipped into a fitful sleep. At first I thought the short, high-pitched sound that woke me came from the phone. I sat up, snapped on the light, and started to answer it. But the sound didn't repeat. And it wasn't the phone.

I heard the noise again and realized it was the alarm down in the laundry room. I snapped off the light and rolled out of bed.

No red-tailed hawk this time, not in total darkness. An owl, maybe? A possibility. But I had a feeling it wasn't an avian creature that had tripped the alarm this time.

In any case, I'd planned for this, and now I was going to check it out.

Chapter Twenty-two

Jake

Two and a half days lying around that hell-hole of a campsite really sucked. But finally the text came through—"loose end" had a name and an address. It was now up to Jake to finish the task. Clean up your mess, he was told. Don't disappoint the Old Man this time.

It felt good to have a job, to know what you had to do. Even a nasty job needs doing. Get in, get it done, get the hell out. That's the way he worked. But at the same time Jake felt like he was carrying a lead brick in his chest. There was that damn little voice, too, the one that kept saying this isn't right, you should stop right now and get the hell out of Oregon.

He wanted to talk to Amy so bad he could taste it. She had more common sense in her fingernail than he had in his entire body. Amy. His mind drifted, as it always did, to their best times, their times in bed. He pictured her lying naked, the curve of her ample hips, the gorgeous tits, the eager look in her eyes as he came to her. The image burned in his head, arousing him.

But he pushed those urges away along with the desire to talk to her. No way he could ever tell her about this. She would never understand. No, this was his secret, and he would take it to his grave.

Jake left his campsite in the canyon around midnight and headed toward Portland. He stopped at a twenty-four hour coffee shop off I-84, just west of the Gorge, that advertised Wi-Fi. He took his laptop inside, ordered coffee, and when he booted up, was encouraged by what he saw. The satellite image of Loose End's location looked damn good. Quick access in and out, and like Watlamet's place it was isolated with only a single neighbor well to the north and separated by a line of trees. Best of all, there was some sort of excavation site immediately south of the house, and it looked like there was a single stand of trees maybe eighty or ninety yards to the east that might provide cover while he waited for a shot. He studied the excavation site carefully and saw no sign that it was active.

After sketching a detailed map, he downed a second cup of coffee and left.

This was supposed to be a reconnaissance run, a quick drive through to scope out Loose End's location. But the layout looked so good that he was tempted to go for it. He glanced at his watch. He could be in place and waiting when the sun came up. His Remington was behind the seat, right where he'd left it.

Why not? Get it over with.

He took off the baseball cap he'd worn low over his face in the coffee shop and put on his cowboy hat. He had a pretty good plan, and he should've felt good. Instead, he found himself fighting that small voice again, the one that kept saying you don't have to do this.

But Jake knew better. A man does what he has to do. That's what the Old Man always told him.

Travelling in the early morning meant little or no traffic, but the flip side was that he'd be more noticeable to a passing cop. Damn lucky the description of his truck in the newspaper was vague. A dark, late model pickup probably described more than half the trucks on the road. Still, he drove well within the speed limit and tensed up every time he came near another car.

Where to park was another problem. The satellite image of the road leading up to Loose End's spread suggested there would be few places to park, and that's exactly what he found. He saw a gap in the trees maybe a quarter-mile below the excavation site and pulled in. He could walk in from there, and his truck would be out of sight. But judging from the beer cans on the ground, the spot was too popular to risk parking there.

The next spot looked a little iffy, too—a narrow space in behind a large patch of blackberries. He pulled in and got out to take a leak while he considered the spot. Good cover from the road, but the path dead-ended. He'd have to back out of there after the shot or go out and back in now. Either way, he didn't like it.

The road leading into the excavation site came up next. Jake slowed down, and as he turned in his lights picked up a series of deep potholes. Looked like the road was no longer in use. He switched off his headlights and used his fog lights as he eased through the potholes and down the road until a gate appeared in front of him. He managed a Y-turn in the tight space, parked facing the main road, and checked his watch. An hour and half to sunrise. Plenty of time to get set.

He removed his rifle—a bolt-action Remington 700 with a Swarovski scope—from its leather case, levered the bolt back, slotted four 7 mm Magnum cartridges into the box magazine, and placed another four shells in a front pocket of his vest. The Remington always felt good in his hands, like an old friend. And he prided himself on knowing its specifications. At twelve pounds, the rifle spit a half ounce of lead at a muzzle velocity of twenty-eight-hundred feet per second, and with its Swarovski scope he was pinpoint at four hundred yards. He'd never tried it, but he was sure he could break the rifle down, clean it, and reassemble it blindfolded. A man needs to know his weapon.

The site was fenced off and the gate at the end of the road locked with a large padlock. The fences on either side would be a tough climb, but the gate had a set of steel crossties that promised good hand and footholds. He slid the Remington under the gate as gently as he could and climbed over. The stand of trees on the rocky ledge of the excavation site was straight in from the gate and maybe a hundred feet to the east. Low in a clear sky, the moon provided just enough light for him to quickly find the trees, but it took a while to pick his way through the twisted trunks to the abrupt edge of a quarry. Loose End's house lay to the west, a faint outline in the shadows.

When Jake looked in that direction, a light came on in the house. It stayed on a few seconds, then went out.

What the fuck was that?

He was in a perfect position, and he wanted to believe that the blinking light was just coincidence. But as he sat there, uneasiness stirred in his gut like a worm. This spot was goddamn convenient, he told himself. Maybe too convenient?

He looked around his perch in the near darkness but saw nothing that looked out of place. He watched in the direction of the darkened house for a long time and saw no other lights or movement of any kind.

But the worm in his gut continued to turn.

He finally sighed, got up, and began backtracking. When he reached his truck he sat in the cab in the darkness, drumming his fingers on the stalk of his rifle as he battled with himself over what to do. *Should I get the hell out of here, or am I overreacting?*

Each time he started to turn the ignition key a voice would kick in. *You've come this far, man. Don't use that light for an excuse. Get this over with.*

Chapter Twenty-three

That high-pitched alarm, so out of place in the dead of night, woke me like a sharp slap to the face. I popped out of bed, and working quickly in the dark put on a black knit cap, a dark sweatshirt, jeans, and hiking boots. I used a small flashlight to navigate the pitch-black back staircase. I kicked myself for hitting the light when the alarm sounded, but it was only on for a second or two. Archie followed me down in a state of barely-contained excitement. It looked like an early jog or hike to him, but his ears fell when I told him to stay as I let myself out the front door.

I stopped at the garage and grabbed an ice pick out of my tool box before heading out the gate. That gun Philip offered me would have been nice, but I wasn't going to need it. My plan was straightforward: while the shooter waited in the trees for the sun to rise and for me to present a fat target, I was going to find where he'd parked his truck, note his license plate number, and use the ice pick to let the air out of one of his tires. That would provide enough time, even for Sheriff Talbot and his deputies, to pick the shooter up.

Simple and rather elegant, or so I thought at the time.

I let myself out of the gate, jogged down to the mailbox, and took a left on Eagle Nest. I took another left at a narrow path that meandered downhill, parallel to the main road, and well out of sight. The firs along the path shaded the waning moonlight, and the going was slow. When I reached the dirt road that led into the quarry, I stood in the shadows and watched the section I could see, ahead of where it curved around and led to the locked gate. There wasn't a sound and nothing moved. I figured the shooter probably parked his truck lower down the hill and walked in. I crossed the road and kept going.

I knew there were only two spots on the main road in the next mile and a half where a truck could pull off and be out of sight. Both were within the next quarter mile. The first was a pullout behind a low berm that had been overtaken with a thicket of blackberry vines. I went off the path and into the trees in order to come up on the spot with maximum cover. It was empty. The detritus littering the second spot, a turn-off through a row of firs, signaled it was a popular place to park. No truck there, either.

Disappointed, I turned around and headed back up hill. Probably a false alarm, I told myself. But there was one more spot I could check. Could it be that the shooter had actually turned onto the quarry road and parked around the curve near the locked gate? I wouldn't have chosen to do that, but maybe he was most interested in having quick access to his truck for a fast getaway.

I wasn't anxious to go in there, because the cover was spotty and the road was bordered on either side by a six-foot fence. At the same time, I'd come this far, and if the shooter was in there, I wanted to know about it. And besides, by this time, I felt pretty sure there was an owl in a tree nearby having a good laugh at my expense.

I stayed low, worked my way around the curve in the road, and took refuge behind a huge oak, the single deciduous tree the mining company had apparently seen fit to spare. The locked gate lay at the end of the road, but I couldn't see it yet. I peered into the darkness. Nothing moved in or around the narrow corridor.

I could just make out the next bit of cover, a shadowy blur on the other side of the road maybe twenty yards further in. A line of scrawny pines, I recalled. At that point I'd be able to see to the gate and anything parked this side of it. I would go to there and no further.

I moved across the road and took maybe twenty or thirty more steps when a blinding light came on directly in front of me. I froze as every adrenaline gate in my body slammed open. An engine roared to life a few beats later. The back wheels of a truck spun in the gravel before taking hold and hurtling forward, right at me. I turned around and dashed for the oak tree. I ducked behind the oak just as the truck roared by, missing me by inches. As the truck's brakes slammed on and it spun into a U-turn, I realized I was trapped in the corridor. I broke into a dead run for the gate, my only means of escape. The U-turn took the truck two tries, giving me just enough time to reach the gate.

I was bathed in the truck's headlights as I climbed the gate. I heard the truck skid to a stop and a car door slam. The shooter was right behind me, and he'd left the headlights on. I ducked behind a stack of rotting timbers just as he fired. The round thumped into a four by four post next to me. I heard the gate rattle, looked over my shoulder, and saw his silhouette as he scaled the gate. I had no choice but to keep running, and there was only one direction—toward the lip of the quarry. I ran in a zigzag pattern that would have been the envy of any NFL running back. The shooter snapped off two more shots, and I felt a stinging in my left arm.

The only cover ahead of me was the lone copse of cedars where I'd rigged the alarm. Even in my panicked state, I got the irony.

I wiggled through the stunted tree trunks and edged out onto the rocky lip of the quarry, my lungs exploding. I heard the shooter's footsteps, then the metallic click of the bolt on his rifle as he chambered another cartridge. "Come on out, Dude. You got no place to go."

He was wrong. As I stepped off the ledge, I wondered how deep the quarry lake really was.

Chapter Twenty-four

I was warm again. That's the first thing I noticed, that and seeing the steady drip of a clear liquid from a plastic bag feeding a tube that ran down to my arm. The bag seemed to levitate above me like an alien spaceship. Looking at it reminded me how full my bladder was. I tried to move my left arm and felt a sharp pain.

"You're awake." The voice came out of nowhere, and a face appeared next to the bag, a face with kind eyes. "I'm Beth, and I'm taking care of you today. How do you feel?"

"Tired. How long have I been out?"

Beth glanced at her watch. "It's close to noon. They brought you in around six-thirty this morning. After the doc stitched up your arm he gave you something to help you sleep. If you're up to it, I'll call the Sheriff. He wants to talk to you as soon as possible."

"Go ahead, but first I need you to do something for me, Beth." I managed to pull Gertrude Johnson's number out of the murk in my brain and recite it. "Please call the woman at this number and ask her to take care of my pup until I get out of here. Okay?" She agreed. As she was leaving I looked at the heavy swath of bandages on my forearm. "How bad is my arm?"

"Something gashed it, maybe a bullet or your fall."

"It was a bullet."

She flinched visibly. "Oh, dear. It's, uh, been stitched up. You'll have an ugly scar, but you'll be fine. You're very lucky, you know."

I drifted off again and thought I heard Sheriff Talbot's voice, but when I opened my eyes sometime later that afternoon

Deputy Sheriff Cleta Grooms' face was hovering over me like a big, full moon.

"Big C. How you doin'?"

She smiled down at me, and her eyes didn't look so steely. "I'm good, Cal. How are *you* feeling?"

"Glad to be alive. How did you get here?"

She laughed. "Sheriff Talbot came here to personally interview you, and you told him to go to hell, that you were going to sue his ass off—"

"I did? I said that?"

"You did. Then you told him to call me, so here I am. It was my day off, anyway."

"Well, I'm not suing anybody, but don't tell Talbot that." I tried to smile, but my lower lip was a fat sausage. "Man, I don't know which was worst, the temperature of that water or the way it tasted."

Grooms laughed again. "The water was in the low fifties. You were hypothermic when they fished you out."

"How did they know I was down there?"

"From what Talbot told me, it was your neighbor. She heard the shots down in the quarry and called 911. There was a patrol car in Dundee and they came in a hurry with lights and siren. They said they could hear you babbling all the way from a locked gate at the entrance to that quarry. They didn't pass any cars coming in. The shooter probably went over the mountain, got away clean."

"That sucks." I shook my head. "I was hoping that pond was deep, and it was—I never did hit bottom. When I resurfaced, he pumped at least two more rounds at me, but it was pitch black down there. I treaded water as quietly as I could, and I guess he either heard the siren or just figured I'd drowned."

"They found you hiked part way out of the water, babbling like an idiot, bleeding like a stuffed pig. You were hanging onto an ice pick. Had it stabbed in a crevasse to anchor yourself. Probably saved your life." She lowered her brows and cocked her head. "An ice pick?"

I managed a slight upward curve in my sausage lip. "I always plan ahead." I went on to sketch in the whole cockamamie scheme I'd come up with and how it had all gone south.

Grooms took some notes, asked some questions, and when I finished said, "Anything else that might help us?"

I tried to focus, but it felt like my synapses were firing blanks. I wondered what was dripping into my arm. "Uh, tire tracks should match the ones Philip found out in Clarno. Maybe some fingerprints on the gate. Several shots fired. He was using a bolt-action rifle, which probably saved my ass. It took him time to reload. Should be some retrievable rounds in the quarry somewhere." I closed my eyes to concentrate and the room took a half-lap. "One hit a four by four post next to a pile of timbers that were maybe thirty or forty feet in front of the cypress trees where I jumped off. There might be one in those tree trunks, too." I sat up a little and fought back a wave of nausea. "Give me a pencil and piece of paper and I'll draw you a map."

When I finished, she said, "That's it?"

The disappointment in her voice irritated me. I massaged my forehead with my good hand and tried to think. The effort felt like walking through deep snow. "Uh, one thing, sort of off topic. I talked to a journalist yesterday who knew Nelson Queah. I got some interesting information and possible leads." When I finished describing the Fletcher Dunn meeting I yawned. "I'm tired. Go get Talbot so I can get this over with."

As she was leaving, Big C turned back to me. "One thing I don't get. If you heard the alarm, why was the shooter in his truck instead of waitin' in the trees to pick you off?"

I shrugged my right shoulder. "I don't know. Only thing I can think of is that when I heard the alarm, I turned on the light for a second or two. Thought it was the damn phone. Maybe that tipped him, and he went back to his truck, and that's when I blundered in. Not my finest hour."

"Well, you beat 'im." She chuckled and looked at me. The steel was back in her eyes. "That boy's gonna be real disappointed when he learns what a good swimmer you are."

I guess Talbot had heard enough from me, because he delegated the interview to two of his deputies. Big C sat in, and she and I made short work of it. Toward the end of our chat she said to the deputies, "There's a gentleman outside who's an expert tracker. He identified some boot prints and tire tracks at the Watlamet murder scene that you folks might want to watch out for. I think he'd be willing to take a look at your crime scene."

The deputies exchanged glances. One of them responded, "We have our own crime scene techs, but if we find anything, we'll let you know."

Grooms nodded. Her expression remained impassive, but her jaw flexed as if she was trying to flatten something very hard between her teeth.

We'll let you know—the quintessential kiss-off.

When the deputies left, I managed to flex my swollen lip into the semblance of a smile. "Lone Deer's here?"

"I called him. He's outside."

My friend came in wearing a look that was one part worry and two parts anger. But when our eyes met he smiled broadly. "This is *Oregon*, Cal. We don't swim in March."

That day in the hospital was a dizzy blur. Philip urged me to call my daughter, but I wasn't about to do that. I knew Claire was busy with classes at Berkeley, and the last thing she needed was to be worrying about me. Grooms had left and I was filling Philip in when his cell phone chirped. He answered and handed the phone to me. "Winona."

"Cal? Oh, my God, are you all right?" Her voice cut the fog in my head like the chime of a bell across a lake. "Philip called and left a message. I'm sorry. I feel like this is my fault."

"It's not your fault, Winona. The sniper seems to have taken a distinct dislike to me. I do that to some people."

"This isn't funny, Cal. He almost killed you. How's your arm? Are you in pain?"

"Definitely not. The drugs here are great."

She sighed in exasperation. "Cal, I want to drop this whole thing. *Now*. I'm sorry I ever brought it up with you."

"That's not an option. I'm afraid it's taken on a life of its own. I'll be watching my back until this guy goes down. When that happens, we'll be in a position to tell the world what happened to your grandfather."

She sighed again. "I'm more concerned about you than my grandfather right now. I guess the police must be all over this, right?"

"Of course. It's a model of interagency cooperation."

"Look, I'm in Seattle. I've got to go into a meeting now. I'll call you back tomorrow. And Cal, I'm glad you're okay."

Later that afternoon I began to feel a little better, and when I asked Philip to swing by my house to check on Archie and pick up a change of clothes for me he smiled and shook his head. "You're not planning a jail break are you?"

"Uh, I'm feeling pretty good now. No need to take up a bed here. Besides, if I can persuade you to stick around, I'd like for us to look around the quarry when Yamhill finishes."

"After those bozos muck it up?"

"It's worth a try. Look what you found last time."

My tone must have had a hint of desperation in it, because Philip shot me a reassuring look. "I'm not going anywhere. I got you into this, not Winona. This guy needs his ticket punched."

We left that evening to the utter disbelief of two shocked nurses and the attending doctor, who had me sign a release.

On the way out, I felt like I was on the deck of a ship in high seas, but I made it to Philip's truck okay.

I had a back to watch and a score to settle.

Chapter Twenty-five

The next morning Philip and I sat on my side porch sipping coffee and watching the crime scene techs finish up their work over at the quarry. Archie lay next to me with his back pushed firmly against my foot in a show of support. He sensed I was injured and was staying close. As we watched, Philip mentioned that, although he hadn't located Timothy Wiiks, he had found his mother, who was living on the Umatilla Reservation. When he told Winona about it, she volunteered to make contact with the mother.

Around mid-morning two men in fluorescent orange vests sawed out a section of a tree that had apparently stopped one of the shooter's bullets. After that, the investigating team left the quarry site.

Twenty minutes later, Archie, Philip, and I slowly worked our way down the narrow corridor leading to the locked gate. Philip led with his head down. The road was rocky and hard-packed. About thirty feet from the big oak tree that saved me from being run over, Philip stopped and dropped to one knee. "That's where he spun a U-turn," I said.

Philip shook his head. "Nothing I can read here."

I pointed up ahead. "He was parked on the right side, next to those trees, facing this way."

After examining the area he shook his head again. We moved to the gate, and Arch and I stood by as Philip effortlessly scrambled over it. I stood there, aching to sit down but knowing if I did it would be hard to stand back up on my own. I held my bandaged arm against my chest, wishing I had a sling. Philip combed the rocky soil that had been thoroughly tramped on by the investigating team, then called back to me. "Nothing here."

We walked back out to the main road and stopped. A strong scent of cedar drifted in the breeze and fast-moving clouds promised rain, an event I hadn't dressed for. I nodded in the downhill direction. "There are a couple of places down from here where I figured he might park."

Archie sat down and cocked his head up at me. Philip placed his hands on his hips and looked me over. "You don't look so good, paleface. You want to go back?"

I shook the question off. "Maybe he pulled into one of those spots before coming up here." I glanced up at the sky. "Let's have a look before it cuts loose."

A large thatch of blackberries marked the first pull-out, a rutted path that wound in between the brambles and a row of mature cedars before abruptly dead-ending. I nodded at the narrow entrance. "I checked in there first, last night."

Philip dropped to one knee and examined the interface between the asphalt and ground at the entrance. "Looks like someone backed out of here not too long ago." He flicked at the fine pieces of gravel on the path with his finger. "See, gravel from the street's been sprayed on the path. My guess is someone pulled in slow then came back out. Could've been our guy."

I told Archie to stay at the entrance and followed Philip into the shaded area between the cedars and the blackberries. The ground was covered with a thick mulch of cedar sprays and seed cones. I walked behind my friend with my eyes glued to the ground but didn't see a thing that caught my attention.

Suddenly Philip dropped to both knees and pointed at a bare spot in the mulch. "Looks like bootprints." He moved in closer, nearly touching his nose to the ground, then looked up at me. "Same pigeon-toed prints I saw at Watlamet's"

I knelt down cautiously and looked where he was pointing. All I saw were two small triangular indentions in the mulch. "*That?*"

"They're *toe* prints. The heel prints are barely visible." He pointed again. "See?"

"Yeah, I think so."

Philip got up and motioned with his hand. "He must have parked his rig right here. He pointed again. "Look, those are tire tracks."

I struggled to my feet, and a wave of dizziness washed over me. All I saw was the suggestion of some faint marks imprinted on the mulch. "Tire tracks? You're kidding me."

Philip rolled his eyes. "White people. So clueless about the natural world."

I pointed at the tire tracks that for me were only a squint from disappearing. "You think we could get a wheel base measurement out of those? That would be a useful piece of information to go with the mold Grooms got of the tire track at Watlamet's."

"No problem. I've got a tape measure in my truck. I'll stop on my way out and phone it into Grooms. What about the Yamhill Sheriffs?"

I laughed. "What we've got wouldn't stand up as valid evidence, and Talbot would be the first to tell you that. Let Grooms worry about what Talbot needs to know." At that point I looked up at the swaying cedar branches and felt the first drops of rain. "We're going to lose it, anyway."

Philip unhooked Archie's retractable leash from his collar. "Here. Take this end." We stretched the leash across the tire marks and using his pocket knife, Philip cut the leash to length. "You don't need a leash for this dog, anyway," he told me with a note of disdain in his voice.

The wind continued to build, and when the rain began it came down at a slant. We were both soaked by the time we got back to my place. I hadn't worn a jacket but managed to keep my bandages dry by wrapping Philip's windbreaker around my arm. Philip made us fried egg sandwiches for lunch, and then on his way out he did two more things. First, he took a stainless steel revolver from under the seat of his truck along with a box of cartridges. "This is a .357 Magnum. It'll stop a mule."

He snapped the cylinder open to show me the gun was fully loaded, closed it, and handed the gun to me. "You need some protection, Cal. Take this, damn it."

Next, he went to my garage and put my chainsaw in the back of his pickup. "I'll be right back," he said.

Not long after that I heard a buzz as the saw came to life in the distance. I went over to the side porch and watched him clear the trees the sniper would have used as cover to shoot me. When he came back, I said a little sheepishly, "Thanks. I should have done that in the first place."

He shrugged. "You know what they say about hindsight." Then he handed me the motion sensor I'd placed over in the trees. "Besides, this wasn't such a bad idea."

That afternoon I took a pain pill and lay down on the couch in my study with Archie at my side and the .357 sitting on an adjacent table. I tried to think through the situation I found myself in, but as soon as a thought formed in my head it would take flight like a bird. In no time, my pain and every care I had dissolved into a slow moving, pitch-black vortex.

I remained there until I heard a guttural noise. It seemed to come through a long tunnel. I opened my eyes to a dark room. Night had fallen. The noise came again. It was Archie. He was in front of the study door, growling—a low, uncertain warning. I picked up the revolver and tried to clear the fuzz in my head.

I told Archie to lie down and hush and then eased into the darkened hallway, shutting the door behind me. I took a couple of steps and froze when I heard the unmistakable creak of the second step on the front porch.

That sound cleared my head in a hurry.

Chapter Twenty-six

I crept down the back hall and let myself out through the kitchen door onto the side porch and slowly circled around to the front. There wasn't much light, but outlined against the white wall I could see the shape of someone at my front door. I extended the .357 Magnum out with both hands and wincing at the pain in my left arm and scarcely believing what I was preparing to do, tightened my finger on the trigger.

I cleared my throat. "Can I help you?"

The figure froze. Even in the weak light I sensed something familiar about the silhouette.

"Cal? It's me. Winona." She peered at me through the darkness. "Jesus, don't shoot me!"

I lowered the revolver and expelled a breath. "*Winona?* Sorry. I was asleep. Heard you on the steps. I'm a little jumpy."

"I just drove up from Eugene. Thought I'd pop in and see how you're doing." She managed a laugh. "You blew it, you know."

"I did?"

"You could have said, 'Go ahead, make my day.'"

We sat in the kitchen with a bottle of pinot between us. Archie was under the table, sleeping against my foot. He liked Winona well enough, but he was still sticking close to me. At her insistence, I was taking her through what'd happened. It wasn't a story I was particularly anxious to repeat. After all, it's embarrassing to be caught in your own trap.

When we'd finished discussing the latest attempt on my life,

Winona said, "I've got some news. Timothy Wiiks is dead. He died on March 9, 1957. That's the day before the falls were flooded, the day before Grandfather disappeared at Celilo. He went off the road into the Deschutes River late that night. Of course, the police found a couple of whiskey bottles in his car." She pursed her lips and shook her head. "Just another drunken Indian."

I sat up straight in my chair. "How do you know this?"

"I talked to his mother, Sarah Morning Owl, over at the Umatilla Rez. She's in failing heath, but her mind's sharp as a razor." She exhaled. "Timothy was her only son. She was the one who told him to talk to Grandfather about the thievery going on at the dam. Timothy didn't drink, Cal. Just like Grandmother, she knew her son had been murdered."

"Let me guess. No one would listen to her."

"Of course not. The police blew her off. There was a cursory investigation. No one, not even the tribal elders could help. An Indian woman had no voice at all in those days."

"Does she have evidence to back this up? A diary, letters, anything that might help us?"

"No. Nothing."

"How did she make the link between her son's death and your grandfather's disappearance?"

"She told me he worked for Cecil Ferguson, kind of a personal assistant. Ferguson wasn't that good with numbers, so Timothy started helping him with the books. That's when he found it—a second set of figures Ferguson was keeping. Timothy was a bright kid and figured out something illegal was going on."

"I see. What did she do after his death?"

She said she tried to contact Grandmother, who was still in the TB ward at Warm Springs. She finally gave up in despair, but she never forgot."

"Did she say anything else?"

Winona picked at the label on the wine bottle and then looked up at me. "She said she had a dream not too long ago that a woman would come to set Timothy's spirit free."

"That would be you?"

The dimples appeared, but the smile was tentative. "Apparently. She said she wasn't surprised that I'd come to see her. In our culture a dream like that is considered a big deal."

"By you?"

She exhaled and stripped a piece of the label off with her fingernails. The nails were painted blood red. "I don't know. I suppose so. It feels like I've set something in motion. Something I can't really control."

I laughed. "Tell me about it. Did she mention seeing a white guy in her dream? I need to know if I'm going to survive this."

She looked up from the wine bottle and met my eyes. "Cal, I'm so—"

I put a hand up. "Don't, Winona. We've already been through this. This is personal for me, too. I'm in for the duration."

We sat in silence for a long time. She shifted in her seat. "Where do we go from here?"

I scratched my eyebrow with the little finger of my good hand while I gathered my thoughts. There was something I needed to get off my chest. "Uh, look Winona, I called Jason Townsend and offered to help in his campaign—"

"I know. He told me. He was pleased. He's very taken by you."

I frowned and shook my head. "I think he's a good man, too, but my motives here aren't pure. I need him to introduce me to his father, Royce. I've got some questions I want to ask him about the construction project at the dam. I need him to cooperate."

"Oh. Well, I guess you have to do that. I'm sure Jason can make it happen."

"I hope so. I don't necessarily want Jason to pass anything on to his dad, you know, about the things we've discovered about your grandfather's disappearance."

"You don't suspect Royce Townsend, do you?"

"I don't know who to suspect at the moment. I just wouldn't want the information to influence his thinking in any way. Memory's a funny thing. Have you told Jason anything?"

Winona brushed a strand of hair from her forehead and widened her eyes. "I told him about the murders of Watlamet and Ferguson. I left out the part about my going to see Ferguson and my brush with the Portland cops. I was too embarrassed to tell him that."

I was disappointed but didn't show it. "That's all?"

She wrinkled her brow and thought for a moment. "Yes. That's all. And you don't have to worry, Cal. I won't say anything else."

"Good."

Winona told me she'd come to cook dinner. The only problem was she couldn't cook. The pain was re-emerging in my arm, so I sat at the kitchen table and gave directions. Soon she had a couple of Chinook salmon steaks sizzling on the grill and red potatoes brushed with olive oil and sprinkled with sea salt baking in a hot oven. "Do you want a salad?" she asked.

"Sure." I pointed to a bowl on the counter, relieved that I had actually done a bit of shopping two days earlier. "Uh, there're tomatoes and a ripe avocado in that bowl, a cucumber and some carrots in the fridge. Just slice 'em up. Simple's good. Oh, and there are some Kalamata olives in the fridge as well." I went on to describe the one dressing I knew how to make—a mixture of olive oil, red wine vinegar, and Dijon.

She smiled and shook her head. "You know your way around a kitchen. How did that come about?"

"I'm a work in progress. If you love food, cooking kind of follows naturally."

She laughed. "Oh yeah? Well, I'm living proof that's not so."

The dinner came together beautifully. We ate with a patter of small talk in unspoken agreement that her grandfather's disappearance was out of bounds during such a meal. Afterwards, she nodded at the bandage on my arm. "That's going to need changing. When're you going back to the doctor?"

In my escape from the hospital, I'd failed to think about that. "I'll deal with it tomorrow," I answered vaguely.

She wrinkled her brow. "Did they give you a sling for your arm?"

"No. I checked out kind of fast."

"I think you need one. I can't believe they let you leave without one."

The sling Winona fashioned from a piece of an old bed sheet fit snugly and relieved a lot of the pressure on my wound. When she finished helping me into it, her dimples appeared and she leaned forward to kiss me on the cheek. I placed my good arm on her shoulder and gently held her in front of me. Her breath was warm on my face, and I suddenly ached to taste her mouth, to hold her in my arms. I pulled her forward, and when our lips touched she opened her mouth and our tongues came together for one white hot instant.

She pulled back. "God, I've got to go, Cal. This isn't a good idea."

"I think you're right."

"I'm not good at juggling men."

I thought of Jason Townsend, picturing his boyish, handsome face. "No problem. I'm the one who's out of line here."

After Winona left, I sat in the study with a book, desperate for distraction. My arm throbbed with pain, but I resisted taking another pain pill. After reading the same sentence for the fourth time, I set the book aside. Not because of the pain, but because of what that flubbed kiss dredged up in me. It wasn't Winona's rejection, either. Hell, she'd done me a favor. Like I told Philip, the last thing I needed was more emotional baggage. I had enough to handle, with a motherless daughter and memories of my dead wife hovering over me, memories that were stubbornly fade resistant. I'd clawed and scratched my way out of depression, and by coming to Oregon, to this ridge, I'd been able to sustain a semblance of normalcy.

Stay with what works, I told myself. Don't rock the boat.

But that night, before drifting off, that fleeting kiss with Winona replayed in my head. I felt the jolt again. It was like touching a downed power line, and as my conscious mind closed down I saw the vaguest outline of new possibilities.

Chapter Twenty-seven

The following Friday I awoke to a thick cloud cover and the smell of approaching rain. Somber light muted the spring colors in the valley but didn't slow a group of rowdy swifts that darted and swooped in my yard after a hatch of insects so tiny I couldn't see them. I'd spent the intervening time getting my strength back after what Philip dubbed "the spring swim in Lake Claxton." I got my arm checked out and redressed at an urgent care center in Newberg and drove on into to Wilsonville to have the back window in my car replaced.

I was having a second cup of coffee when Archie's squeals and yelps marked the arrival of Santos Araya, who'd come on his spring vacation. He was dressed for work this time—faded jeans, beat-up sneakers, and a paint-spattered sweatshirt. Maturity had begun to sculpt his body, but innocence still clung stubbornly to his face. His dark eyes were wary, although perhaps less so than the first time we met. I poured him a glass of orange juice and told him how lucky he was that I was injured. "Otherwise, I'd thrash you on the basketball court."

"I'll play with my left hand in my pocket," he said with the first hint of a smile he'd allowed himself in my presence.

Relieved that he didn't ask me how I got hurt, I threw my head back and laughed. "When I get the stitches out. Now come on, I have some weeds that are dying to meet you."

After lunch, the rain that had threatened all morning finally cut loose, strafing the house with drops the size of quarters and swaying the big firs in the yard. The wind through the trees made a sifting sound, like waves receding on a pebbly beach. I called Santos in out of the downpour and gave him a cold apple out of the refrigerator. He followed me into the study, slouched into my big leather chair and began eating.

"You like to read?" I asked.

He shrugged and used his full mouth as an excuse not to answer.

I pulled a book from the bookcase and tossed it to him. A favorite of Claire's back when she was an early teen, it was the best I could come up with on short notice. He caught it adroitly with one hand, glanced at the cover, and then looked up with a wrinkled brow. "*Hatchet?*"

"It's about a kid who has to survive on his own up in Alaska after a plane crash. You might like it."

His brow stayed wrinkled. "Alaska? The dude's an Eskimo?"

"No. A white kid. You still might like it."

Santos shrugged again but took the book, read the dust cover, and then settled back and began to read the first chapter. The rain continued unabated, and I went back to plunking on my computer with my good hand. The phone rang twenty minutes later.

"Claxton? It's Fletcher Dunn. I read what happened. Been meaning to call you."

I was surprised to hear from Dunn. "Yes, Fletch."

"Are you okay?"

"Yeah, I'm fine. The case I told you about sort of blew up in my face."

Laughter. "I'll say. I read about your mishap. Do the cops have any leads?"

"Not many at this point." I paused for a moment. "Uh, I thought I was *persona non grata* with you."

"Oh, *that*. I'm sorry I went off at you the other day. I was three sheets to the wind. You know what they say, 'never wreck a drunk's pity party.'" He laughed uproariously. "Hell, I'm half in the bag now. But listen, I've talked to some folks about the singer I told you about. You know, Royce Townsend's mistress. Found a couple of things that might interest you."

"Shoot."

"Her name's Sheri North. Don't know whether that's her real name or a stage name."

"She still around?"

"My source didn't know. But I've got more. She left Portland abruptly while The Dalles Dam was being built. Rumor had it she was pregnant. Most people figured Townsend was the father. But get this, my sources tell me she also had a dalliance with Braxton Gage. Apparently, both Townsend and Gage lusted after this woman."

"Did she have the baby?"

"The story was she left to get an abortion. In any case, she just dropped out of sight. A real shame, too."

"How's that?"

"The woman had a real set of pipes, I'm told. Never heard her sing myself."

"So, she never resurfaced?" I asked, becoming curious. "I wouldn't mind talking to her."

"Not that I know of." Dunn chuckled. "In those days, women who got knocked up were *supposed* to disappear."

There was a pause, and I heard the clink of ice on glass. "I also picked up another tidbit on Braxton Gage that might interest you. The old boy's still up to his money-making tricks."

I waited for him to continue.

"He has a growing parcel of land east of Cascade Locks in the Gorge. Rumor has it he's working behind the scenes with the Confederated Tribes at Warm Springs to put a gambling casino there."

"A casino in the Gorge? You're kidding me."

Dunn erupted in laughter. "Afraid not. Word on the street is that the Governor's listening to Gage. And the city fathers in Cascade Locks are salivating. A casino would be a bonanza to them as well as the Confederated Tribes."

"And to Gage, too."

"Oh, yeah. I'm told Gage wants a piece of the gambling action as an inducement to sell the land. Could be huge for him. The cunning old fox."

"A casino in the Gorge. What the hell next?"

Dunn chuckled. "I'm sure Gage's loving this—a sharp stick in the eye of every Gorge loving, tree-hugging environmentalist in Oregon."

I pressed Dunn for details, but that's pretty much all he had. I thanked him again for the information, adding, "So, how are things going with you?"

He sighed into the phone, and I heard the clink of ice against glass again. "Oh, you know, same old demons. I can handle the injury most days. Matter of fact, I find a certain solace in being a cripple. Seems only right since I lived and she didn't." His voice cracked. "But the loss of her, that's what I can't get past."

A wave of emotion blindsided me. I sighed and heard myself say, "Yeah, I know the feeling. I lost my wife a year ago. Suicide."

The line went silent for so long I thought the call had dropped. Finally, I heard a slurp and then Dunn. "I know that, Cal. I did some research on you. Sorry for your loss." More clinking of ice. "Your wound's fresher than mine. It's me who should be giving the advice here. Trouble is, I don't have a clue what to tell you."

I had to chuckle. "No need, Fletch. I'm muddling through," I lied.

"Say," he continued in a bright tone that made it clear we were done with this maudlin topic, "I noticed you had a fine record as a prosecutor in L.A. Reading between the lines, I'd say you had a shot at heading up the whole shebang down there."

I winced inwardly. I wanted to tell him that the price of my lust for success was my wife's death, but I never seemed to have enough breath in my lungs to say that out loud. "Well, it didn't work out that way."

Chapter Twenty-eight

The sun reappeared that afternoon, bathing the valley in splendid light and inspiring a throng of songbirds whose choruses seemed to merge like some improvised jazz tune. I sent Santos Araya back out to continue the weeding. After he left with his father I went out to the garden to look around. I couldn't find a trace of a weed, and he'd even left some tender shoots of something that looked like lettuce that must have wintered over. I'd given him a tough job, a kind of test, I suppose, and he'd done a much better job at it than I could have. He'd left with the copy of *Hatchet*, too, promising to bring it back the following week.

I glanced at my watch and realized it was time to get ready for a dinner party Jason Townsend had invited me to. He'd called two days earlier, saying it was an informal gathering of some of his advisors and potential supporters for his Senate run. Apparently, Winona wasn't kidding when she told me Jason was impressed with me. I wasn't sure why. After all, I wasn't in any position to write him a big check.

I showered, shaved, and put on a striped button-down with long sleeves that covered my bandage, my best pair of jeans and, after giving them a quick buff, my loafers. I fed Arch and headed down to Dundee, where I dashed into my office and grabbed my blazer.

The Townsend estate was on the twisting road that paralleled the Willamette River between Newberg and Wilsonville, twenty-some miles south of Portland. It was dark when I arrived at the gate, but I knew the place, at least from the outside. I'd passed it many times without realizing who owned it.

The massive wrought iron gate had a keypad security system and a camera in a steel tube mounted off to the side like a cannon protecting a harbor. The gate was open, and a man dressed better than me was talking to a couple in a brand new, metallic silver Range Rover. As the big SUV pulled away, I moved up in my twelve year old BMW, wishing I'd stopped at the car wash on the way over. The man found my name on his clipboard and waved me through.

The drive in was maybe a quarter of a mile and on my left several acres of pasture land stretched into the darkness. I figured the half dozen or so horses that normally grazed there were in the stable, a massive stone structure sporting twin cupolas with elegant copper weathervanes. The main house—awash in dramatic landscape lighting—looked like it'd been brought over block by block from a sixteenth-century village in southern France. A steep, slate roof fell away to a stone façade with jutting turrets and a sweeping front staircase that led to an arched portico. The couple ahead of me had already entered, so I rapped on the imposing double doors at the top of the stairs, wondering how many trees in the rainforest had been felled to make them. A slender, elegantly dressed woman with platinum blond hair and eyes the color of the ocean opened the door. Mid-fifties, I guessed. She was so right for the setting, I wondered if she'd come with the house.

I introduced myself, and she flashed a lovely if somewhat practiced smile. "So nice to meet you, Cal. I'm Valerie Townsend, Royce's wife. Please come in. The guests are in the study." She led me down a long hall filled with fine antiques and original art, her lovely hips swaying in the manner of all alluring women.

When we entered the study, Jason Townsend looked up and smiled broadly. "Hello, Cal. Glad you could make it. Come join us."

My eyes found Winona first, and I fought back a lingering feeling of awkwardness over our aborted kiss. Her hair was down, her eyes radiant. She had on a simple, black dress with a delicate silver and turquoise necklace lying just above a hint of cleavage. Royce Townsend was standing next to his son with a glass of wine in his hand. He was as tall and handsome as Jason, although his shoulders were slightly stooped, and he had a full head of strikingly silver hair. His handshake was firm and his pale, gray eyes clear and alert. "Nice of you to join us, Cal. Let me introduce you to these folks."

It was an eclectic group. The couple with the Range Rover turned out to be a local advertising mogul and his wife. She was an artist, and judging from her denim work shirt and the paint under her fingernails, a genuine free spirit. Among Jason's advisers were a black economics professor from Lewis and Clark, the CEO of a high-tech startup, and a Latina woman whom Townsend described as 'a tigress on immigration policy.' She and I were the only lawyers in the group.

After I'd met everyone, Royce said, "We all read about the shooting, Cal. How are you feeling?"

All eyes in the room were suddenly on me. It was clear something had been said before I arrived. "Oh, I'm fine, thanks. That story in the paper exaggerated what happened." Winona started to say something, and I shot her a warning look. The last thing in the world I wanted to do was talk about the fiasco at the quarry.

She caught my drift. "Cal has a charming old place in the hills above Dundee, in the wine country," she said brightly.

It worked. The conversation turned to a lively discussion of Oregon wines, which were being poured in generous quantities by a circulating waiter. When Valerie ushered us into the dining room, I found myself sitting between the artist and someone who looked familiar to me. The artist—sipping maybe her fourth glass of wine—was engrossed in a conversation with Valerie, who'd managed to match her glass for glass.

The person who looked familiar was Sam DeSilva, Jason Townsend's campaign manager. I remembered meeting him at the Celilo Falls commemoration. His shaved head shown in the overhead lights, and his deep-set eyes were definitely not beacons of warmth. I learned he was an executive on loan from Royce Townsend's holding company, Townsend Enterprises. I sized Sam up as a tough-minded, no nonsense type—probably the ideal profile for running a Senatorial campaign.

Another familiar face sat across from me. David Hanson was the Chief Counsel for Townsend Enterprises and was looking after the legal aspects of the campaign, he told me.

So, Daddy Townsend was backing this campaign in a major way.

Unlike DeSilva, Hanson seemed to remember me from the commemoration, at least that's what he said when we introduced ourselves. Tall and thin, he wore sharply creased slacks, a black cashmere sweater, and a perpetually anxious look on his face. Glancing at Sam and then back to me, he said, "Tell us, Mr. Claxton—"

"Call me Cal, David."

"Right, Cal. What brings you to us?" His eyes were skeptical, and I could feel the heat of DeSilva's gaze on the side of my face, as well.

I knew the drill. I was an unknown entity, and they felt obliged to check me out. I smiled affably. "Jason invited me. I like his stand on wild rivers. I'm here to help him get elected."

Sam cleared his throat and shifted in his seat. I remembered him rolling his eyes when this subject came up at the commemoration. David smiled. "That's great. We can use the help. What do you do, Cal?"

"I practice law to support my fly fishing habit." Then to get a rise out of Sam I added, "I'd like to see the Columbia, or at least the Snake, flowing free again before I die."

Sam puffed a breath, shook his head, and with sarcasm dripping from his voice said, "Oh, spare me. Not another dam bomber."

Hanson shot him a withering look, then forced an apologetic smile at me. "Excuse my colleague, here. He doesn't think Oregon's ready for a forward-looking position on dam removal."

Sam snorted. "Read 'extreme' for 'forward-looking,' and it doesn't poll worth a shit, anyway. Oregonians like cheap power more than salmon."

"This is an environmental imperative for Jason," Hanson fired back, as color began to puddle in his pink cheeks.

They were glaring at each other when Jason Townsend tapped the rim of his glass with a dinner knife. Dressed in gray slacks and a maroon crew neck sweater, he beamed his trademark boyish smile. "You can all relax, I'm not going to give a speech tonight." Chuckles rippled through the room. "I think you know where I stand on the issues. I just want to thank you all for coming. I realize it's a lot to ask with the primary still a year away. But politics, being what it is today, requires lots of lead time and planning—"

"And money," Sam DeSilva interjected, causing an eruption of laughter from the well-lubricated guests.

Jason laughed and gestured toward his campaign manager. "Yes, and that, too, Sam. But seriously, I'm humbled by the thought of running for the U.S. Senate and honored that you folks might consider getting in on the ground floor of my campaign. So, thank you again and *bon appétit.*"

After dinner the group adjourned to the library, which looked like something from a movie set—floor to ceiling books, a three-foot diameter antique globe, and even a sliding ladder to reach the highest books. I'd been pulled away from the group by Jason to huddle with his father, where the subject turned to the politics of dam removal. Jason was animated, his eyes lit with obvious conviction as he ran through an argument it was clear his father had heard before. "Anyway, I think we're facing a stark choice. Either dams or salmon, but not both. Trouble is, it's tough to get people to take me seriously." He laughed and put his hand on my shoulder. "That's why you caught my attention at the lunch out at Celilo, Cal. You seem to get it."

Before I could answer, Royce said, "Well, politics is the art of the possible, son. You may have to shelve some of that idealism. The primary race's going to be a dogfight."

"*Idealism?*" he shot back. "Look what's happening on the Sandy River. Marmot Dam's coming out, thanks to pressure from environmental groups like the one Winona works for.

Come October, that river's going to start repairing ninety years of damage."

Royce put his hand on his son's shoulder. "I know, but that's a small dam on a small river compared to the Snake or the Columbia."

Jason moved just enough to free himself from his father's grasp and glared at him. "It's a start." Then he looked at me and said, "Excuse me, Cal," before walking away to join another circle of guests.

Royce turned to me and sighed, his pale eyes the color of fog. "Ah, to be young and idealistic again. I remember those days with fondness, don't you, Cal?" He wore a self-satisfied expression, signaling he had me figured out, that I didn't have the naiveté his son ascribed to me.

I took a sip of brandy and nodded, not wishing to disabuse him of that notion.

"Jason needs to accept the fact that a politician's first duty's to get elected," He went on.

I thought of the mountains of integrity sacrificed on that altar and stifled a sarcastic comeback. Instead, I shifted the subject. "Building The Dalles Dam as a young man must've been the experience of a lifetime."

He laughed heartily. "Oh, it was incredible. Hard work, but far and away the most satisfying job I ever had. All very heroic, too. You know, we needed cheap hydroelectric power for aluminum to build fighters and B-52s, and to make nukes at Hanford, all to fight the Cold War. He glanced over at Winona and lowered his voice, "It was a shame what happened there at Celilo. By the time my brother and I got the contract to build the dam, the die had been cast. Her people didn't really have a chance."

"Jason may have mentioned that I'm looking into the disappearance of Winona's grandfather, Nelson Queah. Would you mind if I abused your hospitality by asking you a couple of questions?"

His face remained unchanged except for a slight narrowing of his eyes and a tighter focus on me. "By all means, Cal."

"I'm interested in a man named Cecil Ferguson. He supervised concrete pours at the dam. Do you remember him?"

"Ferguson. Hmm. Vaguely. I worked with lots of people on that project."

"I have reason to believe he was skimming government money somehow. Did you ever hear of anything like that going on?"

He stroked his chin and paused for a moment. "Yes. Come to think of it, I do remember something about that. Some cub reporter from Portland was nosing around. Nothing ever came of it, though. Didn't Ferguson work for Braxton Gage?"

"Yes he did. Could Gage have been involved in the scam?"

He laughed. "Wouldn't surprise me. That man never saw a dollar he didn't lust after."

"Is there *anyone* else I could talk to about this?"

He wrinkled his brow and ran his fingers through his silver hair. "Fifty years is a long time. I can't think of anyone except Gage. Hell, I'd talk to him if I were you. He was probably up to his eyeballs in the scam." Royce's eyes started to wander, indicating the discussion was over.

"One more question," I pressed. "Can you tell me anything about Sherman Watlamet, the man who was gunned down out on the John Day River? He was apparently a friend of Cecil Ferguson's."

He winced at my words. "Grisly thing, that murder. No, can't say that I ever knew him back in the day." Then he nudged me with his elbow and nodded subtly toward Winona, who was deep in conversation with Jason, the immigration activist and the professor. "She's a gorgeous woman, don't you think, Cal?"

I smiled and nodded in agreement.

"Jason was asking me about family rings the other day. We have a beauty that belonged to his grandmother. I think he's going to ask Winona to wear it. Wouldn't that be something?" With that, he walked off, not waiting for an answer.

Makes sense, I told myself. A real power couple. I drained my drink and stood there for a while, alone. The room seemed to shrink, the buzz of conversation became annoyingly loud, and the air went stale, like someone had taped off the doors and windows. Not wishing to be the first to leave, I hung around until the couple in the Range Rover said their goodbyes. As I was walking out to my car a few minutes later, I heard voices from the other side of a hedge that separated the path I was on from an outdoor patio. The sharp tone of the voices caused me to stop, and when I heard, "Damn it, Jason, I don't care what they say," I slipped into the deep shadow of a large oak and listened shamelessly.

"For God's sake, David, you're just going to have to deal with it." I heard someone moan. "Don't. Not now. We need to get back inside before they miss us. You don't know the pressure I'm under."

The noise of their shuffling feet caused me to miss David's reply, although the tone of his voice came through. It was plaintive, laced with emotion.

When I got in my car, I sat there for a long time in silence. First the news from Royce Townsend about his son's intentions toward Winona and then the weird conversation I'd just overheard. What the hell's going on?

Finally, as I pulled onto the Townsend's driveway and my headlights bored a tunnel across the darkened pasture, I said aloud, "That sounded like a lover's spat."

Chapter Twenty-nine

That night I had a strange dream. I was sitting in a dark room facing the illuminated outline of a door. The thin ribbon of light was unnaturally bright and strangely alluring, as if something desirable burned on the other side. I got up, and as I searched like a blind man for the door knob, the light went out. I awoke with an overwhelming sense of loss. The digital clock showed four twenty, and after tossing around for another half hour I got out of bed and called Phillip.

"What's going on, Cal?" he answered warily. It wasn't like me to call him at the crack of dawn.

"Not much. Couldn't sleep. Did I wake you?"

"Are you kidding? I'm on the way to the Deschutes to meet a couple of developers from Bend. They want to experience the Zen of fly fishing for steelhead. I can't wait."

"You'd better include some deep breathing instructions for when you give them the bill."

"Hey, with the money they're raking in, they can afford me. Real estate in Bend's like a feeding frenzy, man."

"It's called a bubble."

"Yeah, well there's something not right about it. What goes up comes down. But I'm sure you didn't call at five to discuss real estate."

"Actually, I've got a couple of things on my mind. First, what do you know about the Tribes trying to put a gambling casino in the Gorge?"

Philip laughed with derision. "Oh, *that*. Yeah, the Tribal Council's actually considering it. Can you believe it?"

"Is your father involved?"

"Up to his eyeballs. I think it's a stupid idea. Ranks right up there with flooding the falls."

"I heard Braxton Gage's involved in the deal. The guy keeps popping up in this mess you got me into."

Ignoring the dig, Philip said, "Uh, I'm not getting the connection here."

I chuckled. "There probably isn't any. But I need some way to approach Gage. I figured your father might be able to help me. You know, give me some sort of introduction so I don't have to make a cold call."

"I'll ask him."

"Thanks. The other thing is, I need to go fishing to get my head straight."

"What's wrong with your head?"

"Nothing. I just need to think some things through is all," I said, hoping he wouldn't pry. I felt my deck had been shuffled by Winona's visit coupled with that night at the Townsend estate, but I sure as hell didn't want to talk about it.

"What about your arm, man?"

"I'll use Saran Wrap."

"Duct tape might work better."

"What's the Sandy doing right now?"

"Actually, the Sandy might be a good bet. I heard there's a run of native steelies in there right now. I don't know whether they're early summers or late winters. Your best bet's probably below Marmot Dam. It's a pretty good hike in but worth it." He hesitated for a moment. "Uh, you ready to go steelheadin' on your own?"

"Ready as I'll ever be. I've had a good teacher."

Philip laughed. "By the way, you can say goodbye to the dam while you're up there. They're going to breach it in October. You can thank Winona for that. She and the outfit she works for were key in convincing the power company to take it out, and they finally agreed. It'll make the Sandy free-flowing from Mount Hood to the Columbia."

Philip's comment surprised me. Apparently, Winona was as modest as he was. "She didn't mention it to me. I think I'll go have a look."

◇◇◇

The next morning I stood on a boulder with my back to the sun on the edge of the Sandy River. I was looking for steelhead. They're hard to catch, and it never hurts to know where they are, although you're damn lucky if you ever see one. Sluicing off the glaciers on the southwest side of Mount Hood, the water was fast, cold, and clear. The fish would appear as dark shadows against the river bottom. I saw none.

After a hike through the trees, this was my first good look at the river, which swept around a broad oxbow and came rattling at me over a mantle of volcanic basalt covered with loose, gray gravel—prime habitat for steelhead. The firs and cedars still dripped from a rain the night before, and fast moving clouds threatened more weather. Archie was behind me on the bank with strict orders to stay put. There was plenty of wild life up there, even cougars. I didn't want him getting into any mischief.

I waded downriver and stopped about forty feet from a spot where the river darkened, indicating the presence of a depression deep enough to hide fish. I tossed a fly called a Red Rocket at a forty-five degree angle to the bank, watched it sink below the surface, and then worked it across the depression using the tip of my rod. The fly must work by shock value, since the red and pink fluff hiding the hook looked more like something from a Vegas chorus line than any insect on the planet. The water was refreshingly cool against my waders, and the faint scent of fir needles and water hemlock drifted downriver with the breeze.

As I worked the hole, the rhythm of my casts began to relax me. Nothing stirred, which was fine. I'd come here to gain a little perspective. Fly-casting on a spring day—fish or no fish—was my newly discovered way to relax and think. I had to admit I was a long way from the uptight prosecutor I used to be down in L.A. Maybe there was hope.

That damn kiss, I said to myself as I snapped the line forward. Never should have happened. I couldn't seem to get my mind off it, which brought up the question of why I'd chosen to live like a monk. I had good reason. Not just the shock of Nancy's death, but the fact that I wasn't there for her when she needed me. My self-imposed exile was driven as much by guilt and shame as by pain. I swung the fly through another lazy pass across the hole without incident. Nothing doing, so I moved downstream, letting my line drift in the current as Archie followed along on the bank.

A hundred and fifty feet downriver I cast the Rocket into a promising looking series of eddies formed by a line of submerged boulders, a good place for a steelhead to rest and feed. My body continued to relax, but my mind still churned. So, I meet this woman, and suddenly my resolve starts to falter, I mused. What had it been, a year here in Oregon? Come on, you can do better than that, I told myself. The Red Rocket continued to bob along unmolested. I retrieved it and replaced it with a Sandy Blue—its toned-down first cousin—and moved on.

I lost track of time as I worked my way downriver. I thought of the fragment of conversation I'd overheard between Jason Townsend and David Hanson. With the passage of several days, I realized I was no longer so sure what the hell they were talking about. Despite this, a part of me—the self-serving part, I suppose—wanted to say something to Winona. I laughed out loud when I tried to imagine how I would do that. No, I would keep my mouth shut. Jason Townsend's sexual preferences and what he chose to tell Winona about them were clearly none of my business.

Fishing's a lot like life—things happen when you least expect it. I was well below the oxbow, my thoughts drifting with my fly in a soft riffle when a steelhead hit with an adrenaline-releasing jolt. The big fish ran downriver as line tore off my reel, causing the handle to spin into a blur. Afraid all my line would be stripped off, I grabbed at the knob on the crank and got my knuckles rapped for the trouble.

"Ouch!" I cried, and this started Archie barking and spinning in circles.

I thrust my hand in again and managed to catch the knob without further damage. The steelhead slowed down and then stopped. I inched it around to face me, the current magnifying its strength, my rod bent at a worrisome angle, my leader taut as a bridge cable. Archie could barely contain himself on the bank. I worried he might actually swim out to help me.

The fish allowed me a couple of cranks on the reel before breaking for deep water. I pulled up, and it became airborne in a writhing, athletic leap. For an instant it seemed to freeze in front of me like an iridescent sculpture, jaws agape, pink-edged gills flaring. Then it casually tossed my fly with its barbless hook halfway to the bank. As the fish fell back into the river, I could have sworn it looked at me in amusement.

I fished on for another hour, but that was my only strike of the day. Actually, I was glad I didn't hook another fish, since the fight had left my knuckles raw and the stitches in my left arm aching.

Arch and I hiked out on a high trail through the trees that Philip suggested. We stopped above Marmot Dam for a look. The river slid over the spillway in a laminar sheet that shattered at the base like a wave breaking on a beach. A bypass stream around the dam still roared, but the turbines it drove for ninety years were gone. Like a clogged artery, the river above the dam had built up a century of silt and debris. I imagined touching off the blast that would obliterate the structure and wondered how long it would take for the free-flowing river to heal itself.

As Arch and I stood watching, a shaft of sunlight turned a section of water upriver from gray to slate blue. I wondered about the fish down there. I had to believe breaching this dam would stop their decline and give them a fighting chance. I kicked a rock into a swath of sword ferns and started down the trail thinking about Winona and Jason, how they could work together to free rivers like this. Suddenly the idea of their engagement seemed to make a lot of sense.

We were nearly back to the trailhead when my phone rang. It was Philip.

"Cal, where are you?"

"I just hiked out of the Sandy. I'm at the trailhead."

"Do any good?"

"One nice fish, but it got off. Damn near tore my stitches out."

"How's your head?"

"Better."

"Listen, my father says he'll talk about the casino with you, but only in person. You're halfway here. Why don't you come out to the Rez and join us?"

Chapter Thirty

Rain pummeled the car until Arch and I cleared the Cascades and met the high desert, where Route 26 stretched out in front of us like a tapered black ribbon. To the southwest, the snow-clad peak of Mount Jefferson seemed to levitate above the flat plain. I rolled down the windows so we could taste the sage and wildflower scented air. I parked just inside the Reservation, and we hopped into Philip's truck for the drive to the family hunting cabin, which sits on the Warm Springs River near the junction with the Deschutes.

Philip told me once that the land has been in the family since the first Paiutes staggered onto the reservation in 1879 after being ravaged by disease and hounded by the U.S. Calvary. The original log cabin had been torn down and replaced with a modest frame structure after the family received its reparations check in the 1950s for the flooding of Celilo Falls.

George Lone Deer was shorter and stouter than Philip, with close-cropped, silver hair. I could see Philip in his face, although the father's nose was broader, the eyes darker, more brooding. When Arch and I got out of the truck, he smiled with warmth. "Welcome, Calvin." Then he dropped to one knee, and greeted Archie like an old friend. "Philip told me about this one. He helps you fish, huh?"

I smiled and shook my head. "He's a little disappointed in me right now. I lost a nice steelhead this morning."

"I'll bet he can herd some sheep, too," George Lone Deer added, thumping my dog on the back.

"Sheep, cars, deer, you name it."

A younger man standing behind George stepped forward and introduced himself. Isaac Minishut's hair was pulled back in a ponytail like Philip's. His eyes hovered like dark moons behind horn rim glasses with thick lenses.

"Isaac's chief legal counsel for the Rez," Philip said, patting the shorter, thinner man on the shoulder. "He keeps my father and the Tribal Counsel out of trouble."

"More like damage control," Isaac shot back with a droll smile that made me like him instantly.

"We've got the sweat lodge fired up, Cal. Care to join us?" Philip said, his eyes dancing with delight at the knowledge that I hated what he was proposing but couldn't say no.

I winced inwardly and snapped him a dirty look. I'd taken a couple of "sweats"—the homemade steam baths practiced by Native Americans—with my friend, and he knew full well I found them about as fun as a trip through hell with a sunburn. But it would be an insult to say no. "Sure," I answered with false enthusiasm that made Philip snort and swallow a smile.

But I lucked out this time. Once inside the lodge—a rickety half-dome of bent branches covered with canvass and old woolen blankets—Philip's father controlled the ladling of water onto the rocks which had been heated to a dull red. He took pity on me. Every time the steam hissing off the rocks threatened to displace the last molecule of air in the lodge, he would back off and allow me to gulp a breath. The elder Lone Deer mumbled and chanted prayers in his native language, but I really didn't care that I was witnessing a ritual that hadn't changed in eons. I did try to conjure up some spiritual thoughts of my own, but it's hard to think when your brain is melting.

The Warm Springs River is misnamed, because its water is always ice cold. Nevertheless, when the sweat was over I made a dash for the river and when my scorched body hit the water, the shock snatched every ounce of breath from my lungs. But fifteen minutes later up in the cabin with a hot mug of coffee with two shots of whiskey in it, I felt damn good.

Philip had quickly steered the conversation my way, and I was sketching in some of the information surrounding Nelson Queah's disappearance and Timothy Wiiks' accident. I was anxious to see if they could help me in any way but was not anxious to tell them too much.

George Lone Deer was wrapped in a thick robe sipping a beer, his bare feet propped on a stool. He said, "I can't speak about Timothy Wiiks, but as a young man I knew of Nelson Queah. He was a strong man. If he had lived, he wouldn't have taken a dime in reparations. No one believed that he got drunk one night and stumbled into the river. He was a sure-footed fisherman and not a heavy drinker. He had fought long and hard to save the falls. Some thought the loss was just too much for him, that he killed himself. Others were not so sure." He shook his head slowly and studied his feet. "It is good that you're helping his granddaughter find the truth. The truth is important, even after the passage of time."

I met his eyes and nodded in agreement. "I think Wiiks was killed because he discovered a financial rip-off at the dam. Someone was skimming money from the government. Wiiks worked for Ferguson, and Ferguson reported directly to Braxton Gage."

"Gage worked on The Dalles Dam?" Isaac interjected.

"Yeah. He owned a gravel and cement company with his father back then."

Isaac shot George a quick glance and then looked back at me. "Holy shit. You think he's involved in this?"

"Call it a working hypothesis. We may never know exactly what went on at the dam, but it looks like the fear that the cover-up murders might be discovered set somebody on edge."

Philip pointed at my left forearm, which was still wrapped in the same crude waterproof bandage I'd used when I was fishing. "Cal took a bullet from the same guy that got Watlamet."

Isaac's mouth dropped open, but he said nothing.

I looked at him and then at Philip's father and said, "I need to talk to Gage. Can you tell me anything about him that might help me do this?"

"Isn't that risky?" Isaac asked.

"Not the way I see it. If he's in on it, he already knows about me. If not, he might be able to help. It's worth a shot."

"The old bastard won't see you unless you have something he wants," Philip's father said. "He's surrounded by bodyguards and greedy people."

"What about this casino deal?"

Isaac's eyes got bigger. He glanced at Philip's father, then back at me. "How do you know about that?"

The elder Lone Deer raised his hand in a calming gesture. "It's okay, Isaac. We can trust Calvin."

Isaac nodded faintly. "First of all, there's no *deal.* There've been some exploratory talks. Gage has an ideal piece of land and the ear of the Governor, to say nothing of his influence in the Gorge. But he wants more than we're willing to give him."

Philip stood up abruptly and scowled at his father. "Tell Gage to get stuffed. Why do we want a casino in the Gorge, anyway? We're acting like white people. What's next, a new dam on the Columbia?"

His father set his beer can down and massaged his forehead with big, rough fingers. In a low voice he said, "You know the answer to that, Philip. Jobs, schools, roads, bridges, that's why."

Philip stomped across the room, kicked the screen door open and went out on the porch. His father smiled wistfully and shook his head as Isaac dropped his gaze and began studying a knot on the plank floor. The room fell silent and so did my hopes of learning anything useful about Braxton Gage. Finally, I said to both men, "Are you sure there's no way I can get in to see Gage?"

Isaac said, "It would be easier to get in to see the President at the Whitehouse."

My gaze shifted to Philip's father, almost in desperation. He smiled at Isaac's remark like he had after his son's blow-up, as if to say these were things to be expected from younger men.

He said, "I will talk to Gage. He wants this deal as much as we do. I will—"

Isaac interrupted, shaking his head emphatically. "I don't think that's a very good idea, George."

Philip's father put his hand up again, his mouth set in a firm line. "We will do this in honor of Nelson Queah."

I thanked Lone Deer and went out on the porch to join Philip. "Come on," I said, figuring he needed to cool off, "let's hike down to the junction and see if any trout are rising." We were half way to the Deschutes when my cell chirped. It was Deputy Sheriff Grooms. "Hey, Big C." I greeted her. "What's happening?"

"Thought you deserved to hear the latest. I got a probable on the composite sketch. The perp went grocery shoppin' at a gas station out near Clarno last week. A guy who pumps gas there was pretty sure it was him. Didn't see a car. Said he walked out of there with a backpack, headed east on the Shaniko Fossil Highway."

I stopped dead on the trail and Philip eyed me intently. "Nice work. Any idea where he was headed?"

"I've got a hunch. There's a narrow canyon a few miles up from there, runs north off the highway. Used to be a vermiculite mine up in there pretty far. That'd be a good place to hide a campsite. It's a long shot, and the trail's probably cold, but I figured it's worth a look. Listen, any chance you could call your friend, Lone Deer, and persuade him to meet me out there? He might see somethin' I'd miss."

I looked at Philip. "You're in luck. Philip's right here. Hang on a sec." To Philip I said, "Grooms thinks she might know where the shooter camped out. She wants you to come over to Clarno to help her check it out. You up for that?"

"Hell yes," my friend answered.

Chapter Thirty-one

Jake

"Shit. Out of water again?" Jake tossed his Sierra cup, and it clattered against the rocks. There was no one else to blame and no one else to make the hike along the canyon rim to the spring and back. And the stupid question only underscored how much he wanted to finish up and get the hell out of Oregon. He'd been promised a simple job. But it hadn't worked out that way. He'd botched the hit on that lawyer, Claxton, but once again the Old Man told him to stay put and wait for further instructions.

Further instructions? Are you kidding me? This job's snake-bit.

What could they say if he cut and ran? *Nothing.* Well, he wouldn't see the rest of the money for the Watlamet hit, but that might be a price worth paying to be out of this nightmare.

Jake picked up the plastic jug, slung his rifle over his shoulder, and started up the ridge. Twenty minutes later he reached the spring. It burbled up through a bed of mossy rocks, dropped over the edge of the ridge, and flowed noiselessly down the hillside, across the road, and into a dry creek bed. He knelt down and scooped up some water with a cupped hand and drank. It was pure and cold, and its taste brought a rush of memories of his first back-country trip with Amy. They weren't married then, but those five days sealed the deal. She took a big buck on that trip, too. Nailed him from fifty yards. He pushed the memories aside, but the effort blurred his eyes with tears.

The water jug was nearly full when movement down in the canyon caught his eye. It looked like a dust devil scurrying along the hardpan road next to the creek bed. Through the Swarovski he saw it was a Wasco County Sheriff's car with a single deputy behind the wheel. He froze for a moment then shook his head in disbelief that quickly turned to fear.

What the fuck next?

Jake watched through the scope as the patrol car came to a stop. The deputy got out of the car and with a hand up to shade the sun, followed the path of the spring up to where he was crouched behind a line of boulders at the top of the ridge. The deputy's face and upper body were now full-on in the scope and Jake crouched even lower, although there was no chance of being spotted at three hundred yards.

He groaned out loud. "Jesus. It's a woman." Big and tough-looking, but a woman.

She'd stopped where the spring crossed the road in a dark, narrow band. The woman walked around, got down on her haunches for a while and then got up, went to the car and came back with some papers in one hand and a small object in the other.

What the hell's she doing?

She crouched down again and laid one of the papers on the ground and seemed to study it for a while. Then she laid a thin, shiny ribbon on the road using the small object, which he now realized was a tape measure.

"Son of a bitch," he said out loud, "she's found my tire tracks."

The woman retracted the tape, picked up the sheet of paper—which he now guessed was a photograph—and began to scan the steep walls of the canyon. He instinctively hunched down again. A panicked thought of running back to get his truck flashed through his mind, but that was stupid because the only way out was the way he came in. He could bushwhack from where he was, try to reach Clarno on foot and steal a car, but they'd have his truck and know who he was in no time at all.

Fuck. He was trapped.

Cop or no cop, woman or no woman, he saw no choice. *I can't let her get back in her car to use the radio.* He levered a cartridge into the chamber of the Remington, took a deep breath and began sighting-in on her in earnest. The round would sink about three inches at her range, so he would aim to compensate. His pulse rate dropped and a deathly calm came over him as the cross-hairs of the scope steadied on the woman's bulky frame.

"God forgive me," he muttered out of the side of his mouth.

Chapter Thirty-two

Philip and I left Archie with George Lone Deer and were on the road in ten minutes. Before we left, Philip came out of the cabin with a rifle and a box of cartridges and stashed them in the back seat of the extended cab of his truck. I must have looked surprised because he said, "Borrowed the rifle from my dad. We're headed for rugged country, and I don't care if Grooms thinks the trail's cold, I'm not going in unarmed."

We didn't talk much on the drive over. Philip was still fuming about the spat with his father, and I was thinking about the possibility of picking up the sniper's trail and trying not to get my hopes up. Ninety minutes later we rolled to a stop at the turn-off leading into the canyon. The intersection was deserted.

"Huh," I said. "She said she'd meet us right here."

Philip pointed down the dirt road and squinted. "That could be a car in there. Maybe she drove in a ways." He turned his rig onto the road, and we started in. The washboard surface hammered the truck's shocks as we left a plume of fine dust in our wake. A hundred and fifty yards in, Philip said, "That's her cruiser for sure."

My gut began to clench. "Yeah, but where is she?"

We both saw her at the same time. At least we saw what looked like a body on the ground in the middle of the road, next to the patrol car. "Is that her?" We drove a little farther. "She's down," I cried. Philip gunned the truck, and when we slid to a stop we both jumped out and knelt down next to the body.

She was sprawled on her back with her legs pointed in the direction of the west canyon wall like a couple of accusatory fingers. One boot heel lay in the shallow runoff of a small stream angling across the road, and several photographs and a tape measure lay scattered near her body. Her neatly pressed uniform top had a hole punched in it at the center of her chest, her eyes were closed, and blood leaked from her mouth and nose.

Visions of Watlamet's corpse flashed in my head. "What the hell happened? Has she been shot?"

Philip leaned in close. "Looks like it. I think she's still breathing."

I checked her neck for a pulse—a faint flutter, if anything—and looked closer at her chest. The puncture in her uniform looked like a bullet hole, and the torn edge of the fabric rose then fell perceptibly. "You're right! She is breathing, but just barely. "Big C," I said, "it's Cal and Philip. Hang on. We're going to help you."

No response.

Philip nodded in the direction of the west wall of the canyon. "Keep your head down. By the way she fell, the bullet came from that direction. The sniper could still be up there."

I nodded impatiently and unbuttoned her uniform top. "She's wearing a vest." The black, tightly-woven mat was seemingly punctured, an indentation the diameter of my thumb. But it was free of blood.

"It's a Kevlar vest." Philip unclipped the shoulder straps of the vest and lifted off the front section. Grooms coughed, and blood oozed from a jagged hole directly above her sternum.

I winced and swallowed down an urge to puke. "Doesn't look like the vest did her much good."

He held it up. The Kevlar fabric had a bloody protrusion about the size of a finger joint jutting out from the inside surface.

"Is *that* what did the damage?" I said, pointing to the protrusion.

He nodded, turned the vest over, and shook it. A small chunk of something fell out of the tiny pouch and bounced off the toe of his boot. He picked it up and pinched it between his thumb and forefinger. "This is the bullet that hit her, man. Looks like that vest kept it from boring a hole straight through her."

I stripped off my shirt and tee-shirt and bunched the latter into a crude compress. "Is there any duct tape in the truck?"

"Glove compartment," Philip said, springing to his feet. "I'll get it."

Once we had the compress in place, I bent down close to Grooms' ear. "We got a patch on you, Big C. Your vest stopped the bullet. Now we're going to get you the hell out of here." Her eyes fluttered, and I heard a faint gurgling sound as she struggled for a breath.

I flipped my cell phone open. "No service. We need to use her radio."

"I know those radios. I'll call it in," Philip said. When he stood up, he glanced down at a faint wet patch emerging from the streambed. He knelt back down and studied it for several seconds before starting for the patrol car. "Don't worry about the sniper, Cal," he said over his shoulder. "He's long gone." When I asked how he knew that, he waved me off and got into Grooms' car to use the radio.

The dispatcher's response to Philip's account reverberated in the narrow canyon. "I'm sending deputies, an EMT team, and a medivac helicopter," she told us. "Is the area safe?"

"Yes," Philip responded. "The shooter left the scene maybe thirty, forty minutes ago. Probably the same guy who shot Sherman Watlamet. I think he's heading east on the Shaniko Fossil Highway."

"Copy that." Her voice broke as she added, "Take good care of her, you hear." An officer was down, a friend, a colleague. The nightmare of every law-enforcement organization.

When Philip returned, I looked at him, incredulous. "How do you know all that?"

He shrugged and pointed at the wet patch he'd spotted earlier. "That's a fresh tire mark." He dropped down and peered under his truck. "The other one's under here. Someone drove out of here not too long ago. They were in a big hurry." He got up and jerked a thumb in the direction of the west wall. "The sniper shot her from up there and took off. We didn't pass any pickups on our way here, so I figured he headed east."

I nodded. "Well done." My friend never ceased to amaze me.

Grooms coughed again, and I wiped some blood from her lips with my handkerchief. We covered her with a blanket from the truck, and I took her hand. "Stay with me, Big C," I told her. "Help's on the way." There was nothing we could do but wait at this point. I felt a frustrating sense of helplessness interspersed with waves of boiling anger. The sniper had hit another person, a friend, a good cop, and the son of a bitch was still out there. There was something else, too, something more insidious. Come on, I told myself, this wasn't your fault. No guilt trips.

But there it was, that old familiar feeling of guilt I couldn't shake.

Philip stopped his restless pacing and dropped to one knee next to a large photograph lying in the road face up. He looked it over without touching it. "This is a shot of one of the tire tracks I found at Watlamet's ranch." He got up and scanned the stream bed again, stopped and pointed. "There's a track going the other direction, toward the canyon. It's old but pretty well preserved. The mud's thicker there." He knelt back down, studied it, and looked over at me. "Matches the photo." He looked down the road leading into the canyon. "Grooms had the bastard dead to rights, man."

I shaded my eyes and looked up at the canyon wall. "I think that was the problem. He was trapped and knew it. She said the mine was pretty far into the canyon. I guess she thought it was safe at this point." I shook my head. "I wish to hell she'd waited for us."

"For sure," Philip said. "But at least she was smart enough to wear the Kevlar."

The wait was agonizing. I sat talking to Grooms, whose breath came in barely audible gasps so ragged I thought each and every one would be her last. I felt her grip tighten on my hand a couple of times, and I wanted to believe it wasn't a spasm, that she was with me at some level. I kept talking and talking while Philip paced. Finally, he said, "I can't stand this anymore. That bastard's getting away. I'm going after him."

"Cool your jets, man. You told them which way he was heading, and you're a material witness here. Besides, what would you do if you caught up with him?"

He glared at me. "I've got a weapon, too, you know."

I exhaled a long breath. I didn't doubt for a minute that Philip could take care of himself, but the last thing I wanted was to put him in harm's way. "I'd like to chase him, too, but this isn't an action movie. He's already shot two people at long range. Let the sheriff handle this."

Philip kicked a couple of loose stones into the runoff. "Okay. But, damn it, Cal, they're spread so thin out here it's pathetic." He opened his arms. "Wait till you see how long it takes them just to get here."

My friend had a point, but so did I. And as I thought about it while we waited, I couldn't shake the feeling that this thing ran deep, and that it was going to fall to me to piece it all together. This was a long way from prosecuting bad guys sitting in jail cells down in Los Angeles, and it sure as hell wasn't what I expected when I opened my one-man law practice in Dundee.

But on the upside, I felt like I had a purpose for the first time in a long time.

Chapter Thirty-three

We heard the faint wail of sirens out on the highway twenty-two minutes later. Two patrol cars arrived first, skidding to a stop abreast of each other some twenty yards away. An EMT truck stopped well behind them. A deputy got out of each car and stood behind his open door with his service revolver drawn. "Put your hands where we can see them," one of them ordered. "Now," the other one called out.

They holstered their weapons and approached us cautiously, but only after I'd recapped the situation. They both knelt down next to Grooms, their faces twisted in anger and grief. The older of the two, a heavy set man with a florid complexion, bent down next to her face. "It's Hank, Big C. The EMTs are here. You better not die on us, you hear me?"

The EMT crew huddled around Grooms, assessing her injuries. An IV was hooked up, chest monitors and a finger clip were attached, and finally her nose and mouth were covered with an oxygen mask. After what seemed an eternity, she was transferred to a stretcher and loaded onto the truck. "We're taking her south to meet up with a medivac helicopter coming up from Bend, the lead EMT explained. "It's the fastest way to get her into the ER."

As they pulled away, I felt a sense of relief, like a lead-weighted burden of responsibility had been lifted. I looked at Philip and he said, "She's got a good chance, I think. She's strong."

The Sheriff, a man named Grover Bailey, arrived shortly after the EMT truck left. Tall with sloped shoulders and big, strong-looking hands, he came straight up to us, his eyes as friendly as a hawk's. "What in God's name happened here?" He said it in a low, strained voice dripping with anger and accusation.

Both deputies hesitated, so I stepped forward and introduced Philip and myself. "Grooms got a positive on the composite sketch at a gas station near here. She thought the shooter might be holed up at an old mine back in this canyon." I nodded toward the photographs and the tape measure lying next to the body. "She was looking at tire tracks in the mud when she was shot." I pointed at the west wall of the canyon. "Looks like the shooter was up on that ridge."

Bailey looked up at the ridge and back at me, his eyes narrow, his jaw set. "Why the hell were you first on the scene?"

"She called us, and we drove over from the Warm Springs Rez. Philip, here, is the guy who found the boot prints and tire tracks at Watlamet's ranch. Grooms thought maybe he could help pick something up here."

"Why are you so sure it's the same person who killed Watlamet?"

Philip pointed at the photographs lying next to the runoff. "There's one halfway decent tire print there in the mud, and it matches the one I found at Watlamet's ranch. The sniper must've slowed down coming in. Probably didn't want to muddy his rig. And the wheelbase looks right, too."

Bailey nodded and looked up the canyon road. "How do you know he's not still up there?"

"Someone came out of here in a big hurry," Philip answered. "We saw the tracks when we first arrived, but they've dried out. Had to have been him."

By this time, Bailey was a believer. He nodded again, impatiently, and turned to his deputies. "Was she told to wait for backup?"

Deputy Hank looked down at his boots. "She called in, and Elva told her to wait for me. I was over in Clarno on a domestic call. Wendell, here, was out on the highway doing traffic." The second deputy shuffled his feet and nodded.

Bailey blew out a breath, pure frustration. "Why am I not surprised? She never listens to anyone. At least she wore her vest. The EMTs told me it caught the bullet. Otherwise, she'd be on her way to the morgue."

"That's right," I said. We took Bailey over to the hood of Grooms' patrol car, where we had laid out the vest and the flattened piece of lead we'd recovered from it. Bailey picked up the spent bullet and looked at it. "Hard to believe this little piece of lead could do so much damage. The EMTs told me she has a shattered sternum and God knows what kind of internal injuries. He looked at us, his eyes suddenly bright with moisture. "You know, we've only had those vests for a year or so. He rapped on the vest with his knuckles. "This one's got a ceramic plate between the Kevlar. It cost more, and the grant we got from the DOJ only paid for half." He barked a laugh. "Big C bitched like hell, but she finally ordered one." He shook his head. "Kevlar alone will stop a handgun, but without that plate that rifle bullet would have gone right through the vest and right through her."

Bailey turned to his deputies. "Hank, you go on up to the junction at Route 207. I told the State Police we'd meet them there. We gotta find this fella. Wendell, you secure this crime scene. I'm going to take these two gentlemen up this canyon and see what we can find. I'll let you know as soon as I hear anything about Big C."

We located the shooter's campsite near the abandoned mine, and Philip quickly found the signature boot prints, including the pigeon-toe flourish. He'd left nothing behind except a pit full of garbage that was bagged for forensic examination. We also hiked up the west rim of the canyon to the source of the spring, which we figured was the most likely site of the ambush. Philip spotted another boot print in the damp earth adjacent to the source of the spring, but we found no shell casings or other physical evidence.

Other than the hope that a fingerprint or DNA fragment might turn up, it looked like our boy had made another clean escape.

When we got back to the scene of the shooting, Bailey interviewed Philip and me at length. With me, he wanted to know anything new on the case, anything Grooms hadn't already briefed them on. I didn't have much to add, except that the only link I'd found to Cecil Ferguson, Sherman Watlamet, and Nelson Queah was a man named Braxton Gage. I told him about the letters Queah had written, the fact that Ferguson had worked for Gage, and the rumors about the graft at the dam that Fletcher Dunn was investigating prior to Queah's disappearance.

When I mentioned Gage's name, Bailey's eyebrows rose. "*The* Braxton Gage, from The Dalles?"

I nodded. "His dad's company poured the cement for The Dalles Dam. Braxton Gage ran the project."

Bailey whistled. "Now there's a big fish. So, you're saying this mess is to cover up a little financial hanky-panky when the dam was going in fifty years ago?"

"That and the murder of Nelson Queah and a kid named Timothy Wiiks. Maybe Gage was worried the whole thing was coming unglued."

Bailey puffed a breath. "We'll never know, will we. Watlamet and Ferguson are both dead. And I'm gonna need way more than that to take on Braxton Gage. The son of a bitch's richer than God and meaner than a rattlesnake."

I shrugged. "It's all I got."

Chapter Thirty-four

Jake

With 9X magnification, the Z3 Swarovski rifle scope puts the target right in front of the shooter, even at three hundred yards. When Jake squeezed off that single round, the woman went down and violently convulsed twice before going still. He knew she was dead, and the knowledge left him with a numbing sense of disbelief. He had killed a cop. Not just a cop, a *woman*.

He had never thought of himself as a bad person. That all changed when he shot the old Indian and chased that stupid lawyer off a cliff. Now his fall was complete and irreversible.

The only thing stronger than his guilt was the fear of getting caught. It wasn't jail time or the needle he feared so much, but the thought of letting the Old Man down, of fucking up what should have been a simple job, of being called an idiot. The Old Man would be screwed, too. Jake would never talk, but surely the cops would find some link between them.

He double-timed it down the ridge and started breaking camp as fast as he could. By this time, the numbness he felt had been replaced by a sense of raging panic. *She'll be missed in no time. Get the hell out of here!* His breath came in ragged gasps as he tossed everything in the back of his truck. Looking over the scene a last time, he noticed the empty propane canisters lying in the fire ring. "Shit." he said aloud. "Just leave your fingerprints lying around." He tossed the canisters into the bed of the truck, got in, and started his engine. He had studied the area before selecting this particular canyon, so there was no need to refer to a map now.

What he needed was a place to hide his truck in that godforsaken country. No map would help him with that.

Jake didn't look at the body of his victim as he tore past her on his way out of the canyon. He headed east and then swung north on Route 207 in the direction of Fossil, where the country was even more desolate and unpopulated, a moonscape of rugged hills folding down into narrow arroyos, all of them rocky and most of them dry. He slowed down when he reached Route 19, which headed off to Spray. A sign at the junction proclaimed that Spray was The Home of the Best Small Town Rodeo in the USA. When he ditched his truck, he would need another car. He took the turnoff.

Five miles outside Spray he passed a property on his left marked by a rusty mailbox listing at a forty-five degree angle and a weathered gate with the shredded remains of a for sale sign on it. The sign had taken a direct hit from a shotgun blast, probably fired from a passing car. An unpaved driveway led across the mesquite-dotted landscape and disappeared behind a rocky hillock. He checked for traffic, hung a U-turn, and pulled up in front of the gate. It was chained shut and secured with a hefty padlock, and a four-foot barbed wire fence ran in either direction along the road. He tried to spit out the window, but his mouth was dry as cotton. He pounded his fist on the steering wheel and swung his truck back in the direction of Spray.

A quarter mile down the road he saw a spot where the fence sagged. He let a truck pass in the opposite direction before pulling over. He got out and put his shoulder to a leaning fence post until the sagging barbed wire was on the ground. He swung his rig around and drove across the rusty strands. His tire treads were thick. Those barbs were nothing to worry about. Then he hopped out and pushed the fence post back up to reestablish the fence line.

Weaving his way through the mesquite, he joined the driveway well past the gate and followed it around the hillock until he was out of sight from the road. He stopped in front of an old ranch house that looked like a good fart would blow it over. He exhaled a breath of relief. He was positive no one had seen him on his way in, and the place looked like it had been deserted for a very long time.

The barn behind the ranch house was sturdier and its doors secured with a chain and padlock like the one out on the gate. But the double doors to the hayloft didn't appear to be locked. There wouldn't be a bolt cutter in the barn. He wouldn't be that lucky. But a hacksaw or a chisel?

It was worth a shot.

He fetched a rope from his truck and tossed it over a wooden boom that jutted out from above the double doors like the front of an old sailing ship. He tied the rope off, climbed hand over hand, and then pried one of the doors open with his free hand. The hinges yielded with a screech so loud Jake feared for a moment the sound might carry to the highway.

He swung himself into the loft, and after finding nothing of use up there, navigated a rickety ladder to the ground floor. An ancient Ford tractor rested on blocks in the middle of the barn, but there was enough room to squeeze his truck in. He searched the cabinets on the walls and the drawers below a workbench but found nothing he could use to break the padlock. "Damn my luck. anyway," he said, pushing down frustration that was rapidly turning to panic.

He noticed a stack of large canvas tarps and a thick roll of heavy twine in a far corner. He grabbed the two largest tarps and the twine, carried them up the ladder, and tossed them out of the loft.

After climbing back down the rope, he moved his truck behind the barn. Twenty minutes later he had finished covering it with the tarps, which he secured in place with the twine. "Looks like an old tractor under there," he said as he stood back admiring his work. "Won't fool the owners, but hell, they're probably long gone."

He felt a weird sense of betrayal about leaving his truck like that. He loved his rig as much as anything he owned. He had extracted his rifle, backpack, and some tools from it, including a screwdriver, wire cutters, and black tape he would need to hot-wire another truck.

As he moved to higher ground, away from the house and barn, he turned back toward his truck. "I'll come back for you when the heat's off."

He would wait for nightfall and then work his way into Spray. If he's lucky, he figured, the car he steals won't be missed until morning. And by that time, he'll be at the coast and out of sight. Yep, the coast. It was a long way, but he could hole up there, and there was a garage to hide the stolen car.

It was a decent plan. The Old Man might even approve, but no way he was asking permission. He didn't give a shit. That's where he was headed.

Jake was exhausted. He lay back with his head against his backpack, but he was scared to close his eyes, fearing that images of the woman writhing in her death throes would come back to him. But his eyes did finally close, and when they did, an unexpected chain of thoughts, little fragments of hope really, came to him instead—*I never intended for this to happen…maybe with time I can forgive myself and….*

Chapter Thirty-five

Philip lifted a mug of coffee to his lips and took a swallow, his Adam's apple bobbing in the process. We had returned to his family cabin, managed a few hours of sleep that night, and were both up before sunrise. The room smelled of smoke from the woodstove and of coffee Philip had brewed up, coffee so strong I feared it would dissolve my spoon. The flickering light from a kerosene lamp played softly off his ceramic mug. I had just made a comment about how hard I thought it would be for the sniper to hide out in that desolate county. "I mean strangers standout. That's how Grooms found him in the first place."

Philip nodded. "Yeah. He must've run out of supplies and had to show himself. Probably wasn't planning on having to camp there so long. People have to eat."

I got up, walked to the window, and took a sip of coffee, a very small sip. The coppery rim of the sun had just appeared above the knife-edge silhouette of the Mutton Mountains. Stifling a yawn, I asked, "What do you think he'll do next?"

Philip shrugged. "The truck's his biggest problem. If he can hide it somehow he's got a shot."

"He's not Houdini, man. How's he going to hide a big truck in that country?"

"Who knows? But if he does, he can stay hidden during the day, move at night and get outside the perimeter that Bailey and the State Police have put up by now."

"You think he's capable of that?"

Philip nodded. "He's no babe in the woods. Dug a pit and lined it with rocks so you couldn't see the glow of his stove from the road. Rigged a tarp so he didn't need a tent. That's how he cleared out so fast. He's spent some time outdoors. A city boy would have stayed in a motel. No, my guess is our boy's either ex-military or an experienced hunter. The shot that took Grooms down was better than three hundred yards. One round in the center of her chest."

I winced inwardly as the image of Grooms being gunned down like an animal played in my head. "At least the bastard's on the run." Outside, the trees to the east began to appear like apparitions in the diffuse light of the rising sun. I felt no joy in this sunrise.

Philip drank some more coffee. "I heard you mention Braxton Gage to Bailey. You still plan to talk to him?"

I closed my eyes and rubbed them with my fists. "Yep. After talking to Bailey, I'm even more convinced I should give it a shot. Hell, I tried to tell him Gage might be tied into this. He made it clear he wasn't interested, like Gage's someone he wouldn't mess with unless he caught him with a hot, smoking gun."

Philip nodded and smiled knowingly. "Gage could buy and sell Grover Bailey, and his whole damn county, for that matter."

We sat there without speaking. Light from the now-risen sun poured through the window, the beam illuminating the smoke and dust motes like a photographer's flash. Birds began to sing. Finally, my friend spoke. "Cal, what happened to Grooms out there wasn't your fault. You know that, right?"

"Right."

"No guilt, right? No ghosts from L.A.?"

"No ghosts."

"Good."

I didn't like lying to my best friend, but what was I supposed to say?

◇◇◇

After breakfast Philip dropped me at my car and headed back to Madras. "Let me know if you hear anything more on Big C," he said as he pulled away. I had called Sheriff Bailey earlier and gotten an update on her condition. All he could tell me was that she had a shattered sternum and extensive internal injuries and that the ICU docs were mum on her chances of survival. I had a notion to drive over to the hospital in Bend and check on her in person, but it would be a symbolic gesture only, since she was sure to be isolated in the ICU.

It was Sunday morning, and I felt depressed and anxious, depressed about my friend Grooms and anxious about the work I'd put off or lost outright over the last two weeks. My early retirement check from the city of L.A. didn't amount to much, and I needed my private practice, such as it was, to make ends meet and underwrite my growing fishing habit.

I took a couple of deep breaths and pushed the anxiety down. Back in L.A., as an ambitious prosecutor, I fed on stress and adrenaline like a junky. I had a wife, I had a child, but my work consumed me. I was doing it for *them*, I used to tell myself after logging in another late night or forgetting an anniversary or birthday. I didn't face the truth about myself until my wife died. That's when I realized my work wasn't everything. But by then it was too late. Way too late.

I had just pulled away from the cabin when my cell went off. "Cal? It's Winona. I've got some news."

"So have I."

"Where are you?"

"I'm on the Warm Springs Reservation," I told her.

"Oh, good. I'm at Grandmother's in Celilo Village. Any chance you can come over here?"

I glanced at my watch. I was dead tired and a jog over to the Gorge would add miles to an already long trip. "What's your news?" I said, trying to hide my reluctance.

"I found a file of old newspaper articles in my grandmother's stuff. I'm not sure, but I think they might be important."

"Newspaper articles?"

"Yes. They seem to be about the people connected to Grandfather's disappearance. Grandmother collected them. I think you should see them."

She had my attention. "I'm on my way."

Chapter Thirty-six

Celilo Village—or what remained after it was unceremoniously moved by the Army Corps of Engineers fifty years earlier—was jammed against the south edge of the Gorge, the naked cliffs behind it rising like prison walls. I parked in a field outside the fence line, next to a group of aluminum boats stacked on trailers, and let Archie out. Just inside the main gate, four teenage boys scuffled for a loose ball below a rusty rim nailed to the front of a storage shed. Two smaller boys watched from the sideline. On a broad avenue to my right, I could see that the construction of the new village houses was progressing. In contrast, the old, prefab houses looked even smaller and more dilapidated than when I'd last seen them at the commemoration.

The new housing's a decent gesture, I thought to myself, although fifty years seemed a long time to wait for restitution.

Winona's grandmother's house was the third on the left, the one with the boxes stacked on the front porch. Winona was waiting in the doorway holding a broom. She wore faded jeans cinched up with a wide belt, cowboy boots, and a tee shirt with a picture of a leaping Chinook salmon, its body flexed in an inverted U. The words *Got Habitat?* were written below the fish. Her hair was pulled back and tied off, her dimples in full bloom.

"Hi, Cal," she said brightly. "You made good time."

I smiled back. "Traffic was light." Archie left my side and approached her with his butt in full wag.

She bent down and grasped him gently by the ears and made eye contact. "You're such a handsome boy. Yes you are." Then she looked up at me. "Come on in."

The small living room was empty except for an overstuffed couch along one wall, and dust still hung in the air from her sweeping. She steered me to the couch and handed me a thin, discolored file folder when we sat down. She said, "I found this in a photo album my grandmother kept. It was between pages that were stuck together. I missed seeing it when I found her letters."

I opened the folder, began leafing through a handful of yellowed newspaper articles, and looked back at her.

Her eyes were bright, her cheeks slightly flushed. She said, "It looks like Grandmother kept adding to it for several years."

On top were the articles covering the disappearance of Nelson Queah and the car accident that claimed the life of Timothy Wiiks as reported in *The Dalles Chronicle*. The headline of the next article read "Gage Cement Honored for Exceeding Construction Goals." Below it was a photograph of two men receiving a plaque from a man in military uniform. The caption under the photo said the two awardees were Braxton Gage and Cecil Ferguson, who were being singled out for their work on The Dalles Dam by the Army Corps of Engineers. The Ferguson I'd met bore only a faint resemblance to the strapping man standing next to Gage. I skimmed the article and didn't note anything of interest.

Another headline proclaimed "Braxton Gage Re-elected Chamber Head" and was followed by an article praising his civic leadership. Below a couple of articles describing Gage Cement's rapid growth was an item on its move into shipping on the Columbia River. The headline read "Gage Buys Portland Shipping Firm, Plans Major Expansion."

Several more articles chronicled Gage's meteoric rise in shipping on the Columbia River. Toward the bottom of the stack, Cecil Ferguson was back in the news, but it wasn't good news this time. In two separate incidents he was arrested and charged with assault for his involvement in fights at local bars. I had difficulty picturing the frail, wisp of a man I'd met as a barroom brawler.

The articles were interesting, but they didn't appear to give me anything new to go on. I thought about the need to get back to Dundee and fought back a wave of frustration. Winona meant well, but there wasn't anything I could get my teeth into. I said, "The usual suspects. Your grandmother seemed to suspect Braxton Gage as much as I do in this."

"I thought this might give you more incentive for going after him," Winona answered, a pleased look on her face. "It shows Grandmother suspected Gage fifty years ago. Why else would she have saved these? I think she and Grandfather must have talked about it before he disappeared. Not all their communication was written, you know."

"Good point," I said with feigned enthusiasm. I didn't need any more incentive. I needed hard evidence. "'Going after him' is putting it a bit strong, but I am trying to set up a meeting with him."

She raised her eyebrows above enlarged eyes. "Is that wise?"

I opened my hands, face up, and gave her the same logic I used with George Lone Deer—it doesn't matter if Gage's in or out. Either way I'll learn something.

Her face clouded over. "Sounds dangerous to me."

"Laying back's more dangerous the way I see it." I dropped my gaze back to the articles in the folder. Toward the bottom was a grainy picture of two men kneeling on either side of a dead mountain lion. The men were holding the head of the lion up by its ears, smiling broadly. The caption read "Hunters Slay Cougar Responsible for Cattle Kills." The head of one of the men had been circled with a pen. It was a young Sherman Watlamet. I did a double take when I read the name of the other man. I looked at the picture again. It was him all right, although the thick, blond hair threw me for a moment.

I handed Winona the article. "Did you notice this? Watlamet's hunting partner. It's Royce Townsend."

She squinted in the weak light and then put her hand to her mouth. "Oh, I missed that completely. I guess I'm not surprised. Jason told me his father was quite the hunter in his day."

"I almost missed it, too," I said absently, straining to remember what Royce Townsend had said when I asked him about Sherman Watlamet at his party last week. Didn't he say he didn't know him?

As if reading my mind, Winona pointed to the picture. "Obviously, Grandmother was interested in *Watlamet*, not Royce. See, she circled him."

When I finished reading the file, I said, "Can I take this with me? I'd like to copy it."

"Sure. I hope it was worth the trip over."

"Oh, definitely," I replied.

We sat in silence for a few moments. I wasn't anxious to share what had happened to Grooms, so I didn't push it. She said, "Would you like some coffee?"

"I thought you'd never ask."

We made small talk while the coffee perked, the aroma filling the tiny kitchen, which was empty except for a propane stove, a small refrigerator, and a lone house plant hanging in the window above the sink. The plant's translucent leaves glowed softly in the sunlight. "So, what's *your* news?" Winona asked, eyeing me over a chipped mug of steaming coffee.

I dropped my eyes and took a careful sip from my mug. "I'm afraid it's not too good." I faltered for a couple of beats. "Deputy Grooms was shot by the sniper yesterday. She's still alive, but it's touch and go."

"Oh, God, no. Not again," she cried and then slid slowly down the wall until she was sitting on the worn linoleum.

I sat down next to her and began to tell her what happened. I was doing okay until I got to the part about discovering Grooms lying there in the road. I had to stop when a lump the size of a softball formed in my throat, and my eyelids began fluttering to keep the tears back. "We, uh, saw her cruiser on the road in the canyon. She'd decided to look for tire tracks without waiting for us." I stopped again to gather myself. The words were sticking in my throat like dry leaves. "We found her next to the car. She'd been shot at long range just like Watlamet."

There was a long silence, punctuated only by a soft whirring when the refrigerator kicked on. Finally, Winona said, "I'm so sorry, Cal."

"She's a good cop, and I consider her a friend. I should have warned her not to go in that canyon. I should have insisted she wait for us or get backup," I said, barely choking out the last of the sentence.

"It was her job, Cal. Be fair to yourself."

I pulled my knees up and dropped my chin on my chest, the words stuck again. I wasn't about to speak until I had control of myself. There was a click, and the whirring of the refrigerator stopped. A distant shout drifted in from the direction of the basketball game.

After a long pause, Winona said, "Does this have anything to do with the death of your wife in Los Angeles?"

I turned to her with what must have been a look of utter shock. It was the last thing in the world I expected her to say.

She smiled sheepishly. "I don't mean to pry, Cal. It's just that Philip mentioned that you were still mourning the death of your wife. I don't know anything more than that. Maybe what happened yesterday dredged everything back up."

"Yeah, there's probably some truth in that."

"Philip didn't know that much about what happened. Do you want to talk about it? Maybe it would help."

I'd heard the theory that 'it helps to talk' plenty of times but never really bought it. For me, talking about my wife's death was a slippery slope, a third rail, something to be avoided at all costs. I was reminded of the shrink they made me see after her death, the one who worked for the city. I almost smiled at the thought of her. She was one frustrated psychiatrist when I got through with her.

I answered, "I don't think so. I don't think it would help. To talk, I mean."

Silence poured back into the room like a viscous fluid. The refrigerator clicked on, sounding like a diesel engine. Winona put her hand on my shoulder and gently squeezed. "Are you sure, Cal?"

I sat there, frozen in fear and manacled by my own obstinacy. A tear broke loose and burned its way down my cheek.

She kept her hand on my shoulder. I could feel the warmth of her touch. She squeezed again. "Just try. One word at a time."

Maybe it was the second squeeze, I don't really know, but the resistance I'd held all that time suddenly fell away. There was no drum roll or fanfare, just a silent sloughing off, like dead skin. My voice stirred in my throat, although at the same time I seemed to become an observer as well as the one speaking. "My wife killed herself. She was depressed, and she, uh, decided life wasn't worth living anymore." I heard myself say the words. It was the closest thing to an out-of-body experience I'd ever had.

I felt Winona shudder slightly, but she remained silent.

"It was a rainy Saturday. I was, uh, working as usual. That was me—a hotshot workaholic lusting to get ahead. I found her when I got home. Claire got home right after me. Thank God she wasn't the one who found her."

"Claire's your daughter?"

"Yeah." I paused again, trying to check my avalanching emotions. The sight of my wife's body—banished from my memory for so long—hit my conscious mind like scalding water. I could see myself desperately trying to revive her. I could hear myself screaming at my daughter to call 911. But her body was cold. The pills had done their job.

My observer-self watched Winona and I, curious to see what would happen next. I tried to go on but couldn't. "I can't—"

In the softest voice, Winona stopped me. "Yes, you can, Cal. Go on."

My eyes brimmed with tears. "Not much else to tell. The meds weren't working worth a damn, but I figured it was just a matter of time, that her depression wasn't all that serious." I shook my head and scoffed at the notion. "Complete denial. I didn't read the danger signals, didn't understand how desperate she was. After all, that would have required me to focus on something else besides my precious career." I looked at Winona through tear-blurred eyes. "I wasn't there for her when she needed me. That's the long and short of it."

My observer-self watched as she cradled me in her arms. The emotions I'd held at bay for so long finally broke loose, and I wept silently. I have no idea how long this went on. It takes time to drain a deep swamp. When I finally regained my composure, I realized Winona was holding me, stroking my head and chanting softly in my ear in her native tongue.

Awareness of the deep intimacy we were sharing came to both of us at the same moment. She released her hold on me, and I straightened up, feeling light, almost hollow. I exhaled, dried my eyes on my sleeve, and tried to smile. "I don't know what you were singing, but it sure helped."

She rested her eyes on me and smiled wistfully. "Grandmother used to sing those words to me when I was upset, which was most of the time after my mother left." She chuckled. "They're about the only Sahaptin I know. They mean something like "your sadness will end just as the sun ends the night and spring ends the winter."

I suddenly felt awkward and embarrassed as my male ego began to re-emerge. My God, I thought, I just poured my guts out to a woman I hardly know. I've shared my deepest, most shameful secret with her. I said, "Look, Winona, I'm sorry you had to listen to all—"

She cut me off, her eyes flashing. "Don't, Cal. Don't do that. You needed to talk. It was a cleansing. Don't you dare apologize."

Managing a weak smile, I stood up, lowered my hand and pulled her up. "You're right. It *was* a cleansing."

She smiled. "You did all the heavy lifting. And Cal, I'm sorry about Grooms, and I'm sorry about your wife."

She warmed up our coffees, and as we stood in the kitchen I went back to the story of Grooms' ambush. When I finished, Winona took my cup and began rinsing it out at the sink along with hers, her ebony hair rippling with highlights in the sunlight. With her back to me, she sighed deeply. "Timothy's mother called me two nights ago. She'd had another dream. She saw me walking in the desert with a wolf following me. She didn't know whether the wolf was stalking me or protecting me. She told me to be careful, Cal."

"I didn't know a wolf could be a protector."

She turned to face me. "Oh, yes. If a wolf's your totem, it will protect you. And seeing your totem in a dream is often a warning."

"What's your totem?" I asked, but I could already see the answer in her eyes.

"That's the weird thing. It's a wolf. I've been drawn to them for as long as I can remember. I'm sure you noticed the pictures of wolves hanging on my walls."

"I did." I tried a smile, but it only went halfway. I didn't necessarily buy into Indian lore, but for some reason her revelation made me uneasy. "As long as the sniper's out there, you have to be careful. The only good news is that the heat's really on him now."

She closed the distance between us and said, "Am I still on the free hug plan?"

I took her in my arms and held her there as lightly as I could. This is just a hug, I reminded myself. Finally, in self-defense, I stepped back and said, "Speaking of cops, have you heard anything from your friends in Portland about the Ferguson murder?"

"No. Nothing since I got my car and my computer back. But Detective Adams said they'd probably want to talk to me again. He didn't say when."

"Good. No news is good news on that front. It means they haven't found anything to tie you to the scene. If they call you back, don't talk to them without me, okay?"

I glanced at my watch. Leaving now would put me in Dundee by two-thirty. I made eye contact with Arch and let him know we were leaving with a flick of my head. A quick exit seemed the best course. God knows, I needed time to regroup. I turned to her at the door and smiled. "Can you record that Sahaptin chant for me?"

She laughed. "Grandmother's version was better than mine, but if you need it, just call."

As Archie and I walked to the car, I was dogged by a feeling that I'd told Winona more than I should have. Some things are best left unspoken, after all, particularly when they reveal our own mistakes and vulnerabilities. But at the same time, I felt a certain lightness, like a heavy weight had been lifted from my shoulders, and the air had a sparkle to it I hadn't noticed earlier.

A stiff breeze was blowing in a westerly direction along the river. "There'll be whitecaps today, big boy," I said to Arch. "Should be a beautiful drive through the Gorge."

Chapter Thirty-seven

Jake

Jake never should have made it to the Oregon coast. What did the Old Man always say? It's better to be lucky than good? He was lucky, for sure. After stashing his truck at the abandoned farm, he waited in the partial shade of a rocky overhang for the sun to set. At around nine that night the moon disappeared behind a layer of low clouds. He moved into the darkness, staying parallel but well off the highway heading into Spray.

There was no shortage of trucks in Spray, and on a dirt road on the east side of town he found what he was looking for—a mid-eighties Ford Ranger like the one he used to own before his current rig. It was parked in front of a tired looking double-wide with a dead tree in the yard and no lights on. He'd lost the keys to his Ranger once, and a buddy of his taught him how to hotwire it. Those old Fords were simple—remove the plastic cover on the steering column, find the brown wire for the starter and the red wire for the battery. That's all you needed to know. But this Ranger wasn't locked, and he found a key under the floor mat.

He got in it and drove off. Lucky.

He headed east out of Spray and planned to take Route 19 south down to 26, where he would take side roads to skirt around Prineville and Bend, and then over the Cascades via Route 20 and on to the coast. He would be in good shape as long as no one missed the old Ford, he figured. He hoped that would be a long time.

Just north of Kimberly, a motorcycle coming the other way blinked its headlights, the universal signal that a cop or road block was up ahead. *Fuck.* Jake's heart raced as he swerved off the road, turned the truck around, and parked behind a closed roadside stand he'd just passed. He got out and worked his way back up the road in the shadows. Sure enough, a road block had been set up around a sharp bend.

Thank you, dude on the motorcycle. He hunkered down in the shadows off the road and watched as two patrol cars stopped traffic in both directions.

It was a boring, agonizing wait, and it felt like a noose tightening around his neck. *Will they stay there all night? What would I do then?* His anxiety got so bad he thought he might puke. But at around two-thirty, a woman stopped in the eastbound lane who was so drunk she could hardly get out of her car, let alone walk a straight line. She was placed in one of the patrol cars and driven away. Not ten minutes later, a call came in for the second car, and it took off with lights flashing and siren screaming.

End of blockade. *Lucky.*

◇◇◇

It was nearly nine a.m. when Jake reached Depoe Bay, a tiny port city on the central Oregon coast. He was freaked out about driving around in broad daylight, but he had no choice and hoped the old Ford hadn't been missed yet, or if it had, the theft had been chalked up to joyriding locals. The cabin was on the east side of Highway 101 at the end of a dead end street of vacation homes. They all looked deserted. He pulled in the driveway and found the keys under the planter on the left side of the door, just where they should have been. He used one key to put the Ford Ranger in the garage and lock it up and the other to unlock the back door and let himself into the house. He was confident no one had seen him arrive. When he clicked the door shut, he felt better than he had in a very long time.

Lucky. Very lucky.

Chapter Thirty-eight

At the farm that evening the setting sun torched a hole in the cloud cover and lit the horizon in gold and deep red flames. Sipping a glass of pinot, I watched from my study as the flames died and the rose afterglow became indigo then violet, and lights began winking on in the valley. In the background, Thelonious Monk toyed around with "Ruby, My Dear," the fifth track on *Solo Monk*. With Monk you never knew what was coming next. Kind of like my life lately.

It had grown dark without my realizing it. I switched on the lights and brought some wood in from the porch to make a small fire to take the chill from the room. I was hungry, but the cupboard was bare again. I settled for a three egg omelet to which I crumbled in smoked salmon and goat cheese together with chopped green onion and a last slice of bacon that I'd nuked up nice and crisp. I wolfed the omelet down with some delicious bread I'd recently discovered, baked by a guy in Portland named Killer Dave, who'd done prison time and was now into making whole grain breads. Only in Portland.

After eating I opened the folder containing the newspaper articles Winona had found and looked again at the picture of Sherman Watlamet and Royce Townsend with the dead mountain lion. The date of the article—February 2, 1956—meant they knew each other at least a year before Nelson Queah disappeared. Cecil Ferguson may have worked for Braxton Gage, but who did Watlamet work for? I also wondered who'd be in a better position to rip the Corps off, Gage or Townsend?

Maybe Fletcher Dunn would have an opinion on that. I made a mental note to ask him. Clearly, I had two angles to work now.

Later that evening, I let Archie out after feeding him with my usual admonition to him not to get skunked. A few minutes later, I heard him barking somewhere up along the fence line. It was a scolding bark that told me he was warning something off in no uncertain terms. A chill traced its way down my back like an icy finger. I went up to my bedroom and got the pistol Philip had loaned me. It was loaded, and the steel felt cold in my hand. I went back to the front door, turned the porch light off, and stepped out. Arch was still barking, which meant whatever he was upset about was still out there.

"Archie, come here, boy," I yelled into a drizzle so fine the drops hung in the air like fog.

He kept barking.

I called him again, and to my relief he came. We went inside. I bolted the door and did a quick sweep of the house to recheck all the locks. I slept restlessly that night with the loaded gun on my nightstand, secure, at least, in the knowledge that my dog would hear anything suspicious well before I did.

Later that week, Braxton Gage's secretary called to tell me that he would see me for an hour that Friday. I had called earlier and she was quite accommodating. George Lone Deer was a man of his word. We settled on a three p.m. meeting time, and I resigned myself to another trip through the Gorge to The Dalles.

An hour later I got a call from Jason Townsend inviting me to a strategy session of his nascent campaign team. The meeting was scheduled for Sunday night at the headquarters of Townsend Enterprises in Portland. Jason seemed relieved when I agreed to come. He surprised me by asking if I would join him for lunch at noon that day. He was at his dad's place on the Willamette River and offered to drive down to Dundee. I suggested we meet at the Brasserie and gave him directions.

I parked behind the Brasserie and went in the kitchen door. It was eleven-thirty and the place was bustling with activity and filled with the smell of good food. Bettie James stood at the stove with her back to me, stirring a large pot with a wooden spoon. She wore a white apron over a maroon and black African caftan, and her buzz cut was short enough that she didn't bother with a chef's hat. I stopped next to her and inhaled deeply. "Umm, that's gotta be paella."

She dipped a spoonful out of the pot and said, "Taste this. It needs somethin'."

I blew gently on the steaming broth in the spoon and sipped it with my eyes closed. "Saffron, maybe. Not much, though. You're damn close."

Bettie nodded, stirred in a pinch more saffron and offered me another taste. "You're there," I said. "I'm having that for lunch."

She gave me a hug and inspected the fresh bandage covering my wounded arm. I'd gotten the stitches out the day before. I slipped out of the kitchen and into my favorite booth at the corner of the bar. Bettie joined me a few minutes later with a bottle of Lange pinot gris and two glasses. "So, Calvin, what's the latest on this mess you're in?"

I shook my head. "You don't want to know, Bettie." My friend knew about my close call in the quarry, but I didn't feel like going back over what had happened out in that canyon with Big C. Instead, I said, "Is there anything that can't be forgiven?"

She scrunched her brow up, tilted her head back slightly, and gave me a look. "Depends on the forgiver, how big the heart is."

"What about self-forgiveness?"

She laughed and rolled her eyes. Laughter was Bettie's first response to any tough question, and for that matter anything else life cared to toss at her. "Oh, that's a lot harder. That takes a big, big heart. We're always toughest on ourselves." She chuckled and looked past me. "Lord knows, I've done some things in my life that I'm still tryin' to forgive myself for, and I'm no spring chicken." She laughed again, then eyed me for a moment. "You workin' on some self-forgiveness issues, hon?"

I nodded. I hadn't told her much about my past, just that I was a widower. "Early stages. Didn't think it could happen, but I met someone who showed me it might be possible."

Her smile turned a bit sly. "Would that be the tall lady that was in here the other day with you?"

I nodded again, surprised at her insight. "How did you put that together?"

"Oh, I don't know. There just seemed to be somethin' between you two." She chuckled. "I could feel it."

Our conversation was cut short when Bettie was called back into the kitchen. Shortly after that Jason Townsend wandered in from the dining area. "There you are, Cal," he said, extending his hand and beaming his boyish smile, "Good to see you." He was taller than me by a couple of inches and in the manner of some tall, modest men, leaned forward slightly as we shook hands. His eyes were pale blue—like glacier ice—and his blond hair was parted cleanly and combed to the right in a boyish wave. He wore freshly pressed jeans, tassel loafers, and a checkered button-down.

We exchanged pleasantries, and when Bettie came back out from the kitchen ordered up the paella, salad, and some sourdough bread. I poured him a glass of the pinot gris and slid it across to him. He furrowed his brow. "Winona told me there was another incident, a deputy sheriff was shot. My God, are the police doing enough to catch this madman?"

I shrugged. "At this point they don't have much to go on. The crime spree's spread across three jurisdictions. I doubt there's much coordination, frankly. You know how it goes."

He shook his head and shot me a look of frustration. "I see it all the time in the State Legislature—east of the Cascades versus west, liberal versus conservative, environmentalists versus loggers—any damn excuse to draw a line. The gridlock's killing us."

"You'll get gridlock on steroids in D.C."

He laughed, but I saw a fleeting wince of what? Pain? "Oh, for sure. It's a national disease, I'm afraid." Then he grew serious.

"But I'd still like a shot at changing the culture in Washington. You know, I'd like to be part of the solution."

The words were there, if a bit on the cliché side. "How's the campaign shaping up?"

"That's what I wanted to talk to you about, Cal. This meeting Sunday night's pretty important. We're going to brainstorm the key elements of my platform. I'm going to try to stay above the fray if I can. But I want to make sure we get a strong dam-removal plank in there."

He paused, but I waited for him to continue.

"I was hoping you might be willing to make sure dam removal comes up. You know, sort of advocate for it at the meeting."

I nodded. "I can do that. It might piss off your campaign manager, Sam DeSilva, though."

"Oh, no doubt about that. And my father, too." Jason smiled to lighten the comment, but I could see tension in his eyes. "But don't worry, I'll handle them. Look, I'm not some wild-eyed dreamer on this issue. I think we should start with the four dams on the lower Snake. The science is clear—those dams are doing the most damage to the salmon runs. Sure, it'll cause disruptions, but the pumping technology exists to irrigate the wheat fields up there without huge reservoirs. Once that's done, we can consider how to tackle the Columbia. Imagine it, Cal. Imagine Celilo Falls restored. The falls are still down there, you know."

I pictured The Dalles Dam gone and the falls roaring again. The lift it gave me was not unlike the feeling I had after I poured my heart out to Winona. Not all dams are made of concrete and steel, I realized.

Bettie served us lunch, and we went on to discuss the issue in detail. I saw it in stark, gut-level terms. If we let such beautiful creatures as Pacific salmon and steelhead become extinct, could the human race be far behind? I didn't think so. Jason had pretty much the same take, although as a politician he couched his arguments more in terms of economic and recreational benefits. We both agreed that breaching the Snake River dams was a critical step in saving the fish. By the time we'd ordered coffee, I still wondered about his appetite to play down and dirty in Washington, but I certainly liked the man and the way he thought.

I had another item on my mind, too. I said, "Your father has a colorful history. I understand he used to be quite a hunter in his day."

"He was that. Tried to interest me in hunting and shooting when I was a kid, but it never took." Jason laughed and shook his head. "I remember the first and only time he took me hunting. He shot a magnificent elk, and we spent the rest of the day following the trail of blood left by the wounded animal. We never found it." Jason dropped his eyes and studied the tablecloth between us for a few moments. When he looked up there was pain in his eyes. "I spent the next three weeks crying myself to sleep over that poor animal."

"I can understand that."

"Well, my father couldn't. He's had a hard time accepting that I'm different than what he had in mind." Then, as if realizing he'd said too much, he leaned in and added in a conspiratorial tone, "When he married my stepmother, the first thing she did was make him get rid of all his big game trophies. Cleaned them out, every one. I never thought I'd see the day."

When he finished chuckling, I asked, "You remember any of his hunting buddies or guides?"

"No. Not really. I was just a little squirt." Then he gave me a puzzled look.

I took a sip of coffee and waved a hand dismissively. "I thought I might know some of the people he hunted with."

Glancing at his watch, Jason said, "I've got to run, Cal. I told you pretty much all I know about breaching dams. If you need any more technical information before the meeting, call Winona. She knows a lot more than I do. I'm seeing her tonight, and I'll fill her in on our conversation. Oh, and Sunday night you can park under the Tower. Here's a pass."

Since he'd brought up Winona, I decided to fish a little, although a part of me feared what I might learn. I said, "Winona's a real asset for your team. How did you manage to recruit her?"

"Believe it or not, she came to us and volunteered her services. It was a stroke of good fortune for me."

I decided to lay it out there. "I've heard people say you two make a striking couple."

A shadow crossed Jason's face, although it cleared so fast I wondered if I'd really seen it. He smiled a little too broadly. "That's what my father says. I have to admit I'm quite taken with her."

After Jason left, I sat pondering the situation over a second cup of coffee. I hoped to learn a bit more about Royce Townsend's hunting habits, but Jason wasn't much help in that regard. I should've been planning what to do next, but instead I found myself pondering Jason's comments about Winona.

Quite taken with her? Give me a break.

Chapter Thirty-nine

I read somewhere that the name The Dalles is French in origin. In English the city would be known as "The Sluice." French trappers named the area along that stretch of the Columbia River after a narrow channel carved deep into the volcanic basalt, a natural sluice if there ever was one. The channel—later dubbed the Long Narrows by Lewis and Clark—carried the entire volume of the river in a raging, whirlpool-infested torrent nine miles in length. Now, of course, the Long Narrows and its upper terminus, Celilo Falls, lie buried beneath the lake created by The Dalles Dam.

It was Friday afternoon. I was back on Interstate 84 on my way to interview Braxton Gage. I felt good about a call I'd gotten from Sheriff Bailey. Big C was still in critical condition in the ICU, but her prognosis was now "guardedly optimistic." I drove to a staccato rhythm of pelting rain and gusts of wind that buffeted my car. Sheets of water temporarily blinded me as eighteen-wheelers blew by like it was a sunny day. I caught a brief glimpse of the dam before I turned off—an unimposing structure riding low in the water, its floodgates like foaming mouths. When Gage's secretary gave me directions, she mentioned we were meeting at his "other office" and left it at that. I was surprised to find it wasn't located in an office building but a magnificent old Victorian on the west end of town. Meticulously restored, the three story structure was sage green with cream trim and a riot of plum colored gingerbread. A conical tower on the right corner of the building jutted above the two brick chimneys on the roof. A bronze sign at the wrought iron entry gate read

**The Gage House
1887
Private**

A second plaque below it informed me the house had been placed on the National Historic Register by the U.S. Department of the Interior. I was duly impressed.

I let myself in the gate, hit a buzzer at the door, and gave my name through a speaker to an inquiring female voice. She buzzed me in.

The woman behind the voice sat at an antique oak desk in what must have once been the parlor. She wore sketched-in eyebrows, heavy makeup, and lipstick the color of a fire truck. A cigarette smoldered in an ashtray at her elbow. She flashed a half-hearted smile. "Have a seat, Mr. Claxton. Mr. Gage should be free in a few minutes." Across the entryway in the former dining room, a big man with a shaved head wearing a suit coat he couldn't button was talking on the phone in hushed tones. When I sat down, he got up and closed a set of mahogany sliding doors without acknowledging my presence.

"Nice place," I said to the receptionist. "Not what I expected."

She raised the semicircles above her eyes and peered at me through a swirl of cigarette smoke. "This is the old Gage family home. It's kind of a private museum. Mr. Gage has another office at our corporate headquarters down on the river. He spends more time here now that he's retired."

"What's in the museum?"

"Indian artifacts, historical papers and photos, that sort of thing. Oh, and anything relating to the construction of the dams on the Columbia. Mr. Gage feels that that story needs to be preserved."

"Good for him," I chimed in brightly. "The dam building period was an historic time for the Gorge." The receptionist's intercom buzzed, and after stubbing out her cigarette she escorted me up a broad set of creaking stairs to a hallway on the second floor, her hips swaying in a tight dress that displayed all of her contours. I'd worn a long sleeve shirt to cover the wound on my left arm and carried my briefcase in my right hand. The briefcase felt heavy from the weight of the .357 Magnum resting in it.

When we reached the second floor, a tall, statuesque woman wearing a dark dress and stiletto heels met us in the hallway with her arms crossed. She was maybe a decade older than the receptionist, the kind of woman intent on defying the effects of aging and having some success at it. She had streaked blond hair, dark blue, mascara-enhanced eyes, and full lips that were unadorned. She offered her hand. "Hello, Mr. Claxton. I'm Stephanie Barrett, Mr. Gage's business manager." She turned to the receptionist and dismissed her with a ring of authority in her voice. She turned back to me and smiled, pleasing enough but with a hint of November in it. "Mr. Gage is tied up in a conference call. Why don't we go in my office and chat?"

"Sure," I said with a mounting sense that this was some kind of pre-interview, a hurdle I had to clear to get in to see the big guy. A door to an office behind her was open. I figured the door at the end of the hall was Gage's. It was shut. She turned and I followed her into her office. Tight dresses seemed the order of the day at the Gage House. Hers was more conservative, but just barely.

Once thing seemed clear—Braxton Gage was a man who appreciated the female form.

She offered me a chair, slid behind a sleek desk with a black marble top, and smiled again with the same ambiguity. "So, you're a friend of George Lone Deer. How is the chief?"

"Oh, he's fine. I just saw him last weekend. I gave her my best Chamber of Commerce smile. "He's pretty enthusiastic about the possibility of a casino at Cascade Locks."

She smiled back, this time with something approaching warmth. "Well, we certainly think it's a win, win, win." I must have looked puzzled, because she went on, "A win for the

Confederated Tribes, a win for the city of Cascade Locks, and a win for the state of Oregon."

I beamed back at her. "That's the way George is looking at it."

"Well, I certainly hope the Tribal Council listens to him." She shook her head and made a pouty face. "There're some stubborn holdouts at the moment."

"Yeah, I've heard that. Some people think the Gorge's a sacred place and shouldn't become a gambling Mecca."

As if on cue, she launched into a pitch on the supposed benefits of the casino—jobs, tax revenue, income for the Tribes. I must have glazed over because she caught herself. "But you haven't come to hear about the casino. I understand you'd like to talk to Braxton about his early days on the river when he was building dams. What exactly are you interested in, Mr. Claxton?"

This *was* a pre-interview. I flashed the smile again. "It's Cal, Stephanie. Uh, I'd prefer to discuss that directly with Mr. Gage."

She sat back in her seat and crossed her arms. "That's not the way it works here. Mr. Gage is a very busy man. Perhaps I can help you."

I bit back an angry comeback and nodded. Clearly this was going nowhere unless I opened up to her. I did so reluctantly. "Actually, I'm looking into the disappearance of a man named Nelson Queah at the request of his granddaughter." I plucked a card from my shirt pocket, stood, and laid it on her desk. She made no attempt to retrieve it. "Mr. Queah disappeared the night following the flooding of Celilo Falls when The Dalles Dam was commissioned. That was fifty years ago."

I read nothing in her face, but the fingers of her right hand curled into a half fist on the marble slab. "Yes, I've read some about that. I understand you were wounded by that crazy sniper."

Crap, she's done her homework. I nodded and touched my left arm without meaning to. "Oh, I'm fine. I was—"

She cut me off. "Surely this is a matter for the police."

"Oh, for sure. The murders are police business. I'm just trying to help my client find out the truth about what happened to her grandfather. He was a decorated World War II hero."

"This disappearance happened a very long time ago. What could Braxton possibly do to help you?"

I sat forward in my seat. "One of the suspects in the disappearance used to work for Mr. Gage. I'm hoping he can answer some questions about this man and others and what was going on at the dam at that time." I smiled good naturedly. "I understand he's a history buff."

Her eyes went flat. "We're in the midst of some extremely delicate negotiations. The last thing we need is for him to become entangled in something like this. The media would make a circus out of it."

"My inquiry's confidential. I just—"

She stood up, her face set in stone. "Sorry, Mr. Claxton. Braxton will cooperate with any police inquiries, of course, but that's as far as it goes."

I stood up. "Why don't you let *him* decide that?"

She smiled. Winter ice. "We're done here."

That was it. No way I was getting in to see Braxton Gage. Stephanie Barrett walked me to the top of the stairs without saying anything else. As I filed out I walked past the bald behemoth whose coat didn't fit, I now realized, because of his massive chest and shoulders, not his girth. He was standing in the hall in front of the mahogany doors with his hands clasped in front of him. He did not wish me a nice day.

The rain had let up, and the long drive home gave me a chance to think. The casino deal with the Tribes was front and center with Stephanie Barrett. There was no doubt in my mind that she had her mind made up before I got a word out. I wondered if she had consulted with her boss before my arrival or made the decision on her own. Like she said, the publicity could kill the deal, and Gage just talking to me must've seemed threatening to her. It made sense.

I thought about Sherman Watlamet, the first victim, the man who was going to come forward and get something dark and heavy off his chest. Gage was connected through his old employee, Cecil Ferguson, who was at the center of it all. What had Ferguson said when I told him Watlamet was dead? Something like, "Should have kept my fucking mouth shut." He also said that nothing could be proved.

So why take the drastic step of killing Watlamet if the fifty year old crimes could never be proved? It was a question that had been nagging at me from the outset. Maybe the answer was to prevent a 'media circus' that could cause a multi-million dollar deal to crater.

Could it be that simple?

Chapter Forty

"Why don't you go make some coffee, boy?" I said. Archie had just nudged me with his cold puppy nose and planted a slobbery kiss on my cheek. It was Saturday, and the clock on the nightstand read 6:50. I slipped on a pair of jeans and a sweatshirt and went down the back staircase to the kitchen, the stair treads cold on my bare feet. A layer of fog lay across the valley, so thick it looked like you could walk on it. Here and there the tallest Douglas firs pierced the gray expanse like serrated watch towers.

I fed Arch and opened the door for him. He flew across the porch and burst into the yard, barking at nothing in particular except the joy of starting a new day. I chuckled and shook my head. Claire had been right about getting a dog. It *was* therapeutic. I steamed some milk, loaded the espresso maker, and added a double shot to the milk. The cup was warm in my hand, the coffee delicious. I stood staring out at the fog sea and felt, if not at peace, at least not at war with myself.

The cappuccino tasted so good I made a second along with two pieces of toast slathered with Scottish marmalade. I took the coffee and toast into my study and was reading the online *New York Times* when my phone rang. "Hey, Cal, what's up?" The raspy voice was just north of a whisper but instantly recognizable.

"*Big C.* How are you?"

She chuckled then coughed. "Oh, I'm sore as hell but they tell me I'm gonna live."

"Are you out of intensive care?"

"No, not yet."

"You sure you should be calling me?"

She chuckled and coughed again. "Hank smuggled my phone in. I, uh, wanted to thank you and Philip for patching me up out there. I'm real grateful to both of you and kind of embarrassed I got myself shot like that."

"Well, I'm just glad you wore your Kevlar. I—"

"Gotta get off, Cal. Nurse Ratched's coming. Thank Philip for me, okay?"

The line went dead and I laughed out loud. It was good to hear Big C's voice, even if it was barely audible.

I called Philip and described the call, and then I told him about my aborted visit to Braxton Gage. He said, "All that way and you didn't even get in to see to the old fart? Maybe that business manager didn't even tell him you were coming." He said he'd mention it to his dad, but neither of us thought it would do much good. I was groping in the dark and we both knew it.

The last thing he said was, "Eastern Oregon's finest still haven't caught the sniper, Cal. You're watching your back, right?"

The file of newspaper articles Winona had given me lay on my desk. I opened it and looked again at the photo of Sherman Watlamet and Royce Townsend. Another connection from the past. On a notepad sitting on my desk, I'd written the name Sheri North so I wouldn't forget it. She was the singer Fletcher Dunn had mentioned—Royce Townsend's mistress according to Dunn. If Gage wouldn't talk to me, maybe North would. It was worth a shot.

I booted up and began searching the Internet for anything on Sheri North. On an obscure site selling vinyl LPs, I found one reference to a record she'd made in the fifties. Other than that, there was nothing on her. There were a dozen or so listings in the Portland - Vancouver area for the last name North with first names beginning with S. Two were listed as S. North. I had just finished jotting down information on them all when Archie's ears came up, and he began to whine softly. Santos had arrived.

I went down the hall to the kitchen and waived him in from the porch. He set the book he'd borrowed the week before on the table and knelt down and greeted Archie, who by this time was whimpering and wagging his entire backside. He looked at the bandage on my left arm and said, "Get your stitches out?"

"Yep. You ready?"

I pumped up the basketball while Santos swept the driveway in front of the hoop. When he set the push broom aside, I flipped him the ball and said, "First to twenty-two. Take it out."

He took a couple of dribbles with his left hand, feinted left, then crossed over to his right hand and started to drive around me. When I moved to stay in front of him, he switched hands and direction again, this time by flipping the ball behind his back. By the time I recovered he'd blown past me and spun the ball off the backboard into the net with his left hand.

"Two zip," he said.

We battled back and forth, but he won the first game easily. I took the second by one basket, but only because I began to back him down and use my height to score in close.

My left arm was throbbing and I was still breathing heavily when I said, "You're good, Santos. Newberg could use you at point guard. Ever think about playing?"

He shrugged and looked down at his shoes. I could tell by the gesture that he *had* thought about it.

"What's stopping you?"

He continued to study his shoes.

I waited.

He lifted his head but avoided eye contact. "High school sucks, man. You don't know what it's like."

"Tell me."

"I'm invisible there. Anglo kids, Anglo teachers, all in their little Anglo club. He flicked his thumb in the direction of the book on the table. "It's sorta like in that book you loaned me. The dude's trying to survive in a place he doesn't belong. That's the way I feel."

I caught his eyes. "That kid didn't quit, did he."

He shrugged. "I can't play with a police record, right?"

"Wrong. As long as you're in school, you can play. And you don't have a record *yet*. We're going to ask the judge for probation at your hearing. If he grants it and you stick to the terms, they'll wipe the slate clean.

"They do that?"

"Yeah, if you do what the judge orders and you don't screw up again."

Santos didn't say anything, but he looked like I'd just removed a couple of sandbags from his shoulders.

I left him splitting firewood with Archie watching over him and drove to Newberg to run some errands. On the way, I called Fletcher Dunn, but he didn't answer. As I was finishing up, my phone chirped.

"Have they caught that son of a bitch yet?"

"Afraid not," I answered, recognizing Dunn's voice. "How are you, Fletch?"

"I read about the shooting of that deputy in Eastern Oregon. Damn shame."

"Yeah, well, at least every cop in the Northwest's looking for him now."

"That's good, but you're not letting your guard down, are you, Cal?"

I chuckled. "You're the second person who's asked me that this morning. That's why I called. Remember that singer you told me about—Sheri North? I want to find her."

"You think she can help after all this time?"

"I don't know. She was the mistress of the head honcho at the dam. You never know about pillow talk."

"You look over in Washington like I said?"

"I looked in the whole Portland-Vancouver area, then both states. There's no listing for Sheri North. Lots of Sharons and Shirleys, but I have no way to sort them out. Of course, like you said, it could be a stage name."

There was a pause. "You know, the guy you should talk to is Stan Abelman. Know him?"

"The jock on the twenty-four-hour jazz station?"

"Right. He's a walking encyclopedia about the Portland music scene, past and present. He might know something."

I described my meeting with Stephanie Barrett next and asked Dunn for another favor. I wanted the inside scoop on the Gorge casino project, the key players, particularly anything he could find on Barrett, and the amount of money that was likely to change hands. I could have asked Philip to go through his dad for this, but I figured I'd get a straighter story from the ex-newspaperman. Dunn jumped at this like a cub reporter.

After Dunn and I signed off, I drove back to the Aerie. Santos had finished splitting the stack of logs I'd left him with and was weeding the ground around my blueberry bushes. The day had turned sunny, so he ate the lunch I made him out on the porch. I looked up Abelman's number and got him on the third ring. That's the beauty of Portland—its celebrities are in the phone book. He was very cordial. He knew of Sheri North but had no idea where she was now, or whether that was her real name. He did, however, remember the name of her manager—a guy named Harry Voxell—although he was pretty sure Harry had passed away.

There was only one Voxell in the Portland phone directory. I had just about hung up when a woman answered, somewhat out of breath. "Hello, this is Lydia."

Telling her the true reason for my call would have taken too much time, so after introducing myself, I said, "I'm doing a retrospective on the early Portland jazz scene. I'm wondering if you're related to Harry Voxell."

"Um, yes I am. I'm his niece." The voice grew cautious.

"Oh, terrific," I said in a cheery tone to reassure her I wasn't selling anything. "Do you happen to know how I could contact him?"

"He passed away ten years ago."

"Oh, I'm sorry to hear that. I paused, but she remained silent. "Uh, I'm also interested in interviewing a singer he used to manage way back in the fifties. Her name's Sheri North. Do you have any idea how I might contact her?"

There was another pause, as if she were considering the question. Then she answered with finality in her tone, "I'm sorry but I can't help you."

"Do you know Sheri North? Is she still around?" I asked the questions in rapid fire, fearing she was going to hang up on me.

"I'm sorry."

"But, I—"

Click.

"Damn it," I said as I threw my pen across the room. "Good thing I didn't go into telemarketing."

Chapter Forty-one

Townsend Enterprises was nested atop forty-four stories of marble, glass, and steel in downtown Portland. Owing to the tint of the stone, I'd recently learned, the building's called the Big Pink by Portlanders. On Sunday evening I used the card Jason Townsend had given me to raise the bar at the entrance to the tower's underground parking lot. I was running late for the meeting he'd invited me to. I followed a narrow concrete lane down a level and didn't like what I saw. The parking area was poorly lit and deserted. I'd left Philip's cannon back at the farm. After all, I didn't have a concealed handgun license, which meant I couldn't legally carry a loaded gun in my car in Portland. I followed the exit signs out of the place, parked on the street, and walked into the well-lit lobby. Two attempts on your life will do that to you.

After signing in, I was escorted to a key-activated express elevator that took me to the forty-third floor like a bullet train. When the car snapped to a halt and the doors parted, I followed the sound of voices past a row of lavish executive suites to a large conference room that looked down on the Willamette River and out across the patchwork of lights illuminating east Portland. A dozen or so people were chatting and milling around. The meeting hadn't begun.

"Well, well, if it isn't the intrepid, fly fishing lawyer. Or is it lawyering fly-fisherman?"

I turned and saw David Hanson standing alone at a small, self-service bar with a glass of wine in his hand. His cheeks were flushed, his eyes red and overly moist, and there were a couple of wine spots on his pink oxford button down.

I joined him and offered my hand. "Hello, David. Actually, either term fits," I said with a smile I had to force just a little. "How's the campaign team shaping up?"

"Oh, just peachy. Did you come bearing the dam-removal plank, perchance?"

"Uh, yeah, I plan to raise the issue."

He gave me a crooked smile and swayed slightly. "Good fucking luck with that." Then he walked away.

Winona came in a few minutes later wearing a tastefully understated skirt and blouse and high, black books. An uncut chunk of turquoise dangled on a silver chain around her neck. It was the only part of her outfit hinting at the other world she inhabited.

She hesitated as if trying to decide to join me at the bar. Then a voice called to her. "Winona. We're over here, dear." It was Royce Townsend. He waved at her, then scanned his eyes past me like I didn't exist. She smiled tentatively and walked across the room to join him, his son, Jason, and several others. I couldn't help but notice the warm embrace Jason gave her.

I was a little surprised to see the liquor flowing at what was supposed to be a working meeting, and I spotted an open bottle of Beaux Frères Reserve on the bar. I may have been new to the state, but I knew a good Oregon pinot when I saw it. I poured myself a glass and joined a group standing near a wall of windows overlooking the Willamette.

"Mr. Claxton, you decided to come." It was Sam DeSilva. His shaved head gleamed in the overhead lights, and his dark eyes rested on me with something less than fondness, although, in truth, it may have been the look he gave everyone. He stood between the female artist and the economics professor I'd met at Townsend's dinner party. The artist's eyes were slightly unfocused, but it didn't appear that she'd drunk as much as David Hanson had. Not yet, at least.

"I didn't know my attendance was in question," I answered with a smile laced with a measure of ambiguity.

"Well, I know you're a busy man with your one-man law practice way out in, where is it, Dayton?"

"Dundee." I swirled the wine in my glass, took a sip, then held the glass up. "Where this stuff's made."

Sam's eyes seemed to sink into their sockets. He smiled without mirth. "Oh, that's right. Farm country."

I swallowed a comeback. The economics professor, sensing the escalating tension, said, "Do you know Bettie James? She has a great restaurant out your way."

"She's a good friend," I answered, thankful for the intervention. "The Brasserie's my home away from home."

Sam slipped away from the group while the professor and I made small talk. A few minutes later, Sam called to me from across the room to join him, Royce, and Jason Townsend. Royce wore a silver sweater below an elegant black blazer. The color of the sweater matched his hair and eyes, although his eyes were paler and not particularly friendly. His son wore chinos and an open neck shirt. His trademark smile was in place, but the muscles in his face were tight.

Sam waited for the handshakes and greetings before saying, "Look, Claxton, we know you're loaded for bear tonight about the dam-removal issue. We've decided to kick that can down the road for the time being. We've got more critical issues to deal with right now."

I glanced at Jason, whose face had lost some color. I said, "I'd just planned to raise the issue tonight. See what the group thought."

Sam replied, "I know, I know. But we've got some strong enviros here tonight. If you bring the subject up, it'll consume the evening, I guarantee you. We don't want that to happen."

I looked back at Jason, who'd dropped his eyes. "You agree with this, Jason?"

"Uh, yeah, I—"

Royce interrupted his son. "We can examine the issue later in the campaign. We just don't think this is the proper time to raise it."

I watched Jason, waiting for him to finish, but he averted his eyes and said nothing. Finally, I said, "Okay, gentlemen, whatever you say," and with that spun on my heels and walked away.

I saw Winona at the bar and joined her. I offered my hand, and she hugged me instead. After looking me over, she said, "How are you doing, Cal?"

I felt a flush of the intimacy we'd shared at her grandmother's. "Better, thanks to you. Grooms is still in the ICU, but she snuck a call to me. Looks like she's going to make it."

Her face brightened. "That's good news. What about the sniper? How could he have gotten away out there?"

I shrugged. "I don't know. He's pretty resourceful." Her face darkened, so I changed the subject. "I just heard the Townsend campaign's going soft on dam removal."

"*What?* What do you mean?"

Before I could answer, Sam's voice boomed out from the front of the room. "Folks, please grab a seat. We're going to get started now."

"I'll tell you later," I said as Winona made her way to the front to join Jason and his father.

Sam kicked the meeting off with the usual thanks to the volunteers and reminders of how important the upcoming Senate race was for the future of Oregon and the whole country, for that matter. Then he paused with his hands pressed to his lips as if in prayer and said, "I don't want to start out on a down note, but I have an announcement to make." He drew a breath and hesitated for a moment. "Folks, David Hanson's moving on."

There were groans as the collective eyes of the group swung around to David. He was slouched in a chair in the back with a silly grin on his face.

Sam continued, "We knew it would be hard to keep such a talented guy for very long, and well, I guess David got an offer he couldn't refuse. Right, David?"

David raised a nearly full glass of wine. "Couldn't have said it better, Sam."

Sam waited, but David said nothing more.

"Well, we're going to miss you, fella." Then he told the group to stick around afterwards to wish David well, before nodding to Royce Townsend and taking a seat in the front row.

"That was the bad news," Royce said. "Now let me give you the good news. It's probably a truism that politics is not very conducive to romance. But it's the exception that proves the rule, they say. He paused, and I thought for a moment he was going to tear up. Then he looked down at Jason and Winona, who were sitting side by side, and gave them a benevolent smile. "My son, Jason, proposed to Winona last night and she accepted."

The audience burst into oohs and aahs as the bottom fell out of my stomach.

Royce motioned for the couple to stand up, which they did. "Show them the ring," he said to Winona.

She held her hand up to display a big diamond cluster that glittered fiercely in the lights. Jason stood at her side, grinning proudly. For an instant she and I made eye contact. I smiled, and it was only slightly forced. It made sense, after all.

When the group quieted down, Jason said, "Thank you all. You're the first to know about this and, uh, we'd appreciate it if you would keep this news under your hats. We're planning a party soon to make the official announcement. You're all invited, of course."

I don't remember much about the ensuing meeting. Agreement was reached on a proposed platform the candidate would run on, and since I sat in the back and kept my mouth shut, the issue of free-flowing rivers in the Northwest didn't come up. This was just as well, since I was a bit preoccupied thinking about Winona and Jason's surprise announcement. It wasn't about Winona and me. Hell, there was nothing between us but a nascent friendship. And it wasn't what I knew or at least suspected about Jason either. That was none of my business. It was just a gut feeling that they weren't right for each other, that this was some kind of marriage of convenience.

I finally managed to push the thoughts out of my head. Be happy for her. Be happy for both of them. Oregon voters will love such a beautiful couple, and they'll probably take Washington, D.C., by storm.

After the meeting and the well-wishing ended, I was headed straight for the bullet train down when I noticed David Hanson was having difficulty putting his coat on. I walked over to him. "Are you going to make it all right, David?"

He looked at me and squinted. "I'm doing splendidly. But I can't seem to get my arm in this damn sleeve."

I helped him with his coat, and we walked together toward the elevator. Sam had just seen an elevator full of people off. David stopped in front of Sam and swayed slightly. Sam offered his hand while trying hard to put a smile on an otherwise wary expression. "Good night, David."

David gave him the same squinty look and kept his hands at his side. There was a long pause. "You know what you are, Sam?"

Sam dropped his hand and his smile simultaneously. He said very softly, "What, David?"

David extended his arm until his index finger just touched Sam's chest. "You are a scheming little piece of shit." Then he pulled his finger back and shook it from side to side. "No, no. That doesn't quite capture it." He placed his finger back on Sam's chest. "You are a *steaming* little piece of shit."

Sam's eyes went as flat as two worn nickels. He struggled to raise a smile but only managed a quivering ripple at one corner of his mouth. He looked down at David's finger and started to push his hand away.

Like the completion of a circuit in a detonator, the touching of their hands caused David to explode. He screamed with rage, lunged at Sam and raked his fingernails down his face. The move was quick and vicious. I was stunned.

Sam cried out in pain and pushed David away. "You little faggot," he hissed. Then he stepped forward and punched David hard in the face. There was the dull thud of bone striking bone, cushioned by layers of skin. David's knees buckled, and I caught him.

"Stop them, Cal! Stop them!" Winona screamed as she rushed down the hall, a look of horror on her face.

I propped David up and got between him and Sam, whose face was streaked with vertical crimson lines. I extended my arms in both directions. "Stop it. Both of you."

"You scratched my eye, you son of a bitch," Sam said in a high, tinny voice. He was panting and holding his hand over his right eye.

David giggled. "What a shame. I tried for both of them." The skin under David's left eye was beginning to swell around a short, horizontal gash oozing blood.

"Well, the deal's off, asshole," Sam shot back. "You can forget about it."

"I was never going to take your filthy—"

"*That's enough,* David. Shut your mouth and go." It was Royce Townsend, who'd come up behind Winona. He spoke like a man used to absolute obedience, his jaw set in a rigid line, his eyes drawn down to colorless slits. He turned to Sam. "Come with me. Let's have a look at your eye."

David giggled again and lurched toward the elevator. Winona said, "Cal, please take him home. He's too drunk to drive." When the elevator doors opened, she got in and rode down with us. In the lobby, I guided David to a bench, sat him down and said, "Stay."

Winona waited for me next to the elevator, a look of shock and bewilderment on her face. "What's going on, Cal?"

"David's been shown the door. I guess he decided not to leave quietly."

"Why?"

I shrugged. "Why don't you ask your fiancé?"

Her eyes grew large and filled with tears. "Why do you say *that?*"

I didn't know what else to say, so I gathered David up and left her standing at the elevator.

Chapter Forty-two

For a small man, Sam DeSilva packed a wallop. Under the dome light of my car, I could see that David Hanson's left eye would soon be swollen shut and his cheek rendered a fine, if mottled, shade of purple. However, the gash Sam's fist had opened up didn't look that serious.

"The bleeding's stopped, and I don't think you'll need stitches," I told him.

"Oh, damn. I was hoping for a scar. Adds character to a face, don't you think? Like Pacino in *Scarface*."

I laughed despite myself. "Your face's going to have plenty of character, at least for a week or two."

The fight seemed to have sobered David up somewhat, and he agreed to leave his car at The Big Pink and come with me without much of a fuss. He lived in Sellwood, so I took the Ross Island Bridge to the east side. When I turned onto Milwaukie, he said, "Coffee. I need coffee. There's a little bar up on the left. I'll buy you a cup."

I was fine with stopping, because I had some questions I wanted to ask him. The place was bustling with a jovial group of neighborhood types who hardly looked up as we made our way to a table in the back after ordering black coffee and a small pizza at the bar. When we sat down, David started to relive the fight with Sam. I let him go, figuring he needed to get it out of his system. He'd eaten most of the pizza and was on his second cup of coffee when I said, "What the hell happened to get you so upset?"

He looked at me and chuckled. "Well, let's just say leaving wasn't my idea."

"What did Sam mean when he said, 'The deals off'?"

David shook his head. "I wasn't going to take their stupid deal anyway. They think they can just buy people. Take this money, keep your mouth shut, and we'll say nice things about you. I don't need their money or their fucking recommendations."

"How long have you and Jason been lovers?"

David stopped his coffee cup halfway to his mouth. "I beg your pardon?"

I met his eyes and let the question stand by saying nothing.

"How—"

"I notice things, David. So, you're out and Winona's in to bolster Jason's hetero image, right?"

He shrugged. "Sure. That's the way things are done. You can win an election in Portland if you're gay, but a statewide election for a national office? That's another question entirely."

"Who called the shot?"

"Royce. Who else? Sam's just an errand boy. Royce loaned him to the campaign to keep an eye on things. He put me there for legal perspective. But I'm sure Sam's glad to see me go, as well."

"What about Jason? Doesn't he have any say in this?"

David's eyes filled, and he blinked away a tear. "Jason made his decision. He talks a good game about being his own man. But at the end of the day, he wants to please his daddy. And his daddy wants him to be a happily married senator on a short leash. They can all go to hell."

We sat in silence for a while. David dabbed at his eyes with his napkin. I waited for him to calm down before shifting the subject. "I understand Royce was a big game hunter in his day. Ever hear anything about that?"

Hanson made a face. "I don't know anything, except that Jason told me they used to have a lot of disgusting animal heads in their house. You'd have to ask Sam."

"Sam arranged Royce's hunting trips?"

"Sam arranged *everything* for Royce. Still does. He's been with him for years."

"Tell me about Sam."

"What's to tell? His first love's politics, or should I say power—Machiavelli's his role model. He wants to go to Washington worse than Jason does. He's the quintessential sycophant, too. Takes care of all of Royce's dirt. And there's plenty of *that*. Or at least there was. The old man's lost a step or two."

"What kind of dirt?"

David laughed. "You name it—payoffs, bribes, you know, the basic cost of doing large scale construction work." I nodded, and he went on. "The old bastard cut a wide swath in his day." Then something seemed to register in David's eyes. He wrinkled his brow, and I knew the spell was broken. He said, "This is starting to feel like an interrogation. What's your deal, Claxton?"

I took a sip of coffee while I did a quick gut check. I decided not to risk tipping my hand any further. I opened my hands, palms up, and smiled. "I'm just a curious guy, that's all."

"Sure you are."

Chapter Forty-three

I awoke the next morning in a state of agitation. I slipped on a pair of shorts and a tee-shirt, and because it was overcast added a sweatshirt. Archie followed me downstairs, and when I sat at the bench in the entry to put on my jogging shoes he started to squeal and yelp and spin in circles. Running with me was the pinnacle of his existence, and my ears were ringing as proof. But by the time I stepped off the porch and he was halfway down the drive I came to my senses. The sniper was still out there. This was no time to go running in my sparsely populated neighborhood. I called out to Arch, who jerked around and gave me a look, the doggie equivalent of "are you kidding me?"

Archie was still pouting out by the gate when my cell phone went off in the pocket of my shorts. "Talked to my father about Gage." I felt a wave of annoyance and realized it was because Philip seldom bothered to start a phone conversation with any sort of conventional greeting. Fletcher Dunn did the same damn thing, I realized.

"Good. What did he have to say?"

"He said you might get a do-over. He told Gage again that he needed a favor, that you were a good man involved in a violent situation and needed Gage's help to sort things out. My father thinks Gage's a real asshole but no killer. Some kind of grudging respect I don't really understand."

"A do-over? What, I'm supposed to go back out to The Dalles?"

"No. Gage said he would contact you. He didn't know that Barrett had blocked you. Thought the problem was at your end."

"You think he'll follow through?"

"Probably. He's got a four-hour erection for that casino deal—"

"Stephanie Barrett wants it, too," I interjected. "That's why she wouldn't cooperate."

"Well, I think you'll get an audience with the old man, but that doesn't mean he'll open up. You'll have to use your silver tongue to make that happen." Philip chuckled. "Of course, he could be the guy behind this killing spree."

"There is that, isn't there."

"Sure is. Don't turn your back on him."

On that cheery note I changed the subject. "Did you hear about your cousin's engagement?"

"Who? Winona?"

"Yeah. She's wearing a big diamond from Jason Townsend."

"The pretty-boy politician? No. Say it isn't so."

"Afraid it is. They announced it last night at a campaign gig."

"Shit. What the hell's she thinking?"

"She loves the guy, I guess. I'm happy for her. She deserves the best."

"Well, yeah, of course, but..." his voice trailed off. "She's forgotten where she came from, that's what I think."

"I'm not so sure, Philip." He didn't argue, and we left it at that.

I went inside, fed the dog, and had some breakfast. I was sitting out on the side porch with a cup of coffee when the wind began stirring in the Doug firs towering a hundred and fifty feet above me. The now familiar sound—like a receding wave sifting through pebbly sand—soothed me at some primal level for reasons I couldn't begin to explain, except to say that in the listening I began to feel a connection to this piece of land. The rain came next, a gentle patter followed by a hard downpour. Archie came out of the rain, shook himself, and lay down next to me.

A man and his dog enjoying a good Oregon rain.

I spent the rest of that morning getting caught up on paperwork and preparing for what promised to be a busy week of conventional legal work. You know, the kind where people involved don't try to kill you. Toward noon, the motion sensor I'd put back out at the gate buzzed, which sent Archie into a frenzy of barking. I watched out the dining room window as a car pulled in the drive and was surprised to see Winona Cloud. I went out on the porch, and as she got out of her car I couldn't miss the glittering rock on her left hand. Archie yelped and left my side to greet her.

She stopped at the foot of the porch steps and looked up at me with a tired, strained smile. "I was, uh, in the neighborhood. Thought maybe I could bum a cup of coffee."

"I was just going to fix some lunch. Come on in."

She followed Archie and me into the kitchen and went straight to the window above the sink. "Oh, even in the rain the view's magnificent. And this house, Cal. I love it."

"The house needs a lot of work, but the bones are good. It was one of the original farmhouses in the area." As we talked, I ground coffee beans, made cappuccinos, and put bagels in the toaster. Then I sliced a red onion and a tomato and laid the slices on a plate, which I put on a tray along with a carton of cream cheese, a jar of capers, and a slab of smoked steelhead. My go-to lunch.

We kept the banter light while I was preparing the food. I was a little tense about the impending conversation and wasn't about to ask any leading questions. She was here for a reason. She'd get around to it soon enough.

When we were finally facing each other across the kitchen table, she said, "God, what a mess that was last night. Did you get David home all right?"

"Yeah. How's Sam's eye?"

"It's okay, but he looks like he lost a catfight." The comment broke the emotional ice, and we both laughed a little more than we should have. "Jason feels terrible about the way the dam removal issue was handled. He wanted you to know how sorry he is."

I shrugged. "That's show biz. How do *you* feel about it?"

She sipped her coffee and licked a dollop of cream cheese with a caper stuck to it off her finger. "Oh, Jason and I had a long talk about that. He just wanted to postpone the debate until his team has coalesced. You know, with David's departure and all, things are in flux." She searched my face for a reaction. When I didn't give her one, she said without much conviction, "I guess I'm okay with that."

I took a bite of the concoction I'd built between bagel slices and with a full mouth managed to say, "Sam told me dam removal doesn't poll well."

"That's *not* the reason," she snapped, breaking eye contact. "Jason intends to come back to the issue." Then she added, more to herself than me, "He'd better."

I kept chewing and didn't say anything.

The silence in the room was broken with the chatter of small birds at the feeders on the porch. The sun had broken through, and when Winona finally brought her eyes back to mine, they shown with tiny flecks of gold I hadn't noticed before. This softened her stern look. "Cal, did you know about David?"

There it was, the reason for her visit. She'd couched her question in terms of David, but was she really asking me about her fiancé, Jason? I swallowed and dropped my eyes to the tabletop, which was scarred and stained from heavy use. "Uh, I wasn't sure until the other night. I'm not much of a gossip, you know."

She shook her head and chuckled softly. "Well, I was too naïve to see it. Jason finally told me what happened. The fact that David's gay wasn't a problem until he started coming on to Jason. He was becoming an embarrassment for the campaign. Jason didn't want to do it, but he finally decided David had to go."

I looked up at her face. She was watching me carefully. I had this crazy feeling, like she was balanced there on a high wire, and if I said the wrong thing she would come crashing down. The version she'd just told me was the one she wanted to believe. I sensed she was looking for me to allay any doubts she might have about Jason's explanation. I couldn't do that. At the same time,

I couldn't bring myself to tell her the truth. Like I'd decided out there on the Sandy River, it was clearly none of my business.

I nodded and kept my face rigidly neutral.

She waited, and when she realized I wasn't going to speak said, "Cal, he loves me."

"I'm sure he does, Winona. Do you love him?"

She smiled like someone trapped. "I'm not sure. I married once for love, and it failed. Maybe marriage should be more of a partnership." She leaned forward and met my eyes. "Cal, I could help him do great things for the environment, for my people. Imagine the good that could be done."

I shrugged. "I'm a hopeless romantic. I think people should marry for love, not political agendas."

Her eyes flashed with anger. "I don't have that luxury."

That was pretty much the end of that conversation. I wanted to tell her about Braxton Gage's and Stephanie Barrett's lust for the Gorge casino deal, why I was intrigued with the hunting hobby of Royce Townsend, and Sam DeSilva's apparent involvement. But I thought better of it. Despite her vow of confidentiality, I didn't want anything leaking back to the wrong people, whoever the hell they were.

As we walked to her car, I said, "Look, Winona, the killer's still out there, and I don't understand what or who's driving him, so stay on your toes. If you see anything suspicious, be sure to let me know right away, okay?"

I stood watching as she drove down the long drive and out the gate. Archie sat down next to me and whimpered softly, as if to speak for both of us.

Chapter Forty-four

Some nights it's a waste of time to go to bed. After watching the Blazers get thumped by San Antonio, I turned in and tried to read, but the words kept swimming off the page. Yet when I put the book down, I just lay there staring at the ceiling. It was after two when I finally drifted off, only to fall into a troubling dream. There I was, stepping off the cliff edge at the quarry again, this time out of curiosity instead of fear. The green broth was even colder this time. I let the momentum of the fifty-foot drop carry me down without resisting. The promise of something I couldn't name drew me deeper and deeper. Pressure built against my eardrums as my lungs scoured the oxygen from my last breath. I started clawing my way back toward the pale light marking the surface, but it was too late. My breathing reflex kicked in, and I inhaled a lungful of putrid water.

I must have actually been holding my breath, because I awoke coughing and gasping for air. Archie came over to check on me, a concerned look on his face. I put my robe on and went down to the study with Archie at my heels. The house was cold and still except for the soughing of the fir trees in the wind. I sat motionless for a long time, trying to focus my thoughts. Finally, I slipped a piece of paper out of my printer and jotted down the following list:

1. *Sniper: No pro. Outdoorsman. Expert with a scoped rifle. Hunter or ex-military?*

2. *Braxton Gage: Cecil Ferguson's boss. Involved in Skimming money during dam construction? Wants Gorge casino deal.*

3. *Stephanie Barrett: Gage's biz mgr. Calling shots for Gage? Wants casino as badly as he does.*

4. *Royce Townsend: Ran dam construction project. Hunted with Sherman Watlamet (See #1). Had affair with Sheri North.*

5. *Sam DeSilva: R.T.'s right-hand man. Arranged hunting trips (among other things)*

6. *Jason Townsend: Proposed to Winona but risked affair with David Hanson. A tool of DeSilva and his father?*

7. *David Hanson: See #6*

Then I surprised myself by adding:

8. *Winona Cloud: Is she telling the truth about Cecil Ferguson's death?*

At the bottom of the list I wrote: *What does Sheri North know?*

I laid the pen down and leaned back in my chair. If I expected some searing insight as a result of my effort, it didn't happen. The tangled mass of motives and possible interconnections swirled around in my head like leaves in a windstorm. The only thing I felt certain of was that the killer was working for someone on the list. And the only conclusion I could draw at this point was that I needed more information to untangle the mess. *Duh.*

The exercise did have one benefit—I was suddenly so tired I couldn't make it back upstairs, so I crashed on the lumpy couch in the study.

◇◇◇

Between client meetings that morning, I called Fletcher Dunn. "Your timing's good, Claxton," he told me. "I've got some information for you." We agreed to meet that afternoon. I dropped a decidedly disappointed Archie off at the farm before heading off to his place in Lake Oswego. No one answered the bell at his house. I rang again and thought I heard someone in his backyard. I started around the side of the garage and called his name.

"Is that you, Claxton?" he answered. "I'm back here."

I turned the corner and found him sitting in his wheelchair. He wore dark glasses, jeans, and a denim shirt and was holding a pair of pruning shears in a gloved hand. With his free hand, he gunned the motor on his chair. The big wheels spun in place, spraying mud out behind him. He was stuck fast in the soft ground and thick grass that results from the Oregon rainy season.

"Goddamn it, give me a hand, would you?"

I stifled a laugh but couldn't help smiling. "Sure. Looks like you need chains for that buggy."

"Very funny. I was pruning the roses. My wife would kill me if she saw the shape they're in."

I pushed him out onto the driveway, and then at his direction finished up the pruning, raked up the cuttings, and put them into a small wheelbarrow. I said, "I know a young man who could help put your yard back in shape. He might be interested in a job like this."

"Can't afford it," Dunn snapped, averting his eyes.

After we cleaned up his wheelchair in the garage, I followed him into the house. He went straight to the kitchen and made himself a large gin and tonic. I declined his offer to join him. In the study, he swung his wheelchair around and took a healthy swig of his drink before speaking. "A contact at *The Oregonian* finally got back to me on the Gorge casino project. The deal's got legs. The Department of the Interior has just approved the tribe's revenue sharing proposal, a key step in the process, and the Gov's not signaling that he'll veto the damn thing."

"The Governor has veto power?"

"Yep. And an outfit called Allies of the Gorge is lining up to block the deal. Hell, I'm no tree hugger, but a goddamn casino in the Gorge? Are you kidding me?" He chuckled. "But I digress. You asked me about Stephanie Barrett. Turns out she's been quietly buying up land for Gage for some time. They have about fifty-eight acres amassed near Cascade Locks that they're offering to the tribes."

"For big money?"

"Oh, six mil or so. But that's not the *real* payoff. My source tells me Gage wants a piece of the action going forward. Under the table, of course. The Feds would never allow that."

I was sure George Lone Deer hadn't told his son about this twist. "Why would the tribes agree to something like that?"

Dunn shrugged his narrow shoulders. "Sometimes you gotta go along to get along. Gage has enormous political clout, not so much in liberal Salem, but in the Gorge, where sentiment for the deal's pretty mixed outside Cascade Locks. The tribes are going to need all the help they can get to convince the Gov."

"What about Barrett? Anything else on her?"

"One thing—my source mentioned she's got ties to the OPM."

"OPM?"

"The Oregon Patriot Militia, a paramilitary group out in eastern Oregon. Her brother-in-law's supposedly way up in the organization, but it's very secretive. They're arming for the government takeover or the invasion of the Muslim hordes, whichever comes first."

My ears pricked up. "Huh. How secretive are they? Could your source get photos of these guys?"

He shot me a sly smile. "I like the way you think, Claxton. I'll see what I can do. There's something else. My source tells me the anti-casino group has some hotshot hacker, and they're going after e-mail correspondence between Barrett and her brother-in-law. Stay tuned on that one, and keep it to yourself."

"Sure. Thanks."

He took another pull on his drink and wiped his mouth with the back of his hand. "So what else you got?"

"I'm wondering if you could search *The Oregonian's* archives for old articles on Royce Townsend and anything having to do with his hunting exploits."

Dunn laughed. "Now it's Townsend. Shit, you don't mess around, do you? Well, this won't be hard. Townsend's always been a media darling. Anything specific you're looking for?"

"Yeah. Who he hunted with, both friends and guides and any hunting lodges he frequented, that kind of thing. I know he hunted with an Indian named Sherman Watlamet in the late fifties, but I'm more interested in what he did later, in the seventies and eighties, before he hung it up. The sniper's considerably younger than Townsend."

Dunn nodded, put his wire rim glasses on, and turned around to face his computer. The archives covered nearly everything printed in *The Oregonian* and the newspaper that preceded it, *The Portland Journal*. Dunn quickly located and printed out three articles on hunting that mentioned Royce Townsend. Two articles in the late seventies described trips to Alaska. One article showed a picture of Townsend posing next to a huge bear stretched out on scaffolding. The caption read: "Local Hunter Bags Trophy Kodiak in Alaska."

"They don't dare print shit like this anymore," Dunn remarked. "They'd lose circulation."

The second article covered a successful caribou hunt and featured a picture of Townsend and Sam DeSilva posing with their weapons. Both articles mentioned the trips were led by Alaskan Wilderness Guide Service, but no other information on them was included.

The third article covered a hunt in Idaho in 1989. Townsend had shot a world record elk dubbed "Old Granddad" with the help of an outfit called Idaho Adventure Guides and Outfitters. The article pointed out the guide service used a spotter airplane and a small army of trackers to find the legendary animal, who'd avoided being shot by ordinary hunters for as long as anyone in that part of the Idaho could remember.

Once Old Granddad's location had been pinpointed, Townsend was flown in to make the kill. A world record was claimed. The piece included a photo of Townsend crouched behind and enveloped by the dead elk's rack, which must've stretched a good eight feet across.

"What a shameless prick," Dunn said after taking a long pull on his drink. "How could anyone shoot an animal like that? And they flew him in, for Christ's sake."

I swallowed back a lump of something, anger tinged with disgust. We sat in silence for a few moments before I said, "Not much to go on."

"What the hell did you expect?"

"A picture of the sniper with his name under it would've been nice. Short of that, names, I guess, someone to talk to."

Dunn logged out of the archives and onto Google. We found nothing on The Idaho Wilderness Guide Service. "Probably gone out of business," he said. On the other hand, Idaho Adventure Guides and Outfitters had an elaborate website, which included a map showing the location of their hunt camps. I jotted down the name of the owner and the telephone number, although I didn't have a clue how I might use the information.

I leaned back, stretched, and watched as Dunn drained his gin and tonic.

I must have telegraphed my concern, because Dunn said, "*What?* Why do I always get the feeling you're judging me, Claxton?"

I raised my hands in a gesture of surrender. "No offense. I just need you to stay with me, that's all."

"Don't worry about it," he shot over his shoulder as he motored off to the kitchen. When he returned, he held up his glass and said, "Half the usual gin. Satisfied?"

Next, I explained how I had struck out with Lydia Voxell, and Dunn agreed to scan the archives for anything on the blues singer, Sheri North. He found several articles. Dunn expanded a photo of her on stage with a piano, drum, and upright bass trio. "You can see what all the fuss was about. She could sing, and she was one gorgeous woman."

I had to agree. She had a willowy body, long, flowing black hair, and a set of cheekbones that would have made Lauren Bacall envious. But all the articles were written in the fifties about her singing engagements in Portland. Nothing after that.

Her deceased manager, Harry Voxell, appeared in a smattering of articles over the years. But only his 1996 obituary contained anything useful. The piece mentioned that Sheri North had sung a moving rendition of "Amazing Grace" to end his memorial service.

"So all I've got is that Sheri North was living in '96, but there's no record of her anywhere."

"Must be her stage name," Dunn said.

"She used her stage name at the funeral?"

"Sure. She was performing again. Show biz habits die hard."

I nodded. "Maybe so."

"The only way you're going to find her is through a detective agency. Or maybe you should try talking to Voxell's niece in person. You know, turn on the charm, if you can find any."

"Very funny."

A few minutes later, Dunn saw me to the door, and as I was about to step outside said, "That kid you mentioned who does yard work, can you set something up?"

"Sure. I'd be happy to. And thanks again for the help, Fletch."

Back at the Aerie around four, I was thumbing through the mail out on the road when I noticed a car coming from the direction of Dundee. It was a black Hummer with deeply tinted windows and a gleaming chrome grill that looked like the bared muzzle of a pit bull. Its nose dipped as it began to brake, and I stepped off the road warily, putting a fir tree between me and the oncoming vehicle. It stopped in front of me, and the back window came down, releasing a cloud of blue smoke.

"Are you Cal Claxton?" a voice said from within the car.

I nodded. "Yes I am."

"I'm Braxton Gage. I understand you want to talk to me."

Chapter Forty-five

I felt exposed but wasn't about to show it. "Mr. Gage, it's a pleasure to meet you. Thanks for stopping by."

"George Lone Deer tells me you're a man with a problem. Why don't you get in and we can talk about it."

There it was—one of those put up or shut up moments. I could either get in and chance being abducted or play it safe and miss out on talking to someone who might help me blow this thing open. I decided to risk it but not before buying myself some insurance.

I put my mail back in the box. "Just give me a minute to make a call." With Gage watching, I flipped open my cell phone and speed-dialed Philip Lone Deer. I got his voice mail, but that didn't matter. I said in a voice that Gage could hear, "Philip, this is Cal. I'm here in front of my place talking with Braxton Gage. I just wanted to thank you and your father for making this possible. We're going for a ride in his Hummer to talk things over. Talk to you soon." It wasn't much of a deterrent, but it was the best I could come up with on short notice. If I went missing, Philip would know Gage was the last person to see me alive. And Gage would know he knew.

Gage wore a burgundy golf shirt with some sort of logo on it, cream colored slacks and expensive, hand-tooled shoes. Not the attire of your typical abductor. He must have been in his eighties, but he looked much younger. He had fleshy jowls, an off-kilter nose, and moist eyes from either age or cigar smoke, I couldn't tell which. I had a fleeting sense that his face, around his eyes, looked familiar, but it passed. His chest and shoulders were thick and raised veins lay on his stout forearms like snakes.

"You want a cigar?" When I declined his offer, he said to his driver, "We're going to talk for a while, Jerome. Just drive through the vineyards, please." Jerome—the guy who had trouble finding jackets big enough to fit him—nodded and swung the big Hummer back onto the road. A faint, metallic beat began to bleed out from speaker buds stuck in his ears, assuring me Jerome wouldn't be eavesdropping on our conversation.

Gage flicked the soggy remnant of his cigar out the window and turned to face me. His eyes had narrowed a bit, and the tight line of his lips formed the faintest of smiles. "I understand you drove all the way out to The Dalles to see me, but Stephanie threw up a roadblock."

I nodded. "She told me you were tied up in a conference call."

He chuckled. "God save us all from bossy women. Steph's afraid some skeleton from my closet will rear up and bite my ass." He laughed again. "I told her not to get her panties in a bunch. I know what I can say and can't say."

I smiled and nodded. "Guess I can't blame her. She was convinced I was going to screw up your casino deal with the tribes."

"She means well, but nobody can screw up the deal except the Governor." His eyes narrowed again. "Now what in the hell's on your mind, son?"

I started at the beginning. "A Wasco Indian named Nelson Queah went missing the day The Dalles Dam floodgates were first closed and the falls at Celilo flooded. Queah was an influential member of the tribe there and an activist in the effort to stop the dam construction. I have reason to believe he was murdered and thrown into the lake that night. I also believe he was killed by a man named Cecil Ferguson, a man who worked for you at the time." As I said this, I watched Gage closely.

The muscles in his face remained relaxed, and his expression didn't change for a couple of beats. Then he smiled knowingly and shook his head. "Ferguson," he said with derision. "Wouldn't surprise me if he did what you said. Where is the old fart, anyway?"

"He's dead. Someone beat him to death in Portland a couple of weeks ago. The day before, someone shot a friend of his, a man named Sherman Watlamet. Watlamet had told Ferguson that he was going to talk about some things that happened fifty years ago at the dam."

Gage's eyebrows moved up a few notches. If he knew about the killings—and I'm sure he did—he didn't show it. "I figured that's the way it would end for Cecil, just not so late in life. I cut him loose after we finished The Dalles Dam. He was a good worker, but I got tired of bailing him out of jail for drinking and brawling. Why would he have killed this Indian fellow?"

"An employee of Ferguson's, a young man named Timothy Wiiks, discovered he was somehow siphoning money off at the dam. Wiiks father was Scandanavian, but his mother's a Umatilla. He went to Queah for help. Wiiks was found dead in the Deschutes River the night before Queah disappeared. I believe Ferguson killed him, too."

Gage fished a fresh cigar from his shirt pocket and went about the obscene ritual of wetting it with his lips and tongue before he lit it. His expression had gone pensive. "I don't remember anyone named Wiiks or Wat-the fuck, and I can tell you that no one in my organization was skimming *anything*. I watched my books like a hawk back then. Still do. If there were any financial shenanigans going on, it came through Royce Townsend's organization, that hypocritical little fucker."

"Why do you say that?"

Gage pinched a fleck of tobacco from the tip of his tongue and rested his eyes on me. I sensed he was gauging how much to divulge and waited for him to continue. After what seemed an interminable pause, he said, "Townsend ran The Dalles project on a pay to play basis. If he awarded a contract, he expected a kickback, a generous one, and not any one-time payment. He liked regular installments. He and his older brother were the golden boys as far as the Corps of Engineers was concerned, so none of the subcontractors dared fuck with him."

"Did you pay Townsend a kickback?"

He lit his cigar, blew a cloud of smoke through a gap in the window, and shot me a satisfied smile. "Nope. There was no way in hell I was going to kowtow to that son of a bitch."

I smiled with what I hoped looked like admiration. "How did you manage it?"

"Pretty simple, really. See, Townsend was supposed to be the devoted husband and father, but it was common knowledge that he was banging a babe from Portland. I hired a private detective to follow him around and get some nice pictures of the two of them." He laughed. "The rest was easy. Matter of fact, I sent Ferguson to see Townsend with an envelope full of pictures. No siree, we didn't pay any kickbacks." He leaned back and smiled with pride. "Pretty creative solution for a young buck just starting out in business, don't you think?"

I stifled a laugh at Gage's take on business ethics. "Creative, for sure." He's talking, I told myself, keep him going. "Uh, so maybe what Wiiks observed was Ferguson working the deal with Townsend?"

Gage took a puff and shrugged. "It was a long time ago, Claxton. I *can* tell you no money exchanged hands in my deal."

"Okay, suppose for minute that Ferguson was working a scam. How would he do it if he worked for you?"

Gage fingered his cigar absently and gazed out the window. "How sure are you about this money being stolen?"

"*Very.* The story from my source was confirmed by a newspaper reporter who'd been contacted by Queah. I talked to him a few days ago."

He brought his gaze back inside the Hummer, still pensive. "Maybe Ferguson and Townsend were playing me."

"How do you think they worked it?"

"Hell, I don't know. Ferguson probably billed our work out at an inflated rate and then kept the difference between that and the lower amount he deposited in my account based on the actual invoices. So, I probably didn't lose any money, but they would've made out like bandits." He shook his head. "I'll be a son of a bitch."

"How can you be sure it was Townsend working with Ferguson?"

Gage studied the rows of newly leafed grapevines passing by outside while he considered my question. "Can't say for sure, but I sent Ferguson to cut the deal with Townsend. Maybe that slimy bastard found a way to turn Cecil. Cecil was no tower of virtue, you know. And it would have taken someone high up in Townsend's organization to grease the skids on a scam like that. Who better than the boss himself?"

We drove for a while in silence. Then Gage turned to Jerome and told him to turn around. I said, "The woman Townsend was involved with—she was the blues singer, Sheri North, right?"

His eyes got bigger for an instant. The question had obviously caught him off guard. He inhaled deeply on his cigar and blew the smoke slowly out the gap in the window. "Where in God's name did you dredge that up?"

"Sorry. I have to keep my sources confidential." He nodded slightly, and I continued, "Do you think she would know anything about this?"

Gage looked down at his big, gnarled hands and then back at me. I saw a depth and softness in his eyes that wasn't there before. He exhaled and said in a low, suddenly weary voice, "I don't know what she knew. I suppose there could've been pillow talk between her and Townsend about his business dealings. I can tell you one thing, though, she's a good woman and Townsend didn't deserve her."

I nodded. "Do you know where she is now?"

His looked up at me, and his eyes had gone hard as flint. "What do you want with her? You got what you need, don't you?"

"What you've told me is useful, but I'd like to know what she remembers, if she'll talk to me. She was right in the middle of this thing."

Gage gazed out the window for so long I didn't think he was going to answer. When he finally turned to face me, his eyes had softened again. He sighed. "Well, if this'll help bring that bastard Townsend down, I guess it's worth it. Sheri North's her stage name. Her real name's Shirley Norquist. She lives down around the Salem area."

Jerome brought the Hummer back around to my mailbox and stopped, the motor idling silently. Gage tossed his cigar butt out the window into the weeds. I started to thank him, but he waved me off. "Listen, Claxton, I don't want to be associated with this in any way. If you try to quote me I'll deny we ever had this little talk, and you'll have more trouble than you ever dreamed of. Are we clear?"

"We're clear," I said and got out.

"One more thing," he said through the open window. "Sheri North's a fine lady. If you talk to her, treat her with respect. Got that?" I nodded, and he tapped Jerome on the shoulder. The big black Hummer pulled out and headed back toward the Pacific Highway.

I jogged up my driveway, grateful to pump some clean air into my lungs. Archie met me at the gate with a tennis ball in his mouth. I threw and he fetched for ten or fifteen minutes, and then I took him inside and fed him. While Arch ate, I opened a cold bottle of beer and went out on the side porch to think. The sun was out, but a bank of dark clouds was heading up the valley, towing a band of rain that hung below them like smoke.

I finished the beer but not my thought process. I had either been given an incredible gift of information or had been lied to by a master. I couldn't decide which.

Chapter Forty-six

Jake

Staying out of sight at the beach cabin was boring as hell, but Jake managed it. Don't even think about doing anything for at least a week, he told himself. Deep cover, just like a spy movie, man. His luck was holding, too. Okay, the piece of shit TV didn't work, and there was no beer in the fridge or I W Harper in the cupboard, but there were plenty of staples in the pantry. He wouldn't starve. He'd wavered a couple of times, thinking about how easy it would be to slip on his shades and ball cap and go out for a couple of bottles and a carton of Camels. But he stuck to his vow and even began rationing his cigarettes.

He had quit sending texts. He wasn't sure why. It just seemed like the smart thing to do until he got his head straight. Maybe he'd just slip out when the dust settled and never contact them again. Fuck 'em. He had his fifteen thousand dollars. The incoming texts arrived every couple of hours for the first two days, then stopped. They probably thought he was dead or had lost his phone. He could only imagine what they were saying about him, how he'd screwed up a simple, well-paying job, made a mess of it. But he saw it differently. He had made it out of eastern Oregon—no easy task with every cop in the state looking for him—and his truck was hidden, the car he stole was out of sight, and he was in a safe house.

Not a bad piece of work.

But on the eighth day, he woke up with the Old Man on his mind. He'd had a vague dream about camping with him, and that brought to mind a trip to the Sawtooths they'd taken when Jake was fifteen. It was just the two of them. And it wasn't just the hunt. Hell, they both got an elk on that trip. No, it was those nights around the campfire. Jake cooking, the stars so low you could touch them, and the Old Man stretched out, telling stories like only he could. It was the closest he ever felt to having a father, and the thought of it now caused him to blink away stinging tears.

Time to break the silence, he decided. He sent the following text:

In a good place now. Would like to talk.

He was microwaving the last package of instant oatmeal when his phone pinged:

Where are you? The Old Man wants a face to face.

He knew he would have to give up his address, but when it came down to it, he hesitated. No one knew where he was, and he liked that. Just do it, he finally told himself. The Old Man knows what he's doing. The link they're using must be secure. He sent a text with his address and directions for where to park and how to approach the cabin without being seen.

Ten minutes later this response came back:

See you late tonight. We will park and approach per your instructions and knock on the back door.

The hours dragged by that day. There was a stash of books in the bedroom, mostly romance novels but some mysteries, too. He had read all the mysteries by then, so he tried one of the romance novels, a steamy one by the looks of the cover. But it was useless. He couldn't focus. Not even a good George Pelecanos would have held his attention. He was about to reenter the world, and that stirred up thoughts about what he'd done. He had kept those thoughts at bay for a while, but now they were back like big, ugly ants crawling around in his head.

He had killed two people, one was a woman, and he'd forced a third off a cliff. Could he ever put that behind him? Or is there a point at which you can't go back, when things you've done are just too terrible? He wasn't a religious man, and he wasn't worried about burning in hell. It was the hell inside his head he was afraid of. He was sorry for what he had done, and if he had it to do over again, he would have left that fucking money sitting on the table at the guesthouse. Was that enough? To be sorry and to promise yourself never to kill again?

He had no answers to these questions, just the incessant churning of his guilty conscience. Time will quiet your mind, he told himself. Somehow he knew that. And maybe the Old Man will give you some credit. After all, you may have fucked up, but you pulled it out.

Amy will get her back alimony, too. *I'll deliver the payment in person so I can see the look on her face.*

He managed a nap and ate another crappy dinner, Hormel beef chili and creamed corn. A front blew in and rain drummed on the roof of the cabin the rest of the evening. At 11:53 p.m., he heard a knock on the kitchen door.

He went to the door, opened it, and stepped back in surprise. "Oh, it's you. Where's the Old Man?"

Chapter Forty-seven

Archie lobbied hard to come with me the next morning, but I left him standing at the gate with his ears back. I found two Shirley Norquists in a computer search the night before. One listing was for a woman living on the coast. I ruled that one out. The second was in Independence. I had to look it up on a map. Another small town like Dundee, it was located just southwest of the state capitol, Salem. From what Gage had told me, that had to be the one.

Independence was straight south of Dundee, and I got there in less than an hour. I pulled up to the curb a few houses down and across from the place at eight-twenty. It was a modest, ranch-style house with a couple of comfortable looking wicker chairs on the front porch. I'd fretted all the way from Dundee that she wouldn't be home, but a Honda Civic in the driveway and a couple of lights on in the interior gave me hope. I waited until nine and rang the bell.

A woman opened the door but left a screen door in place between us. She had a book in her hand and looked at me a bit warily, fearing, no doubt, that I was selling something. I recognized her immediately. Her hair was gray now, but the fine sculpting of her face was still evident below pale skin that had yet to show its age. She wore a black, cable-knit sweater and a pair of jeans that probably would have fit her equally well twenty years earlier.

"My name's Cal Claxton," I said, holding up a business card and smiling affably. "Are you Shirley Norquist?"

"Yes I am."

"The jazz singer who used the stage name Sheri North back in the fifties?"

She hesitated for a couple of beats. "Uh, yes, but—"

"I was hoping I might speak to you about your singing career in Portland and some of the people you knew back then."

She put on a pair of glasses that hung on a cord around her neck and read my card through the screen door. "You're an attorney?"

"Uh, yes. It's a cross I bear every day."

She tried to contain a smile but failed.

"I represent a Native American woman who's trying to find out what happened to her grandfather. He disappeared fifty years ago at The Dalles Dam. I have reason to believe you might be able to help us."

"Fifty years ago? You can't be serious. I can't help you with something like that. I don't even know any Native Americans."

"I realize you don't know my client or her family. It's a fascinating story. Give me a chance to explain. Your help would mean a great deal to her."

She looked down at my card again and then back at me. "What's your client's name?"

"Winona Cloud. She's the first Wasco Indian PhD ever. She's doing great work for her tribe and for the Columbia River."

She hesitated while seeming to ponder something weighty. My guess was she didn't necessarily want to revisit that time in her life. I waited, knowing her willingness to talk hung in the balance. Finally, she unlocked the screen door, stepped out on the porch, and shut the door behind her. "I doubt if I can help you, Mr. Claxton, but I guess I could try to answer a few questions."

I sat down next to her in one of the wicker chairs. After I'd outlined the story of Nelson Queah's disappearance, I said, "We know from letters Mr. Queah wrote to his wife during this time that he had learned of a plot at the dam to steal money from the Corps of Engineers by using deceptive accounting procedures. We think he was killed to keep him from going public with the story."

What I was about to say next would show my hand completely, but I was convinced it was worth the risk. "The construction project for The Dalles dam was being run by a man named Royce Townsend." I paused again and met her eyes. "I know that you were seeing him during this time."

Her eyes registered surprise. "My, you've done your homework." Then she looked down at her hands in her lap and added, "I'm a very private person, Mr. Claxton. I'm not comfortable at all talking about my past."

"I know it's difficult, and I respect that. But what if you could help rectify a great injustice? Mr. Queah was a tribal leader and a decorated war hero. The police who investigated his disappearance concluded that he got drunk and either fell into the Columbia River accidentally or killed himself. This has brought great shame to his granddaughter and his tribe. And of course, the person who murdered him has gone free all these years."

She avoided my eyes and remained silent.

Fearing I was losing her, I quickly added, "This is a just cause, Ms. Norquist. And of course, what you tell me will be held in the strictest confidence."

"Are you suggesting Royce Townsend had something to do with this man's disappearance?

"Let's just say I have reason to suspect him. Nothing's been proven, however."

She stared out at a spot on her front lawn for a while. Finally, she sighed deeply. "The singing was good. But the life wasn't. Smoky bars, lecherous drunks, patrons who didn't know blues from opera. God, I hated it. Yeah, I had a fling with Royce Townsend. I'm not proud of it. He was married." She returned her eyes to me and smiled. "I was young, self-absorbed, and very naïve."

"Weren't we all," I replied, and we shared a laugh together. "I know it was a long time ago, but do you remember Townsend saying anything about an illegal scheme at the dam, or about keeping two sets of books, anything like that?"

She rolled her eyes and laughed. "You're not kidding about it being a long time. No, I don't remember anything about *any* scam. Royce never talked shop with me." She fell silent. I could only imagine the avalanche of memories that had been triggered by my questions. When she came out of her reverie, she said, "You know, what you're implying doesn't really surprise me, at least the stealing part. Royce was always looking for the easy way, and he had a gift for getting people to do his bidding. But killing someone's a different matter. I don't think he would've gone that far."

"What if he had someone else do the killing?"

She considered the question for a moment. "Maybe, if the stakes were high enough."

"Did you know anything about Townsend being blackmailed over his affair with you?

Her eyes enlarged, and she put her hand to her mouth. "You're not serious."

"It happened. Does the name Braxton Gage ring a bell?"

The question hit her like a body blow. Her face drained of what little color it had, and her eyes narrowed down. "*He* was blackmailing Royce over me? You're kidding."

"Afraid not. He used pictures of you and Townsend together to get a fat contract at the dam and to avoid paying the kickbacks Townsend was demanding of all the other contractors."

She blew a breath out and shook her head. "I told you I was naïve. I was swimming with sharks and didn't even know it."

"How did you know Gage?"

She clenched her jaw and drew her mouth into a thin line. Her eyes smoldered. "I didn't, really. He came to several shows, seemed to like my stuff. Royce and I were having a spat at the time, so I was on the rebound. I only went out with him a couple of times."

I knew there was more. I waited.

Looking down at the table, she said in a voice I could barely hear, "That was a mistake. Braxton Gage was *not* a gentleman."

There was a long pause broken only by the whir of a neighbor's lawnmower and the cawing of a crow in the backyard. "I'm sorry," was all I could think to say. There was little doubt in my mind about what she was implying. A disgusting image of Braxton Gage forcing himself on a young and beautiful Sheri North flitted across my mind like an ugly porno clip. I wondered why Gage had put me in contact with her in the first place. Apparently, he never dreamed she'd reveal his dirty little secret.

At this point she offered me coffee, which I readily accepted. When she returned with a tray, I could see that, like a passing cloud, her anger was gone. I found myself admiring this woman. I said, "Why did you leave Portland?"

She took a sip of coffee and shrugged her shoulders. "I got pregnant. I didn't want to bring my kid up in the life, so I moved here, had the baby and got a real job." She laughed. "The rumor was I left to have an abortion, but that never entered my mind. I stayed out of the limelight and never bothered correcting the rumor. I didn't care what Portland thought of me."

She didn't mention who the father was, and something told me not to press my luck. She told me how she became a paralegal secretary and about the struggles she had bringing up a son as a single mom. She wasn't forthcoming about her son, and I saw no need to press her on that, either.

By this time I was feeling pretty disappointed. She had more or less reinforced what Gage had told me, but she sure as hell hadn't given me the smoking gun I was hoping for.

She seemed to read my mood. "I'm afraid I haven't helped you very much, have I."

"Of course you have. And I appreciate your being so candid. Remember, the confidentiality works both ways. I'm counting on your not discussing this with anyone, even your son or closest friends. Okay?"

"I was a paralegal secretary, Mr. Claxton. I understand the importance of confidentiality."

She stood, and I took my cue that it was time to leave. In the vein of small talk, I said, "Any grandchildren?"

She frowned. "No. My son was married once, but it didn't work out." Her looked turned wistful. "He lives in Idaho, and I don't get to see him nearly enough."

"Beautiful state, Idaho. Where's he located?"

"Boise, mainly, but he moves around a lot. He's a hunting guide."

I arrested a double take just in time. "Really," I said as casually as I could while I frantically tried to remember the name of the guide service Townsend had used. "I've hunted in Idaho. Used one of the guide services out of Boise, but I can't remember the name. Does he guide for one of them?"

She eyed me for an instant, and I thought maybe I'd telegraphed something. Then her look turned embarrassed. "He used to work for the Idaho Wilderness Guide Service, but they went under a while back. I've forgotten the name of his new outfit."

Her answers were vague, either because she was withholding information or she simply didn't know. I felt it was the latter, but I wasn't sure. I risked another question. "What's his name?"

"Jacob, after my father.

I gave her my broadest smile. "Well, I'll ask for him the next time I'm hunting in Idaho." I left it there, fearing that if I kept probing she'd get suspicious, if she wasn't already. I had a name and a state. That should be enough.

I thanked her again, got into my car, and as I drove away there was only one thought in my mind—*Jacob Norquist. Could he be the sniper?*

Chapter Forty-eight

When I got out of sight of Norquist's place, I pulled over and called the Wasco County Sheriff's Office in Shaniko, Oregon. Sheriff Bailey would be the right man to contact first since both Sherman Watlamet and his own deputy, Cleta Grooms, were gunned down in his jurisdiction. The other reason I called him first is that I knew he wanted the man who shot Grooms as badly as I did. Bailey wasn't there, and I left a message for him to call me. "Tell him it's urgent," I told the dispatcher at the other end.

I had a child custody hearing at the Yamhill County Courthouse that morning. I took the 99W straight north to McMinnville, and by the time I found a parking space in the courthouse lot I was wound pretty tight. Bailey hadn't returned my call. I tried him again and left a lengthy voice message this time.

When I finished I realized that my case against Jacob Norquist wasn't all that compelling and wondered how Bailey would react. Sure, as a hunter Jacob Norquist fit the profile, and Norquist was probably Townsend's illegitimate son. I knew Townsend had used guides from Idaho, too, and thanks to Braxton Gage, I had a possible explanation for the skimming at the damn, which had set this whole thing in motion. Then again, Norquist could be Gage's son, and Gage could be a clever liar.

Clearly, without a photograph to confirm he was the man I saw in Clarno I was way ahead of myself.

The custody hearing was gut-wrenching. Both parents let their antipathy for each other cloud their judgment on what was the best for two beautiful kids. I got through it, but honestly I wanted to crack their heads together.

Bailey called while I was in the hearing and left the following message: "Thanks, Mr. Claxton. I agree it's probably best to keep the mother out of this at this point. I'll try to secure an Idaho driver's license picture of Jacob Norquist. If there's more than one, I'll e-mail them all to you. If we get a match, call me at this number, and we'll go from there. Maybe the mother knows where he's hiding, since we sure as hell can't find him. Nice work."

I had to skip lunch to prepare for a DUI case that afternoon, which turned out to be a waste of time, because my client got the book thrown at him. A client who plows into the back of a police car while intoxicated is tough to defend. When I got back to the farm I was hungry but still tight as a coiled spring. I took Archie for the long run up to the Pioneer cemetery with my cell phone in tow. No calls came in, and when I got back, nothing on the computer from Bailey, either. *Damn, damn, damn.*

I was low on groceries and berated myself again for not shopping more often. After feeding Arch, I fried up two eggs in olive oil and wolfed them down with couple of pieces of toast and a beer while checking my notes from the research Fletcher Dunn and I had done. The guide service Royce Townsend had used was called the Idaho Adventure Guides and Outfitters. Of course, even if Norquist worked there, it would only *suggest* a link between him and Townsend. In any case, it would be something Bailey could check out.

Norquist's picture was key, damn it. *What the hell was taking Bailey so long?*

I checked my e-mail again. A small, spinning circle on my screen indicated an incoming message was downloading. I waited and waited, and it kept spinning and spinning. If Bailey sent me too large a digital file my computer would choke on it. My DSL phone line didn't have all that much bandwidth, after all. Sure enough, I got an error message stating that an incoming e-mail had timed out. *"Shit."*

I called Bailey again, but of course he didn't pick up. I left a message for him to only attach one photo per e-mail, and then I waited some more. Nothing happened, so I dragged my laptop upstairs, propped myself against the headboard of my bed, and tried to get caught up on my e-mail. But my mind kept turning back to the possible link between Jacob Norquist and Royce Townsend, which brought me around to another concern—if I was right about the connection, then Winona was swimming with sharks just like Sheri North fifty years earlier.

I decided to call Winona just to check in. "Hello, Cal," she answered, sounding a bit surprised to hear from me. "How are you?" I felt better just hearing her voice, although it stirred something in me better left alone.

"I'm okay." I was brimming with news but didn't dare share it with her. I figured the less she knew at this point the safer she would be. "I just wanted to check in and see how things are going."

"Oh, I've been busy collaborating with a professor up at U Dub who's studying orcas. He claims they can't survive in Puget Sound unless the salmon populations are saved. Salmon's their main food source. Now, get this—he thinks the key is removing the four dams on the lower Snake River. I've seen his data. He makes a compelling case."

"Sounds seditious. Have you cleared this with Oberführer DeSilva?"

Laughter. "Oh, shut up. I'm going to show this to Jason just as soon as I get the whole picture worked out. This is a completely new angle. I mean the fate of salmon and orcas intertwined? Think of the power of that argument, Cal."

"I see your point. Maybe something as emotionally charged as threatened orcas would stir up enough anger to get something done. After all, they're warm-blooded mammals like us." We kicked this around, and she plied me with more data and statistics than, given my agitated state, I was up for. I finally changed the subject, saying for no particular reason, "Has Timothy's mother had any more wolf dreams?"

She laughed again but with less levity. "I don't think so, but I haven't talked to her in a while. Actually, I've had a recurring wolf dream myself. I'm walking on a deserted beach and see this wolf in the distance. He turns and looks at me for a while and then trots back into the trees. That's it. Pretty weird, huh?"

"Well, I guess your totem's warning you to be careful." I tried to make it sound light, but I meant every word of it.

"Could be," she said before changing the subject. "Still nothing on the sniper, huh?"

I puffed a breath. "He seems to have vanished into thin air."

"How could he do that? I mean the terrain out there's so barren."

"It's barren, but it's vast, too. And he knows the high desert. But if he hasn't slipped out of the perimeter they've established he'll eventually run out of food and water, and they'll catch him."

She signed heavily. "Well, I hope that happens soon. God, will you ever forgive me for getting you mixed up in this?"

"Not your fault, Winona. I, uh, feel like this thing's going to break open any time now."

"Do you still feel like Braxton Gage might be behind it?"

I forced a light tone. "Oh, I certainly don't have any evidence of that. That'll be something for the police to unravel once they catch the sniper. Speaking of police, have you heard anything from your friends in Portland?"

She sighed. "Yes. As a matter of fact, I have to go back tomorrow for another interview."

"What did they say?"

"Oh, some details in my statement needed checking. I suggested we do it by phone, but that didn't go over. I talked it over with Jason and Royce, and Royce offered to have one of his attorneys sit in with me." She paused. "Do you think that's a good idea?"

"A second interview is fairly common, but I would use the attorney, Winona. They might get more aggressive this time around."

She laughed. "That's not possible."

The conversation drifted off into everyday things, and before I knew it we'd talked for over an hour. Somehow, this engendered an intimacy neither one of us intended nor expected. I was still under her spell when she apparently realized the impropriety of our lengthy, late night chat and said a hasty, almost flummoxed goodbye.

Afterwards, I lay there thinking about how nice it was to hear her voice, although I had the damn dream she described stuck in my head for some reason. Every time I closed my eyes to sleep I saw that wolf on the beach. The funny thing was, it wasn't the wolf that drew my attention. It was the beach.

I had nearly drifted off when it hit me. "*The beach!*" I cried out so loud that Archie came out of his corner barking at the top of his lungs.

I flipped the light back on, logged back on my computer, and pulled up the white pages. I'd completely forgotten about the *first* address I'd found for a Shirley Norquist—the one in the beach town of Depoe Bay. I'd skipped over it, because Gage had told me she lived inland, near Salem. What if Jacob's mother owned that house, too? A small cottage in a tiny coastal town would be an ideal hiding place for someone on the run. I pulled up a satellite image on the computer. The cottage was on a narrow, isolated road off Highway 101.

Could Jacob Norquist have slipped out of eastern Oregon and be hiding there?

I still hadn't heard from Sheriff Bailey and thought about calling him but decided against it. My hunch was a long shot, and even if he bought it, I was sure things would move at glacial speed at best. He'd have to arrange to send in some local cops or the State Police to have a look, and he wouldn't do that without some kind of confirmation from me.

I wasn't in a glacial speed kind of mood.

I thought about the fact that Shirley Norquist had brought her son Jacob up in the small town of Independence. He must have gone to the local high school. High schools have yearbooks with lots of photographs. A few minutes later I was scanning a montage of photos for the Central High School Panthers' yearbook on the Internet. I found a formal picture of Jacob from 1979, his senior year—a nice looking kid with a narrow face and large eyes, like I remembered. But I wasn't positive. Then I found a candid shot of him bearing his nickname, Jake. His face was turned to the side, revealing a prominent nose. The smiling kid I was looking at was maybe twenty-five years younger than the man I'd glimpsed that day near Watlamet's ranch. But I was pretty damn sure he was the guy.

It was an easy decision. I could be in Depoe Bay before the sun came up to see if I could spot Jacob Norquist and seal the deal. Hell, I wasn't going to get any sleep now, anyway.

Chapter Forty-nine

I made a thermos of coffee and put Philip's .357 Magnum, a flashlight, and a pair of field glasses in a backpack. The satellite images showed a small, square house and stand-alone garage well south of the Depoe Bridge on a narrow road on the east side of Highway 101. There were several other houses on the road with ample space between them. About a quarter mile south, another narrow road ran parallel to the one of interest. A patch of densely forested land lay between the two. If I parked on the second street, I might be able to work my way through the trees and find a spot to watch the back of the cabin from a safe distance.

The plan made sense, but I was mindful of my last encounter with this guy. I paused for a moment and had to chuckle. What was that old military saying? Something about battle plans never surviving contact with the enemy. Well, my plan was once again to *avoid* contact with the enemy.

I made great time on Highway 18 and after cresting the Coastal Range began to follow the twisting path of the Salmon River. Except for a barred owl that flapped through my headlights like a low flying drone, I had the road to myself until an empty logging truck roared up behind me and rode my bumper clear into Otis, where I turned south on 101, and he thankfully turned north. I crossed the bridge into Depoe Bay shortly after five a.m., but it took another ten minutes to find the road the cabin was on, which was set off from the highway and unmarked. I missed it twice. On the third pass, I cruised by and turned left at the next road, which had only two summer rentals on it, both of which looked vacant. I parked at the cul-de-sac and walked back to a point that would put me roughly in line with the Norquist cabin one street over.

I could barely see my hand in front of my face as I moved into the forest understory. Using a couple of short bursts of the flashlight, I saw what I was up against—sword ferns, silal, dense patches of Oregon grape, to say nothing of closely-spaced cedars and hemlocks. I saw no poison oak, but who knew going forward? I tried to plod straight ahead, but the going was tough, and I found myself zigzagging so much I almost lost my bearings several times in the thick undergrowth.

I was a good way in when a faint light flickered through the trees from the direction of the cabin. I moved another step, stopped, and it went off. *Shit. Is that light moving toward me?* I took another step, and the light winked back on. I stopped and pulled the Magnum out of my backpack as the hair on the back of my neck turned to wire. I stood still and watched. The light remained stationary. I took a step, and it went out again. I relaxed and let a breath out. The light wasn't moving. It was *my* movement through the trees that created the illusion. I put the gun in my belt and trudged forward as quietly as I could.

I reached the edge of the forested area maybe fifteen minutes later. The light that had guided me was above the back door of the Norquist cabin. The rest of the structure was shrouded in deep shadow. I found a spot behind a red cedar whose trunks had twinned, leaving a narrow gap affording what I hoped would be a good view of the cabin. A thick patch of silal further concealed my perch, which was maybe forty yards out.

I took off my backpack and poured myself a steaming cup of black coffee. I sipped the strong brew, although I didn't need the caffeine. If I had been any more wired, I would have been glowing. There were no sounds except for the occasional high-pitched *creek, creek, creek* of a colony of frogs, which overlay a rhythmic chorus of crickets. The low wattage bulb above the back door stared back at me like an indifferent eye, and nothing moved in or around the place. The light meant there was a good chance someone was home, I told myself.

Let's see what the morning brings.

The first hint of dawn came when I noticed the bloody scratches on my forearms from the hike in. I was crouched behind the double-trunk cedar with what turned out to be an excellent, if sharply angled view of the back of the cabin. I watched through a pair of binoculars as the structure began to slowly emerge out of the shadows like someone was pulling a curtain back. Features closest to me revealed themselves first—a wrought iron table and chairs, a gas barbeque, a kitchen window. The barbeque was uncovered, another hint someone might be staying at the cabin.

My pulse ticked up when a vent pipe on the roof began emitting a thin wisp of steam. I checked my watch. It was six-thirty on the nose. It could be someone had awakened or the response to an automatic timer on a thermostat. A set of French doors that opened onto the patio appeared next, then another window, and finally, the back of a freestanding garage next to the house. As the light came up, I focused a gap through the curtains on the French doors, which promised a partial view of one room inside the house, probably the dining room.

As the shadows resolved into shapes, I made out a couple of chairs at a table with two glasses on it and what looked like an armchair in the far corner of the room. I put the binoculars down and waited for more light. When I looked back I stopped breathing for several beats.

Was someone sitting in that chair?

I couldn't quite tell. I retreated back into the woods for better cover, moved fifty feet to my right, and repositioned myself. The light and the angle were better now as I focused the binoculars again on the inside of that room.

Someone *was* sitting there. The head of this person was still not clearly visible, but it was lolled to one side at a disturbing angle. I moved in a little closer, waited for more light, and refocused.

The image, now sufficiently clear, made me flash back to the grisly discovery of Sherman Watlamet. A man sat in that armchair, and the side of his face and most of his shirt were stained the color of oxidized blood.

Chapter Fifty

From the front page of *The Oregonian* the following day—

Body of Suspected Killer Found

DEPOE BAY, Oregon—An Oregon State Police spokesman reported that a man named Jacob Norquist of Boise, Idaho, was found dead inside a house in Depoe Bay on Wednesday, April 3. The body was found by state troopers at approximately 8:45 a.m. following a tip from an undisclosed source. The spokesman said that the cause of death was under investigation, but initial indications suggested that the victim used a handgun to take his own life with a single shot to the head.

Dubbed the "Oregon Sniper" in the media, Norquist was the subject of an intensive manhunt in the Northwest. An itinerant hunting and fishing guide, he was wanted in connection with the recent murder of one person and the wounding of another near Clarno, Oregon. Both victims had been shot at long range with a high caliber rifle. The victims were Sherman Watlamet, killed on March 16, and Deputy Sheriff Cleta Grooms, wounded on March 24. Norquist is also a suspect in the bludgeoning death of Cecil Ferguson of Portland and the attempted murder of Calvin Claxton III of Dundee, Oregon. The spokesman said the motives for these crimes have not been fully determined at this time, and it is not known whether others were involved.

A rifle matching the caliber of the weapon used in the shootings in Wasco County was recovered at the scene along with undisclosed physical evidence connecting Norquist with at least one of the crime scenes. The house in which the victim's body was found belongs to his mother, Shirley Norquist, of Independence, Oregon. According to the spokesman, Ms. Norquist is cooperating with the investigation and stated that she was not aware her son had taken refuge at her beach cabin. Ms. Norquist could not be reached for comment. The spokesman also indicated that a witness has positively identified the victim as the man seen leaving the murder scene in Wasco County.

Asked to comment on the death of Norquist, Oregon State Police Captain Harvey Patterson said, "Thanks to the diligent police work and outstanding interagency cooperation between the Oregon State Police and other jurisdictions, we believe another criminal is off the streets of Oregon. We were closing in on Mr. Norquist, and apparently he realized this and decided to take his own life. We're all a little safer now."

Anyone with information related to these crimes is encouraged to contact the Oregon State Police or the Sheriff's Department in Shaniko, Oregon.

Chapter Fifty-one

Two Weeks Later

An irritating sound began ricocheting down the deep well I was in. I tried to will it to silence, but it was insistent. *My phone.* The first thing I thought of was my daughter, Claire. Has something happened? It wasn't Claire. It was Philip. "Can you bust free?" he said the moment I quit fumbling and managed to put my ear to the phone.

"*What?* Jesus, Philip, what the hell time is it?"

"It's four-thirty. You want to fish? I had a party cancel on me and sent my guides home. I'm on the Deschutes with an empty boat."

I exhaled a breath and tried to clear my head. "Uh, I don't know if I can get away."

"Aw, come on, Cal. The weather looks great."

My mind started to clear. "Is the salmon fly hatch on?"

He chuckled at my fishing naiveté. "No. It's too early, but the fishing's still good, man."

"I, uh, would have to rearrange some things and get Gertie to feed Archie."

"No problem. I've got some repairs I can work on, so I'll just hang here until you arrive."

He left me no out. Philip had a way of doing that. "Okay. See you in three hours."

After sending off a volley of e-mails to clear my schedule, I began to pack my gear. When the inevitable feelings of guilt and anxiety arrived, I took a breath and told myself my business would be there when I got back. After all, this was the Deschutes River. It occurred to me that my old self—that uptight prosecutor lusting for glory down in L.A.—would have never, ever agreed to something this spontaneous.

Apparently, I was starting to get the hang of this Oregon thing.

◇◇◇

We put in at the Warm Springs Reservation, which stretches better than twenty miles down the west side of the river, a pristine section of the Deschutes off limits to all but tribe members and their guests. Our plan was to amble downriver with the intent of catching some native rainbows, called redsides for the hue dominating their iridescent sides.

It turned out Philip had exaggerated a bit—the fishing wasn't that great, at least for me. The fish were "looking down," as they say, meaning they weren't looking up for bugs on the surface of the river, where we hoped to fool them with Philip's hand-crafted flies. But that was okay. There would be plenty of time to talk, something Philip and I hadn't done face to face since I discovered Jacob Norquist's body in his mother's beach house.

I was back at the boat after working what looked like a good stretch of water but without any luck. I poured myself a cup of coffee and watched as Philip fished his way upstream along a grassy bank. Meanwhile, an osprey across the river was busy building a nest atop a bone white, forty-foot snag. I turned back to Philip just as his four-weight rod bent double. It was the second redside he'd taken along the bank. Apparently the fish were only looking down for me. He held the fish up for a moment before releasing it.

I called across the water, "You gave me your defective flies, didn't you."

He shrugged, showing his palms. "They were free, weren't they?"

I laughed. "I'm hungry. Let's eat."

We found a place to eat out in the open, the spring sun warm on our skin. "So how does it feel not to have to watch your back?" Philip asked as he took a bite of sandwich.

"Good. There's something about the threat of getting your head blown off that wears on you. By the way, I forgot to give you your Magnum. It's in my car. Thanks for the loan."

He shot me a look bordering on exasperation. "You know, you really ought to get yourself a gun."

I rolled my eyes. "Why? The damn things make me nervous. Actually, I ought to feel a lot better than I do about having Norquist off the board, but this isn't over. And he didn't kill himself, either."

"The gun that killed him was found in his hand. What more do you want?"

"Oh, right. A cheap thirty-two with the serial number filed off. No way Norquist uses a street gun like that, even to kill himself. You, of all people, should understand that. I mean, they found his rifle in the house, meticulously cleaned and oiled. No suicide note, either." Philip flashed me a skeptical look that annoyed the hell out of me. "I talked to Norquist's mother at length afterwards. She's not buying the suicide, either."

"So what happened then?"

"Someone shot him, then put the gun in his hand and squeezed off a second round. That way he's got powder residue on his hand."

"And then they replaced the bullet to make it look like only one shot was fired?"

"Something like that. It's done on TV all the time."

"Where'd the second round go?"

"Who the hell knows? They didn't find anything at the cabin. The killer probably opened the French doors and popped one into the woods behind the cabin."

Philip nodded and paused for a couple of beats. "What about his truck? They ever find it?"

I shook my head. "Nope. He stole another one in Spray. Drove it right through their roadblocks. Go figure."

We ate in silence for a while, and then I said, "At least the evidence proving he was the shooter is tight. I saw him leaving Watlamet's ranch, the boot tracks you picked up there and in that canyon matched the boots he was wearing when they found him, and the bullet that killed Watlamet was fired from his Remington. The one you found in Grooms' vest was too flattened for a match, but it was the right caliber. By the way, Bailey said that was the slickest tracking job he'd ever seen."

Philip allowed himself a modest smile. "That wasn't much. My grandfather tracked a wounded elk in a rainstorm once." He sipped his coffee. "You identified the body, I guess."

I exhaled. "Yeah. Funny thing about that. I didn't feel the anger I expected when I saw him. Just pity. He, uh, looked like he was at peace, you know? And I got this feeling—it just came over me—that he'd been manipulated somehow. It was weird."

Philip nodded knowingly. "The dead speak to us sometimes, Cal." He paused to unwrap another sandwich. "So, what are you going to do about the rich dude in Portland and Braxton Gage and the whole mess at the dam fifty years ago that started this?"

I shrugged. "I don't know. Truth is, there isn't much I can do. Everything I have is hearsay or came from someone who's dead now. I told the cops everything I dug up."

"And they're stymied?"

"Completely. Bailey told me they're taking a hard look at Royce Townsend, but he has an ironclad alibi for the night Norquist died, and nothing else has turned up showing any recent contact between him and Norquist."

"What about Ferguson? He made that first call to *someone*, right? No record of that?"

"No, and that fits because Ferguson bragged to me that he used a pay phone."

"But he wouldn't tell you who he called, even though Waltlamet was his buddy?"

"Right. His screwed-up code of honor wouldn't let him. Anyway, Townsend admitted to using Norquist as a hunting guide numerous times over the years. But there's no law against that. I told Bailey he could be Norquist's father, but Shirley Norquist isn't talking about that, and there isn't probable cause to force a DNA test. I assume they're also questioning Townsend's son, Jason, and his political team, but that'll take some time."

"What about that son of a bitch Gage? Maybe he was the one Watlamet was going to expose. That kind of publicity, even if it came from some hermit Indian, would ruin his chances at doing a casino deal with the Tribes. My father tells me the Governor's on the fence. A piece of bad publicity about one of the players would help kill the deal."

I nodded, thinking not only of Braxton Gage, but his business manager, Stephanie Barrett, and the fire in her eyes when she warned me about making trouble for them. "You're right, the stakes are high for Gage, too, but there doesn't seem to be any connection between Norquist and him, except that he knew Norquist's mother back when the dam was being built."

Philip smiled, but his face turned grim. "Yeah, well, I'd like to see that bastard go down in flames and take the casino deal with him. I have the greatest respect for my father, but a casino in the Gorge is the worst idea I've ever heard of."

We kicked this around for a while, and then Philip changed the subject, saying out of the blue, "What's going on with you and my cousin?"

I shot him a look. "*Nothing's* going on. She's engaged to be married."

He raised an eyebrow and smiled. "I meant your *business* arrangement. You still working for her?"

I managed to suppress a sheepish smile. "Uh, not officially. But I'm worried about her because of her proximity to Royce Townsend. She's going to be a member of his family, for Christ's sake. I don't like it."

"Have you told her what you suspect?"

"Well, she knows about the connection and all, from the newspaper accounts. She called me, and I filled her in on the details but didn't connect any dots. She seemed relieved that the sniper was dead, but that was about it. I think she's in denial, what with the engagement and the Senate race and everything."

Philip considered this for a long time. "Maybe you've done enough, my friend. You've brought Winona the peace of knowing what really happened to her grandfather. You figured out who the sniper was and where he was holed up. Maybe it's time to let it go, and besides, Winona's a big girl. She can take care of herself."

"Maybe you're right."

At the time I think I really meant it.

Chapter Fifty-two

I found myself buried in court appearances and depositions during the following week. I was locking up my office after a particularly busy day when the phone on my desk rang. I dashed back in and caught it on the fourth ring.

A familiar voice said, "Cal? I'm glad I caught you. It's Jason Townsend. How are you?"

He went on to invite me to what he described as an important meeting of his closest advisors for that Friday night. I told him I hardly qualified as an advisor, let alone a close one, but he insisted I come. He was evasive about the purpose of the meeting but managed to pique my curiosity. I told him I'd be there.

The meeting was at his father's estate on the Willamette River. It was seven in the evening, and the horses were in the stable, although stable seemed an inadequate term—'palatial equine structure' would be more accurate. Plum trees in full flower lined the drive, and the manicured pasture to my left looked like a fairway at the Masters, even in the fading light. I parked my car on cobblestones, followed the murmur of voices around the side of the house, and let myself onto the patio through a gate covered with English ivy.

I knew some of the players by now, but the throng of supporters had grown considerably. The professor from Lewis and Clark was huddled with the emigration activist and the Portland artist.

They were speaking in low, conspiratorial tones. The rest of the group, including Winona, was gathered around Sam DeSilva. I didn't see Jason Townsend or his father, Royce. When DeSilva saw me, he broke from the group and came toward me like a heat-seeking missile.

"You've got a lot of nerve showing your face here, Claxton."

"It's nice to see you, too, Sam."

The color in his neck deepened a shade, and the healed scratch marks on his face turned purple. "You're the one who suggested to the police that Royce might've had some connection to that crazy bastard Norquist, aren't you?"

"What I told the police is none of your business."

"Well, we kept the lid on the publicity, but it could have crippled the campaign. Why don't you just turn around and get the fuck out of here?"

"I'm an invited guest," I answered and brushed past him.

Winona saw the encounter and came up next to me. "What was *that* all about?" She looked anxious, but there was a fragment of something new in her eyes as well, something I couldn't read.

"Oh, just Sam being Sam. So, this doesn't feel like another political strategy meeting. What's up, anyway?"

Her smile turned bittersweet. "I'll let Jason tell you."

As if on cue, Royce Townsend and his wife came out of the house with Jason Townsend walking between them. The gathered supporters of the campaign turned to face them and fell silent. Obviously, they'd sensed the same vibe I had. Winona took her place beside Jason, taking his hand.

Jason cleared his throat, let go of Winona's hand, and stepped forward. "Good evening, folks. Thanks for coming on such short notice." He glanced back nervously at his father, who stared straight ahead like a stone statue. His stepmother had a glued on smile that hinted something awkward might be afoot. In contrast, Winona looked serene. "I also want to thank you for the support you've given me over these past months. The advice, the hard work, the campaign contributions, it's all been incredible. I'm deeply honored that you find me worthy to represent you in the U.S. Senate, and that's what I want to talk about tonight. I, uh, have an important announcement to make and wanted you to be the first to hear it."

Out of the corner of my eye I saw Sam shift his feet nervously, a puzzled look on his face.

Jason focused on something behind the group, and the easy, boyish charm he'd always exuded seemed gone. In its place was the look of a man who'd come to terms with a difficult decision. "I believe it was Plato who said, 'The life which is unexamined in not worth living.' Well, I've examined my life and decided to make some changes and own up to some things." He paused for a moment and brought his gaze back to the group. "Effective immediately, I've decided to drop out of the race."

The group gasped in near perfect unison and then went silent. I heard a horse whinny out in the barn. *"What?"* Sam DeSilva said, stepping forward. Smiling in disbelief, it was clear he hoped what he'd just heard was a joke. The smile disintegrated as he and Jason stood looking at each other. "You can't do this," he said, shifting his eyes to Royce Townsend. "Royce, what the hell's going on? Tell him he can't just up and quit. He's a lock to win this damn thing. Tell him, Royce."

Royce Townsend looked straight ahead and didn't answer.

"What about the money these people donated? Have you thought of *that*?" Sam's face was flushed. A glistening thread of spittle dangled from the corner of his mouth.

Jason wrinkled his brow and shook his head as if he were dismissing the antics of a small child. He said, "Sam, would you be quiet, please? You know very well we haven't spent that much from our war chest. We'll be glad to refund people's donations. But I'm not finished." He turned and offered his hand to Winona, who took it and stepped forward, a nervous smile on her face.

My chest tightened, and I swallowed hard.

"Winona and I have made a joint decision to end our engagement."

A collective groan rippled across the group. The Hispanic activist cried out, "Oh, no!"

Jason raised his hand in a calming gesture. "Please, it's the best thing for both of us. We remain the best of friends." Then he turned to Winona and added, "We both know now that we entered into the engagement for the wrong reasons."

Winona smiled and nodded her encouragement.

The economics professor said, "What are you going to do now?"

Jason stood there for a moment as if he'd been waiting for that particular question. His lips traced a faint smile. "I plan to serve out my term in the Oregon Senate and then decide what's next. I, I'm really not sure I'm cut out for politics." He paused for a couple of beats. "And I plan to live my life as an openly gay man."

The room went completely silent. Jason continued, "I want to be clear about one thing—I'm not dropping out because I'm gay. I'm just not sure politics is what I want to do the rest of my life."

By this time, Sam DeSilva looked like a balloon with its air let out. He stepped unsteadily up to Jason and said in a low voice, "After all I've done for you, this is how you repay me? I was handing you a Senate seat on a platter, and this is how you react? You're going back to that little faggot Hanson?"

A collective groan rose from the assembled guests. Jason stood his ground, regarding Sam with a look of pity. Then another voice said, "Sam, I think it would be best if you left now." It was Royce Townsend. His tone left no room for misinterpretation.

Sam spun on his heels and walked out, muttering to himself.

I looked around just in time to see Winona disappear into the house with the Townsends. I stayed around, hoping she'd come back out of the house. I wanted to reassure myself she was okay. None of the others left right away, either. There was a need to talk, the jarring news seeming to forge a new level of camaraderie among Jason's spurned supporters. It was safe to say no one saw this coming.

I gave up after fifteen minutes. I was fumbling for my keys next to my car in the darkness when I heard a voice behind me. "Cal, is that you?"

It was Winona.

Chapter Fifty-three

I turned and saw Winona's silhouette backlit by a landscape light. I said, "Oh, hi. I was just leaving."

She wove her way through a bed of rhododendrons, and when she stopped in front of me I caught a hint of lavender from her hair. "I'm glad I caught you, Cal. Jason and his father are having another, um, discussion. I came with him tonight, and I'm exhausted. Do you suppose you could give me a lift home?"

When we got out to the road, I said, "Look, we're closer to my place. Why don't you come to the Aerie? You can sleep in my guest room, and I'll take you back in the morning, after I feed you a proper breakfast."

"Do you make pancakes?"

"I think I can manage that."

"Okay, the Aerie it is."

She was asleep before we reached the Pacific Highway. When we got to the Aerie, I nudged her gently to wake her and led her up the stairs to the guest room. I started to leave, but she turned and put her arms around my neck. I kept my distance for a few awkward moments as my resolve left me like so much smoke in the wind. She tugged softly on my neck, and our bodies met, tentatively at first, and then full on with a hungry urgency. I could feel her heart pounding, her breath entering and leaving her lungs. I began kissing her face, her hair, her eyes, the soft hollows of her neck. We rolled on our sides and undressed each other, flinging the clothes on either side of the bed, and then we were joined. I abandoned any hope of slowing myself down, the end coming like the breaking of a dam on some river in my mind.

Afterwards, there were few words. We slept deeply, pressed against each other. In the morning we made love again, this time more slowly.

While I made breakfast, Winona began pouring her heart out about Jason Townsend and the decision they'd finally come to. To me, it was something personal between them, and I wasn't sure how much I really wanted to hear, although I listened without protest. At one point, though, curiosity got the better of me. I said, "If he hadn't come out, would you have gone through with the marriage?"

She was sitting at the breakfast table, looking fresh and beautiful. The valley pulsed with color, and highlights from the morning sun rippled in her hair. She paused for a moment. "I don't really know. I loved Jason in an admiring kind of way—not romantically—and I thought he loved me. I figured that might be enough, that it would be something to build on. But when you and I talked after David left, I began to look at the situation differently, although I think on some level I already knew. There was something about David, you know? He and I agreed on the issues, but I always got this vibe from him. He was so, so protective of Jason." She paused again, wrinkled her brow, then chuckled. "At the time, I chalked it to loyalty, but it was jealousy, wasn't it."

I nodded. "It went way beyond loyalty."

She smiled, shaking her head. "You were carrying quite a secret around. How did you find out about Jason and David in the first place?"

"I happened to overhear a conversation between them that made me wonder. Then when I took David home after his fight with Sam, I got him to admit he and Jason were lovers."

"Why didn't you tell me?"

"I struggled with that. Part of me wanted to, you know, maybe break you two up. But I couldn't do it. It just wasn't any of my business. Hell, for all I knew, Jason was being perfectly open with you."

Winona came over to the stove and hugged me. "Well, thanks for the discretion. I'm afraid I might have shot the messenger."

I laughed. "That possibility certainly crossed my mind. At the very least, I wanted to keep you as a friend."

We polished off two batches of pancakes while managing to keep the banter light. Afterwards, Winona went to the window and gazed out at the valley. Not one to shrink from delicate subjects, she said, "This place is beautiful but so *isolated*, like you've been exiled or something." She turned around and faced me. "But I can understand wanting to be alone after what happened down in Los Angeles."

I swallowed hard and nodded. "I had to get away from myself. At least the self I used to be." I made a sweeping gesture with my arm. "This seemed to be the best way to do that. Arch and I have everything we need up here."

She smiled and met my eyes. "Is this the new Cal speaking?"

I thought for a moment. "You'll have to be the judge of that." Then I asked, "What caused Jason's epiphany, anyway?"

She hesitated for a moment, considering, no doubt, whether to let me get away with changing the subject. She shrugged. "I began to see how he was being manipulated by his father and Sam. The last straw for me was when he caved on the dam removal plank. We had a long talk after that. I told him if he didn't start standing up to them, I'd break the engagement and quit the campaign."

"I'll bet you didn't expect him to go as far as he did."

"Oh, my God, no! I was shocked when he told me. But now I'm so proud of him. He's determined to find out who he really is." She hesitated and then added, "And I'm relieved, too."

I hoped she might elaborate on the last part, and I knew she was like me, so I waited. Matters of the heart didn't come easily for either of us.

Reading my mind again, she made a face at me and sighed. "Of course, things got complicated after I met you. I tried really hard to shut you out, but it didn't seem to work."

"I have that effect on women."

Her laughter put to flight two towhees at the feeder out on the deck. "In your dreams, Cal Claxton." Then she tossed a wet dishrag at me.

We were out on the porch having coffee when my cell phone rang.

"Mr. Claxton? This is Shirley Norquist. I hope I didn't call too early."

"Not at all," I told her, my mind snapping to attention. Why was Jacob Norquist's mother calling me?

"I wanted to thank you again for your kind words after I lost Jacob. You had every reason to be angry, I suppose, but you showed forgiveness, and I appreciate that."

"If what I said comforted you, I'm glad."

She paused before going on. "But that's not why I called. I just received two boxes from the guide service my son worked for over in Boise. They contain some of his belongings from the last camp he stayed at before he came to Oregon. There're some papers, too. I opened the boxes but couldn't bring myself to sort through it all, but I figured someone should. They might shed light on what really happened to Jacob."

"Have the police gone through the stuff?"

"I have no idea."

"Have you talked to the State Police about this?"

"No. And I don't intend to, at least right now. They've made up their minds about my son. Besides, if they find anything embarrassing, it'll wind up in the papers." She paused again, and I knew what was coming. "I was hoping you'd be willing to take a look at the boxes, Mr. Claxton. Maybe advise me about what to do."

I agreed to have a look and told her I'd drive over that morning. I could imagine the Idaho guide service wanting to shed themselves of any and all things associated with Jacob Norquist and wasn't that surprised that the belongings had apparently been overlooked by the Idaho police. Shirley Norquist was mired in deep denial, too.

I snapped my cell shut and turned to Winona. "Want to take a ride?"

Chapter Fifty-four

On the way down to Independence I began filling Winona in on what I'd learned just before finding Norquist's body. "Thanks to Philip's father, Braxton Gage met with me to discuss the events at the dam fifty years ago. Gage's a crusty old bastard, but he managed to convince me that Royce Townsend was the most likely person behind the money skimming operation."

Winona sucked in a quick breath. The significance of what I just said wasn't lost on her. "My God, you mean Royce could have been the one who ordered Ferguson to kill my grandfather?"

"That's my best theory. But the trouble is, it rests on my believing what Gage told me, and that's not exactly a safe bet. Gage's version gets byzantine, too. He hired a private detective, because Townsend was rumored to be sleeping with Shirley Norquist, who was a very hot blues singer at the time. He used some juicy photos of the two of them to get the major cement supply contract at the dam." I had to chuckle. "Gage bragged about it to me. But Townsend apparently outsmarted him and talked Ferguson into keeping a double set of books on Gage's accounts. Gage thinks it almost had to have been Townsend who turned Ferguson."

We rode in silence for a considerable distance. I could only imagine what was going through her head. She said, "All this time, I've focused my hatred on Cecil Ferguson. But he was just a pawn in this deal. Is there other evidence pointing to Royce?"

"He used Norquist as a hunting guide back in the day, but he denies any recent connection. There's a good chance Norquist is his illegitimate son."

"Oh, my God. That can be checked, right?"

"They certainly have Norquist's DNA, but they'd have to compel Townsend, and there's no probable cause at this point. And it's a link, not a smoking gun."

"What about his mother? She must know who the father is?"

I exhaled a breath in frustration. "I told her to tell the police about the affair and all, but she's frozen right now, doesn't want anything coming out about her past. Hell, she hasn't really accepted the fact that her son was a cold-blooded killer."

Winona leaned back in her seat, her face suddenly pale and drawn. "How many times has Royce Townsend hugged me and called me dear? And, you know, his touch always felt strange, almost creepy." A noticeable shiver coursed through her body. "I just chalked it up to him being a fading lady's man. Should have gone with my gut."

"Nothing's proven," I reminded her.

The color returned to her face along with that warrior look of resolve that I'd seen before. "Yeah, well, not everything needs to be proved."

I was shocked when Shirley Norquist opened the door. Sad-eyed, pale, and wan, she'd aged a dozen years. Burying your son after having his picture plastered across the newspapers with headlines screaming that he was the "Oregon Sniper" will do that to you. She led us to a back bedroom that had obviously been her son's when he was growing up. Instead of athletes and rock stars on the wall, there were pictures of big horn sheep, grizzlies, and elk. The trophies on a shelf above the bed had rifles and targets on them, not balls and bats. She waved at two large boxes on the bed. "It's all there." Then she excused herself. I didn't blame her. The room must have been haunted with memories.

I shut the bedroom door, relieved that she had left the room. I didn't want her witnessing us handling her son's possessions, which could turn out to be state's evidence. My intent was to look things over without disturbing anything. If I saw something of potential interest, I'd advise her to call in the police, despite her misgivings.

I pulled two pairs of latex gloves from my briefcase and handed Winona a pair. "Better wear these."

She gave me a conspiratorial smile. "Gee, this is getting exciting."

I opened the top of the box on my left and nodded toward the other box. "Take that one. Remove everything gently and lay the contents on the bed. When we finish, we'll put everything back the way we found it." I winked at her. "This never happened."

My box contained a pile of scruffy clothes that needed laundering, an assortment of camping gear—including a propane stove, day pack and small espresso coffee pot—and a half empty carton of Camel cigarettes. There was a large collection of creased and dog-eared paperbacks, some Hemingway and Clancy, but mostly George Pelecanos. Norquist's name was scrawled in each of them. **Jake Norquist.** I thumbed through the books and found a couple of snapshots of him with a woman I took to be his former wife. In one, he knelt next to a five-point buck, and she stood on the other side of the dead animal cradling a rifle. They looked very happy.

"Not much here," Winona said, looking over the items she'd unpacked—a heavy jacket, a pair of mud-encrusted boots, and an assortment of toiletries. She fished out a bulging, legal-sized envelope, opened it, and removed the papers. "Looks like bills and correspondence." She peeled off half the stack, handed it to me, and began leafing through the other half. "What am I looking for?"

"Any connection between Norquist and the outside world, especially Oregon. Names, dates, anything unusual. Bear in mind that he shot Sherman Watlamet on March 16th. That's when it all started. Whoever hired him to hit Watlamet had to have contacted him just a few days earlier, because that's when Watlamet called Ferguson, which set the whole thing off."

She nodded and started sorting through her stack. I sat down in a chair in the corner and began going through mine, a collection of bills, receipts, and lists of things that needed doing around the campsite. The lists were in Norquist's handwriting, and most of the items were dutifully checked off. I scanned his credit card and cell phone bills carefully but saw nothing that caught my attention. "Nothing here," I finally said.

Winona looked up and frowned. "I'm not finding anything either. This is all local stuff. He was close to the edge financially. His checking account shows a balance of $108.52 at the end of February. There's a letter from his ex-wife, too, complaining that he's four months behind in his alimony."

"Sounds like a man who could use a good payday."

She nodded. "I'll bet they knew he needed money." She sifted through the last of the papers and found a folded piece of notepaper on the bottom of the stack. She unfolded it, and her eyebrows went up as she read it. "It's dated March 14th." She handed it to me. "Look at this."

In the now familiar scrawl, I read—

1. *Clean rifle and pack ammo*
2. *Tell Jimmy to feed horses*
3. *Pack light camp gear*
4. *Guesthouse 9 pm*

"Huh," I said, "the last entry says he planned to meet someone at a guesthouse on the night of the fourteenth. That's probably where he got his marching orders on Watlamet."

Winona looked up, her eyes suddenly larger. "*Guesthouse?* Oh, my God, Cal."

I looked at her. "What?"

"There's a guesthouse on the Townsend's estate in Silverton. I know. I stayed there once."

I put the slip of paper down. "Silverton? Near the park with all the waterfalls?"

"Yes, the Townsends have acreage there, on the road between the town and the park. Their country estate," she said, enclosing the last phrase in air quotes.

"They refer to it as 'the guesthouse'?"

"Yes. That's what Jason called it. *The* guesthouse."

I nodded. "Could be the place. Norquist didn't jot down an address, which implies he knew the location. He'd worked for Townsend. He could have known where it was."

Her eyes flashed with excitement. "Yes, and he probably stayed there for at least one night. The police should search it. Maybe Norquist left something behind—a fingerprint, DNA, *something*. That would prove the connection between Townsend and him right before the killings started, wouldn't it?"

"It would make him a prime suspect, for sure. But I doubt there's a judge in Oregon who would issue a search warrant on the basis of that one reference. Besides, if he was there, it's been a while. They may have cleaned up the place."

We finished our search a few minutes later without finding anything else that looked even remotely interesting. I showed Shirley Norquist the note and told her it could be important because of the date. She read it, then looked up with a furrowed brow. "This is all you found?"

I nodded. "But the reference to the guesthouse might mean something to someone, you know, a useful lead." I didn't want her to know anything more than that.

She looked at me, a flicker of hope stirring in her eyes. "So I should tell the police."

"Definitely."

She glanced at Winona, then back at me. "Should I mention you?"

"Tell them you found the note and showed it to me and asked my advice. Better not to say we found it."

She sighed. The hope in her eyes faded as fast as it had appeared. Deep down she must have known the truth, that her son was a murderer, and that this scrap of evidence would do nothing to alter that harsh fact. But she seemed to hope against hope for some kind of miracle. The duty of a mother, I suppose.

"I'm sorry, Ms. Norquist, but that's all we found."

As we were leaving, she placed a hand on my arm and met my eyes. "Jacob was a good man, Mr. Claxton. I just can't believe he did something like this." Winona squeezed her hand, and I hugged her. I liked this woman, even though her son had nearly killed me twice.

◇◇◇

We rode in silence for a while, and then Winona turned to me. *"That's it?* That's all we're going to do?"

"Look, let's give her some time to report this. I'll call the police this afternoon and tell them I asked you about the note, and you came up with the guesthouse connection. That'll close the loop. Maybe it's enough to motivate them to go for a search warrant." My response felt frustratingly weak, but I couldn't think of a better course of action.

Winona didn't respond, but I could feel her glare on the side of my face as I watched the oncoming traffic. I knew damn well she wasn't the type to let the grass grow under her feet, and I should have known she'd take matters into her own hands.

Chapter Fifty-five

I dropped Winona at her place in the Pearl. "I'll call you just as soon as I talk to the police," I told her. She kissed me and got out, then looked back at me after she'd climbed the steps leading to her loft. Her look made it clear she was disappointed. Who did she think I was, some kind of Rambo private eye? *Jeez*

When I arrived at the farm, Archie was up on the north fence line with Santos. Not one to sit around and wait for instructions in my absence, Santos was busy trimming a row of unruly forsythia bushes. My dog made a beeline for my car and when I got out and knelt down to greet him, nearly knocked me over before slathering me with kisses. He was getting big and strong, that pup of mine. I greeted Santos and told him about the employment opportunity with Fletcher Dunn. "Lake Oswego?" he said. "Uh, how would I get there?"

"If you want the job, we'll work something out. It's not that far from where you live in Newberg." He said he could use the money, and I even got a smile out of him.

I called Sheriff Bailey that afternoon and explained the situation surrounding the discovered scrap of paper dated March 14th. He listened quietly until I finished. "We sure as hell know that Norquist didn't act on his own, and I know you think this fella Townsend's behind it. But what you got here's pretty thin, Cal. Tell you what, I'll call the State Police and see what they think. They'd have to generate the warrant to search that guesthouse. By the way, they asked Townsend for a cheek swab, and his lawyer told them to pack sand."

I thanked him and signed off. It was pretty much what I expected. Winona didn't pick up, so I left a message. I tried to sound optimistic that something would get done, but I doubt if I did. Spin was not one of my strong suits.

Santos and I got in a couple of basketball games before his dad picked him up, and I sent him home with *Endurance*, the story of Shackleton's Antarctic voyage. "This'll show you what real toughness is," I told him. I called Winona, and the call went to voice mail again. I wondered why she wasn't answering. Archie was lobbying hard for a run, and when I finally sat down on the porch to put on my jogging shoes he began barking and spinning in circles in front of me.

The hill leading up to the pioneer cemetery seemed especially steep that day. By the time we summited, I stopped, hands on hips, gasping for air. The sun was out, but a line of dirty gray clouds skimmed across the valley, and I figured there was a good chance I wouldn't beat the rain home. Sometimes I wondered why I came up there because the place invariably reminded me of the day we buried my wife in L.A. Penance. That was it, I reminded myself.

My thoughts turned to Winona. No question, when she was around I felt a lift, like what a clear morning or a soft breeze at twilight does for my psyche. She had a way of opening me up, too. The truth was, I had told her more about my wife's death than I had any other human being. I trusted her, which was saying a lot for me, and there was a side of her, too, her Native side, I suppose, that I didn't fully understand. I liked that mystery, too.

And the sex last night—oh, man.

The leading edge of the clouds reached the sun, and the light fell, taking my mood with it. I started back down with Archie out in front. It's only been a year, I told myself. What would Claire say if she knew about this? How could you be so goddamn selfish?

◇◇◇

I had just stepped out of the shower when my cell phone chirped. I wrapped a towel around me, dashed into the bedroom, and fished my phone out of my shorts.

"Hi," Winona greeted me. "Guess where I am?" Her voice sounded mischievous.

"Uh, I have a feeling I'm not going to like this."

She laughed, almost a giggle. "I'm in Silverton. I drove out here to check out the Townsend country house, see if anyone was at home."

"And?"

"No one was there. The drive-through gate was locked, but the side gate was open. Did you know I left my favorite earrings in the guesthouse, Cal? Anyway, I remembered the spare key was hidden in a little ceramic rabbit by the door. The rabbit was there, but the key wasn't, and the place was locked."

"Where are you now?"

"I'm in Silverton having a coffee at a Starbucks."

"That's a relief."

She laughed again. "There's more. I'm waiting for a call back from Jason's secretary. She'll know where the key is."

"My God, Winona. Even if she knows, how do you know she won't say something to the wrong person?"

"Norma and I are buds, Cal. I told her it was awkward with the breakup and all and swore her to secrecy. Women understand about favorite earrings."

I blew out a breath. "Look, Winona, would you at least not do anything until I get there?"

Chapter Fifty-six

No brief squall, the front that moved in unleashed a pelting downpour. I fed Arch and left him pouting at the front door. "Guard the castle, big boy," I told him, and he did the doggie equivalent of rolling his eyes. I took the Pacific Highway to Newberg and then the 219 across the St. Paul Bridge and south through the heart of the Willamette Valley. Even in the rain and low light, the spring fields pulsed with more shades of green than there were names for. I pulled into Silverton fifty minutes later, a prosperous looking little burg named, I guessed, after Silver Creek, which cut through the west side of town.

It took one lap around town to find the Starbucks, and I scored a parking place right in front. Winona wasn't there. I called, and her phone went to voice mail. "Damn it, Winona, pick up," I said in a tone that caused a couple at a table to look up at me. I turned to the barista. "This is the only Starbucks in town, right?"

She smiled. "The one and only."

I had to assume the worst—that Winona had gone without me. "Uh, do you know a big estate around here? It would be on the road that goes down to Silver Falls State Park?"

She smiled again. "You mean the Townsend estate?"

"*Yes.* That's it."

"It's about twelve miles straight south on Silver Falls Highway, left-hand side. My brother used to do landscape work out there. You'll see a humongous iron gate and a freaking mansion set way back. Can't miss it."

I thanked her, put five dollars in the tip jar, and tried Winona's cell again. She answered this time. "Where the hell are you?"

"I'm in the guesthouse," she said, with an edge of excitement in her voice. Norma got back to me on the key. Sorry, but I couldn't wait. I figured I had a pretty good excuse to be in here, anyway. Listen, Cal, I've found something important. Are you in Silverton yet?"

"Yes. I'm standing in front of the Starbucks."

"Come straight sou—"

"I know where it is, Winona. Don't touch a goddamn thing. I'll be there in five minutes."

I got in my car and headed out of town, muttering all the way. My odometer just clicked past eleven miles when I saw her car pulled off on the right side of the road. I pulled in behind it. The Townsend estate was a bit further down the road. I hadn't bothered with a raincoat, and by the time I got to the gate I was wet, starting to get cold, and feeling very grouchy.

The main house was set back and I could barely see its outlines in the failing light. I let myself in the side gate, stopped, and took a breath. This wouldn't constitute breaking and entering, I told myself. Winona had permission to enter the guesthouse to look for her earrings, and I'm just popping in to assist her. A shaky rationale but defendable.

A light burned at the front of the two story structure to my left, which had to be the guesthouse. I followed a path lined with boxwoods to the front porch and knocked softly. Winona came to the door wearing the latex gloves I'd given her and holding a small white garbage bag in one hand.

She held the bag up, her eyes wide with excitement. "He was here for sure, Cal. Wait till you see this. I searched the bedrooms first. There's three of them. They were clean as far as I could tell. I was getting set to leave, and then it occurred to me to look in the trash out back."

"Good thinking." I was starting to get excited myself.

"Anyway, I found this bag." She led me into the dining room, opened the bag, and spread the contents on the table—an empty

fifth of IW Harper whiskey, four cigarette butts, a paperback—
Shame the Devil—written by George Pelecanos, and a squeezed-
flat tube of toothpaste. She picked up the paperback, which was
stained and swollen. Clearly enjoying this, she smelled it and
smiled. "He spilled whiskey on the book, so he left it behind."
She held up one of the cigarette butts. "Camels." She pointed at
the filter. "See? The little camel's right here on the filter. Probably
got his DNA plastered all over it."

I looked at her and smiled. "This will do nicely. The bag was
in the trash, right?"

"Yes. It was loosely tied off. I—"

The front door clicked open and we both swung around.
David Hanson walked in, looking dapper in a blue blazer, gray
slacks, and tassel loafers. "Oh, hi guys." He smiled broadly. "I
heard you needed the key and drove over. Any luck with the
earrings, Win?"

Winona casually stepped in front of the table to block his
view. "Nice to see you, David. Yeah, we're good." I nodded in
agreement. She said, "Uh, Norma must have called you."

He laughed. "Yeah, she did. I was the last to use the place. Mis-
placed the key. My mistake." He stepped forward, leaned to one
side, and peered past Winona. "What's all the mess on the table?"

"Oh, nothing," Winona said, swinging her hand in a dismis-
sive gesture. "We were just sifting through some trash, you know,
to find the earrings."

He took another step, his eyes fixed on the table. I think it
was the IW Harper bottle and the book that tipped him. He
straightened up. "Oh, good grief, what a slob. I told him to clean
up after himself." He rolled his eyes dramatically. "I should have
known." Then he brushed his blazer back, pulled an automatic
from his waistband, and shook his head. "Damn, I was hoping
it wouldn't come to this."

Hanson? I said to myself. Didn't see that coming.

Chapter Fifty-seven

Winona put her hands on her hips and glared at Hanson. *"David,* what are you doing? Put that gun down, *now."*

He raised the gun a little higher. "Shut up, Winona." He swung his eyes to me. His face had grown taut, and a muscle twitched below his right eye. "No heroics, Claxton. I'm very proficient with this weapon, and I will shoot you if you try anything."

I extended my hands in a calming gesture. "Take a breath, David. We were just leaving. We found the earrings. The rest of this stuff means nothing to us."

He waved us away from the table with the barrel of his gun and moved in for a closer look. He shook his head and said more to himself than us, "Oh, Jake. I never should have trusted you with this. You were in over your head."

I said, "Look, David. All you have to do is destroy this stuff we found and it'll be our word against yours. No one can prove you killed Norquist, either. You got away with it clean, man." A flicker of something, not quite a smile, crossed his face. And besides," I went on, "most of the evidence points to Royce Townsend, not you."

He exhaled a loud breath. The eye twitched again. "Royce had nothing to do with this. I'm freelancing here. When Ferguson called that day to warn about Watlamet, Sam wasn't in and I happened to pick up. I'd helped Ferguson out of a couple of legal scrapes as a favor to Royce, so he opened up to me." He shook his head again. "Sam thinks he's a hard ass, but I knew he wouldn't have the guts to shut Watlamet up, so I took care of it myself. It was simple, really. All I had to do was tell Norquist the Old Man needed a favor. And pay him well, of course. The bastard son would do anything to please his father."

Winona took a half step forward. "David, why? What were you thinking? Jason would never, ever have wanted you to do something like this."

He glared back at her. "Jason doesn't always know what's best for Jason. His election bid would have been toast. And listen to *you*," he sneered. "You wanted to go to Washington as much as I did." He raised his chin slightly, his face beaming with self-righteousness. "You had an agenda—your pitiful people, your precious salmon—but I did it for *love*, Winona. *Love*. Something you wouldn't understand." His smiled bitterly. "But I was betrayed by Sam and Royce." He swung his eyes back to me and opened the palm of his free hand. "What could I do?" He pleaded. "By the time they sacked me, everything was in play. I had no choice. I had to see it through."

"You're wrong, David."

I saw something stir in him, the tremor of a face muscle, a flaring of his nostrils. But a breath later it was gone. His face grew rigid, and his eye twitched, twice this time. "I, I need time to think this through. He drew a breath and wagged the barrel of the gun. "The wine cellar's off the kitchen. There's no way out, so don't even try. And don't drink any of the wine. It'll piss Royce off." He stopped us at the cellar door. "Give me your cell phones and your car keys, please. Just drop them on the floor." He swept them aside with a foot and opened the door. "Inside."

He clicked the door shut and locked it with a key that must have been resting on top of the door frame. The cellar was pitch black and reeked of wine—that smell of mold the French call *pourriture noble*—noble rot. I found the light switch and after descending the steep steps, we hugged each other, and I felt Winona shudder.

She said, "Oh, Cal, I think you got to him. Do you think he'll relent?"

I pushed her away gently and looked her straight in the eye. "No, I don't. When he comes back, it'll be to kill us. He won't do it here. Too messy. He'll take us somewhere down the road, probably in his car.

She nodded. Her eyes narrowed, and she got that warrior look. "Well, we need a plan, then."

We spent a couple of minutes scouring the place for anything we could conceal as a weapon. One wall held a wine rack nearly full of bottles of well-known vintages from Oregon, California, and France. A rich man's wine cellar. There were cases of wine stacked here and there, too, and a utility sink on the wall opposite the wine rack. We found a corkscrew in no time, the kind with a fold-out screw. I tucked it in the small of my back, under my belt.

Winona frowned. "He'll find that in a heartbeat."

"I know." I took a bottle from the rack, walked over to the sink, and tapped the neck on the bottom of the sink. *Chunk.* The neck broke off, and the wine glugged into the sink.

In a hushed voice, Winona said, "Cal, what are you doing?"

"You'll see." I held the jagged neck up and examined it. "Not quite."

"Oh," she said with a knowing look.

I broke six more bottles of 1986 Romanee Conti, probably the most expensive wine Townsend had in the cellar. Might as well really piss him off, I figured. I finally found what I was looking for. I held the neck of the seventh bottle up. It was maybe five inches long with a sharp, dagger-like blade.

"He might not be looking for this," I said.

Winona looked at me, her face as hard as marble. "Cal. Give it to me. My blouse's untucked. He might miss it. He under-estimates me." I handed the weapon to her and she tucked it gingerly into her waistband, under her blouse. She turned in a circle with her hands up. "What do you think?"

"Could you use it on him?" I asked the question, but I knew the answer.

Chapter Fifty-eight

We talked through various scenarios and how we might use our weapons against Hanson. We agreed on the simplest of plans. It was laughable, really, but it was all we had, and the act of making it gave us a shred of hope. Now there was nothing to do but wait at the base of the steps for our would-be executioner.

I put my arms around her and pulled her gently to me. She said, "Oh, Cal, how can you ever—"

"Shhhh," I said. "This was nobody's fault but Hanson's. We've still got a shot."

She looked at me, her eyes laced with a tenderness that made me want to weep. "I'm glad I bummed a ride from you last night."

"Me too. It was worth the wait."

"I'm sorry I've been so conflicted, I—"

"Don't. I understand. *Conflicted?* Hell, that's my middle name."

She hugged me and chuckled softly. "The walking wounded, both of us."

The trapped, fetid air hung heavy in the cellar. Time passed like the movement of a glacier. An hour in, Winona said, "Maybe he took off, Cal. Maybe he doesn't have the courage to go through with it."

A flicker of hope stirred in my chest. "He'd kill me with no compunction. Maybe your presence has given him a moral dilemma."

She puffed a derisive breath. "Doubt it."

I nodded. "He's probably moving our cars further down the highway, maybe to the park. That could take a lot of time."

We fell silent, straining our ears for any sounds coming from above, and at the same time, trying not to dwell on what those footsteps would bring.

Winona sighed deeply. "This reminds me of when I was living with my mother. I used to lock myself in my bedroom with the lights out."

"Why?"

She sighed. "My way of trying to disappear, I guess. Mom used to get drunk and bring men home. One night she passed out, but she must've said something about me to the guy she'd picked up. Anyway, he knocks on my bedroom door and tries to sweet-talk his way in. Then he starts to force the door. I got behind it with our big old iron. When he came in, I hit him with it, hard, and then ran to my cousin's house."

I waited, but she didn't continue. "What happened then?" I finally asked.

"The next day I moved in with Grandmother. Mom went into rehab for a month, the first of many. Grandmother told me later that the man had to be hospitalized."

"A warrior, like your grandfather, huh?"

"Funny. That's what Grandmother said."

"Where's your mother now?"

"Last I heard, Spokane. She calls and leaves messages, but I don't return her calls."

It was my turn to sigh. "She probably feels guilty for the way she treated you. She wants your forgiveness."

Winona stiffened visibly. "You don't know that."

"I think I know what she feels like."

We lapsed into another long silence. Winona began sobbing softly, and I did my best to console her. Finally, she stirred against me. "If we get out of here alive, maybe I'll call her. What do you think?"

I took her hand and kissed it. "I think you should."

She looked at me and smiled demurely. "Can I ask you something else?"

"Anything."

She shook her head. "You'll probably think this is dumb."

"Try me."

"In October, they're going to breach Marmot Dam on the Sandy River. Will you hike in with me to watch it go?"

I squeezed her hand. "I wouldn't miss it." I hesitated for a moment, then added, "I, uh, have a question for you—"

"Anything."

"Did you kill Cecil Ferguson?"

She withdrew her hand from my grasp. "*No*. I didn't kill him."

"I know you lied to me about what happened."

She smiled and dropped her eyes. "Okay. After that staff member questioned me outside the center, I left. But I came back and got in the second time. Ferguson's door was ajar, so I went into his room. He was dead on the floor." She raised her eyes. "Maybe I would have killed him, I don't know. But that's what happened."

I nodded. "Fair enough. I believe you, Winona."

It wasn't long after that exchange that we heard the front door slam and the sound of approaching footsteps. She took my hand, and we stood up to face the cellar door.

Chapter Fifty-nine

Hanson stood looking down on us, the line of his mouth tight and straight, his eyes gleaming and feral looking. My stomach dropped. "Claxton, you come up first," he said in a voice straining to sound commanding. He greeted me at the top of the stairs with the metallic click of steel on well-oiled steel as he cocked the automatic and leveled it at me. "Now, take the corkscrew out from wherever you've hidden it or I swear I'll shoot you right now. There was one down there. I'm sure you found it."

I pulled the corkscrew from my belt and offered it to him in my outstretched hand. "Drop it," he said, and when I did, he kicked it aside while keeping his eyes and gun trained on me. "You're next, Win." When she got to the top of the stairs, he looked her over carefully but didn't pat her down. Okay, we're going to take a drive. You're the chauffeur, Claxton. Win will be in the back with me. If you do anything stupid, I'll shoot her, of course."

On the way out, he picked up the white garbage bag, which he'd apparently repacked with Norquist's left-behinds. To be disposed of once and for all, no doubt. The rain had let off and a cold wind had blown the clouds, exposing a partial moon that cast a pale light on the courtyard.

When we reached his car, I turned and he tossed me his keys.

I caught the keys and threw them over my shoulder in one motion. They cleared the fence and landed in the thick underbrush. "*Hey,*" he shouted as his eyes left me momentarily, following the arc of the keys. I lunged at him and missed grabbing his gun, but deflected the barrel enough that the round he squeezed off whizzed past my ear. The explosion deafened me. I lunged again, but he pulled free.

He must have been a tennis player, because the backhand he hit me with was perfectly placed, the barrel of the gun catching me square on the side of the jaw. My head felt like the clapper of a bell. My knees buckled, and as I sank to the ground I heard a scream and thought I saw Winona with an arm up out of my peripheral vision. Then I fell down a very dark elevator shaft.

When I came to, I was lying in a deep mud puddle. I came up on my hands and knees, and my nose drained muddy water. I coughed up some gravel, too, along with one molar and a mouthful of blood.

I looked around like a cow in a pasture, my head spinning, my ears ringing. Winona and Hanson were gone!

I struggled to my feet and looked around, trying to clear the wasps swarming in my brain. I could just see the side gate in the dimness. It was open. I tried to run, but my legs were like rubber. I shook my head and tried again.

I stopped on wobbly legs in the middle of the road, my breath coming in gasps. *Which way to go?* I screamed to myself. Then I heard a single gunshot. It came from the forested area directly across the road. I took off in that direction and found myself on a narrow trail.

It was darker under the canopy. I moved as fast as I could, trying to be as quiet as possible. Don't think about the gunshot, I kept telling myself. *Just find her.*

The trail steepened as it descended into the Silver Creek watershed. I was moving at a good clip when I saw a shadowy form in the trail. *Too late!* I tripped on the object and went sprawling. I got to my hands and knees, turned around, and gasped.

A body.

I crawled back to it. David Hanson lay face down in the trail, one knee pulled up, one arm outstretched with the gun still in his hand.

Moonlight shone softly off the bottle neck sticking deep and firm in his back. I checked for a pulse on his wrist and his neck. If it was there, it was weak. He moaned.

I pried the gun out of his hand, stood up, and called out. "Winona, are you okay? Come out. Hanson's down. You got him."

I heard a couple of twigs snap up the trail. "It's okay," I repeated. "He's down. I have his gun."

She came up the trail and hugged me so tightly I feared for my ribs. "Oh, Cal. I thought you were dead." She laughed almost hysterically. "You tossed those damn keys and I was trying to get the bottle neck out of my pants. I thought he shot you."

I laughed, too, as the stress drained out of me. "I heard you scream, I think, before I went out."

She peered at my face, then turned it into the moonlight and wiped my chin with her fingertips. "You're bleeding."

I shrugged. "The bullet missed, but he clipped me good with his gun." I rubbed my swelling jaw. "He owes me a tooth, damn it, and maybe a hearing aid. What happened after I went out?"

I felt her shudder. "I stabbed him, that's what. It staggered him, but he stayed on his feet." She opened her hands, palms up, as if to apologize. "I had no choice but to run."

Hanson groaned again. She knelt down next to him. "He's lost a lot of blood. We need to get him out of here. I don't want him to die." She looked up at me, her brow knotted in surprise. "I asked you for that bottle neck, but I wasn't sure I could actually use it..."

I smiled. "I was. You're a warrior, Winona. You did your grandfather proud."

Chapter Sixty

Marmot Dam on the Sandy River
October 19, 2007

It would have been a perfect day to watch a dam being breached if my heart hadn't been so heavy. Archie and I were hiking east along the ridgeline above the Sandy River. Old growth hemlocks and Douglas firs still dripped from a rainstorm the night before, and the trail was heavy with mud. But the river below gleamed like polished silver in the afternoon light, the air crisp and cool and filled with forest scents.

We were hiking in to witness the final step in the removal of Marmot Dam. I had been tied up in court that morning, so we were hurrying to catch at least part of the show before it got dark. It was a promise I intended to keep. After today the Sandy would join the small but exalted ranks of rivers in the U.S.—or the world, for that matter—that flow freely for their entire length. Of course, the Marmot Dam wasn't that large, but as my friend Jason Townsend said once, "It's a good start."

I couldn't help but think of the ceremony Winona had organized to honor her grandfather, Nelson Queah. It was held at the little park across the highway from the new Celilo Village, where Winona and I had first spoken of the events of March 10, 1957. Tribesmen from up and down the Columbia River came in cars, trucks, and even canoes. There was drumming and chanting, speeches and food. A bronze plaque was unveiled. I remember exactly what it said:

Nelson Queah
June 9, 1920 to March 10, 1957
Fearless defender of his Tribe, his Country,
and The Columbia River. May his soul rest in peace
below the falls he loved and fought so hard to preserve,
and may it come to pass that the mighty roar of the
falls will be heard again.

As I hiked on under the dripping canopy, my mind drifted back to the events that took place after our confrontation with David Hanson. It'd been close, but he pulled through. After we told our story and connected all the dots for the police, Winona was not charged with anything. In fact, several articles in the media referred to her as a hero, a term that made her eyes flash with anger. "My grandfather was a hero, but I'm not," she was always quick to point out.

David Hanson is a guest of the state now. The charges against him include multiple counts of murder, attempted murder, kidnapping, and assault. He considered himself a pretty bright guy, but the burner phone he used to communicate with Jacob Norquist was found in his car. Hubris always trumps intelligence. He's trying to duck the death penalty by offering to implicate Royce Townsend in the murders of Nelson Queah and Timothy Wiiks back in 1957. There's no statute of limitation on murder.

The fact that Hanson took that call from Cecil Ferguson that day last March proved fateful not only for him but for Townsend as well.

There may not be enough evidence to get an indictment, but the accusations look pretty ugly for the elder Townsend. To make matters worse, word has gotten around that he's the father of "The Oregon Sniper." That pretty much shit-canned what was left of his social standing in Portland, and there's a rumor his wife has left him.

Townsend's legitimate son, Jason, took a dim view of all this and severed ties with the family. Incidentally, I had lunch with him last week, and he told me he's decided to leave Oregon politics to go trekking in the Himalayas for six months. Can't say that I blame him for wanting to get out of town.

The icing on the irony cake came when I got a call from Shirley Norquist after all this broke in the paper. Turns out Jacob Norquist's father was really Braxton Gage, not Royce Townsend. "You can tell by the eyes," she told me. "Jacob had Braxton Gage's eyes." I thought back on my first encounter with Gage and realized that's why he looked familiar to me. "Even though Royce never treated Jacob very well," she went on, "I figured my son was better off thinking he was his father rather than Braxton's. I guess I was wrong about that."

When I asked if she intended to set the record straight, she replied, "No. Let Royce twist in the wind like me."

The casino deal in the Gorge tanked last month. The Governor nixed the deal after learning of Gage's plan to fund the Oregon Patriot Militia using casino proceeds. Apparently the cyber attack Fletcher Dunn had told me about worked because a string of incriminating e-mails between Stephanie Barrett and her brother-in-law, a high level OPM operative, got plastered across the Internet. Of course, the hacking was illegal, but the Governor couldn't ignore the posts.

Smart move by the Gov, I'm thinking. If he had okayed that deal, he ran the risk of being confronted with a pitchfork-wielding mob of Oregonians outraged by the prospect of a gambling casino in their beloved Gorge.

Philip and I would have been in that mob.

Speaking of Fletcher Dunn, I drove him over to the Hazelden Center in Newberg two weeks ago. He's decided to do something about his alcoholism. He'd called and asked for a ride but didn't tell me where he wanted to go. Just like him. The last thing he did was hand me fifty dollars and say, "Santos is taking care of the yard while I'm drying out. Make sure he gets this. It's a bonus."

I rounded a sharp bend in the river and heard the whine of an engine and the faint sound of people shouting before I saw the sand and gravel dam. It had been constructed to hold back and divert the river while the concrete behemoth below it could be blown up and carted away in huge trucks. That job was finished and all that remained was to breach the massive, yet temporary structure.

I wasn't sure how much I'd be able to see before it grew dark. The experts couldn't agree on how long it would take the river to have its way. But they had already blocked the diversion channel, which meant the full force of the river now waited to be unleashed, a river that stretched from the dam up to the glacier fields on Mount Hood.

As I watched, workers cut a channel into the top of the dam, which allowed the river to commence its work. The flow began with a trickle but built with amazing speed. Soon it became a fast stream, which became a torrent, and then a waterfall. Huge chunks of the dam broke away and washed downstream, releasing rock, sand, and gravel held captive for ninety-four years and opening miles of new habitat to the runs of salmon and steelhead that had called the Sandy their home.

The light faded slowly, and when the sun touched the horizon behind the trees it set it afire. By this time, the dam was nearly gone, the river free.

As I hiked out, my heart ached for Winona. She wanted to be here as much as I longed for her company. That wasn't possible. Her reward for saving my life and catching the man behind the Oregon Sniper was to be arrested by the Portland Police for the murder of Cecil Ferguson. The Portland crime lab had found a speck of his DNA on the bottom of one of her shoes.

Whoever said that no good deed goes unpunished wasn't kidding.

Tonight, the midnight oil will burn at the farm as I prepare for a meeting with her lawyer in the morning. This will not stand.

Author's Note

Four historical events underpin this story:

On March 10, 1957, the falls and the village at Celilo on the Columbia River, a Native American cultural and trading hub for more than ten thousand years, were inundated with the closing of the floodgates of the newly commissioned The Dalles Dam.

On March 10, 2007, a commemoration of the event was held at the relocated Native American village, which lay across I-84 from the original site.

On October 19, 2007, the Marmot Dam on the Sandy River was removed, allowing the river to flow freely again from the glacial fields on Mt. Hood to the Columbia River.

An attempt to site a gambling casino in the Columbia River Gorge—the so called "Bridge of the Gods" project—was active during 2007. It failed to get traction when numerous citizens, citizen groups, and the governor came out against it.

The rest of the story was derived solely from the imagination of the author.

To receive a free catalog of Poisoned Pen Press titles, please provide your name, address, and email address in one of the following ways:

Phone: 1-800-421-3976
Facsimile: 1-480-949-1707
Email: info@poisonedpenpress.com
Website: www.poisonedpenpress.com

Poisoned Pen Press
6962 E. First Ave. Ste 103
Scottsdale, AZ 85251